W9-ABM-913

Also by Nancy Means Wright

Harvest of Bones
Mad Season

Poison Apples

NANCY MEANS WRIGHT

Thomas Dunne Books
St. Martin's Minotaur
New York

Grateful acknowledgment is made to reprint three lines from *Deliverance* by James Dickey, on page 94.

 For information, address St. Martin's Press, 175 Fifth Avenue, New York, N.Y. 10010.

www.minotaurbooks.com

Library of Congress Cataloging-in-Publication Data

Wright, Nancy Means.
Poison apples / Nancy Means Wright—1st ed.
p. cm.
ISBN 0-312-26220-5
1. Women farmers—Vermont—Fiction. 2. Vermont—Fiction. I. Title.

PS3573.R5373 P65 2000
813'.54—dc21 00-024755

First Edition: July 2000

10 9 8 7 6 5 4 3 2 1

For Joan and the late Dr. Ted Collier
and their wonderful Windfall Orchard

Acknowledgments

For help on this novel I owe thanks and gratitude to the following:

Aerial sprayer Doug Daugherty for his time and invaluable information on spraying, insecticides, apple predators, et al.

The late Dr. Ted Collier for generous apple expertise, and his wife, Joan, for the loan of reference books, including *Apples* by Peter Wynne and *The Apple Book* by Rosanna Saunders.

My daughter, Catharine Wright, and farmer Bob Piggott for reading early drafts of the manuscript with a critical eye.

Barney Hodges Jr. and T. Tall for allowing me to visit their apple trees and to interview their delightful Jamaican pickers.

Mike Brinkman and Bob Pannozzo for a dramatic spraying demonstration in Bob's Cornwall orchard.

Apple growers Ruthven Ryan, Art Blaise, and Dick Bates for good talk about their experience on the former Edgewood Orchard.

Eric Neil and Spence Wright for sharing their adventures with tractors.

Burlington Free Press reporter Sally Pollak for her delightful piece on the Rattlesnake Show at the Champlain Valley Fair.

Fellow writers Kathleen McKinley Harris and Julie Becker for news clippings, friendship, and moral support.

Copyeditor Dave Cole for keeping me in line through his forest of perceptive green Post-Its on my manuscript; and editorial assistant Julie Sullivan and my agent, Alison Picard, for cheerfully responding to my numerous E-mails.

And of course my wonderful editor and role model, Ruth Cavin, whose knowledgeable insights, sense of humor, and enthusiasm for this book carried me along to publication.

And finally, to my husband, Dennie, and my extended Vermont family for constant encouragement and support.

A goodly apple rotten at the heart.
O, what a goodly outside falsehood hath!

—William Shakespeare
The Merchant of Venice
(I, iii, 124)

Poison Apples

One

Moira Earthrowl was Irish enough to know that a bird that tried to enter your house meant death. And here the cardinal was, flinging itself at the living room window again, thud, thud, thud at the glass: a stout red bill, a rush of scarlet feathers.

"Get away, get, you crazy bird!" She waved her arms at the intruder. How could she concentrate on her weaving, with a foolish bird assaulting her window? It was the third day in a row it had come, and she was mystified. More than that, she was downright worried.

Now, she didn't really believe that a bird could bring death, but twice already the superstition had come true. A blackbird had flown into her grandfather's workshop in Ballyvaughan, Ireland, and the next day the old man was dead of a massive heart attack. And at Aunt Bridget's funeral a sparrow darted through an open window, circled the casket three times, and flew out. Of course, Bridget was already dead, so it wasn't quite such a concern. But it proved the superstition; her mother had reminded her of that.

Here it was again: wham! bam! dashing its crimson side against the glass, then its fiery red beak. She half expected to see a spot of blood on the glass. But there wasn't any. At the very least the bird must be brainless by now, she thought, all that bashing and smashing!

What she really worried about, though, was her husband Stan. Not that he was superstitious, oh, not at all. He was a pragmatic man. But he was so sensitive, so vulnerable these days. Always, it seemed, in a bad patch. There he was, out in the orchard now, arguing—or so it seemed—with the orchard manager, Rufus Barrow. Stan was practically a foot taller than short, stocky, soft-spoken Rufus. And yet Rufus seemed the more powerful one, feet planted on the grassy triangle between cider barn and house, arms folded, head tilted slightly back to make eye contact with Stan.

And not stepping back, she saw, when Stan shook his fist. What was the matter now? The cider press not working right? The local pickers dropping too many apples? They were slower than the others: After all, the Jamaicans were professionals. And the locals were young: the Butterfield twins, Rolly and Hally; a tall athletic young woman named Millie Laframboise from East Branbury, who had an ailing mother and three other part-time jobs; Adam Golding, tall as a Knicks player, his ponytail gleaming in the sun like a mass of spilled coins—he was aptly named. Then Emily Willmarth, from the farm on Cow Hill Road. It was Moira who'd argued with Stan to hire the girl, but she might have made a mistake. Just this morning she'd seen Emily and Adam whispering together, looking quite chummy. Yes, she'd better keep an eye on that one. The boy was in his twenties, the girl still in high school.

Now Rufus was wheeling about, moving doggedly off. He was upset, it was obvious. He wanted things to go right. There was something almost maniacal about the way he ran the orchard: not a minute to be wasted. He knew exactly what he was about, and he resented Stan butting in. She watched Stan stride down into the orchard, stop short at the first tree, where Bartholomew, the Jamaican Number One man, was standing on the third rung of a ladder, picking; Stan shouted up at him, his cheeks red as the apples.

Now, she couldn't have that. She couldn't have Stan taking out his anger on Bartholomew. The cardinal flung himself at the window again and fueled her with purpose. She dropped the loom stick, dashed out of the house to intercede.

"Stan," she cried. "Stan, can we talk? We have a problem, sweetheart, I'm going mad with it. Stan?"

The old Jamaican's face was inscrutable. He was a tall, proud-looking fellow, sixty-one years old, but still picking, a fisherman by trade who boasted twenty-one children. He was on his third wife now, she knew, a younger woman, who was always pregnant, it seemed—but by her husband? The younger men joked about it. And Bartholomew had to support them all. He'd been working this orchard for ten years, seven years before she and Stan had bought it. She was fond of these Jamaicans: They brought, well, vibrancy into her world. Jamaicans singing in the trees, like a chorus of sleek dark birds: "Papa save my body, Papa save my soul. . . ." The ripe red apples, hanging like shiny Christmas balls in the green-leafed trees—oh, she loved the autumn. She loved the orchard. It was Leonardo da Vinci, it was Michelangelo. If she could only paint!

Her ruse worked. Stan was turning around, Bartholomew going on with his work—though he'd stopped humming. She took Stan's hand. "Hot coffee for you, love. The coffee cake you like, fresh from the oven."

"He's gone and done it over my head again," Stan said, jerking his head toward the apple barn where Rufus—bossman, the Jamaicans called him—had disappeared. "You'd think he owns this place. You'd think I was one of the local pickers."

"Oh, he does *not* think so," she said. "You're getting paranoid. He respects you. He knows you're a naturalist. He's a reasonable man. Only yesterday—"

"So what's this big concern?" She could hear him taking deep breaths, trying to cool down. At least he was aware he had a problem. Actually, he'd had a problem for three years now, since Carol's death. Devastating though it was, Moira had come to terms with that death; Stan never had. And then the poisoning last spring, a fifth of the trees destroyed, those budding apples. A mistake, they said, someone using the wrong spray, an herbicide called Roundup, in spray tanks used to apply a fungicide. No one could say how, why it happened. The sprayer himself was horrified, had no idea how it got in there. He'd put in Diazinon himself, the night before. It was evidently the wrong herbicide in the wrong canister. No one to take the full blame.

She told Stan about the cardinal, led him to the window. Of course it wouldn't appear when Stan was there; he waved away the worry. "I'll cut an owl out of cardboard, if it really worries you. They're scared of owls, those birds. It's just being territorial, that's all."

"Would you do that?" She threw her arms around him. They needed more touching, more feeling; she pulled him close. Stan Earthrowl: She'd laughed at the name when she first met him. He rather resembled an owl himself, in fact: those round, black-rimmed glasses, the solemn look. They'd been so much in love!

He was tense in her arms. She could feel the nerves, like wires, tightening in his body. She pulled back. "I'll pour your coffee, Stan. I'll warm the cake in the toaster oven."

"Cake, yes. Coffee, no." He was heading for the liquor cabinet—at three in the afternoon. The gray-bronze hair bristled on his head, his back was a brick wall. The cat, Ben Blue, followed him, meowing; mechanically, he threw a handful of dried food in its dish, then fixed himself a Manhattan, glugged it down, kissed her quickly on the cheek, and ran outdoors again. She went back to her loom. Soon the apple barn would open up, children coming from the local schools to watch the cidermaking process—a neighbor had volunteered to operate it. Finally, customers coming to pick drops, buy cider and bags of apples. There'd be no time for her own work. She leaned into her weaving, into the bright pink and mauve threads. She craved sunshine in her life. Dream time.

She was just getting up to stretch her back—at forty-three she couldn't sit and concentrate for hours anymore the way she used to—when the phone rang. It was Annie May, Stan's sister-in-law, down in Houston, Texas. Her voice was breathless. She called only when there was a trauma—what now? "In the hospital! As a patient!" Annie May shouted. "Lindley's in the hospital and I got to be with him. The heart thing, you know—I tol' you about it. They got to do an angioplasty! How bad is that?"

She didn't wait for an answer—not that Moira could tell her much. "They're going in," she screamed, "sticking in a tube, a balloon. Imagine. A balloon in his heart!"

"I've heard it works, though," Moira said. "He'll come out all right, I'm sure of it. He's a doctor, he'll know how to take care of himself afterward." She felt a balloon inflate in her own heart, squeeze her ribs. Lindley had met Annie May when he was interning in a Houston hospital and Annie was an aide. She was lovely: eighteen and ready to nest; Lindley thirty-six and newly divorced. Annie got pregnant; they married after a six-month whirlwind courtship.

"Lindley's a gynecologist," Annie May was shouting. "What does he know about hearts?"

"He'll be all right, I'm sure. Do you want to talk to Stan? He's out in the orchard. I can run out with the phone."

"No, no, you can tell him. I got to talk to you." Annie May's voice was jarring in Moira's ears. The bird was crashing into the window again; the sounds joined in a cacophony that made her head drum. It was Opal, Annie was talking about now, the daughter she'd had with Lindley. Moira hadn't seen the girl in years; they'd sent her away to boarding school when she was twelve. Moira had never understood how they could do that. She and Stan had kept their own daughter Carol at home through high school; even then, she wished she'd spent more time with the girl. She'd been so self-satisfied, so laid back in those days. . . .

". . . to your place, up there in Ver-mont." Annie May always divided up her words, giving the same emphasis to each syllable. "You got room, don't you? Stan says it's a big house, just the two of you. I mean, just for a few weeks, a month maybe, till Lindley recovers. Opal's home now from that school, she doesn't want to go to col-lege. After all we done for her education. She's too much for Lindley. She wears him out, you know? Will you, Moira?"

What could Moira say? For a moment the house was quiet, the windows mute, the voices of the pickers far away, remote; she heard the distant honking of geese—Stan's acquisition. It was lovely, that quiet. She could work on her weaving, that's what she'd come up here for. With Stan it was apples, though she was determined to learn about those, too, so many varieties! She'd take one each day, read about its qualities. Stan was learning how to graft: maybe four kinds of apples on a single tree—a true act of creation. Her first love, though, was the weaving: shawls, scarves, they were selling them now down at the State Craft Center. It was a way of meditation, a way of healing.

"She'll fly to New York, take a bus from there. She hates flying! I wish I could come, but you know I can't. She can help around the house if she'll do it, she can pick apples."

Picking apples was a skill, not everyone could do it, but there was no point explaining that now. Annie May was in a "dash" to get back to the hospital, she said; Lindley needed her. Moira agreed to meet the bus. Day after tomorrow. The five-ten.

Annie May said, "Thanks, I'll pay you all back, maybe we can come get her when Lin's better. I'll send plenty of clean underwear. She'll throw it in your washer, you know? And make her work, she's not crazy to work, but make her."

When Moira hung up, the cardinal began dashing its body at the window again. It was more than territorial, she was sure of that. It wanted to come in. It wanted something from her. It wanted to take something from her. With Carol gone, she had hardly anything left to take—except Stan, the orchard. What—what did it want from her?

She banged her forehead with her fist to dismiss the superstition.

Two

Stan paid off the last Jamaican—the men were going into Branbury to shop. They were all slicked up: hair brushed and greased, clean bandannas, fresh cotton shirts—Ephraim, the one they called the "scholar," wore a bright red tie, although the others teased him. Stan paid them by the bushel, it kept them hustling. He sank down on a stool in the apple barn. He needed to be alone. Things were getting beyond him this year. The Jamaicans demanding a goat for the harvest supper, for one—where in hell was he supposed to get a goat? They didn't sell them in the Grand Union. The men had gotten their own last year and now they wanted him to supply it. Rufus complaining about Bartholomew, who was too old, he said—couldn't pick his limit. The younger men had to pitch in for their elder and then the whole output was less. Two hundred forty bushels a day, that was what Rufus asked for, and yesterday they'd picked only two hundred thirty. And Rufus expected Stan to do what—fire Bartholomew? Where was he to get another Jamaican, with the season already started? He'd had to cut back by four men this year as it was, with a fifth of the orchard destroyed last spring.

He dropped his head in his arms, was suddenly overcome by the tart smell of pressed apples. The orchard was supposed to have been a cure for his troubles. To have filled up his life with

Carol gone. He'd needed to get out of Connecticut, out of teaching high school biology—after Carol's death he couldn't look at those rosy-faced girls, and Carol not among them. He needed to take on something completely new. And it had worked—for a time, anyway. Until that spraying fiasco. A deliberate poisoning, he was sure—never mind what the police said about some bungler. Roundup! It was a weedkiller, for God's sake! It was no mistake, no sir.

Worse, they knew he was a flatlander, they wanted him to fail. Someone did, anyway! Someone! Who?

He labored to his feet, banged both fists against the barn wall. Leaned there, groaning, feeling the blood boil in his brain. Knowing it was bad for his heart, this anger, but what could he do about it?

"Stan? What are you doing in there, Stan? Dinner's ready. You said you'd make the salad. And I need your help because—"

"Everyone wants my help! I've got that school board meeting tonight and where in Christ's name do I get a goddamn goat?"

"A goat?" Moira put a hand on his shoulder, rubbed it. "Oh, for the Jamaicans, you mean. Well, there's a goat farm up in Panton. That's where they found it last year. . . . Oh, come on, Stanny. Cheer up. I'll get the goat. If you don't get mine first."

He was too upset to acknowledge the pun. He needed a drink. Never mind the school board meeting. That woman would be there, the one he was fighting. That damned right-winger. Trying to oust that English teacher. She'd be a ball of fury, lashing back at him, every point he made. Who was the angry one now? He was a newcomer, she said, his first year on the board, what did he know? Well he'd had a hell of a lot more experience in schools than she; they'd voted him in last year, hadn't they? They'd liked the way he campaigned, door to door, shaking hands. Never mind that no one else had wanted to run for the post. Of course his school board experience had been years earlier. Before Carol's death. BC and AC: Before Carol and After Carol. He coughed. Something in this barn he was allergic to. He hoped it wasn't the apples.

"Come on, Stan. I've got a salmon loaf, you like salmon. Besides, your sister-in-law called, she—"

"Don't tell me." He let her lead him up the path to the house. "Lock up, will you?" he yelled at Rufus, who was with Derek, one of the younger men, dragging along a last crate of ripe apples, and the manager nodded. He had a look of long suffering on his square stolid face, as if he could barely tolerate this upstart owner. Rufus was a Vermonter. He'd let it drop once—eyes cast down shyly, of course—that one of his ancestors had fought at Ticonderoga. Well, Stan couldn't fight that; his ancestors had come over from Russia in steerage—he was Jewish on his mother's side. It would be easier just to leave the management of the orchard to Rufus. But he, Stan Earthrowl, was the owner, damn it! He had an M.A., almost a Ph.D. He knew more about biology in his little finger than Rufus in his whole brain. About apples? Well, he was learning, anyway. He had a chart up on the refrigerator of one hundred kinds of apples. He was learning. He had to admit, Rufus had him on that score. Rufus knew apples. He had to respect the man for that.

Back in the house he mixed a stiff Manhattan, swilled it down. It burned hot and startling in his chest. He fixed another. "So what'd she call about?" They might as well get it over with.

"Lindley's back in the hospital. Another heart attack. But minor. They're doing an angioplasty. Stan, your face is flushed. I wish you'd see a doctor, have your blood pressure checked. . . . That last episode—where you blacked out . . ."

He ignored that. There was no time to go seeing doctors. He was only forty-eight. Lindley had just turned fifty-five, after all, the older brother. Things would go better—they had to! He'd leave more to Rufus, he knew he had to calm down. After this term he'd resign from the school board. He didn't need the extra hassles there—that crazy woman, Cassandra Wickham. But he wanted to help that English teacher. For one thing, the man was Jewish. Stan worried that Vermont was so *WASP*.

"He's supposed to have complete quiet afterward and so she wants to send Opal up to us." Moira helped herself to salmon, passed the platter. He took some, a little spilled on the place mat. He scraped it back onto the plate. He was beyond worrying now. Pile on the complications! Throw another goat at him! He could handle them, as long as he had the Manhattans.

"I suppose you said yes." She nodded, and he sighed. "Well, we can put her to work around here. Send the girl to the local school. How long she staying?"

"Annie May mentioned a few weeks, maybe a month. And Opal's hardly a girl anymore, she must be twenty at least. She quit college, Annie says. She's not easy, I gather."

Something was banging at the window. "What in hell?"

She had to laugh. "It's that cardinal I told you about. I suppose I should put up curtains. But I want the light for my work. You said you'd make an owl."

The thing came back and back, like a flashing red light, like the throbbing he'd been feeling in his head. Thud thud thud. He could hardly stand it. He shoved his chair back. "I'll make it now, the damned owl."

"Have your dinner first."

He wasn't hungry anyway; it was the thought of that meeting, that woman, Cassandra Wickham. Maybe he'd just skip the meeting and stay home and watch TV. Though he couldn't let her oust a teacher—a good teacher, he'd heard from others. He'd been involved in a similar case down in Waterbury, Connecticut. A group of right-wingers had tried to get some of the classics off the reading lists: *Grapes of Wrath*, *Catcher in the Rye*. Stan had won, too, the books were kept on the list. If a parent didn't want the kid reading a certain book, that was his problem. The school wasn't going to deprive others of the experience.

Now it was *Deliverance* by James Dickey; Aaron Samuels, the English teacher, was teaching it. It was vulgar, according to Cassandra and her buddies, overtly sexual. "Unfit for children," she claimed. On top of that she was accusing Samuels of sexual harassment. That was the worst. He balled his fists. "I'll do the owl when I get back. That bird'll quit anyway when it gets dark. It's almost seven. I've got to go. When's she coming anyway, that girl? Uh, woman. My niece . . ." Well, it was the least he could do for his brother. Blood kin.

"Day after tomorrow. On the five-ten bus, up from New York."

"Jesus," he said, and jammed on his cap and stalked out of the house.

The pickup was losing its muffler, it sounded like a growling lion. A pair of geese rose up in front and threatened the car with their spread wings. He'd bought the geese for Moira, thought she'd like them, thought they'd be a watchdog for the orchard. Hadn't Caesar used them to warn against an enemy attack? Now they, too, had turned against Stan.

How much could a man take?

He roared down Cider Mill Road and out onto the highway. A local oil truck blared its horn, but he raced out in front, just in time.

Three

A thunderstorm coming, he could hear the distant thunder; already it was spitting rain. Perfect. They wouldn't hear the geese if they squawked—or would think the geese were afraid of the thunder. He pulled the stocking cap down over his hair and face, adjusted the eye-holes; hefted the axe he'd taken from his car. Lightning blazed, illuminating the trees; the apples shone blood red. He chose his trees in the next flash; he didn't need any other light. They were older trees here, he could tell, taller than some of the others, but still yielding. He had nothing against the trees themselves, the apples: He just needed a way to show that he was here, that he was dead serious. He waited for another flash; it came almost at once, a jagged knife of light. Already it was raining hard, but it was all right, he swung and hacked at the trunk. Again, and again, and the tree groaned and cracked and fell sideways into the grassy path. He could hear the apples smacking the ground; in a fit of anger he stamped on them, felt them squash under his boots. He axed a second tree. The rain was driving down on his head now, he was soaked through his jacket and pants. Two trees were enough. For now. He ran on back to his car, opened the back, tossed in the axe. Already the rain had washed it clean of bark and pith. They'd find the downed trees tomorrow, maybe the following day when they went to pick in that section. He smiled grimly, to think of their stunned faces.

Four

Moira took her jog through the west orchard at six the next morning and found the trees. "Omigod!" A pair of apple trees toppled, and seemingly in their prime; most of the apples smashed on the ground—not even good for cider. There'd been a storm the night before, the thunder had woken her up, the geese. But was the storm powerful enough to uproot a tree? She couldn't imagine it. She looked closer, examined one of the stumps. An axe cut, it looked like, not jagged the way lightning would leave it. "Omigod," she said again, and clapped a hand to her mouth. She wanted to clean up quickly, sweep away the debris, the way she did when a young Carol had broken a favorite cup—before "daddy" saw it and chastised his chubby daughter.

But already she heard them, the Jamaicans, singing their morning welcome, parading out of the bunkhouse, ladders over their shoulders, arms swinging in time to a gospel tune: "I'm so 'frai-aid I could sit down and cry-y-y . . ." The words suited her mood. The men were splitting up now, moving to the assigned trees; the second oldest of them, Zayon, coming closer, the feed cap sitting high on his dreadlocks. She ran to him. "Zayon, look!" She pointed.

She could see his eyes, widening, shining like lakes as he

viewed the damage. He leaned down, ran his hand across the cut, turned his lean brown face up to her. With surprise she saw he had blue eyes. What rapacious forebear had given him those?

"Somebody dey done dis," he said in that melodious island patois that was a synthesis, she'd read, of old English, Spanish, African, even Irish dialect. She loved to hear it.

She nodded. "You'd better get the bossman," referring to Rufus. "Just don't tell Mr. Earthrowl. Not yet." They could chop up the trunk, scoop up the smashed apples; maybe Stan wouldn't notice that this had happened. He was in the apple barn, making cider.

Zayon turned and ran, his legs like propellers, the bucket bouncing on his chest. "Bossman!" he was shouting. "Hey, boss!"

She waited by the felled trees, as if they wouldn't find them if she left. Who could miss? She picked up a couple of drops that were still whole: yellow green apples, with a crimson flush. They weren't Macintosh or Greenings or Golden Russet—almost the only varieties she could distinguish at this point. She polished them on her jeans; they were bruised on the side where they'd struck ground, it was a shame. She'd cook them into applesauce.

Rufus was there in minutes. His face, as usual, was expressionless. Even after the Roundup fiasco last spring, Rufus hadn't changed expression. He'd quickly terminated the relationship with that sprayer, although the man had claimed innocence. Now he turned and glared at Bartholomew, who was close behind. Bartholomew looked back, equally fierce. Surely Rufus didn't think Bartholomew had done it—that sweet old man! She touched the Jamaican's arm, and Rufus's eyes narrowed. "We better clean it up," he said. "You get back to work." He nodded curtly at Bartholomew. "I'll get some of the locals. Golding! Butterfield!" he shouted. He never used the twins' first names: just seemed to treat them as the same person.

A moment later Adam Golding came loping along. There was nothing quick about the young man, although he picked well enough, and he seemed to have stuck with it, in spite of his rather thin build. He seemed to Moira a pleasant, self-assured fellow. Something about the accent suggested a monied background. He'd attended Branbury College for a year, he'd said, then dropped out for one reason or other. It wasn't unusual for former students to gravitate back to the area; the town was full of them—urban dropouts. And here was Emily Willmarth, right behind: a pretty dark-haired farm girl—anything but self-assured. Emily made Moira think of Carol, always eighteen, it seemed, naive, trusting; and her nose filled.

"You'll be late to school," she reminded Emily.

The girl flashed a smile at her. "I don't have classes Friday mornings, Ms. Earthrowl."

Moira said, "Oh," and patted the girl on the shoulder. "Your mother's coming over for cider this morning. She called us to save her some. Your little brother having a scout troop over or something."

"Vic, yeah. He's working on some badge. Birds or stars, one or the other he's always into."

"Good for him. Involvement's important." If Carol had been more involved with birds or stars . . . she might not have taken up with that boy, the one who killed her. No, she mustn't say "killed." It was Stan who'd used that word. She'd never seen the boy again after the accident. Yet what torment he must have gone through, what remorse! Who was to say he wasn't really in love with Carol, young though she was? But she couldn't convince Stan of that.

"Rufus, you tell Stan," she started to say—then changed her mind. One more chance for a confrontation, for accusations. Stan had come home impossible to reason with after the school board meeting last night. He could only rant about the Wickham woman this, the Wickham woman that—she was a narrow-minded bigot, he claimed, she had "gall enough for twenty people." Moira had given up trying to placate him.

"I'll tell him myself," she said, changing her mind. "I'm on my way to the barn this minute." She swiveled about. "Or don't you think he'll notice?"

Rufus turned his brown-cow eyes on her. His face was immobile, she couldn't read him—his shyness, perhaps. "He'll notice," he said. "You better tell him." A glint in the eyes said that he didn't want to be the one to tell.

She found Stan in the apple barn, cranking out drops into cider with Don Yates. Don was a tall, lean man with close-cropped white hair, a laid-back demeanor. He was a former engineer, now retired to the area, and the quintessential volunteer: church, hospital, library, apple orchard. She was glad of Don's calming presence: A third person might hold back an explosion.

"A little accident," she said, "over in the west quad. No, maybe more than an accident." She had to admit it. "A pair of trees, cut down. Mature trees, someone might have thought them ready to go. Rufus had been marking the old ones. I don't know the variety." She held out the drops.

"William Crump," Don said. "It's a dessert apple, crisp and juicy. You don't see it around here very often. I've a couple trees of it myself."

Stan was staring at her. He was unusually quiet. Suddenly he threw up an arm and Don raced over to catch him from falling. Moira rushed a stool under him. Stan's face was as patchy red as the apple skins.

"It's been a shock, these . . . accidents," she told Don, and he nodded, he knew.

Stan came slowly to life then. "Accidents, hell," he muttered. "Malice. That's the word you want. Malice. Someone wanting to do me in. That woman on the school board. Cassandra Wickham."

"Oh, for heaven's sake, Stan. Just because she holds a different opinion from you."

It was the wrong thing to say. Stan staggered up, knocking the stool sideways against the barn wall. Before she could open her mouth to warn him back, he was striding off into the orchard, into the west quad, toward the debris. She prayed the young people would have cleaned it up by now. She heard him shout, "Rufus!"

Don grabbed her elbow, held her back. "Let him go," he said. "He'll have to see it sooner or later."

"You saw it?"

"No, Zayon told me—I was on my way here. It wasn't one of the marked trees, he said. It was still yielding." Don looked worried. “Stan should see a doctor. He doesn’t look good. Anyone check his blood pressure lately?”

“It was high when we came here. You knew about our daughter.” Don nodded; everyone knew. “He was just beginning to heal when that spraying accident . . .” She looked at her neighbor. “If it was an accident . . .”

Don was silent a minute. “I hope it was. I hope to God it was.”

Five

Emily Willmarth's mother was already at the door when Moira got back. Ruth was a tall, robust-looking woman . . . well, robust, yes, but lithe, dressed in loose-fitting jeans, a yellow denim shirt open at the neck, brown leather boots redolent of barn. She was most likely in her mid- to late-forties. She lived on a hardscrabble farm on the road behind the orchard—they'd met off and on at the local food co-op. Ruth was divorced, Moira knew, with two children still in the house, if you could call Emily a child. She must be at least seventeen, maybe eighteen. The girl's breasts were bursting out of her denim shirt as she ran up behind her mother to collect a packet of sandwiches Ruth had brought.

"I have to go now, Mom. I haven't got to the picking yet, we had a little . . . accident. I'm helping to clean up."

"Uh-oh." Ruth smiled. "I hope it wasn't anything you were involved in."

Emily glanced at Moira. "Most definitely not," she said, and raced off, her denim shirttail flapping behind her.

"Someone cut down a couple of our trees," Moira told Ruth. She paused, coughed, she hardly knew this woman. Then, seeing Ruth's interest, her concern, she went on. She recalled something Don Yates had told her about Ruth's help with other victims—an abused woman, an elderly farmer and his wife, that eccentric old

Glenna Flint on Cow Hill Road, who'd been kidnapped but, remarkably, survived.

"Come on in," she said. "Emily left your cider in the kitchen. Have a cup of coffee with me. I need to talk to someone. Can you spare the time? I know you have all those cows."

"I have a good hired man. He can cope for a bit." Ruth had a nice smile, it lit up her face. "I live on caffeine. One day it will do me in. But for now—it's fuel, energy, a way of coping. Thanks. I hear you weave, too, something I've always wished I could do. I used to do a little pottery. But now—I don't have any hobbies. Just those thirty cows. Thirty-one, to be exact. We just had a birth."

Moira smiled back. She could use a friend. She almost asked, *Will you be my friend?* They'd been so busy with the orchard these last few years, she hadn't taken time to join a group or make friends. "Sugar? Cream in your coffee?"

"Black." Ruth planted herself down on a kitchen stool, looked comfortable, as if she belonged there. "No frills. So tell me about this latest, um, accident. You look like it might help to talk about it."

Moira poured the coffee, stuck her elbows on the kitchen table, stared down at the old pine boards, wondered where she should begin. With the school board, maybe? Or was she paranoid herself, beginning to believe what Stan had said, that perhaps the vendetta between Stan and that woman Cassandra Wickham had something to do with the malice—there was that word again—in the orchard?

So she told about the vendetta. "He came home last night in a fury. Had three Manhattans—he holds his liquor better than most, but by golly, there's a limit! The woman's trying to ban a book, she's 'crucifying' some English teacher, he said. Stan's been involved in censorship before, it's one of the reasons we chose Vermont; you're supposed to think for yourself here. No one to dictate: do this, do that. But then he found himself in the middle of another row. The woman is archconservative, she wants us to think her way. She belongs to some church called the Messengers of Saint Dorothea. I'd never heard of it before! I mean, she has a right to her beliefs, but Stan's afraid she'll bring a whole group of the religious right onto the school board. They're the ones who voted her in. They're organized!" She stopped, drew a breath. Was she getting worked up herself, like Stan?

The cardinal was slamming at the window again. Ruth was watching it, her tongue stuck in her cheek, looking thoughtful.

"Bertha belongs to that group," Ruth said. "My sister-in-law. Or was. Pete and I are divorced now, but Bertha hangs on. Well, she has a right, I guess, my kids are her nieces and nephews. Anyway, she's been writing letters to the editor. She's taken an interest lately in the school board. I wondered why. I guess I was naive. I mean, I've got a child in that school! I've got to get out of the barn now and then, find out what's going on." She squinted at the window. "What is it with that bird?"

"It wants to get in," Moira said. "It wants to get in and that's a bad sign." She laughed to lessen the solemnity of the words, but Ruth was taking her seriously.

"We won't let him in," Ruth said. "We'll keep him out. I promise you that. I'll keep tabs on that crazy Bertha. See what I can find out about the school board woman." She grimaced, then smiled, and swallowed her coffee.

Six

Stan had them lined up in the barn: Rufus, the eight Jamaicans, four of the five local help. The Jamaicans, headed by Bartholomew, stood stiffly against the barn wall, their caps shading their downcast eyes, hands loose at their sides, their work pants stuffed into tall rubber boots. The locals appeared more relaxed, more confident, in jeans and caps stuck on backward the way the crazy kids wore them these days. There was Adam Golding; the twins, Rolly and Hally Butterfield, who had never finished high school and were exercise freaks—lifted weights, the muscles bulged under their tight-fitting T-shirts; and six-foot-tall Millie from up on the mountain, seated cross-legged on the barn floor. Emily Willmarth was the only one absent: Most days she had a class; today she had a dental appointment. She couldn't pick on a regular basis—his wife had hired Emily in spite of his concerns for the girl's inexperience.

Rufus stood silently beside Stan, arms folded across the barrel chest, heavy legs wide apart as though the stance gave him more authority. Stan could hear his harsh breathing, the occasional cough. Rufus was a smoker; Stan had seen him once or twice in town, a cigarette hanging out of the corner of his mouth—though he never smoked on the job. He'd come to Stan with consummate credentials, had worked the orchard seven years before

Stan acquired it. It was as though Stan were an interloper. Stan cleared his throat, began the interrogation.

"You all know by now that two of our trees were cut down, destroyed. I want to hear from anyone who knows anything about this." Stan glared at the assembled group. The only one who made eye contact was Millie; she seemed amused. No one spoke. Stan hated doing this, interrogating in this way. Back in Waterbury, when a student cheated on a test he'd send him at once to the principal, wouldn't deal with it himself. He didn't want to accuse anyone without proof. Absolute proof. You're innocent until proved guilty, that's the way he felt about things.

And that boy, the one who killed Carol—the guilt was absolute. The blood rose up again in his chest. He couldn't always make Moira see it his way, though. Carol's death had driven a stake between him and his wife. He'd bought the orchard to help pull up that stake. And now someone, inside or outside this orchard, was driving it in again.

"Well?" he said. "Cat got your tongues?"

Rufus coughed. The twins shifted position, seemed less composed. The Jamaicans remained a solid core—until Number One man, Bartholomew, nudged the shorter, leaner man beside him. It was Zayon; Zayon was a Rastafarian, whatever that was—Stan always meant to ask the Jamaican about it. The dreadlocks reminded him of an ancient apple tree, the way the black hair was knotted up in ropelike clumps. It was all but impossible, he'd heard, to unravel them.

"Those trees were deliberately slashed. Now I want to know who did it. I'm not accusing anyone here. . . ." Stan had to be careful with this. He adjusted his glasses where they'd slipped down on his sweaty nose. "But someone might have seen, heard something last night. I mean, other than a little thunder and rain. Or early this morning."

Again, there was silence. He'd been through this before, back in April, after the Roundup spraying. He didn't like it. He didn't want to be put in this position. He could feel the red pushing out on his skin, the familiar heaviness in his chest. But he had to go through with the questioning. He wanted to work this out himself—no police, no reporters who would alter the public's view of the orchard. He'd ask each picker individually. Start with the locals. "Rolly and Hally," he began, then checked himself—they were two young men, not one. But he always got them mixed up. "Hally," he said, and the twin on the left stared back at him with wide blue eyes.

"We sleep sound," Hally said, answering for them both. "Didn't even know there was a storm."

The other one said, "Nope. Slept right through it."

"Golding?"

Adam Golding shook his head. He was a quiet, good-looking fellow. Stan didn't care for the long hair, but at least Golding had the decency to tie it back. "Nothing. I was with them," he said, nodding at the brothers. The trio slept together in the smaller of the two bunkhouses. "Though wait," he said, and the heads swiveled. "I thought I heard the geese—I was half awake. But it could have been part of my dream."

Millie spoke up before Stan could question her. She didn't live on the orchard; there was probably no point having her here. Still—you never knew. "I heard the storm. It woke Mother. She got under the bed!" Stan heard the others snicker. "But I'm afraid I can't tell you anything about those trees." She gave Stan a winning smile. There was something schoolgirlish about her, straightforward. He smiled back—or tried to. Seemed he couldn't really smile anymore.

Bartholomew spoke for the Jamaicans. He had been to a British school on the island and spoke British English to the Earthrowls. "Nobody allowed out nights. My rule," he said. "Sometimes Derek, here." He nodded at the youngest Jamaican—barely of age, it would appear—a gold earring dangling in one ear. "Derek walks in his sleep. I find the door open, he tracks in leaves after I sweep nights. But last night—no. Derek was gone from this world." The others chuckled; one of them, Desmond his name, pointed a finger at Derek, and Derek giggled.

Zayon, who was standing next to Derek, gave him an elbow. Derek gave it right back. Bartholomew glared at Zayon, and the latter grimaced. Those two didn't always get along, Stan had observed—some vendetta from the home island.

The interrogation was over then; it had gone nowhere. Stan gestured and the crew filed out of the barn. Rufus followed, already giving orders in his bullfrog voice. "Rufus," Stan called, and the man turned, waited politely—too politely, Stan thought—in the doorway. He wanted to ask, *Where were you last night, Rufus? How late did you stay at the orchard? How early did you get here this morning?* But Rufus's hazel eyes were squinting at him, challenging, so Stan gave in and said, "Keep an eye out, then, will you, Rufus? For anyone acting suspicious around here? Maybe a stranger?" And he thought again of the woman on the school board, although why she'd want to destroy his orchard, he didn't know. But someone had slashed those trees. Someone! A fist squeezed his heart.

Rufus gave a curt nod and went out. Stan saw him break into a run, catch up with the Jamaicans. In moments his arms were waving, his head waggling as he barked out orders. The men shouted, "Yeah, bossman, yeah," exuberant now, like schoolboys released from the classroom, and trotted off in different directions, the white apple buckets bobbing on their chests. Rufus, Stan had to admit, knew how to get the best out of the pickers. He'd been working with them much of his life, in this orchard or other orchards—never his own.

Maybe Rufus felt it was time for his own place, his own orchard; after all, he must be fifty years old. If Stan were to sell, if this orchard were "jinxed," so to speak, if it sold at a lower price, Rufus could maybe afford to buy it.

Stan would keep an eye on Rufus.

Seven

The five-ten bus was fifteen minutes late and Moira had forgotten to bring a book. Her head was in too much of a spin anyway to concentrate on printed words. Stan had taken the latest bit of mischief hard. He'd stomped back in the house minutes after his interrogation, shouted at the encroaching cardinal, banged on the window as though he wanted to break it; then gone directly to the liquor cabinet and poured a stiff one. She'd put a hand on his shoulder, tried to sit him down to talk, but he'd waved her away. That was a bad sign, she didn't like that. If he wouldn't talk, if he bottled it all up inside—there was sure to be an explosion. At her; inside himself. No, she didn't like it at all.

The bus was here and she wished it wouldn't stop, that no one would get off it. It was not the right time for a visit from a niece. All the same, she must try to act normal, keep things on an even keel, keep the girl busy. She'd introduce her to Emily Willmarth. They might be of an age—though, no, Emily would be younger. Would Moira recognize the girl? She hadn't seen Opal since Carol's death three years ago when Annie May had brought her, looking morose, to the funeral. And Moira had gone through that service in a daze—partially sedated. It had been crowded with Carol's friends, it seemed the whole high school was in mourning. Annie May and her daughter were just two more shadowy figures weaving in and out of the crowd.

The bus doors were swinging open; for a moment it seemed as though no one would get off, and she was almost relieved. Then down came an old woman, fiercely resisting the arm of the bus driver, her hair a cloud of white around her shoulders—it was Glenna Flint from the derelict farm on Cow Hill Road. She scuttled into the bus station calling loudly for a "place to pee." A young man came next, a seeming redneck with bare tattooed arms, an earring dangling from the left ear. He was met by a heavy-breasted girl in a stained blue sweatshirt.

Finally a slim girl got off, in black tights and T-shirt with a peregrine falcon on it that outlined her round apple breasts and the wires of her bra; a colorful Guatemalan bag was slung over one shoulder. Her thick black hair was short about her ears but then shaped into a long pigtail. She had a piquant oval face, pale complexion, and huge sunglasses that hid half the face. Was it Opal? Moira took a step forward. The girl—or young woman, she should say—was scowling at the driver, who was slow to pull out the suitcases. Finally two overstuffed cases stood on the pavement, along with a backpack and—what was it?—a guitar in its case, yes; she could tell by the shape. The girl was evidently prepared for a long stay. Moira felt a pang of anxiety, a moment of breathlessness. How would she cope? She took a step forward, thrust out a hand. "Opal?"

The girl whirled about. "I'm done in," she said. "It was a stinking trip. I had to get up at four in the morning to get to the airport. The bus was crowded with smelly people. I wish Uncle Stan could have met me in New York."

Moira mumbled something about the busy orchard and took one of the suitcases. She reached out for the guitar, but Opal cried, "No! I've got a broken string. I got to get it fixed. I don't suppose anyone does that in this cow town."

"I think we can find someone," Moira said, trying to sound cheerful, and heaved the suitcases into the trunk of her old Honda Civic; she let Opal place the backpack and guitar case in the backseat. Moira was getting a headache, she definitely felt it coming on. It was like that red bird pecking at her forehead, peck peck peck, trying to get in under her skin.

Home, the girl stomped up to her room and shut the door. Well, Moira wasn't going to entice her down; she'd let her rest, get over her mood. Opal didn't want to be here, she'd made that clear in the car. "I'm not staying long," she'd said. "As soon as I have enough money I'm getting my own apartment down home. I'm going back to Houston."

"How will you earn the money?" Moira had asked, trying to sound concerned, and the girl was quiet a minute, squinting out the window.

Finally she'd said, "I have a friend. He'll help me."

"Oh," said Moira, and the subject was closed. They rode the rest of the way back to the orchard in silence.

She could hear the girl now, in the upstairs bathroom, running a bath. Moira had forgotten to leave a towel on the bed she'd made up fresh, so Opal would have to find her own on the bathroom shelf. It didn't take many brains. When the water stopped running, she heard a splash as the girl lowered her body into the tub, and then all was quiet.

Except for the answering machine. "Hello, you have messages," it announced for the dozenth time (she must shut off that insistent voice) and, sighing, she pressed the red button. There were four messages. The first was from a developer, wanting to know if they'd thought "oh, just a teeny bit," a female voice murmured, "about selling the orchard. I mean, we're here if you'd like to talk." We? Who was we? "Crows," Moira said aloud, "coming in on the kill." The second was from Ruth Willmarth, a crisp voice thanking her for the coffee and cider from that morning, reminding her to call about any "further developments" in the orchard. She was obviously worried about her daughter Emily working there. The third message was something of a shock. A guttural voice, almost a grunt—she could hardly concentrate on the words. Was it was a passage from the Bible—Ecclesiastes? She'd heard it from the minister at Carol's service: "The Lord giveth and the Lord taketh away." And then: "Let this be a lesson to those who heed not his Word." She clenched her fists. Who was this? What "Word" wasn't she heeding? She walked away—but there was a fourth message. It was the same gruff voice as before. "Satan is in this town," the voice growled. "He's turning it into a Sodom and Gomorrah. Oppose the forces of evil or you and yours will perish."

She sank into a chair. What religious nut was this? What evil forces were she—or Stan—supposed to oppose?

Then she remembered the woman on the school board. The one who was trying to censor that young English teacher for having the students read James Dickey's *Deliverance. Deliverance* was one of two books their own Carol had defended to the end, had stood up for in a fight in their Connecticut high school. There was something else, too, about that English teacher—she couldn't think, she was too rattled by those messages.

She was sorry now she'd derided Stan for fighting this woman, for getting so upset, for letting the woman dominate his thoughts. He had every right to be upset. Of course Moira would back him up! The hearing was tonight, in executive session: only the school board and the teacher. She couldn't go, but she'd encourage Stan. Calm him down first, yes, but tell him she was on his side, that her heart and spirit would be with him in that room.

They had to work on this marriage. They couldn't just let it atrophy.

She decided to let the messages clear. Stan didn't need to hear them; he was angry enough without throwing more fuel on his fire.

Then, fixing herself a cup of hot tea—caffeine, to be sure—she wondered, did the school board woman have anything to do with the orchard-spraying last April? Stan had had his first run-in with the woman in March. Did it have anything to do with this morning's felled trees? With a group of women she'd stumbled upon, down by the small cemetery where they'd buried Carol's ashes, on their knees and praying? She hadn't known what to do, just stood there and watched, then hurried away before they saw her.

Of course not, she admonished herself, how could it? All the same, she shoved a stool over by the phone, called Ruth Willmarth. She needed someone to talk to about these messages. She tried the barn phone, it was after five. It rang four times and then Ruth's breathless voice came on the answering machine: "This is Ruth. If I don't answer, I'm milking or I'm out in the pasture or Lord knows where I am. Just leave your message. Thanks."

"Please call me," Moira told the machine. "But if I don't tell you why I called, you'll understand. It means Stan's around. I don't want him to hear."

"What can't Uncle Stan hear?" a voice said, and there was Opal, in the same skinny black tights, with a clingy red sweater this time, and shiny black vinyl knee boots. She was going out in the orchard for a walk, she said.

"You'll get those pretty boots muddy," Moira said, ignoring the question about Stan. "It rained last night. You haven't got any sneakers? I can lend you some rubber boots."

Opal shook off the thought of sneakers or rubber boots and flung the door wide; stepped back with a shriek.

Moira ran to see what was wrong. But she saw only the men parading back to the bunkhouse: Bartholomew in the lead, the others behind him, jostling, humming, laughing over some private joke.

"What are *they* doing here?" Opal pointed a trembling finger.

"Why, they work here. They're professional apple pickers. We couldn't make the orchard pay without them."

"Mother didn't tell me this. She knows what happened to me!"

"Oh? What was that, Opal?"

"Never mind," Opal said. "You wouldn't want to know. I hope you lock your doors." She faced Moira, leaned in close with a shaking finger, like a mother warning her child.

"At night," Moira said, "we do. But not because of the Jamaicans. We trust these men absolutely."

"Then I'll need a key to my room," and Opal waltzed out onto the porch. A moment later Moira heard her voice sweet as maple syrup, introducing herself to someone. It was Adam Golding, she saw through the window, striding along with an apple crate, his ponytail lifting with each footstep. It was like a scene out of TV with the mute on: Adam standing there with the crate in his arms, a small surprised smile on his face; Opal tapping a shiny foot on the path, not caring that she was digging up mud, her head a little to one side, then nodding back and forth—was she giving a life history? Then Emily Willmarth swinging along with an aluminum pail, halting when she saw Adam with Opal; glancing at Adam, moving quickly past, head down as though she'd just lost a race. A race we all seem to be losing, Moira thought.

Emily was passing by the front porch now, her pace slackened. For a moment she was Carol, after losing a battle at school—her favorite teacher chastised for teaching *Deliverance*. "Hey," Moira called, and the girl swiveled her head. But it wasn't Carol, of course. It was Emily Willmarth. If Moira were to run out and hug her, the girl would think her mad. So she waved, smiled encouragement, and went back in the house. The cat was curled up on her weaving chair, and she patted it, stood a moment, listening to it purr, letting her heartbeat go slack.

Eight

Amelia, the new heifer named for Amelia Earhart, one of Ruth's heroines, was in heat for the first time. She was humping the other cows, and they were humping her. A child would have thought they were playing leapfrog. It was early, though, for Amelia to breed, she wasn't yet six months old. Now she was in a standing heat, remaining immobile while one by one the other cows mounted her. She was enjoying it, Ruth thought, looking through the barn window—Ruth, who hadn't made love to a man since her husband Pete went off with that actress, leaving Ruth with three children, one of them a ten-year-old. Not that she hadn't had her chances, of course; her old friend Colm Hanna would have gladly obliged. He made that eminently clear each time he came to the house.

But the divorce had come through only two months before; it was a matter now of signing a paper, making a brief appearance in the local courthouse. Yet she felt like the bull calf she'd sent away to slaughter just before the signing—axed, cut into pieces: legs, thighs, liver, a side of beef. That was Ruth.

She'd determined then that she wouldn't get deeply involved again. To get involved, it seemed, was to get hurt, and so—for a time, anyway—she would close herself off, remain celibate. Watching Amelia, though, she wondered—was humping natural? Common sense told her it was, in the spontaneous animal world. Amelia was antsy, Amelia was in heat. In the old days she and the others would have run with a young bull. Who cared that he was a loser, a stuck-on-himself egotistical jerk? You were carried away by your body's instincts.

Today, though, there was no bull. What up-to-date farmer could afford to let any old bull impregnate her heifer? The offspring needed a better set to the leg, more curve, a greater milk flow. And so the artificial inseminator would come: He'd have you and a couple of your siblings in a chilly test tube. He'd pooh-pooh the idea that Pete's granddad had about being sure to align your cow with her head to the north and tail to the south to ensure a heifer calf. He'd squeeze the syringe, shoot it in.

Why was she thinking all this? Was she horny herself? A farmer in heat? She went to the barn sink and dashed her face with cold water. It helped, a little. She pushed her hair back behind her ears, lifted her chin. And uh-oh, here was Emily now, running across the pasture, glancing at the mounting cows, looking disgusted, angling across to push Zelda off of Amelia. And suddenly—oh no!—Amelia leaping up on Emily, knocking her flat. Ruth dashed out of the barn, hollering. A ring of cows gathered about Emily, watching her. Guarding her? Amelia was off to one side, nibbling a black-eyed Susan, looking innocent. Emily jumped up, ran toward her mother, swerved at the last minute. "Mother! Get him here, that inseminator. I can't bring my friends home to see this. It's too awful. The whole day has been awful!" She burst into tears, raced—yes, raced—back to the farmhouse, Ruth in pursuit.

"What is it, Em? Talk to me, Em."

Already Emily was on the steps; upstairs, her bedroom door slammed. It meant: *Mother stay out*. Ruth sank into a kitchen chair. Its upright back dug into her spine, but she couldn't afford new chairs, the farm was barely making it, milk prices dropping—when they usually went up in the fall. She could ride it out if her family would cooperate. If they'd stay healthy, cheerful, contained. But Emily was in crisis this year, or so it seemed. Her boyfriend Wilder Unsworth was away in private school for a postgraduate year; her parents were divorced in spite of Emily's trying to patch the unpatchable. Her grades were dropping—and now she was spending every extra minute over at the Earthrowl orchard: to make money, she said, for a trip between graduation and college. She wasn't ready, she claimed, for college, she needed her "journey." A journey, Ruth thought, how lovely. But the only journey Ruth had made was up the aisle of the local church, to marry Pete at the end of her sophomore year at the university.

The answering machine was blinking and she picked it up, pushed the play button. She was thinking of simplifying her life, giving the machine away; she didn't need the world blinking at her, pulling her away from her work. There were two calls: Colm Hanna wanted to take her to the local diner for dinner; this was Colm's idea of a grand evening; would she call him as soon as she got his message? Well, she might, she might not. Then there was Moira Earthrowl, asking her to call. Moira's voice sounded breathy, hoarse. She'd respond to that one.

But when she called, Moira said Stan was there, in the living room with Opal, their visiting niece, she couldn't talk. Could she call Ruth back? Her voice dropped to a whisper: "It was a hate call," she hissed, and hung up.

Then Vic ran in, with two friends; they left triangular cleat marks of mud on her scrubbed linoleum floor. Before she could speak three words they were on their way upstairs, two steps at a time. After that the phone rang; it was her older daughter, Sharon, wanting to know, "Can you baby-sit, Mom? Seven-thirty Jack and I are going out to a movie. We haven't seen a movie in months, Mom, it's a Jack Nicholson film. Emily can take over for you. You don't mind, do you?"

She did mind, but she said yes. It would be an excuse, anyway, to give Colm when he called again to ask her to go to the diner. She was especially tired tonight, she didn't know why.

"But it wasn't just the diner," he said when she called back. "That was a lure to get you to go to the movies. There's a new Jack Nicholson film on, I thought you might—"

"I'm baby-sitting," she said. "At seven-thirty. So Sharon and Jack can go see it."

"Then I'll be over at six," he said. "With dinner. That new

Chinese restaurant in town. They have a great takeout combo. You like asparagus and chicken?"

"No," she said, staring at the muddy tracks on the floor.

"Something else, then. You'll have a choice. Besides, I want to hear more about that orchard. I hear that guy Stan is going bonkers over there. Complains to everyone who'll listen about the censorship case. Though he's got a point, don't you think? Tonight's that meeting, with the teacher they're trying to incriminate. But it's a closed meeting. Too bad. It might be better than the movies."

"Moira's had a hate call. That's the latest. She couldn't talk much, Stan was there. She didn't want to upset him."

"Shrimp and noodles," he said, "with broccoli."

"I don't eat shrimp," she said, "you know that. I break out." But he'd hung up, he was coming over anyway, he'd bring pork and beef. Now Emily was stomping downstairs, her face a red fury. "Those boys," she said, "they've made a mess out of the bathroom. They let the tub run over. You better go up, Mom."

Ruth couldn't face it. She drew a bottle of Otter Creek Ale out of the fridge. She needed it. She wasn't about to clean the floor, either; Colm would have to see it the way it was.

"I need one, too." Emily held out a glass.

"You do not."

"I do. If you could see that girl, that niece or whatever she is, you'd need one, too. She's a vamp. It's obvious. She practically layed Adam Golding, right in front of me."

"Oh stop."

"She did." Emily poured herself a small glass of beer. She swallowed it in a gulp, sat at the table, dropped her head on her elbows. "Everything's wrong in my life. Everything! This girl vamping Adam just when he and I . . . well. Then my favorite teacher—they're trying to throw him out. I don't believe one word about him coming on to Harry Rowen. Or if he did, it was to comfort him, Harry's been failing, you know. There's all that bad stuff going on at home."

"You like him, Mr. Samuels."

"I do. I like him a lot, everybody does. Well, almost everybody. There's a small group in class—well, hardly a group, only three of them. Their mothers go to some weird church. They report everything, every word he says. Harry's own mother is one of them. Now they want to crucify Mr. Samuels!"

"I can't believe they have that kind of power. There are only two right-wingers on the school board, according to Scuttlebutt. The others are perfectly sane, open-minded people. They won't let anything bad happen."

"Says you. Mr. Samuels says people are too relaxed, they don't interfere, they don't care. They don't vote. Did you vote in the last school board election, Mom?"

"Well I . . ." She thought a minute; it was the time Jane Eyre was giving birth, she'd meant to go, she couldn't. She couldn't afford the vet, she needed to be here herself.

"Then don't be surprised if there's a takeover," Emily warned. "We've been talking about that in my American history class. People are passive and the next you know it's a fascist state." She banged down her glass and threw on a jacket. It read BRANBURY HORNETS on the back in large orange letters.

"Where are you going now? You just got home. Colm is coming over with Chinese."

"Count me out. I'm going to Amigo's with Adam Golding. Though I may be back. If he has that vampire with him."

Ruth had to laugh. She wouldn't be too upset herself if that happened, would she? She'd heard too much about this Adam Golding. He was twenty-three years old, according to Moira. Too old for a going-on-eighteen-year-old. Definitely too old—at this stage, anyway. Ruth was secretly glad the niece was there. It might create an even balance.

The front door slammed. The three boys dashed down. Before she could open her mouth to protest, Vic hollered back, "The cows are humping, Mom, we're going out to watch."

She felt suddenly left behind. Her children growing up, Emily graduating in June, Vic starting middle school. Two grandchildren to watch while her daughter and her husband went out and had fun. Ruth was a leftover, a has-been. Only forty-eight and she was a has-been. She sat down, dropped her chin into her elbows. The front door slammed again, and again. The slamming entered her temples.

Nine

It was like a witch-hunt, something out of long-ago New England. Stan had to keep breathing hard, pulling the breath up out of the lungs, letting it go with a sibilant hiss. He popped an aspirin. Without the deep breathing, the aspirin, there'd be a heart attack, he was certain of it. There'd been pains lately, in his chest; sometimes they traveled down the left arm. He knew what it meant, he wasn't one to lie to himself. Breathe in, out, in . . . keep on breathing.

Still she talked on, in her high wispy voice: a plump blond woman in a pink pantsuit; she piled up the accusations like dirty underwear in the laundry basket. Aaron Samuels listened, or appeared to listen, his eyes cast down, his slender hands gripped in his lap. It was the inquisition, the pogrom, the holocaust. An aunt on Stan's mother's side had died, a girl of fourteen, in Buchenwald. He had her smiling picture at age ten, tucked away in a drawer.

"This boy," she said, "this Harry Rowen, you had your . . ." She paused, the matter was delicate, she wrinkled her nose as if she smelled something bad. "Your arms around him, you were embracing him. Someone saw, a classmate, oh yes, you were seen. Touch-ing this boy." She gave the word "touch-ing" two syllables, as though it were a dirty word, the sexual act itself.

Let him speak! Let the man defend himself! Stan wanted to shout, but the man beside him, another moderate, he knew, put a restraining hand on Stan's arm. Was it that obvious? Could they hear what he was thinking?

Already she was on to the next count, the book *Deliverance*. "On page one-fourteen," she was saying, "there is a scene where one man makes another man kneel over a log. . . ." She read the passage aloud, breathing between words, as though she were smelling each one, collecting them to stir into her cauldron. Bubble bubble, toil and trouble . . . He almost smiled; would have smiled if he hadn't been so upset, so deep-down angry in his bones.

"It's disgusting," she said in her wispy voice, her pink arms flailing the air like pinwheels, "it's abnormal, it's immoral. Men doing that to men. And our children reading this filth! And their teacher . . . well, you can draw your own conclusions."

Stan couldn't take it. He leaped up, shouted, "Let the man speak for himself! Let him tell you about that book. It's not filth. It isn't fair to take a passage out of context. Dickey's a poet. It's literature! My own daughter read it, she liked it, she . . ." His breath gave out.

The woman stared at him, waved a finger as if he were a mosquito whining in her ear. The man in the next chair pulled Stan back into his seat. "Samuels will have a chance. When she's done," he said. "This is a hearing." The young woman on Stan's other side said, "Ssssh," and Cassandra combed her fingers through her dyed pinkish hair and went on.

"Touching a student, teaching a prurient book—and it's not the first, oh no, not the first. Last year—"

"Ma'am," warned the board chair, and she sighed, and added quickly, "Inciting a rebellion, over to New Hampshire, defending that elementary teacher who—"

"Ma'am." The board chair spoke again and Cassandra sat down, curled up, it seemed, in her chair, like a cat full of forbidden cream.

But the damage was done. Even Stan saw visions of teachers seducing their students, maybe falling in love, like that Oregon teacher. He'd wondered himself: How could a grown woman fall in love with a thirteen-year-old? But now he was being seduced himself, he was being brainwashed. If so, then what of the others? He glanced at his neighbor. Ralph Lotti was staring down at his hands, wiggling the fingers slightly. Thinking what? Ralph had a boy of his own in the school. Thinking this man, Samuels, might be guilty? Of seducing a sophomore boy? It was crazy, crazy. "Let him speak," Stan shouted again. "Let the man speak for himself."

Samuels looked up for the first time, and there was a moment of knowing, of sympathy between them. Here is a man, Stan imagined Samuels thinking, who understands, who has been through the mill himself, been broken on the rack. Did he know that Stan was half Jewish?

Finally Samuels spoke—not about the novel, but about the boy. "He'd failed a test," he said. "He's a farm boy. He had chores, he didn't have time to study. The father didn't understand, he's illiterate, Harry says. The mother belongs to some Bible church, she doesn't want her son reading *any* book, much less *Deliverance*. Hey, she wanted to pull the boy out of school altogether! Harry's a bright boy, he needed someone to turn to, someone to talk to. . . ."

Cassandra made a squealing noise and was shushed by the board chair.

"He was crying," Samuels said, his slight body visibly trembling. "I embraced him, that was all. I couldn't let him just, well, go on crying." He sighed. "That was all," he repeated.

Samuels stood there, as though if he moved, he'd lose his balance and fall. He was a small-boned, dark-haired man of forty or so, with large brown penetrating eyes. He was wearing jeans and an open blue denim shirt; there was a hole in the toe of one sneaker. He might have dressed up a little, Stan thought, for this interrogation; the man seemed determined not to help himself. Stan wished suddenly that Carol were there to hear this, to talk to, to add her perceptions. She'd be old enough now to be on the school board. She'd be twenty-one. She would understand this man. She wouldn't tolerate that two-faced, biased prude of a witch-hunter.

"I believe him," Stan shouted. "He was comforting, not seducing a kid, for God's sake! My own daughter, my—my daughter had a friend who . . ." The board chair was staring at him and he slumped back in his chair. Ralph patted him on the arm and Stan pulled away. He didn't need sympathy.

Finally it was over, the hearing. Samuels hadn't defended himself well at all. As for the novel, he'd simply said, "It's well written, it's literature. This is 1999," and sat down. He had a point there, Stan thought. It was 1999. Not 1699. Or hadn't things changed that much in New England?

Samuels had been dismissed—why the devil had he walked out head down like a kicked dog? Stan wanted him to stand up and fight. He grimaced. Was he doing that himself? Was he fighting the mischief that was going on in his own orchard? His anger was a snake, gripping his throat, tightening around his chest, weakening it. Was this the way Samuels felt?

He couldn't stay for the rest of the meeting. He couldn't listen to the small talk, the petty disagreements. He had to find Samuels. He had to warn him before it was too late. *Stay and fight*, he'd say. *Fight, man! You're not alone. You have an ally.*

But when he got outside the meeting room, the corridor was empty. "Samuels!" he shouted. The classrooms were locked, a janitor leaned on a mop in one corner of the hall. "Down the stairs," the man said, lifting the mop to indicate where. Stan ran down. In the main hall the double doors were shut. Through the glass he saw Samuels climb into an ancient hatchback. The man sat there for a moment, humped over the wheel, as if he'd just had a heart attack. Stan felt his own chest burning. But when he got outside he saw the car moving slowly through the school parking lot, down the drive, toward Main Street. Stan couldn't go back to the meeting. He was done in, he wasn't even angry anymore, just numb. Walking out to the Blazer, he had the illusion that the night was closing in on him, the Norway pines that surrounded the parking lot were moving toward him, like Birnam wood to Dunsinane—something out of *Macbeth*, Carol had had to memorize it. Inside, he locked the car doors against the encroaching pines. He sat a moment, trying to calm his breath. Finally he turned the key and the car sprang to life. He took another deep breath, didn't let it out until he reached Main Street.

Ten

When Aaron Samuels stumbled out of his car and up onto his front porch, he found it full of women. They were kneeling, mewling like cats, the high-pitched sounds crossing and recrossing, rising and falling. He caught words: "Show him the light . . . Save him from Satan . . ." Who were they talking about? For a moment he thought he had the wrong house; it was dark, he was depressed—that meeting, those accusations, like something out of *Brave New World*. Big Brother is watching you . . . He'd taught that book, the kids liked it, they'd had great discussions. *Deliverance* too, it was a good book, James Dickey was a poet. He got the kids to read the poems along with the book—what was so bad about that? That boy, the one they accused him of harassing, seducing—he didn't know what the right word was—Jesus! Was this the inquisition? Couldn't you comfort a student anymore? Touch him—her? Couldn't you give a kid a book and let him draw his own conclusions? What did these people want from him? His soul?

He thrust past them, through them, there must have been a dozen, all women. No, one man, maybe, he heard the voice, as if the man were regurgitating gravel. A woman caught at Samuels as he fumbled for his keys; then they were on him, clutching his sleeve, pulling at his shirt till it ripped up out of his pants. Still praying. No, preying, he thought, the irony of it almost making him laugh. At last he was through the door, shutting it on their fingertips; he drew the bolt. But they wouldn't go away. It was a keening sound, as if he were dead already. And he was, he felt the numbness in his feet, creep up to his waist. His wife lost to him, their young son—now maybe his work. . . . He was a dead man from the waist down.

"Shut up!" he screamed at the closed door. "Shut up! You have no business here! Leave me in peace!"

Still the voices rose, circled his head; it was as if they were inside: disembodied voices, swirling in a vortex about his brain. He was hot, he was angry, they were driving him crazy. He ran to his study, yanked open the desk drawer, snatched up the pistol he'd kept there since his early teaching days in Brooklyn—why had he brought it up here to rural Vermont? Vermont, which had once been a republic? He'd loved that idea, a republic where all men were equal, Jew and Gentile, black and yellow and white, straight and gay.

One shot and he'd frighten them off—he didn't care about the consequences—let them call the police. What did it matter anyway? He'd as good as lost his job. He wasn't cut out for teaching: He was too emotional, he took things too much to heart. Rachel always said that.

They were banging on the door, calling to him. "Repent, repent!" Repent of what? Repent that he was a Jew? That he'd come to believe in nothing now, no God except in his heart—though even that One seemed to have deserted him? The pounding grew louder, the voices crowding his ears, persecuting: "Satan! Deliver him. . . ."

"Out of here! Get out of here!" he screamed, and when they didn't, desperate, at his wits' end, he picked up the gun.

Eleven

It was three o'clock Sunday morning, an hour when most working people were still asleep. The geese were quiet; he'd slipped a powder into their feed. He moved down into the south quad of the orchard, far from the bunkhouses. A sliver of moon wove in and out of the clouds to guide his path. He would concentrate only on the outer block of trees, six or seven of them this time. He was carrying a cardboard box and a large glass jar, which he placed carefully on the grass. He removed the cover of the first and peered in at the wriggling mass of small greenish brown worms. He had bred them himself at home, off season, so they would be ready to feed in early fall. He took out handfuls of the squirming things and laid them on the branches of three trees, just above where the apples were clustered. The worms would spin a light web, rolling several leaves together, enclosing the clusters of fruit.

He took up a glass jar and unscrewed the top, waiting a moment before opening it all the way. Inside were a hundred apple maggots, a native pest. Smaller than houseflies, they had black bands on their clear wings, a white spot on the back of the thorax, a black abdomen with light-colored crossbands. The design was quite beautiful, he had to say so. He had been breeding the maggots for a whole year now, in preparation for this night. The females would deposit their eggs singly under the apple skin, and then the larvae would burrow in and feed on the flesh. Soon the brown decayed areas would show, and bacteria would cause the fruits to rot internally. They were mostly Cortlands in this block, the apple most susceptible to maggots.

Of course, it was already the second week of September and the apples were ripe and ready for picking. But the flies on the few trees they would strike would cause damage, the apples would be unsuitable for eating. Besides, this part of the orchard had been sprayed with malathion throughout June, July, and August; no one would expect the maggots to appear in September. This was all the more pleasurable to contemplate. He imagined the confusion, the anger, the hysteria. What next? *Earthrowl would say.*

What next? Well, he had bigger things in mind for what next. The leaf rollers, the maggots, were only a beginning.

He opened the lid all the way and the flies rushed out. He didn't have to lay them on the branches. They would know exactly where to go.

Twelve

Moira took Opal with her to pick up the goat for the Jamaicans. She thought the girl might enjoy the outing, have a chance to see the area. Everywhere in Vermont, it seemed, there was a view. In Branbury it was the mountains—the blue curve of Adirondacks to the west; the rolling Greens to the east. And below, the pastures alive with cows and horses, their necks bent to feed on the succulent grasses; and then the open cornfields where the September corn was as tall as—what—an elephant's eye? She smiled, remembering the musical *Oklahoma!*, hummed a few bars. The local high school had put it on, Carol had played a small part; she'd looked so fresh and homespun in her jeans and pale pink shirt that it had made Moira's eyes water.

And here she was, at it again. Moira wiped her eyes with a denim sleeve, willed herself to stop thinking about the past.

Beside her, Opal sat, looking sullen. She hadn't wanted to come, of course; she was reading a book, a paperback romance. The cover depicted a hairy hand pulling back a diaphanous shower curtain. And of course one could see the woman's perfect white body shining through.

"So what do you think of Vermont?" she asked Opal, and heard the girl give a small groan. "Dullsville," the girl said. "This book, too. It doesn't live up to its cover. Page sixty-two and they haven't gone to bed yet."

"Branbury's a small town," Moira admitted. "But there's plenty to do if you look for it. Take Emily Willmarth, now: She belongs to 4-H, a couple of clubs in school, she plays softball—there's a town team of girls at the rec park."

"Softball. God," said Opal, and sighed again.

Moira gave up. For the time being, anyway. They were already in Panton, at Atwood's goat farm. Opal was staring out the window, her face a pale mask. "Hello there," Moira called.

Old Mr. Atwood emerged from the barn, a short cheerful man with hairy sunburned hands and a fringe of white hair on his pinkish skull. "Got her here for ya," he said. "You just drive round now t'back of the barn."

Opal didn't want to get out, so Moira helped Mr. Atwood entice the goat over to the pickup. It was a small, white-faced, black-nosed goat; she could hardly bear to look at it herself, thinking it would soon become curried stew. It clambered up the walkway Mr. Atwood had prepared for it, but then balked; it didn't want to get into the truck. They might have to leave it there, forget about goat stew—Moira almost hoped so. But she remembered how eager the Jamaicans had been, how important the goat was to the harvest supper. They had to get it in the truck.

"She'll go, she'll do it, give her a push now," said Mr. Atwood, and finally, with a concentrated effort and a few giggles on Moira's part, they were able to shove it up in. He locked the tailgate behind and tethered the goat to the side of the pickup.

"So," the old man said when they were done, when she had paid him, "pickin' goin' well up t'the orchard?" She glanced at him to see if there was a deeper meaning behind the words, but his round pleasant face was innocent of innuendo.

"Well enough," she said, "though there's been a lot of rain lately just at dawn. All they're picking today is brushwood and drops. We don't need our Jamaicans for that." She wasn't going to say any more. Everyone knew about last spring's spraying fiasco, it had been in all the papers. Stan hadn't reported the most recent incident. He wanted it kept quiet.

"Guess not," he agreed. "Don't help the haying none, either." Mr. Atwood had a dozen cows along with his goats, and a huge garden full of corn and pumpkins and green vegetables. His farm was an example of self-sufficiency farming at its best.

They were off then, with Opal holding her nose as if, even up front, she could smell the goat. Back at the orchard, where they'd parked down by the Jamaicans' bunkhouse, she scrambled out of the pickup and raced up to the house. Moira heard the screen door bang behind her.

"He's a good 'un," Bartholomew said as he came running up when Moira honked. He still had a bucket of drops around his neck; he slipped it off to help untether the animal. "Ex-cell-ent stew, oh, you see." The whites of his eyes shone in the dark brown face. He had a red cotton bandanna wrapped twice about his thick neck, though it couldn't be any less than sixty degrees outside. She could see the drops of sweat on his wrinkled forehead.

"You be sure to save us some of that stew," Moira said. "We don't want to miss out on the feast."

"Oh, we make a big potful, don't you worry, mum."

"That's what I'm afraid of," she teased. "Poor goat!"

"I got a new recipe," he went on. "Lot of spice, my wife make it up. But first we got to fatten her up more, you know." He grinned, and trotted on to the bunkhouse with the goat, his free arm swinging.

It was raining lightly again; there wouldn't be any picking until it stopped. She heard a harmonica playing a lively tune inside the bunkhouse, then a shout, and laughter. Then Adam Golding came down the path from the barn, with Emily Willmarth. The girl was wearing a cotton shirt, a bright green bandanna—no coat in spite of the rain. Her face was rosy, it seemed her cheeks would crack with the smiling; Adam's face had a look of satisfaction, the way boys looked when they'd made a conquest. Moira knew the look; she'd seen it on Hilly Winner, on Jake Candido's face, when they came looking for Carol, and Carol gave them all the same warm smile, the same close attention—but then she always kept something to herself. She didn't give her full self until . . . that last boy, the one who caused her death. The boy with the handsome face, the shock of dark brown hair that fell almost into his eyes so you couldn't tell what color they were, what the boy was looking at, thinking. And Carol believed in him; Carol, who was so discriminating, whose judgment of people rarely erred, who saw through a teacher when that teacher tried to throw the bull, or the parent who tried to dismiss a teacher who was hardworking, teaching what she considered meaningful. To that boy, Moira worried, Carol was merely a conquest. And yet she was wholly taken with him; she thought, for the first time, she was truly in love.

The pair passed by, laughing. Emily seemed so caught up in the romance of it she didn't even acknowledge Moira. They moved on out past the farmhouse. Opal was standing on the porch with her guitar, pretending she didn't see the couple. She had changed her clothes, she was wearing something hot pink, her hair was freshly washed. She was pretty, as her mother had been pretty before she had Opal and gained all that weight, those facial jowls.

When Emily had moved out into the road, on her way home, Opal called out to Adam and he halted, went to the corner of the porch. Was Emily out of earshot? Moira thought she saw the girl's back slump slightly forward. Emily had been disappointed once before in love, Ruth had told Moira, her boyfriend taking up with some city girl. Emily had never wholly forgiven him, and now he was away at school.

Moira wanted to run and hug her.

But here was Stan, calling to her from the barn doorway. "Where've you been, Moira?"

"I told you. Getting the goat. It's outside the bunkhouse, Bartholomew's tied it up."

"Let's take a walk. I need to talk. Christ, you don't know what's happened?"

Now she was alarmed; she felt the hairs prickle on the back of her neck. She ran to him, took his arm. He was rushing her down the path, away from the bunkhouse. She stumbled on a fallen apple. "What, what?" she said.

Stan's face was contorted. He looked as though someone had given him a blow on the head.

Finally he stopped, grabbed her hands. "It's Samuels," he said. "He shot himself. Last night. After the hearing. He went home and shot himself. He's in a coma now." His voice rose with each sentence. "And that bitch did it. It was her fault. It was—it was murder, Moira. Attempted murder."

"Wait a minute. *She* didn't shoot him. . . ."

"She might as well have. She was his tormenter. He was sensitive as hell. Everyone says so. He couldn't take the hammering she gave him. Oh Christ, Christ, that poor fellow. . . ."

He pushed his damp face into her shoulder. Her left shoulder was soaked, and not just from the rain.

Thirteen

Ruth was swabbing down the barn floor when Emily ran in, breathless, her face streaked with grime and tears. The floor was Emily's job, but now that the girl was picking apples, Ruth was doing it. Emily flung herself at her mother; the mop in Ruth's hands went flying. "Emily! What—what is it?"

Emily sank down on a sawhorse. She was openly sobbing now. Ruth knelt beside her. And heard the news about Aaron Samuels.

"My friend Cissy Harper told me, I met her on the way back from the orchard. It was all because of Harry Rowen's mother. She's a fundie. She complained after that school board woman tried to—to persecute him." She blew her nose loudly into a tissue. "He was so wonderful—is! He's such a great guy. We all love him. He understands us. He liked that short story I wrote, the one about being a farmer's kid. . . ." She broke down again. Her hands were trembling where they gripped the rough sides of the sawhorse. Ruth squeezed in beside her daughter, put her arms around the girl.

"I'm sorry, so sorry," she said. She'd only met Mr. Samuels once, at a school open house, and liked him. He'd been divorced a year or two ago, she'd heard; his wife had left for the city, taking along their young son. There might have been more to the shooting than just that school business. But Emily wouldn't see that. She'd see it as persecution. Everyone was persecuting everyone else in Emily's world. The British persecuting the Irish. The Israelis persecuting the Palestinians. The government persecuting the farmers. The Republicans persecuting the Democrats. Someone persecuting the orchard next door. Emily was upset about that, too; she'd talked incessantly about the latest incident, the destruction of two trees. And now the school board had been persecuting her favorite teacher. And the teacher was unable to fight back. Or lacked the courage. . . .

Ruth was mad at him suddenly for taking an easy way out; for trying to kill himself when he could have stood up to his tormentors. Unless there *was* a relationship between him and that boy . . . was there?

Emily answered her question. "Harry's all broken up about it, he thinks it's his fault. That's what Cissy says, she lives next door. Harry loved him, he really did—I mean, in an innocent way. He went to see Mr. Samuels every day after school, he was Harry's anchor, his anchor, Mom. His parents are so strict, all that religious stuff Harry doesn't believe in. They don't want him to read anything except the Bible! Mr. Samuels was all Harry had. He's such a shy kid. And now . . ."

Now the phone was ringing. "Tim," Ruth shouted at her hired man—he was just coming in the door, back from the first cut of corn. Tim pushed back his cowboy hat, wiped his brow with a sweaty hand, and nodded. He sized up the situation and answered the phone. "Hang on a minute, I'll see if she's here."

Ruth started to signal no, but Emily was up, running to the door. "Adam Golding is coming over—we're going out. I have to wash up, change."

Already, Ruth thought, the girl was back to life, thinking of a boy. The young got over things quickly. Well, more or less. There was the divorce, of course: Emily hadn't got over that.

She nodded at Tim and went to the wall phone. She was suddenly overwhelmed with the smell of cows and manure. Usually she hardly noticed the odor, except when she first came in from the outdoors. Tonight, for some reason, it was potent. She stretched the phone line as far as it would go, kicked wide the barn door; breathed in the evening air. What day was it? She couldn't think. Saturday, yes. Saturday night. Emily would want to stay out late, the pickers had Sunday morning off. "Hello?" she said.

Moira's musical voice filled her ear. There was the slight hint of Irish: Moira had been born in Ireland, came over with her parents at age ten. "I'm sorry, I'm sorry I haven't got back to you," she was saying. "Things have been hectic here. You've probably heard some of it. My niece arriving, and then those messages I told you about. And now . . ."

"Now?" Though Ruth couldn't remember what messages. Moira hadn't told her exactly, had she?

"Now that teacher has gone and shot himself . . ."

"I know," Ruth murmured. "Emily told me."

"And Stan's in an uproar. He's gone off to see that woman. That school board woman who was persecuting [there was that word again] the teacher. Cassandra, her name is. I don't recall the surname." She paused, caught her breath.

"And you're afraid Stan will do something rash."

There was a silence, a slight laugh. "Yes. These days . . . I hardly know him. He's so mad at the world. I tried to stop him, tell him to think things through, but he stomped out. He knows where she lives. I just hope . . . she won't be there."

"I'll come over," Ruth said. "Tim's doing the milking tonight. We can talk. You haven't told me yet about those messages, after you picked up your niece."

"I'll make you a hot cup of tea. Or wine—would you rather?"

"Tea will be fine," and Ruth hung up.

Emily was still upstairs when Adam Golding arrived. His shoulders were slightly forward as he entered the kitchen door, as though he were afraid of what he'd find there—a cross mother-of-the-girl, a smell of manure, a chicken scurrying across the pine floor?

Ruth looked at him, appraising. But he smiled, an easy, pleasant smile that tried to tell her how at home he felt in her kitchen. "We thought we'd take in that new movie in town."

"What is it?" she asked, for something to say.

But he couldn't remember, just knew it was something about weddings. He laughed, shrugged. Weddings weren't exactly his thing, the shrug said. But Emily wanted to see it. That, of course, was precisely what Ruth worried about. Emily had college to think about. Ruth didn't want her to take a year off after high school, was afraid she'd get sidetracked. She wanted her to finish college and graduate—unlike herself, married after two years, plunged into farm life, into motherhood. Even Sharon, her first-born, had quit three years into college, run off with a man nine years her senior. She'd promptly divorced him and married a man four years her junior. You couldn't control your children's lives!

Ruth surrendered, offered a soft drink. But Adam spread his hands, that easy smile again. Where in hell was Emily? But she could hear the water running in the upstairs sink. The girl was brushing her teeth, most likely, to a pearly white.

"Where are you from?" she asked Adam. She might as well give the inquisition. Of course he'd anticipated it. The answers came quickly.

The family hailed originally from the Midwest, came east when his mother died. Ruth said, "Ah."

"But Dad remarried, they settled down in, uh, the Boston area."

"Brothers? Sisters?" Ruth asked.

"Sisters? Oh sure, two older sisters, Ellie and Esther. They're married now, with kids. I have no brother," he said, as though it was something he regretted. And Ruth could understand that, she'd had no brothers herself, only an older sister who'd moved to California, whom she rarely saw. Adam looked less confident now, he was biting his lower lip with his teeth. He looked vulnerable. Ruth decided that she liked the boy—if you could still call him a boy.

Emily came dashing down the stairs, her eyes lighting up to see Adam. She was wearing a pale blue mohair sweater Ruth had never seen before. A recent acquisition? Because of Adam? "Hi," she said brightly. "Mother, you've met Adam?"

You know I have, Ruth wanted to say, but nodded instead and smiled. It was Adam's second visit. The last time he'd only come to the front porch, whistled up at Emily's window. How had he known which window? Was this a real romance? Something out of Romeo and Juliet? Oh dear. Ruth didn't care for that.

"Remember you have morning chores," she called after Emily. "Don't be out late," and knew that Emily would hate her saying that.

But Emily just waved a hand in the air as though the reminder had gone right over her head, and they were gone, racing off in Adam Golding's white Volvo. It looked well traveled, a dented fender, but it was a monied kind of car. Ruth worried about that. Now the phone was ringing. And she'd promised Moira she'd go over. And she had to pee, all those things at once. She should give in, buy one of those cordless phones she could take into the bathroom with her. But there were other priorities. There was a sprawl of unpaid bills on the kitchen table.

Upstairs in the bathroom she could hear the phone ring. It was such a tyrant! Well, let it ring, she thought. Seconds later the voice boomed on the answering machine. It was Colm Hanna. He wanted to come over. He was coming over. Where was she anyway? He'd tried the barn phone, Tim said she was in the house. "Not answering the phone? That's a bad sign," Colm's voice said. "It means you're getting antisocial, withdrawing." Of course, he didn't say where he was calling from. The real estate office? His father's funeral home? The police station, where he worked part time? "Moonlight in Vermont" was Colm's motto. "Moonlight in Vermont—or starve."

"My God," she said, "that man." She washed her hands, then put in a call to the mortuary—but it was his father who answered: "Hanna's Funeral Home," sounding weary, and so she left a message. "In case he comes there first. If not—he'll have to find me gone," she said, and William Hanna said, the usual non sequitur: "When's Colm gonna stay home and take over for me here? Is he waiting for me to drop in my tracks?"

Well, she couldn't answer that.

Fourteen

Stan rammed the pickup into the curb in front of the Wickham woman's house. This was the place, all right, he'd driven past a dozen times since last spring, his chest heating up each time, and always it was the same: immaculately kept lawn with one of those cheap pink plastic flamingos stuck in the center of it, a row of stiff orange marigolds lining the straight stone walkway, pink impatiens thick in the two window boxes. The house was a bland white ranch with black shutters, no character to it, according to Stan, who loved his orchard farmhouse—anyone at all might be living here. A chameleon. A criminal. A Medusa with her snaky dyed red ringlets.

He'd yank off that wig, expose her for what she was. A killer in the name of God, in the name of morality. A hate crime, that's what it was. He slammed the car door, strode up to the front door, rang the bell. It gave off a high shrill sound that split his eardrums; it was the bell Cassandra Wickham would have chosen, a dead ringer for her own voice. He rang again. And again. Then rattled the door. It was locked. Like Cassandra Wickham's mind. Locked tight, so no new idea could get in. He went to a window, peered inside. The living room was neat, bland as the house: a yellow flowered sofa, a matching yellow chair, matching mahogany end tables, a large TV set on a stand on wheels. Sears, Montgomery Ward—one of those. Bought to match. He rang, again and again. No one answered.

He was annoyed, as though he'd made an appointment and the person had missed it, deliberately so. He ran back to the Blazer, revved up the engine; it raced, like his heart. He was out of vermouth for his Manhattan; it was five-fifty, the liquor store would still be open. He sped through a yellow light, it turned red when he was halfway—why were there three traffic lights in this small town? And a fourth about to go up. Lights, traffic, this was one of the reasons he'd left Connecticut. And of course to find peace, to work with his hands, to calm his heart. And now—this woman.

The liquor store was in the Graniteworks, down by Otter Creek. It had once been a gristmill, he'd read, built by the town's forefather, Gamalial Archer, with, he supposed, a waterwheel to utilize the falls that rushed just beyond. The miller wouldn't recognize the place now, an electric gathering of shops: a pharmacy, a fish store, the Vites Herbs shop, Dr. Raymond Brace, dentist. And next to the liquor store, the Planned Parenthood building. Seemed an irony, as though liquor helped make the babies, and Planned Parenthood undid them. Well, he had nothing against the latter—they helped women in trouble, Moira said, she gave them money now and then.

There were a dozen figures in front of Planned Parenthood. They were carrying homemade crosses, and placards with huge Magic Markered lettering. MURDERERS, KILLERS, they were labeling the people inside. GOD LOVES LITTLE CHILDREN, one placard read, as though He didn't love the woman who was walking out now, with her man, her head bowed to avoid the eyes of the protesters. Even the man looked sheepish, as though he'd committed a crime. The protesters were praying audibly, a crew of mostly women. They'd been on a Samuels's porch, he'd heard, before he shot himself. What business did they have there? When the man and woman got into the car, when the lights went out inside Planned Parenthood, the group moved over in front of the liquor store.

The leader was a man in black: black shoes, black tie, black jacket. Only his shirt was white. Was he some kind of minister? Black and white, that said something about him. The women followed, one of them—yes! the Wickham woman. Protesting the liquor store now. Trying to shut it down. Trying to take away what he loved, what he needed; to leave him dry, thirsty, his lips parched. He got out of the car, ran over, tried to wrench away the sign from the Wickham woman. When she hit him with it, he shoved her against the side of the door and she cried out. He grabbed her arms and shook her: "Who's the killer?" he yelled. "Who's the murderer here?"

Someone grabbed him from behind. He pushed the person off, raced back to his car. His heart was slamming against the walls of his chest, the landscape was a purple bruise. He had to calm down or he'd have a heart attack, his doctor brother had warned of that. He laid his head on the steering wheel, gulped in air. Looked up finally to see them coming, a dozen of them, like blurred ghosts, waving their signs, coming at him from the side. He didn't want anything to do with them now, he'd be the next victim. Where in hell was the key to the Blazer? He fumbled in his pocket; finally found it. He backed blindly out, then forward, hit something—a curb? He heard the squeal of tires behind him, a lot of hollering; he drove off.

Then he realized he'd never gone into the liquor store, and he wheeled about in someone's driveway. A black SUV passed him, full of people, almost sideswiped him, blundered through a red light. Stan stopped at the light, heard cars honking behind him. He was surprised now to see it had gone green. He lunged ahead. A police car passed to his left, sirens squealing. They were breaking up the picketing, he supposed, down in the Graniteworks. He didn't want to be there. He'd drive to Argennes, there was a liquor store there. And no one praying at it, he hoped.

Fifteen

A red car was in the orchard driveway when Ruth arrived—she'd walked the mile and a half from her farm. It wasn't that she needed the exercise: Exercise was all she got all day, every day, milking, graining cows, calves—she had muscles! But she needed to think. She couldn't think in the pickup. Cars went too fast. It was the feet that helped the thought process. Left right, left right . . . clear the brain! But Moira had another visitor, someone in a shiny red automobile. Ford, Corvette, Suburu—Ruth didn't know the difference, she didn't know cars. Unless it was a John Deere, and who'd ever heard of a John Deere sports car?

But Moira expected her, and so she knocked. And was practically yanked through the door, the woman was so glad to see her. "She didn't phone first," Moira whispered. "It's a developer. Someone wanting our orchard." She looked frazzled, her cheeks were apple pink.

Ruth had to smile. "It's routine, I've learned that by now. They're always after my farm. I say, 'Thank you, but no thank you.' 'But you deserve a rest, dearie,' " she mimicked in a loud whisper. " 'Go to Florida, we'll pay a good price.' Sure," she said to Moira. "Sure. They'll screw you, turn you into fodder for the pigs."

The woman, who'd overheard, gave a false laugh. "Oh no, no, that's not it at all. We have a business just like you do. I mean, we're just giving you an opportunity—if you're interested. . . . I just happened to be in the neighborhood," she told Moira. "I'd heard about your, well, troubles. I just thought, um . . ."

Moira was too polite. She nodded, took the card the woman offered. Ruth would have got rid of the woman at once. In the dairy business you had to be straightforward—no time for small talk. Moira was from downcountry. She was still starry-eyed about Vermont living. The good life: apple pies and tofu. Ruth's flatlander friend Carol Unsworth had been that way, but now she had one hundred sheep, her hands were like work gloves. Carol Unsworth's sheep on Ruth's land helped keep the farm alive.

"There haven't been any troubles this couple can't take care of," Ruth said when Moira just stood there, gazing down at the developer's card. "Now, if you'll excuse us, we have an appointment here, Ms. Earthrowl and me." She nodded the woman off. The woman looked somehow familiar—why was that? The red clock stockings, the red jumpsuit, the red lipstick. Or did they all shop at the same mall? The developer who'd been partly responsible for those barn fires three, four years ago had left town. A short jail sentence, then parole. She was let go to set more fires. Ruth found it unconscionable. Maybe she was prejudiced. Even so . . .

"But it has your name on it," Moira said when the woman had gone. "Her partner, I mean—one of them—they call themselves Three Partners, though only two are listed. Mavis Dingman, Peter Willmarth. Isn't that—isn't he . . . ?"

Ruth snatched up the card. Peter Willmarth. How many Peter Willmarths were there in the world? Peter, her ex-husband, ex–dairy farmer, a developer now? But he lived in New York with that actress. Or would-be actress. The one who'd once ridden elephants in the circus—my God. Was that the way she rode Pete, in bed? Ruth had never met her, didn't want to. Would the woman have the gall . . . ?

"I'll find out what this is about. Believe me, I'll find out," she told Moira. "This is the first I've heard. Whoa . . . now how about that tea?" Someone was knocking on the window; it seemed to be decorated with black cardboard owls. She squinted.

"It's that cardinal again," Moira said. "The bird just plain disregards the owls Stan made. It circles the whole house now, like a wake-up call. Like a warning."

"Nice owls," Ruth said, and they were: cleverly drawn.

"Stan has a knack for drawing. I've told him he should take a class, do something with it. But he . . ." Her sentence trailed off. Moira waved her arms as if to say, *What can you do with men?* And she went after the tea. Outdoors, in an evergreen, the cardinal stared at Ruth with a beady eye and then flung itself against the window glass.

"Someone should wring its neck," a voice said, and Ruth looked around in surprise. A girl paused in the archway between rooms, dark frizzy hair with a pigtail in back, a guitar in her arms—the niece, Ruth supposed. The girl gave a little smirk and then walked with dignity out the front door. Ruth heard her on the porch, tuning up the instrument, then singing to it in a high sweet voice that negated her words about the bird. She recognized it as a Joan Baez protest song. So Joanie was still around. Ruth found herself humming in spite of herself.

"You, too?" Moira said, coming out with a tea tray. She set a plate of brownies on the kitchen table.

"It's almost suppertime," Ruth murmured, but took one anyway. It was rich and sweet in her mouth. "And, yes, I did the sixties thing. Well, actually the early seventies. I was in college then. But it ended when I got married. Pete supported the war I'd protested. He loved any war, actually. Battle of Saratoga, Battle of Shiloh, Iwo Jima. Armageddon. No, I'm kidding about Armageddon. But he took his maps and books with him when he left." Left, she thought. But was he back? He'd come back for the divorce proceedings, then left for New York again. He'd said nothing about forming any partnership with a developer. Here was a new twist. "I'll definitely look into it." When Moira looked confused, she added, "Pete's being a developer now, I mean. It figures, in a way. He still owns half the farmland here, it was part of our settlement. I get the profit from the milk sales—when there is a profit; he owns half, pays his share of the taxes that I can't afford. Which makes things . . . complicated. Of course, he wants me to sell. Maybe that's why he's become a developer! My God. Maybe that's it."

Moira looked sympathetic. "The developer's the least of our worries here. We can always say no. Though I don't know what Stan would say. He might get discouraged with all this mischief going on. I still haven't told him about the message from that minister."

"It was a minister?"

"Oh yes, I think so. Some kind of minister, anyway. He's called twice now. Quoting from the Bible. Sinister kinds of things, apocalyptical—speaking of Armageddon. I'd call the police, but Stan doesn't want them. That's why I was glad when you said that you might, well, help a little. I don't want to exploit you." She gripped her teacup in two hands as if to steady it.

"Don't worry, I won't let you do that," Ruth said, and smiled. "That minister's a charismatic fellow, I gather—at least to my sister-in-law. We won't convince Bertha to speak against him, though—he might send her straight to hell!"

Moira was still gripping the cup. In a minute, Ruth thought, she'd break it. Ruth told about Emily. How upset she was over the scandal, the teacher's pogrom. "Emily thinks he was genuinely trying to help that boy. That he wasn't . . . coming on to him, it wasn't sexual harassment."

"I'm sure not. Once Carol had a crush on a history teacher. She stayed practically every day after school to get help. It's hard. It's hard for the teacher. To know exactly how to handle a crush like that. I taught a couple of years myself. The student-teacher relationship is a funny one. Intimate, rewarding. But dangerous. Can be, anyway. You going to eat that brownie? Come on, Ruth. You'll never get fat in your work!"

"I'm getting to that age." Ruth patted her stomach, then sucked it in. It was still pretty taut, after all. There. She'd talked herself into it. She did love chocolate.

Outside, a car pulled up with a grinding of brakes. "It's Stan," Moira said, getting up. "I know the Blazer. It needs a tune-up. Thank God he's back."

Ruth rose with her. "I have to be off anyway. I have to get supper for Vic."

"No, wait. I don't know what kind of mood he'll be in—it'll be easier if you're here. Just a few minutes more?" She reddened, sat back down, and Ruth waited, patted the cat that was rubbing against her leg—smelling cream, maybe.

Stan looked agitated, his shirttail was out. There was a bruise on his left cheek. He nodded at Ruth, went to the refrigerator, yanked out a tray of ice. The women were quiet. He pulled a bottle of whiskey out of a paper bag and shakily poured—and poured—or so it seemed to Ruth.

"She wasn't home?" Moira said, sounding hopeful.

Stan looked at her, as though for a moment he didn't know who she was. Then he said, "No, no, she wasn't there. She—I saw her down at the Graniteworks, picketing."

"That's all?"

"What do you mean, all?"

"You didn't do anything? Try to interrupt the picketing or something crazy like that? They resort to violence sometimes, you know."

"I did. Of course I did. You know I would. I didn't come up here to be kept out of any store. Drugstore, liquor store, whatever."

The door opened and the niece came back in with her guitar. "We can see that, Uncle Stan," she said, nodding at the glass in his hand, and he glanced at her, started to retort; then he tightened his lips, sank into a chair, drank. It was as if he'd been walking in a desert, he seemed that thirsty.

"Opal," Moira said, "I want you to meet Ms. Willmarth, she's Emily's mother. You know Emily, who works here?"

"Oh yes," Opal said. "I know Emily. She home?" she asked Ruth, with a sly look. The girl was pretty, Ruth thought, but there was something defensive about the way she thrust up her chin, crossed her arms over her breasts—as if she wore a coat of armor under the red ribbed sweater.

"I've been out of the house," Ruth said, wary, not wanting to give Emily's movements away. "Last I knew, she was home."

A fleeting smile came over the girl's lips. She wheeled about and ran upstairs.

The phone rang. Ruth got up to go. Moira rose, too, spilling her tea into the saucer. "I'll get it," she told Stan.

Ruth waved good-bye. She was glad of a break so she could leave. She had to get home to make supper. Besides, it wasn't exactly comfortable with Stan here. "Thanks, thanks so much," she said, and kept going even when Moira said, "No, no, it can't be!" into the phone.

Back at the farm, Ruth found Colm's ancient two-toned blue Horizon parked by the silo—an amateur paint job at best. It was missing a hubcap and a few other essentials. How long was he going to keep driving that thing? She was glad to see Colm, though, she wanted to tell him about Pete. She didn't like the sound of it, Pete's involvement with this developer.

But he had news for her, too. "Moira called," he said, putting an arm around her waist. His fingers dug a little into her body, like a cat kneading flesh.

"Moira? But I just came from there."

"She said. There was evidently a phone call just as you left. She thought you should know."

"What? Know what?"

"It was from that minister. It seems that woman is dead. The one with the Greek name: Cassandra, the one who was harassing Samuels. She was hit by a car. According to the minister—Turnbull's his name—it was Stan Earthrowl's Blazer."

"No!" Something struck Ruth in the pit of the stomach. "Oh God, poor Moira. What did Stan say? Was it really his car? I just saw him. He seemed . . . all right." She thought a minute, saw his white face, the way he threw down that drink, his hand trembling. He wasn't all right, not at all.

"She didn't say." Colm was holding her impossibly tight, and she didn't object. A moment later she heard Vic skipping down the stairs, too fast, the way he always did, and she pulled away from Colm.

"What's for supper?" Vic asked.

"Misery pudding," she said, and Vic said, "What?"

Sixteen

Morning, and Stan was sleeping like a baby beside Moira. He was making sonorous sounds. One would think it was just an ordinary Sunday morning, church perhaps—though Stan was a nonpracticing Jew, and Moira didn't attend St. Mary's very often now. Though today she felt the need. She needed to sink to her knees and mumble the liturgy, feel the good numbness, chant along with a hundred others, the priest in his fatherly white robe. He would take care of her. He would keep the birds out of the house.

They'd gotten in late last night from the police interview. It had all happened so fast: the phone call from that minister, the police wanting to take Stan into custody. They hadn't been able to hold him, there was no proof—"Not yet," Chief Fallon had said, quite ominously—that croaky voice! The minister had been a witness, but admitted he hadn't *seen* Stan run the woman down. He'd described Stan breaking up the picketing at the liquor store, pushing Cassandra into the door front. Then when they went after him, a matter of defense, the man said—a handsome gray-haired fellow with blazing blue eyes, a deep melodious voice that would mesmerize his flock—Stan peeled off. Cassandra, foolish woman, the man said, had run at the car and Stan knocked her down. At least it had to have happened that way, the man—Turnbull—said. He'd gone back into the store to leave pamphlets. The next he knew, he heard a scream, he turned to look, and the woman was down on the pavement. He'd run to her, she was lying in a Z—

"In a what?" the chief had asked. "Curled up," Turnbull responded, "like a fetus, she was struck in the back. The back!" he'd hissed, the voice warmed up to a fine pitch. "The back!" as though she'd been exploited, martyred, in her innocence. He'd called an ambulance; then he'd left in Cassandra's car. The rest of his group had already taken off, he explained, in the church vehicle. "I went to the hospital. To pray," he added, with a hard look at Stan.

And all Stan could do was shake his head. The woman was nowhere near his car when he left. Well, she must have been, he conceded. He did recall seeing her, at one point, run toward the road. "She was crazy!" he shouted. There was a slight slur in his voice. The chief was smiling a little, or so it seemed; it was hard to tell, there was a single dim light bulb hanging from the ceiling. "Was there anyone else in the parking lot?" he'd asked. "Any people getting in or out of their cars?" He was so relaxed, so laid back, that chief. The faster and louder the minister spoke, the softer Chief Fallon's voice sounded. Once the chief turned to smile at Moira and somehow she was calmed. It was as though they were in the office of Stan's old high school principal: Stan had inadvertently thrown a piece of chalk out the window of his classroom, hit a young girl in the neck. She was bruised, but everyone knew it wasn't intentional. Of course not!

And then, to Moira's surprise, Turnbull had turned to the chief and said what a nice person the chief's wife was, how spiritual. And the chief's nose and cheeks got red, and he said it was late and everyone could go home now, at once; they'd all be in touch. How had that minister known the police chief's wife?

But the facts were damning. Stan had a grudge against Cassandra Wickham. That it was well deserved wasn't the question here. A death was a death, a murder was a murder. Murder? Stan was no murderer! She looked down again at his sleeping form, at the way his nose squashed into the pillow where he lay on his side. At the soft dark hairs on his arms and chest. The slow, even breathing.

But last night—he was still an angry man; late in the interview the anger had pushed through again. He admitted interrupting the vigil; he wanted the woman to realize the magnitude of what she'd done. She was a busybody, he'd said, "She's a two-faced bigot"—as though she were still alive.

And Turnbull, she recalled, just gazed at him with those fiery eyes. "You were angry enough to kill," he said in his sonorous voice. "God will punish you." A key ring, or maybe it was a pen, fell off the chief's desk, as if dislodged by the minister's words; it clattered to the floor and rang in Moira's temples.

Finally they left in a taxi. The police were keeping the Blazer: They'd examine the tires, look for blood, fibers, flakes of flesh, she supposed. She lay back on the pillow. "Please, God," she prayed, "please don't let them find any blood. Please. Please. . . ."

And Stan slept on. He'd gone to bed full of drink, it was his way of coping. She'd tried to jog his memory, but there was no memory. He'd drunk up his memory. And what do we have to go on, she thought, but our memories? Without them it's like living with a stranger.

He seemed a stranger today, this sleeping man who might have killed a woman—accidentally, perhaps, that's what they would have to conclude, in spite of the minister's testimony. But if Stan couldn't remember—how could he help himself? How could she help him?

The cardinal thudded against the bedroom window, like a rooster announcing dawn, and she staggered up and waved her arms at it. Below she saw Rufus walking, stony-faced, up the path with a jar in his hands. He was coming toward the house. Why was he coming here on a Sunday morning? The pickers had Sunday morning off. She threw on her bathrobe and went, barefoot, down the stairs. Already Rufus was knocking. It was her turn to be angry. She'd come up here for a quiet life among the apples and the mountains. Now that quiet life had gone awry.

She opened the door and Rufus thrust a jar of insects at her. Dear God! What were they? "Maggots," he said. "Apple maggots. Down where we planted the Cortlands. We sprayed 'em. Now they're back. You tell Stan he better go have a look."

Before she could speak, he'd turned on his heel, was quickly swallowed up by the trees.

Seventeen

Stan woke to a web of sunlight in his face. It seemed to tie him to his bed; he couldn't move his body. He was still in that half dream and he wanted it back, he didn't want morning in his life. He squeezed his eyes shut, concentrated on the dream. He was in the Blazer, it had Connecticut plates, he was driving along a back road, there was no one in sight. He was on his way home. He was a schoolteacher, his life was simple, he had a lovely, creative wife, a beautiful daughter. He had Hester, the old yellow collie, beside him, her nose stuck out the crack in the car window. It was spring. The trees rushed by: the maples, the willows, the pear trees in pale delicate bloom. That was the dream: the driving home, the wonder of it, the almost thoughtless joy of it.

The dream was slipping away, he tried to hold on, he couldn't. The web of light was catching his neck, enveloping it, forcing his eyes open, wide. Bringing reality into the room. Making him see, making him remember. Was it only last night? That woman, Cassandra. Turnbull, the man who called himself a minister. He, Stan, had been angry. He couldn't help it. They'd driven him to it. He hadn't always been that way: As a child he'd been the one to settle his parents' disputes, resolve the vendettas of his peers. But that woman! Her bigotry, her obtuseness, her interference. . . .

Something else about that woman. He couldn't think. The sun was in his eyes now, like a pillow on his face, smothering. Suddenly he sat up. She was dead, that was it. The woman was dead. Someone had struck her with a car. They said it was him. But he . . . had he? He'd wanted to kill her, it was true, but he wouldn't have, not consciously, unless in anger . . . He sank back into the pillow. It felt hard, like a stone. The pair had come at him, the woman and the minister—or was it just the woman? He couldn't think, he couldn't remember. After that, after that . . . The sun was bright on his body, flattening him, holding him down on the bed. Numbing his brain. When his wife came up, a glass of orange juice in her hand, he waved her off with a limp wrist. He wanted to sleep. It was the way he'd felt after Carol's death. That was all he wanted to do. To sleep . . . to forget.

Eighteen

Moira went down herself to see the apple maggots. Someone had to oversee the orchard; Stan was in no state. With the future in flux, she had to live and work inside the moment. Rufus was already there, among the Cortland plantings, with Bartholomew beside him. Cortlands had become one of her favorites: a sweet-flavored apple with a shiny red cheek. She loved them in salads, the flesh was slow to turn brown. She resisted the urge to pick one off a tree, bite into it. But not with Rufus looking! There was something stern and ministerial about the orchard manager, as though he were the owner and not herself and Stan. Don't touch. *Don't touch my apples*, she could imagine him muttering under his breath.

But here he was, expressionless as usual, picking off the maggots one by one; dropping them, plunk, plunk, into a pail. A crow was perched on a top branch, eyeing them, as though waiting for something dead to pounce upon. She stood behind Rufus, but he seemed hardly to notice her. Bartholomew, at the next tree, gave her a shy smile. He was wearing a green UVM baseball cap with a panther on it, the usual red cotton bandanna around his neck, a lavender shirt with striped sleeves, ripped a little at the top. Cats, the university athletes were called up in Burlington. Catamounts, extinct now in the Green Mountains—or were they? People claimed to have seen droppings, tracks. Somehow she believed there were panthers, skulking around, reminding the world that there was danger out there, yellow eyes watching, observing, hiding. Unlike the cardinal that knocked boldly on the windows, trying to get in. . . .

"How many trees are infected?" she asked Rufus, and he held up two fingers. He wasn't one to waste words. "But leaf rollers on that'un." He pointed at a third tree. "Hard to see 'em, they get on the underleaves." He glared at her a moment and went back to his task of pinching off maggots.

"Two trees, I find the worms," said Bartholomew. "Mum, look." He held up a plump greenish brown worm. It appeared so innocuous. But she knew what it would do, she'd read Stan's handbook. It would slowly munch away at the leaves, denude the trees, kill the fruit. "Bad, bad," Bartholomew said, his leathery brown face, wrinkled like parchment, turned compassionately toward her. "Too many to be accident." He dropped the worm, wriggling, into a galvanized pail.

"Then who could have done this, Bartholomew?" she asked, and he cocked his head thoughtfully. "Obeah," he said, "somebody practicing obeah. Someones don't like us. Want to harm us, you, me, us all." He looked gloomy, his grizzled head bobbing, the broad nose flaring at the nostrils as he spoke.

She'd read about obeah: It was an African-rooted belief, similar to voodoo. "But I didn't think people practiced it anymore. Do you really believe in it, Bartholomew?" As she spoke, she thought of the cardinal, her own family superstitions. It's inside all of us, she realized, these fears.

He gazed at her out of eyes like dark oceans. "It happens, oh yea, it happens. I don't make it! No! But there's ones that do. Oh yea. Happen anywhere. Right here in this orchard."

She shook her head. She didn't want to hear any more about it. Obeah was just that, superstition. She'd had enough of superstition from her mother, her Irish aunts. The worms and maggots could have gotten here by accident. She wanted to believe that. The south quad bordered on an old orchard, unused now, the trees unsprayed. She turned back to Rufus; he was rational, knowledgeable. No obeah for him. "They might have come from over there?" she asked, her arm sweeping in the derelict orchard.

"Maybe," he said, shrugging. "Maybe they did. Maybe not." And he went back to pinching off the maggots, as though they were bits of filth on his sleeve.

Nineteen

Emily Willmarth saw Moira coming up the path and ducked behind a tree. Not that she wanted to avoid her—she was a very nice lady, in fact. It was just that Emily had overheard her mother talking to Colm Hanna about Mr. Earthrowl and that woman who'd been killed, and she wouldn't know what to say. Besides, it was Sunday morning, and she didn't have any business here, really, they weren't picking until afternoon. That is, she did have a reason for coming, but it wasn't apples. It was Adam Golding. When he'd brought her home the night before, he'd kissed her. That is, she'd kissed him first. They were out by the barn, it was a beautiful starry night, he'd pointed out Venus to her, it was floating in the sky above the silo. He knew a lot about stars, Adam did, he knew a lot about a lot of things. He'd been to Branbury College for a year. But then he wanted to see the world, and he did—for a summer, anyway. He and another boy had hitchhiked through Greece and Afghanistan—though Afghanistan was full of pirates, he said, who would rush down on tourist buses and take all the money. They went to India together, and then to Katmandu.

Emily wasn't sure where Katmandu was, but it sounded terribly romantic. She'd look it up on a map when she had the time. Adam told about how his mother had practiced Zen Buddhism before she died and always wanted to go to Katmandu—as a child he remembered her sitting in meditation, and then Emily was so choked up she just flung herself at Adam and kissed him. She was amazed at herself! She'd never done that with Wilder Unsworth. Wilder seemed so prosaic, so ordinary for all his city background. Whereas Adam was a romantic hero by contrast. He reminded her of the Shakespeare play they were reading in English, that melancholy Hamlet. Would she be his Ophelia? She didn't know. They were only now finishing Act One.

Three of the Jamaicans were squatting on the steps of the bunkhouse when she passed by. One of them, Derek, waved at her. Derek was her favorite, he teased her about Adam, he seemed to have noticed that she was sweet on him. "I know where you go," he said now, shaking a dark finger, and she blushed and waved him away. The others she felt awed by, a bit uncomfortable with; there were no black students in her high school, though there were several at Branbury College. She would like to get to know the Jamaicans, but they didn't always return her interest, as though they, too, were uncomfortable in this milk-white state, as her mother called it. Zayon, who sat beside Derek, was polite when she passed by, and though she admired his dreadlocks and would like to know more about his Rastafarian religion, she felt gauche in his presence.

She wondered if Zayon was unhappy with her being there, for receiving pay for picking apples when she couldn't come close to his expertise. Surely, he knew she'd receive less pay, since they were paid by the bushel. But still, he seemed distant. The third man, Desmond, was more friendly. He was stroking the goat that was tied up nearby. Poor thing! It didn't know what it was in for. Desmond glanced up at her and said, "Goat fritter, goat soup, ummmmm, la-dy," and laughed. She smiled feebly; she didn't want to offend him. But she didn't like the idea of goat soup! A fourth Jamaican was coming out the door now, grinning at Desmond's comment about goat soup, and she moved on past, taking a long way around so it wouldn't be quite so obvious where she was going.

She hadn't gone fifty feet when she came upon that girl Opal, standing by a tree, with a sketching pad. She didn't want the girl to see where she was going, so she slowed down, pretended she was just taking a walk.

"Hi," she said. "I love this orchard, don't you? All those shiny apples. You should see it in the spring, though, the pink apple blossoms. It's like a perfume bottle got spilled and spread the fragrance all over." She paused. Opal didn't seem impressed with apple blossoms. She just kept on sketching, her face tight with concentration. Emily stepped closer. The girl was drawing a Jamaican. He was holding on to a goat—the goat looked pretty realistic, but it had big curving horns, like a ram, and the Jamaican—Oh, no! The Jamaican had horns, too. Emily didn't know what to say, so she just said, "You're a good artist. But why those horns?"

Opal kept her eyes on her sketchpad. "That's the way I see things. With horns. With cloven feet."

Emily looked again at the sketch and saw that, yes, the Jamaican's feet were cloven. It was as if he were some kind of devil. It was Derek! She recognized the single gold earring he always wore. Her favorite, Derek. There were no horns on Derek.

She must have shown her consternation because Opal laughed and said, "Just a joke, that's all." She ripped up the sketch and sent the pieces flying, then ran back down the path without a good-bye.

Emily thought of the night before when she'd seen Opal down by the storage shed. Emily was to meet Adam just beyond there, by the toolshed, and she wasn't exactly happy to see Opal. Adam had his blue bandanna loose around his neck, and Opal was lifting her arms as if to tie it for him. Until she saw Emily, and then Adam stuffed it in his pocket and spoke briefly to Opal, and walked away from the two of them. Emily hadn't known what to do: She waited by the toolshed anyway, and after a short while Adam came, and they sat and talked, and then he'd walked her home, and then . . . She stumbled on a tree root, remembering.

Adam lived with the Butterfield twins in the smaller of the two bunkhouses. They all seemed to get along, and she liked that about Adam, he was friendly with everybody. She'd never heard him bad-mouth anyone or anything. He was polite even to Rufus, whom, personally, Emily didn't care for—Rufus was too matter-of-fact, too distant somehow. He'd look right through

Emily like she was invisible, or just a girl who couldn't pick apples fast enough and he was only tolerating her because Ms. Earthrowl wanted her here.

Adam had said to come by at nine-thirty and they'd take a hike on Snake Mountain. Emily had made up a picnic, she carried it now in her backpack: cheese, lettuce, and peanut butter sandwiches, corn chips and wine. She'd bummed a bottle of white Zinfindel from her sister Sharon. Sharon was nursing the new baby and bossing her husband around all at once; she'd said, "Go ahead, but don't get loaded," and went on telling her husband how to mop the kitchen floor—he never did it right, she said. In Emily's opinion, Jack should tell Sharon to take it or leave it. But Jack just winked at Emily and started mopping. He was crazy about the new baby girl, of course, and even changed her poopy diapers. Emily liked that in a man. She wondered if Adam would—but that was looking too far ahead. And Emily was still going out—more or less—with Wilder. But Wilder was away at that fancy school now. She wondered who he was dating down there.

She tossed a handful of pebbles at Adam's window and he grinned out at her. "C'mon in," he called, and she entered, although she felt a little embarrassed at the thought of the Butterfields in there, too, who might still be in bed. But they weren't there at all. Their bunk beds were neatly made up. Adam was sitting on his unmade bed, pulling on his jeans, like he'd just woken up. His chest was bare, and not hairy at all—unlike Wilder, who had a thick nest of brown hairs on his neck and breast.

"I'm so-oo sleepy," he said. "I had a nightmare last night—couldn't sleep. That old one I told you about. My mother's putting a rope around her neck, only it was me this time, my rope, my neck. . . ."

He looked so woeful, so stabbed in the very heart, like Hamlet after his dear father's death, that she didn't resist when he suddenly pulled her down beside him on the narrow bed. Any minute, she felt, any minute he'd start to weep, and then she would comfort him, in any way she could.

"Comfort me with apples," he said, and buried his head in her breasts.

Twenty

It was a beautiful late afternoon, leaves spinning gold on the poplar trees, Queen Anne's lace and wild purple aster carpeting the pastures; and Ruth was out in the middle of it all, getting ready to bring in the cows. But Emily still hadn't come home to grain and prep them. She was apple picking, yes, but she'd promised to be home for chores. Tim had Sunday off and Ruth was alone with the thirty-odd cows. She was trying to get the herd back up to forty as it had been when Pete left, though she might have to sell the two calves born last week. One of them was Bathsheba's calf, dropped out in the burdocks. Bathsheba was one of the wild ones, second only to Zelda: No one was going to tell *her* what to do! Only last spring she had leaped over a pair of barbed-wire fences and taken to the road. Three months pregnant, she trotted down Cow Hill Road, forded the Otter Creek, and crossed a trafficky Route 23 before Ruth and Tim could find her and bring her home. Pregnancy kept her quiet awhile, but she ignored the calf after it was born, and Jane Eyre had to play surrogate mother. Ruth should sell the cow, but couldn't bring herself to.

Moving up beside her now was Moll Flanders, another problem cow. She thought Ruth was her mother. Ruth would sit by her in the barn and she'd lay her head in Ruth's lap. Even now, as

Ruth walked back, Moll was shoving her big black head under Ruth's arm. Ruth didn't mind, really, it was a sign of affection; she needed affection these days. Emily was ready to move out into the world, Vic, in middle school, was impatient of any company but his peers, and Sharon was wholly absorbed in motherhood. As for Colm—well, too much attention there. He'd read a Dorothy L. Sayers mystery novel, and, like her Lord Peter Wimsey, had begun proposing to Ruth once a week. She couldn't accept, of course, not yet. She'd grown used to her freedom, too, hadn't she? Did she ever want to marry again?

Colm wasn't discouraged, though; Wimsey did finally get the girl. But Ruth wasn't going to conform to some woman in a mystery novel. Oh no.

Free of Moll, she shooed the cows into the barn, got the first four ready for milking. Just as she was about to disinfect the teats, Emily ran into the barn, breathless. "I went [gasp] for a ride [gasp] with [gasp] Adam. We had a flat tire, Mom, on Snake Mountain Road [gasp]. Adam didn't have a jack, we had to hike to somebody's house."

"Yes," Ruth said, not wanting to hear the tale. She was tired, her back was aching; she needed help, not excuses. "You can tell me later. Prep those cows, will you? Then we'll milk. The cows won't wait. Molly's getting antsy."

She knew she should listen now. But she was everybody's mother here: not just to Emily, but to three dozen cows and calves! Seeing Emily's lips tighten, she relented. If Emily couldn't confide in her, what crazy thing might the girl do? She thought of the Rowan boy whose parents had deserted him for work and religion.

"I'm sorry, Em. I really want to hear all about it. At supper, okay? I've made a meat loaf."

"Meat loaf again?" said Emily, sounding world-weary, and Ruth sighed, turned back to the cows. Immediately, of course, the barn phone rang, and mechanically she picked it up. "Hello?" she said, hearing her own voice hard, and then harder still when she heard who it was. "Pete? What do you want, Pete?"

It was Pete who should be here milking these cows; angry tears squeezed out of her eyes. "What are you into now, Pete? You're a developer, are you? Buying up people's dreams? They've had problems at that orchard, Pete, they're good people. They're trying to make a go of it."

"Wait a minute, wait," he said, sounding laid back as always, making her seem the shrew. "I'll explain."

She heard him clear his throat, heard the change jingle in his pocket. She remembered that about him: He always cleared his throat when he was nervous, jingled the change in his pocket. Good. She'd wait it out. Why was she still bitter? She'd have to get over it. She should accept separations, accept divorce. "This is the twentieth century, Mother," her daughter Sharon would remind her. "Divorcees are civilized to each other." Yet when she saw Pete, heard his voice, the old shock of his leaving welled back up in her.

Finally Pete said, "This woman, she's a friend of Violet's." (Violet, oh yes, that was the woman's name—she kept forgetting it.) "She . . . I . . ." He was confused now; she relished it. "She knew I farmed for a time."

"A time? Twenty-two years," she said.

Ignoring the comment, he went on. "I, um, know the area. I said I'd help out. The friend is from downstate New York. Trying to get back to the land, you know, has some capital."

Back to the land all right, she thought, and waited again.

"Well, that's it. I'm helping out a little."

"You're a partner."

"Well, that was her idea."

"You told her to go to that orchard. You knew they had some, well, problems?"

"I did read about the spraying last spring. I get the local paper, like to know what's going on." He chuckled. "I am a native here," he reminded her. "My parents and grandparents are—"

"Buried here, yes."

She heard him pull in a breath. "I think I've explained," he said stiffly. "And it wasn't just because they've had 'problems.' We—she—has called on *other* orchards and farms."

"Not this farm, Pete. I don't want her coming around here."

Now it was his turn to be silent. Then, "The land's half mine, I believe. Last I knew. Are you planning to buy me out?"

"You know I can't. Not yet."

"You could get married. That whazzisname, the mortician."

"You know perfectly well what his name is. You were in high school together. Colm Hanna."

He laughed. "My memory's slipping. I've been away, you know."

"I know. Where are you calling from, anyway?"

"Branbury Inn. I'm up for a few days. That's why I called, before you decided to give me the third degree. I want to take Vic and Emily to Montreal, a little outing. Violet and I. . . ."

She felt a chill wind blow through the open barn door. Beyond, the early evening mountains were an icy blue. It was mid-September, winter was breathing in on them already. "You'll have to ask them. Emily?" she called, and the girl came running.

"Dad," she said eagerly, and Ruth went back to the cows. The hum of the milking machine, the grunting and salivating cows, drowned out Emily's voice. When Ruth straightened, ready for the next group of cows, Emily was back. "I'll take over, Mom."

"Are you going, then? To Montreal with your father?"

"I'd like to, I really would. But I have the apple picking. And next Sunday morning Adam and I are renting a canoe. We're paddling down Otter Creek, having breakfast at Mister Ups."

Emily sounded happy. She pushed her mother aside. "Go in and check that meat loaf, Mom. I'm fine." And Ruth did just that.

But when she opened up the oven, the meat loaf was burned. It was that damned electric stove Pete had bought before he took off. It overheated, it burned everything. What was wrong with the old gas stove? At least she could count on it.

She decided to call Colm. She needed to talk to a friend. Colm was in real estate; she'd ask him to look into this developer. Only she'd forgotten the woman's name. So she called Moira Earthrowl. And Moira said she'd call back, the woman's name was on a card somewhere and she couldn't look that minute. "Things are a madhouse here. The goat's gone! It happened while the Jamaicans were picking. Someone cut the rope. The Jamaicans are all in a tizzy. And I'm darned if I want to go get another goat!"

Ruth called Colm anyway. But he wasn't home, he wasn't in his real estate office, and he wasn't at the police station. Wholly frustrated now—was there no one to talk to in this town?—she dropped the phone into its cradle, and poured herself a tall mug of Otter Creek Ale.

Twenty-one

Moira calmed the Jamaicans with a promise to get another goat. More or less calmed them, that is. They were accusing one another of letting the animal go. Derek was pointing a finger at Zayon, the goat "keeper." "He let 'im go, yeh, he wanns see um run, he let um go." And Zayon: "I neber let um go, you know dat. Why I do anyways? You crazy, mon. Someone cut um loose, de rope cut, right?" He held up an end that was still attached to a tree in front of the bunkhouse, shook it under Derek's nose. Bartholomew laughed, and Zayon turned on him. "Laugh, laugh, mon, go 'head. I tink you de one cut 'im loose. To spite me. Make me look bad." He made a movement toward Bartholomew and the old man jumped back, responded in the patois. "Hey! You watchit dere. I do nutting of de kind, you know dat."

"Stop it, stop it now," Moira shouted, and Derek sidled up to her. "Jus' an ole hate," he confided in her ear, "ober a woman. Bartolomew he took away Zayon woman, ten year ago, but Zayon he don't forget it. Neba mind now, bosslady. I calm he down." He took Zayon's arm and led him back into the bunkhouse, although the latter was still muttering, "Trick, trick, dey play on me trick."

So she'd have to get another goat. She made Bartholomew promise not to mention that the rope was cut. She'd told Stan that the goat broke away, and he'd accepted that with a shrug. He didn't need anything more now on his plate. She was worried sick about him, to tell the truth. He was obsessed with all that had happened: the spraying—though it could have been an error; the maggots and worms—though she argued they might have come from another orchard; the felled trees—well, where was the explanation for those? A disgruntled picker? Surely not the Jamaicans, whose livelihood depended on the work. If not—then who? Rufus Barrow, who obviously wanted the orchard for himself? The local pickers, those cheerful young people? she couldn't imagine it. The Three Partners, who wanted the orchard sold? That Messengers minister, who resented Stan's interference with Cassandra—and the woman dead and Stan accused of running her down? Not true! Not her Stan!

Though he had changed over the last three years, she had to admit that. He was like her bootlace, fraying more and more until just this morning, it broke. It could have been Stan who ran down the woman, she had to face the possibility. Her body trembled with the thought. But no, surely not deliberately. The Stan she'd married twenty-six years ago would never kill, not in his right mind. Not that Stan. But this new Stan?

Think positive, she told herself. He didn't do it. He didn't kill that woman. No.

"Well, Opal," she said—the girl was on the porch, tuning up her guitar; it was like a fingernail running over a blackboard—"looks like the goat is just plain gone. We'll have to get another. You want to come with me?"

Opal looked at her blankly. "Goat?" And went on tuning. *Zing zing zong zung . . .*

"You didn't hear all the whooping and hollering? Someone cut the rope and the goat's gone. They searched all over last night but couldn't find it. So we'll have to get another. You want to come with me?"

The girl's frown gave her the answer. She sighed, pulled on a jacket; she'd go alone. But before she could reach the door, the phone rang. It was old Glenna Flint from the Flint farm on the road behind the orchard. A goat on a raveled piece of rope had blundered into Glenna's pasture and got caught on a fence. "We've got enough trouble with a greyhound dog and a pain-in-the-ass rented cow," Glenna said. "We don't need a goddamn goat! I been calling around. I want somebody to come and pick it up. Now."

Moira whooped. They'd come at once, she promised. "Don't let it get loose! It belongs to our Jamaicans. We'll send over a bowl of goat soup for your trouble."

"Don't trouble yourself," said Glenna, who was known for her outspokenness, and hung up.

"We've found the goat," Moira told Stan, who was coming through the door, with a Cortland apple in each hand. "This," he said, holding them out, "is what that worm does." She saw where the flesh was undermined, bruised and brown.

"How awful. But we were warned when we bought the place. You have to worry about weather and worms and maggots and—"

"People," he said. "People who have an axe to grind. And grind it on us. That goat didn't break away, the rope was strong. Zayon told me that; I believe him. Someone deliberately cut that rope. It's one more link in a chain of malice."

He sank down in a chair, dropped the apples—he was dropping things a lot lately, she'd noticed—and Moira picked them up, sat on the chair arm beside him. He didn't look at all well: His skin was as bruised-looking as the apple where the worm had burrowed. The worm that was burrowing into their lives, eating away at their hearts, their marriage.

She stroked his hair. "Stan, Stan, sweetheart," she said. "We'll fight it. Ruth and her friend Colm Hanna are helping—Colm works part-time for the police—"

"No police!" he said. "No reporters!"

"No, no. It'll be like having a private detective. They'll keep our troubles as quiet as they can. Things will come right, you'll see. You'll see." He closed his eyes then, while she stroked and murmured, and moments later he was sound asleep in the wing chair.

Twenty-two

When Emily arrived at the orchard after school, she found Derek crooning to the goat. "Ole billy goat," he told her, "he heb hisself a good time 'fore he turn to soup."

"Oh," said Emily, "how could you do that anyway? To a poor goat? You've given him a name, right?"

"Who name him? Not me," he said, winking at Desmond, who was emerging from the bunkhouse in his black rubber boots, the apple bucket strapped to his chest. He looked like he was ready to march off down the road, beating a drum.

"Well, I'll name him, then," she said, watching the goat nibble the grass, which was already considerably thinner in the area where he was tethered. "I'll call him . . . Munchy. Munchy the goat. Hello, Munchy," she said, and patted the goat on his hairy head. It felt surprisingly soft.

"We munch 'im, all right. At de harvest supper," said Derek, guffawing, and Emily sighed. It was like the young bulls she and Vic would grow fond of at home, and suddenly the bull would be gone, and she knew where—to the slaughterhouse. Her mother was a softie, of course, she always managed to be in town when they came to take the male baby away.

"Don't serve me any of your Munchy," she said, making a face.

Derek laughed, of course, and spotting Adam striding down the path, Emily ran off.

They were working in the southeast orchard today, Adam told her, he and Emily and Millie were picking together. The Butterfields were in a different quad. "I need to talk to you. I have an idea," he went on, and something leaped in her throat, like a bird wanting to get out and fly.

She strapped on her bucket and followed him down through the orchard. Millie was already there, waving at them from a ladder. It was a beautiful day; it had rained at dawn and now the air was sweet and fragrant as perfume. No, sweeter. The apples seemed larger and redder this year, perhaps because of all the rain in May and June. It was as though her whole world were an apple: Golden Delicious, thank you, and she had only to bite into it to taste the universe.

She waved at Rufus as he drove past. His tractor was pulling a small wagon filled with crates, into which they'd unload the picked apples. He looked straight ahead, granite-faced as usual. Adam stuck an elbow into her ribs, and she laughed. "I've tried telling the guy jokes," he said, "and he just nods and grunts. I don't think he knows how to smile."

"Too bad," she said. Nothing could break her good mood today. She'd gotten an A on an American history test—her teacher would recommend her for any college she wanted to go to, if she decided to go next year, and *if* she could get a full scholarship; the sun was out; and she was with Adam. Adam, who thought she was pretty—he'd told her that only yesterday.

"You're a pretty girl," he'd said. "You going to run that farm yourself one day?" And right then she decided that she wasn't—though he meant it in a positive way. "I don't intend to farm," she'd said. "Mom says we can choose, Vic and me. We're not committed. I mean, my dad has already quit the farm. He doesn't want anything to do with cows." Adam had smiled. He understood the lure of the city, he said.

"So what do you want to do with your life?" she asked him now, as she picked the lower branches of a Macintosh tree, taking care to ease the apple gently off the tree as Rufus had taught, and into her bucket. True, she thought, it wasn't a day for thinking ahead; rather, for living the moment—as her sister Sharon was always repeating, although Sharon had two children now and *had* to live moment by moment, diaper by diaper. Emily didn't think she wanted that life, either—at least, not for a long time.

"Join the Marines," Adam said.

"What?"

"Just kidding. I don't know. Go to New York, I think. This winter. After I save up enough money. Get a pad there. Greenwich Village, Soho. Do some music. Make some money."

"How? Doing music?"

He shrugged. "I'll think of something. Things happen in the city. Opportunities. You don't get them in a place like this."

"What brought you up here, then? To this orchard? If you like the city so much?"

But he was being silly now, doing a little dance step with the ladder over his left shoulder, looking like a fireman about to throw it against a burning building. His ponytail danced behind him. She could imagine him in fringed leather breeches and beaver cap, the way her forebears had looked two hundred years ago. They cultivated apples on their land, too. For now, though, Adam was gorgeous in his jeans and the periwinkle-blue shirt that matched his eyes. "The wind," he threw back over his shoulder, "the wind blew me here. The wind will blow me back."

She laughed, and ran after him as he moved to the next tree. "But what's that idea you had, that you wanted to talk to me about?"

He turned suddenly, looked serious, his eyes blue-green lakes. "A trip. A little trip. Not far. To the Valley Fair, up in Essex. It starts next week. I have a friend there, we can spend the night. Maybe go to Montreal Sunday."

She gasped. "But the apple picking? How can we stay the night? They need us here."

"Oh, just for a short weekend. We can beg off."

She took a quick breath, her heart galloping in her chest. "When?"

"Week from Saturday? We get Sunday off anyway—half of it. There's a guy in Montreal I want to see, he has a band. I sing a little, you know. I drum. I was in a band back home. I thought he might need an extra guy. After apple picking, I mean. I need to earn some bucks before New York."

She was thrilled. "I didn't know you were in a band!"

He smiled, came toward her, kissed her lightly on the lips. She heard Millie hoot, up in a tree. "Mmm, nectar," he said. "So you'll come along?"

She thought of her mother, the chores. She couldn't tell her mother she was going for a weekend with a boy—with a man, she amended. Where would they sleep? Her mother would want to know that. And then she'd look into Emily's eyes and Emily would back down. She couldn't tell her mother she'd already slept with a guy, with Wilder, before he'd left for private school—though they hadn't gone all the way. Wilder had wanted her to, but somehow . . . she couldn't. For one thing, he didn't have a condom, and she didn't want to get pregnant! And then Wilder got mad, and she was angry, too, that he didn't understand her concerns, and they parted with hard feelings.

No, she couldn't tell her mother she was going to Essex, and then Montreal with Adam. But she was going, she knew that, oh yes, she was going, all right. It would be fun—more fun than she'd ever had with Wilder, who was so serious. He wanted to be a dull old lawyer—unlike Adam, who was a musician, an artist, a poet . . . well, as good as. He was grabbing her two hands now, looking deep into her eyes, and, "Yes," she said, "yes, I will. I'll find a way."

"So let's get picking," he said, boogying off, as if he were hearing a rock beat in his head, and she danced after him, the bucket bumping on her chest, echoing her heartbeat. She would pick, pick, and with every apple she'd make a wish.

And every wish would have Adam Golding's name on it.

Twenty-three

When Colm Hanna stopped at the Willmarth farm he found Ruth with Tim and Tim's foster boy, Joey, planting hemp. They were putting in a dozen plants in a square foot of earth; the result, according to Ruth, who looked flushed and perspiring in a blue cotton shirt, would be tall, thin, reedy plants that would produce "a modicum of THC."

"Meaning 'Tender Heartfelt Care'?" Colm asked facetiously. And Tim, an aging hippie in a cowboy hat that Colm found an amusing antidote to the traditional feed cap, explained, "Tetrahydrocannabinol. What gives you that marijuana high."

"Ah," said Colm. He'd read about the controversy in the legislature. Hemp and marijuana were the same plant; it still wasn't legal to plant hemp in Vermont. "My conservative dairy farmer," he said, putting an arm around Ruth. Her shirt was damp in the center of her back; she smelled slightly bovine. Even so, there was that corn and milk fragrance about her throat—it was on her breath. He withdrew his arm, squeezed her elbow.

"Heck, industial hemp has less than one percent THC," she said. "And it's only a matter of time before they legalize it. We're just getting ahead of the crowd, that's all."

"But in September? I mean, who plants in September?"

"That's just it. They won't think of looking now."

"We'll cover 'em up good," said Tim, packing in dirt around the roots.

"Cover 'em up good," said Joey, who loved to repeat Tim's words, but with a slight whistle because of missing teeth. Tim pulled a packet out of his pocket. "Hemp brownies. Try one?"

"Jeez," said Colm, "better not. I'm off to Dad's. He needs help laying out. A new body. I can't be . . . like, on a buzz." Colm had been in college in the sixties, he'd tried it all: pot; LSD—once, though he was still subject to panic attacks; speed to get him through those physics exams. . . .

Ruth smiled, and winked at Tim. "Green Horizons Hempseed Snackfoods Company," she announced. "They sell brownies, edible hemp seeds, sneakers, hats, you name it. That new hemp store in Branbury—I bought Vic a pair of socks. Look, I'm not going out of dairy farming. I just need to diversify. They use industrial hemp for food, cloth, rope. We're starving here, Colm, you know that. Pete's making noises about my buying him out. Now eat the damn thing and relax. And tell me what body you're laying out. I hope it's not Aaron Samuels. Or is it that school board woman?"

He nodded. He was on his way over now, he'd dropped in for a quick cup, hoping she was between milkings; didn't know about "this illegal stuff. I'll call you, Ruthie." He started off across the field, waved.

She ran after him. "Colm. Sorry about the coffee, but we have to get these plants in. Look, that woman—Cassandra. It's Moira Earthrowl's husband who's being accused of running her down. They're investigating now. Have you heard anything about it down at the police station?"

"They've got a new detective on it, I think. Guy named Bump." He grinned. "It figures."

"Well, see what you can find out. There's something weird going on in that orchard. A lot of stuff that might be accidental, might not. I worry about Emily, for one thing."

"What's the orchard business got to do with the dead woman?"

"I told you, didn't I? Stan is paranoid. According to Moira he thinks Cassandra's church is behind some of the shenanagins. He's had hate calls from that Messengers minister."

"Jeez. I'll talk to Fallon about it." Though the chief was talking retirement again; more and more he was off fishing or bowling, leaving it to the underlings.

She held out her open palms in a gesture of not knowing. "Oh, and Colm, check out a developer named Mavis Dingman, would you? I'll tell you more when I've time to sit down." She ran lightly back to where Tim was stamping in the plants.

Hemp, he thought, Ruth was crazy. Someone would tell, she'd be fined, or worse. He imagined visiting her in the local lockup. He'd take her hemp brownies. Where'd she say they made them? Some snackfoods company? He laughed out loud and bit into the brownie Tim had given him. It was damn tasty. One percent pot, but hell, he'd chance it. He jogged over to the blue Horizon—his Irish cap blew off and he chased it down an incline, clapped it back on. Then stepped into a puddle that splashed his new plain blue Lands' End shirt.

Now it was striped with mud and cow shit.

Home at the mortuary, he found his father and the cosmetic woman putting the finishing touches on Cassandra Wickham's face. It was oddly unbruised, considering the fact she'd been hit in the back, they said, and would have fallen face down. Though she might have fallen on her side. At any rate, he had his father photograph the body front and back, just in case. It was to be an open casket, of course, her church would want that; it would want the blooming cheeks, the lipstick, the eye shadow. After all, she was a martyr now.

"Gorgeous," he said, and Fern, the cosmetic woman, beamed. His dad scowled, he knew an ironic tone when he heard it. "We're doing our best. This is the way they want it," his father said, sounding tired, off his sense of humor. When the phone rang: "Answer that phone, Colm, will ya? And then I need help setting up chairs."

It was Roy Fallon. "You're just the one I wanna talk to," the chief said. "Afraid I'd get your dad, he never gives a straight answer. Not that you do," he added. "Anyway, just wanna say, Stan Earthrowl's car hit something, all right—marks on the front bumper. We'll check 'em out. But we need the body, want an autopsy. It can't go underground yet."

"The church won't like that," Colm said. "The wake's tonight, funeral tomorrow. You should've told them right away."

"Hey, we thought it might've been an accident, you know that, Colm. But we got a witness, see? Some woman called up, saw the whole thing, she claims. She says Earthrowl deliberately swung around to hit her—that dead woman, I mean. So it's murder. We gotta investigate, um, we might find the way the tires—the way the body, um . . ."

Roy Fallon seldom finished his sentences. It drove Colm nuts. It reminded him of his brief schoolteaching days where he never finished a sentence himself, left it open for the students to respond. "In the Battle of Gettysburg, the South . . ." And the students would shout out, "lost," or "fought like madmen," or whatever. Jeez, it was a zoo. The principal came in one day and accused Colm of losing all discipline. He'd quit before he was fired.

But his father was hollering. "What was that call, Colm? Not another body, I hope. I mean, Fern here says she can't do any more this week. And I can't put on lipstick. Jesus, Joseph, and Mary! I can hardly bend over to do the embalming, Colm. This arthritis, it's in my right hip. Sometimes the leg just collapses. Collapses, Colm! Hey, you got a tongue? Who called?"

"I'm trying to tell you, if you'll stop talking. It was Roy Fallon. He wants an autopsy on the body. They suspect homicide."

"What? My God! They're coming at seven tonight for the viewing. She's all ready for them. That minister will sue, you watch, he'll hit the ceiling. He'll sue, I said."

"Go ahead and have the wake. But the burial will have to be postponed. Dad, it might be homicide. You can't obstruct—"

"Justice," his father finished. "Justice, hell. Why didn't he tell me in the first place? Before Fern came all the way down from Winooski. Right, Fern?"

"They don't care," Fern said, snapping shut a tube of red lipstick. "They don't care about nobody but themselves." She pushed away "the police" with both hands. The pointed fingernails, Colm observed, could gouge out anyone's eyeballs. It was fortunate she was working on a corpse.

The phone rang again and Fallon said, "I forgot to say, they're coming for it now."

"It?" said Colm, although he knew. There wouldn't be any seven P.M. wake. The Messengers of Saint Dorothea would be hopping mad. He rather wished he could be there to see the reaction. But he had to show land. Some New Jersey executive wanting ten acres "to play around with." As though the earth could stand up and dance. He chuckled to himself. Then remembered that Vermont was on a fault, they'd had one minor quake already in his lifetime. There could be another.

"Quit the police and run this place, will ya, Colm?" his father pleaded when he stopped swearing about the sudden change of plans.

He might as well tape the response, he'd said it often enough, but Colm said anyway, "Sell it, Dad. Sell the place. Buy a condo. They'll mow the grass, shovel the snow for you. You can go to Ireland. You've always wanted to see the homeland."

"Nobody over there anymore, Colm. Nobody who knows me. I'll stick to Branbury. Play with the grandchildren." He squinted meaningfully at Colm.

There were no grandchildren, wouldn't be. Unless Ruth—her kids. Her own two grandkids. How long could a guy keep the faith? "Guess you won't need those chairs set up after all," he told his father. "So I'll be taking off. Let Fallon call that minister. Let him take the gaff. You take a nap after lunch."

"That's just what I'll do, damn it." His father sank into an easy chair with an "Oh boy, oh boy."

"I get paid anyway, right?" said Fern, sticking her skinny arms through the sleeves of a black vinyl jacket, and William Hanna said, "Oh boy."

Twenty-four

The students and friends of Aaron Samuels were holding a vigil in the Unitarian Fellowship Hall, where he was a member. He was still in a coma, could "go either way," according to the report Moira had read in the local *Independent*. If he lived, she hoped there'd be no brain damage. He wouldn't want that.

The bland wooden building had been built originally by Jehovah's Witnesses, a small irony, in view of the ocean of difference between the two denominations. Moira recalled that many Jews, disenchanted with the more orthodox regimen of their faith, turned to the liberal Unitarians—Stan himself had attended a few services and felt comfortable there. The hall was jammed with people. She spotted Emily standing in the back with her classmates—one young boy was virtually propped up by his peers; Moira wondered if it might be the boy Stan had told her about, the one Aaron Samuels had befriended. Her eyes watered to see the anguished lad.

Stan kept his head down, his lips moving as though he were talking to or arguing with someone—Cassandra perhaps, he couldn't seem to get over that obsession. When she nudged him, he looked up, startled, as though he'd just wakened out of a nightmare and found himself in an unfamiliar place.

Toward the end of the vigil one of the students, a lanky boy with dark unruly hair and wide-set eyes, got up and read a passage unfamiliar to Moira. It was about a river that seemed to run only in the writer's head.

" *'In me it still is, and will be until I die, green, rocky, deep, fast, slow, and beautiful beyond reality. I had a friend there who in a way had died for me, and my enemy was there.'* "

Yes, the enemy was still there, Moira thought. But the friend who *in a way* had died, could that be her Stan? A metaphoric death after Carol, and then his confrontation with the "enemy"? She drew in a long breath. Moira could hear the students weeping openly now, and when the reader announced the title of the piece, she understood. "James Dickey, from the novel *Deliverance*," he said, and stood a moment, chin lifted, as though in silent prayer.

She heard a noise beside her, and saw that Stan was weeping, too. She reached over for his hand and he took it, and squeezed, until she wanted to cry out from the pain. He seemed calmer then, and they walked out together, behind the crowd. There was a feeling of solidarity here: that there were still feeling, thinking people who opposed censorship, who wanted an open, democratic world where one could choose for oneself; who respected the views of others: who would live and let live.

It was almost a euphoria—until they left the hall, and then there they were: maybe seven women and that minister from the Messengers of Saint Dorothea, on their knees in a circle, praying. Praying what? she wondered. That Samuels would remain in the coma? Or that he would live, virtually brain-dead, perhaps, and become one of them? Or were they simply here to torment Stan? She tried to steer her husband in a different direction, but too late, he'd seen. She felt him stiffen.

"They've no damn business here," he muttered, and for a moment she thought he was going to fling himself on the minister. But he let her pull him back, and she was relieved.

Just as they were almost past the group—the students steering a wide berth—one of the women cried, "Murderer!" and pointed a pale finger at Stan. Stan yelped, and lunged at the woman. But Emily—thank God for that girl—and one of her male classmates pulled Stan back, each taking an arm, and by the time they got to the car he was quiet again—more or less, but deeply flushed and clutching his chest as though there were pain there, and she worried that there really might be.

She embraced Emily, thanking her—she was headed back to school, the girl said, and Moira and Stan drove, in silence, home to the orchard.

Twenty-five

He quickly found what he was looking for: the paraquat, a dark, almost black liquid, in a large white plastic container. It was exactly what he needed now. Paraquat was used for burning the tall grasses that grew up around the trees. If sprayed on the trees, it would turn the leaves brown within days. The leaves would fall off and make the apples inedible. If ingested, it would burn the stomach and intestines, cause vomiting, diarrhea, and giddiness. It could even affect the heart, according to the fine print. Did he want to do that to someone? He sighed. He had to think of his long-term objective. The herbicide wouldn't kill the trees, though it would look to the untrained eye as if they were dying. That was scare enough; he had nothing against the trees.

He locked the storage shed door, returned the key to his pocket, and loaded the liquid into the plastic sprayer. He strapped on the backpack and plodded down into the west quadrangle, pausing every few feet to listen. It was three in the morning, the deepest, darkest time of the night—an hour almost not part of the day or night at all; an hour outside of time, an unnatural hour. He heard only the hooting of an owl, the rustling of leaves, a fox maybe, stealing through the trees. Something brushed against him, and he jumped. But it was only a barn cat, a tom, looking for game, for sex maybe. He leaned down to stroke it. He had nothing against any animal—he liked cats, in fact.

He chose his trees, pumped the handle at his side to build pressure, then squeezed the trigger on the spray wand. It was a quiet method of spraying, he couldn't have used a ground rig—the motor would have awakened someone. Anyone hearing this might think it an airplane on its way to the Burlington airport, or a squealing rabbit, caught up by an owl. He'd be quick. He would do only this section for now, six or seven trees: to frighten, to turn the wits. So that he wouldn't have to destroy the orchard completely: He'd accomplish his purpose before then. Though if he had to—if they hung on—he would complete the destruction, oh yes. He had access to an airplane. He'd do it without remorse—he had good cause.

He could smell the stuff even as he sprayed. It stank, it made him want to throw up, he didn't like that. He didn't want the smell on him, though it would probably fade out with the wind. When he was done, when he'd defoliated seven trees, he returned the spray rig to the storage shed where he'd found it, looking about carefully to be sure he wasn't seen. Next time, maybe, they'd initiate a night watch, he'd have to use a friend's Cessna to do the job.

It would be several days before they would discover what he'd done. Maybe weeks before they caught the full effect. One apple alone wouldn't harm, would it? He didn't think so. But make cider out of several, drink a gallon of it—it would do the job. Make life difficult for one certain person.

Off in the woods beyond the orchard there was a squealing sound; then a humming noise, like something chuckling, triumphant. Even though he identified with that, the sound made him shudder. It was like a nail scraping a blackboard, a machine gone askew. He hurried off.

Twenty-six

It was nine A.M., the milking done and the cows out in the pasture. That was one of the pluses for this time of year, Ruth thought, as she walked slowly back to the house: With days growing shorter, one could milk later in the morning. The second hay cutting was in, and Ruth and Tim had stacked most of the split wood in the basement. It was a glorious fall day: goldenrod and blue vetch springing up along the roadside and in the uncultivated fields. The mountains were soft gradations of purple: One could see the Adirondacks to the west, the Green Mountains to the east. Who could ask for more?

But then there were the minuses. In the kitchen she found Vic's dirty boots where he'd dropped them in his race for the schoolbus, Emily's breakfast dishes in the sink because she'd been late for school, and a note from Tim, in the capital letters he always used for writing: "CORN CHOPPER BROKE, BLEW UP AFTER THE FIRST WAGON LOAD, NEEDS A U JOINT. CAN'T GET IT IN TOWN." So she would have to order one through a dealer—which might take a week or more and slow up the whole proceedings. Then there was Tim's P.S.: "COONS IN THE CORN AGAIN."

She poured a cup of strong coffee. One day, her older daughter Sharon said, the coffee would do her in, but Ruth lived day by day, milking by milking, calf by calf. This was another concern: Bathsheba was nearing the end of her pregnancy and that would make three dry cows this fall—definitely a financial burden. The Holstein had to store up her milk for a good two months and be treated with antibiotics in the bargain to prevent mastitis. Ruth hadn't figured right this fall about the inseminating. Less milk, but at least higher prices in the fall—a plus, after all. She guessed she'd come out even in the plus-minus category. But lately Emily had been talking about going out of state to college—how on earth could Ruth afford that? She'd have to have a serious talk with Pete—if he was still in town.

She finished the breakfast dishes and swept the kitchen floor. She didn't mind, she had energy to burn. Afterward she pulled her boots back on to check the corn that the pesky raccoons had knocked down—and heard a car careen into the drive. She knew who it was even before the woman got out—she could sense her sister-in-law by the way the hairs bristled on her own neck.

"Oh, Ruth, I just saw Pete. He's staying with me a few days, did you know? Just until Violet gets here. Isn't it wonderful he's doing business up north again?"

Ruth had no answer for that. Pete's sister, Bertha Willmarth, came tripping up the steps in her shiny heels and polyester pants and bobbing bonnet. One would think she was off for a cruise instead of a trip to a hardscrabble farm.

"I know, Bertha. He called. Look, I was just heading out in the fields. We can talk on the way if you want to." Of course Bertha wouldn't want to—the holes and rocks would make short work of those pinky-red shoes.

But this time Ruth was foxed. Bertha said, "I've got some galoshes in the car, just wait a minute now. I need to talk to you." Back at the car, she stuck out a stockinged leg to pull on a pair of rubber galoshes that might have been a legacy of her deceased mother.

"I hear you've been on your knees a lot lately," Ruth said as Bertha followed her into the field. Moira and Emily had told her about the praying women of the Messengers. And Bertha belonged to that group. Aaron Samuels was improving; she supposed Bertha would want to take credit. She could hear Bertha panting, though—her activity on her knees evidently didn't keep her in shape.

"What? Please, Ruth, slow up, I don't want to fall, I've got a weak left hip, you know."

Ruth slowed; she needed information from Bertha about the Messengers, but it was hard. Hard to deal with this woman, to forget Bertha's past, her transgressions on the family. Well, she'd let the woman talk. She might learn something.

"It's that apple orchard up the road, Ruth. I hear Emily works there. Does Pete know that?"

"He will when you tell him, Bertha."

"He'll want to discourage that, I'm telling you. It's a godless place now. It used to be so beautiful. It was my Uncle Howard on my father's side owned it, you know, Pete and I played there as children before Howard sold it. But now that man Earthgrowl—"

"Earthrowl."

"He's a murderer, oh yes. He ran poor Cassandra down. On purpose, Ruth. On purpose! Oh, he knew what he was doing. And now he's taken the body. Cassandra's body. Ruth—slow up, will you?"

"What do you mean, he's taken her body?" Ruth turned to face the woman. "It's the police—forensics, not Stan Earthrowl—who have the body. They're trying to find out what—well, what really happened." Now she was confused. She didn't know herself what had happened. They were checking tire prints, Colm had told her; there was something about a witness. They were walking past the hemp patch now, she saw Bertha peer closely at it—there were still handwritten HEMP tags Tim had tied on some of the plants. Ruth walked faster. Then she stopped again. "Where were you when Cassandra was struck, Bertha?"

"I saw. Oh yes, that's what I was coming to tell you. I've been to the police. I saw that man start up his car, and Cassandra close by. She ran toward him. He'd broken up our vigil at the liquor store, you know, he'd assaulted our minister! That godless man."

"Stick to the point, Bertha. What exactly did you see? After she supposedly ran toward him?" Ruth started walking again, she didn't want to seem *too* eager.

"Not 'supposedly,' Ruth. She *did* run toward him. Ruth, can't we go in the kitchen? This ground is all uneven. I don't remember it this way when I was a girl."

"It was worse, Bertha. We've filled in a ton of woodchuck holes since then. What did you see?" Ruth did want to hear what Bertha saw. Or thought she saw. Bertha was impressionable: You could plant an image in her head and it became "reality." "Answer me, please, Bertha."

"If you'll stop walking—"

"All right, I'll stop. Now speak. Please."

"Well, Cassandra ran toward him and—oh, it was terrible, she was lying there on the ground, all bloody, she was hit in the back—"

"But you said she ran 'toward' Stan. He wouldn't have hit her in the back, then."

"Stop being so technical, Ruth! Maybe she turned her back at the last minute, I don't know. Anyway, I got out of the car after I heard the scream, I felt her pulse. Our minister went to call an ambulance. But when it got there it was too late. She was, she was . . ." She drew a large flowered hankie from her purse, blew her nose loudly into it.

"Wait a minute, Bertha, back up. You were in a car? What car?"

"We were going back to the church. I mean, we hadn't left yet. I was sitting in the back between Gertrude and Alma. We had cushions, you see, it was quite comfortable, though I kept telling our minister we needed a larger vehicle. . . ."

"If you were in the back between two women, you couldn't see, then, could you? You didn't see the actual moment of impact? You can't say it was definitely Stan Earthrowl's car that struck her? You can't prove she wasn't, well, pushed in front of his car?"

"Of course she wasn't pushed. Who on earth would push her?"

"But you didn't actually see the moment of impact. Answer me that, Bertha."

Bertha looked about her wildly, her orangy hair was flying on end in the wind, her hat had blown off; she went back to retrieve it.

"Answer me, please, Bertha."

"No," Bertha shouted back. "No, I didn't see that very moment! I was looking at something else, I don't recall exactly. We were all, well, talking. But it had to have been Stan Earthrowl. That's what Reverend, um, Turnbull said."

"Then tell the police that, Bertha. If you don't, I will. You tell them you didn't actually see her hit by Stan Earthrowl's car. This is a human being you're accusing, Bertha. A man who has lost his own child to an automobile accident. Maybe he was wrong to break up your damn vigil. I can't figure that one out in my mind. But maybe you and those other women were wrong to go on Aaron Samuels's property and pray! I mean, right on his porch? Oh, I heard that, yes I did. A neighbor saw it, she told the police. You weren't praying *for* him, but *against* him. He's out of the coma, I hear—lucky it was a low-velocity bullet—but it will be a slow recovery. He'll give up teaching, he says. Is that what you wanted, Bertha?"

She turned on her boot heel and stalked on ahead through the pasture; put distance between herself and this officious woman.

"That's enough, Ruth," Bertha shouted after her. "I won't listen to that talk. I only came here to warn you about Emily working in that place. I thought you cared about . . ." Her voice grew thinner, the wind blew the words back in her face.

Ruth walked on into the cornfield. Several rows had been knocked down, chewed, the corn stripped and bare. It was annoying, yes, but they were only raccoons. They were hungry, Ruth was willing to share. She'd take a raccoon any day over Bertha and her group of exterminators.

Twenty-seven

Bertha trudged slowly back across the pasture. She was upset, oh she was. Ruth had no right to speak to her that way, no, to put down her friends, her fellow parishioners. They were her life now, since she'd found Christ. All those years growing up on this farm, the blur of days that followed—mundane jobs, charities, endless trips to the grocery store, the beauty parlor—were nothing compared to now. She was doing important things: keeping babies from being murdered, men from taking to drink—at least she was trying. Sometimes it was discouraging, oh my, so discouraging. Why, they shoved right past her and into the liquor store!

Ruth didn't understand. Ruth would never understand, she was too hotheaded, too . . . too—Bertha searched for the word. "Godless," was the word she came up with, "godless." Yes, openly godless. What was this she was planting now? Bertha leaned down, broke off a stem, sniffed it. It didn't smell like corn. The tag said HEMP. Wasn't hemp illegal? Yes, she'd read about it in the paper. She'd take it to Pete, that's what she'd do. Let Pete decide. Or her pastor. Should they go to the police? Should she warn Colm Hanna? But Colm was in league with Ruth. That was what hurt the most. Her wonderful Colm, who'd danced with her, kissed her once by her locker. Back in high school it was, she'd never forgotten it, never. It was near Christmas, someone had hung mistletoe in a doorway. She'd stood under it and suddenly there was Colm, his dark fuzzy head bending over her. Was it a long kiss? She couldn't remember. She'd gone over and over it a thousand times through the years. Had he spoken? Had he said he'd . . . loved her? How, why had he changed? Why did he ignore her now? Oh, Colm, Colm . . .

Pete wasn't there when she got home. She kicked off her heels, they pinched, her feet had expanded over the summer. She fixed herself a cup of herb tea—they weren't allowed caffeine, Christ called it a stimulant, like wine, like whiskey, like cigarettes. That had been the hardest, giving up her cigarettes! They were to be pure, like their Christian saint, Dorothea.

She gazed at the print of Dorothea she'd hung on the living room wall. The reverend had given them each one, he'd had it copied from a portrait by Francisco de Zurbaran; she rolled the name over on her tongue. Fran-cees-co de Zur-bar-r-ran. How beautiful Dorothea was, in her rich red gown with the pale yellow sleeves, her dark hair flowing like water over her shoulders, and in her hands, the tray of apples. Golden Delicious, they looked like, yellowy, with a cheek of red. Uncle Howard used to grow them in the family orchard: She remembered her own dear mother slicing them up into salads. The orchard that was being contaminated now by that murderer, that Jewish Antichrist!

How innocent Dorothea looked. How sweet, how courageous, as she walked to her execution, her martyrdom. Her path to paradise. For it wasn't this life that counted, no, but the next. Christ had taught them that. Good deeds in this life—joy everlasting in the next. As though Heaven were an orchard full of sweet-tasting apples, like nectar.

She imagined meeting Colm Hanna there, sharing an apple with him. If she could only loosen Ruth's hold on him, show *him* the true light! She sipped her raspberry zinger tea and closed her eyes. And there was Colm . . .

Twenty-eight

Now Emily knew who had let the goat go that first time. Because it was happening again. It was seven o'clock Thursday evening and she was on her way to the tool hut in the east quad of the orchard where she and Adam had a trysting place (she loved that word, "trysting," she'd come upon it in a nineteenth-century poem they were reading in English class). And just as she was coming through the trees she saw Opal—well, not exactly cutting the rope, but, knife in hand, shooing off the goat. Only the goat didn't want to leave; it kept coming back to the grassy spot where it had been feeding. So Opal grabbed it by the rope fragment and pulled it down the path. "Nasty thing," she hissed, and gave a little shriek when it suddenly backed up and banged into her thigh. Emily stifled a laugh.

Opal was wearing a red T-shirt and cutoff jeans, in spite of the evening chill. Her black pigtail bobbed like a feather where it was pinned up. Several times Emily had caught Adam looking at the girl, and Emily didn't like that. Adam was hers. Weren't they planning a trip to Essex, and then Montreal, the very next weekend?

Emily coughed. And Opal shrieked again. "You're following me!" she shouted. "You've no business. I was just—"

"You were just letting that goat go. For the second time, right?

And I know why. It's because of the Jamaicans. What do you have against them, huh? What?"

Opal didn't answer; she just stood there, her dark eyes blazing, her pigtail quivering with her indignation. Suddenly the goat lunged and broke free; this time it loped ahead through the trees.

"Look what you made me do!" Opal cried.

Emily was floored. It was Opal's fault that the goat was loose. "Help me catch it," she told the girl. "We'll bring it back to the bunkhouse. I think you'd better do that," she said when Opal stood motionless, her mouth open, a bit of spittle on her sallow chin. "Where'd you get that lethal-looking knife, anyway?"

"From the Earthrowls' kitchen, of course," Opal said, as though it were the dumbest question she'd ever heard, and dropped the knife in the grass. It gleamed there like a streak of moonlight.

"Well, you better put it back," Emily snapped, and started after the goat. She heard Opal tramping slowly behind her. Hearing voices, she turned, and there were Derek and Bartholomew, Derek's gold earring glinting in the waning light. She saw that Don Yates was nearby as well, picking up drops.

"It broke its rope," Opal told the men. "I saw, I came after it." Emily was stunned at the lie, but said nothing.

"It a feisty one," Derek said, "it know what's comin'. Smart ole goat."

"It went that way," Emily told the men, pointing into the darkening trees. "Opal and I were chasing it." She glanced at Opal, but the girl was staring straight ahead.

The chase went on for another fifteen minutes until they found the goat chewing on a clump of grass under a tree. Derek laughed and caught it up. "You don't get away dis time, ole goat," he said. "You mek my harvest soup, oh yea." Bartholomew laughed, too, and snatched an apple off a tree and bit juicily into it. "Bossman won't miss one," he said. "Maybe two will make good luck," and he put another apple in his pocket.

"Good luck get dis here goat bek," said Derek, picking one of the apples for himself, and he and Bartholomew trotted with the goat back up toward the bunkhouse. Night was coming on quickly now. Don Yates followed, carrying a bag of drops he'd picked farther down. "Good evening, ladies," he said, doffing his tweed cap. "I'm sure the men appreciate your help."

Opal grabbed Emily's elbow. "If you don't tell on me, I won't tell where you're going—what you all are up to." She pointed in the direction of the toolshed. Then her voice got all husky. "Someday I'll tell you why. Why I really let that goat go."

"Because you like goats?" Emily said, still shaken by Opal's insinuation about the toolshed.

But Opal only motioned with her hand as though she'd swat a fly and ran off to retrieve the knife, like an Amazon charging an enemy.

Twenty-nine

When Moira went to the bunkhouse Friday evening with a special dessert she'd made—apple strudel with whipped cream and cherries on top—she found the group playing a quiet game of dominoes. The raggedy lines of dominoes seemed to have been built up in virtual silence. It was odd; usually the men were laughing or arguing or chattering about their women and children. But when she asked why they were whispering, Desmond pointed to the bed in the far corner and said, "Ole fellow sick," shrugged as though it were somehow expected of an "old man" like Bartholomew, and went on with his game.

Zayon came up behind as she stood by Bartholomew's bed. "He eat too many apple, that why. Got a bellyache." He clutched his stomach and made an oohing noise.

"Bartholomew?" she said, and he opened his eyes. "It's your stomach that hurts?" He nodded, then pointed at his throat, telling her that, too, was causing pain.

"Open," she ordered, and when he did, she saw that the inside of his mouth was scarlet, as though a fire had been kindled in his throat. His eyes were oozing a yellowy liquid; he clapped a handkerchief over his nose, then bolted out of bed and over to the bathroom in the far corner of the bunkhouse. The men chuckled, as though he were a small child and had the runs.

"How many apples did he eat?" she asked, and Zayon held up two fingers, still smiling.

"Well, that shouldn't make him so sick. After all, we can drink several glasses of cider and not get ill."

"Mebbe other ting, don't know, he tek medicine, too." Zayon pointed to an array of small bottles on the stand beside the bed. "Too old now, too sick fer be picking. He belong home wid his childrens. Can't pick like us," he confided to Moira, and she turned away, she didn't want to hear a complaint against another picker. Anyhow, she was fond of Bartholomew, he was there when they bought the orchard, he was always cheerful. She glanced at the bottles. Aspirin, warfarin—warfarin? A blood thinner? She remembered her Aunt Eileen, who had a heart condition. There were things one couldn't mix with warfarin. Bartholomew had gotten them, she saw, at a drugstore in Florida, where he'd been picking oranges before he came to Vermont.

He staggered now out of the bathroom and fell heavily into the bunkbed, a lean, dark figure in overalls and a T-shirt that read, REGGAE MIAMI. He'd gone to bed right from work, Zayon told her, he hadn't changed into his nightshirt or whatever he wore to bed. She glanced at her watch. It was only seven-thirty now.

"That's all you ate—two apples?" she asked. "What did you have for supper?"

"A few beans," he whispered. "Then the apples. I get them off a tree las' night. Derek eat one, too."

"Derek?"

"Yes, mum," Derek said. "I make a run for it." He pointed at the bathroom. Zayon smiled.

"Where? What tree did these apples come from?" Silly question, she knew, but she was paranoid herself these days. She didn't want anything else to happen to the orchard. Stan's thin psyche couldn't take it. At least there had been no more visits from the police. Ruth's sister-in-law, the so-called "witness," turned out not to have seen the moment of impact at all. Ruth had called to tell her that.

Bartholomew was groaning now with pain, he was perspiring profusely; she saw it was serious, this heart condition. She ran back to the house to call the hospital. She'd take him there in her car. She remembered, as a child, the doctor coming to the house when her mother had pneumonia. That didn't happen anymore. Too bad. Even in Vermont, life was in a fast spin. Sometimes—sometimes, she just couldn't keep up with it.

When they'd pumped out Bartholomew's stomach, when he was back in the bunkhouse sleeping—and she prayed there would be no other far-reaching side effects—she found Stan and the Butterfields down in the west orchard flashing a lantern at a group of Winesap apple trees. The leaves were turning brown, it appeared; it didn't seem to have been caused by maggots or worms. One of the Butterfield twins had discovered the trees earlier that evening when he was taking a jog through the orchard. It was quite dark now; they'd look again in the morning, Stan decided, not wanting to think that anything else had happened here. Besides, he didn't know what it was, he'd have to ask Rufus. She knew, of course, he didn't want to have to ask Rufus: Rufus made him feel "dumb," he'd complained at lunch that day. "It's the way that man looks at me," he'd said, "the tone of his voice, like, what am I doing here anyway? Why aren't I back in the classroom where I belong? Let the orchard men take care of the orchard."

"They're older trees in this quad, aren't they, Stanny? They're taller than most? Don't leaves turn brown when apple trees get old?"

He didn't think so, but then, he'd only read a couple of books. He was tired, he told her. He needed a drink. He took her hand like an obedient child and they plodded back up toward the house. The path forked, and Emily Willmarth appeared suddenly with a flashlight.

"Just taking a walk, I hope you don't mind," she said, and Moira said of course not, though she wondered why the girl would "take a walk" in the orchard when she had acres and acres of her own to walk in.

"It's Adam Golding, I bet," she said to Stan after they'd passed by. "The pair are getting thicker. I wonder if I should say something to Ruth. The girl's still in high school."

Stan grunted. "She's a farm girl. Seems a sensible kid. Adam doesn't give any trouble here. Don't worry."

"You said that about Carol. She was just in high school, too, when she met that boy."

Seeing his face in the glow of the kerosene lantern, she regretted the allusion. She was the worrier back then, as well; Stan hadn't been concerned about the older boy Carol was dating. It wasn't that he was so much older—there were only a few years' difference, and he seemed amenable enough when he'd come to the house to pick her up. But he was a city boy, he'd had more experience. He was into drugs, too, she'd suspected. Hadn't she smelled pot on him one time? She knew that sweet sickly smell of pot, oh yes! But Stan said not to worry. Until it was too late. And then he was devastated. Angry at himself for not intervening earlier.

"I'm sorry, darling, I didn't mean to say that. It's just that Emily is so naive. I know that Ruth worries about her."

"It's all right, it's okay," he said, sounding ambivalent. Entering the house behind her, he went straight to the liquor cabinet.

There were two messages on the answering machine, but she couldn't bear to press the button. If she didn't hear them, the world might stop for a moment, leave her and Stan in peace. And when he asked her if she wanted a drink, maybe a whiskey sour, her favorite, she said, "Oh, why not? Fix me one." She'd sip it while she worked her loom. She was making scarves for the men. Stan thought she was foolish, of course. "They wear scarves down in tropical Jamaica?" he'd teased. But these were cotton, with glittery bits of red and orange threaded through the blue or green. They could wear them over a shirt, a kind of decoration. So she was making them anyway.

But there wasn't to be any peace, any evening quiet, because the phone shrilled, and it was Annie May, wanting to talk to Opal. She'd found something that her daughter had hidden from her.

"What right d'you have going into my drawers?" Opal shrieked, and the fight was on. It happened every other night now.

"Let's sit in the kitchen," Moira whispered to Stan, and for once he didn't argue. They huddled together on two stools and commiserated. "That sister-in-law of mine," said Stan. "That niece of mine," said Moira, and they broke into giggles. It felt good, like old times. "Let's go to bed early," Moira said, stroking her husband's thigh, and for the first time in two weeks, he looked interested.

Thirty

It had rained all night and into the morning, and dampened Ruth's spirit. Pete was coming over to talk "business," he said, and Ruth was behind in everything. The woodpile she and Tim and Joey had heaped up against the winter was damp and there were only a few dry sticks in the cellar for the woodstove. The raccoons had attacked the corn again—none of Tim's makeshift scarecrows worked. But at least the hay cutting was complete, and the hay done up in their round bales. She was at her desk paying bills—or portions of bills; there was never enough money for full payment. Dues to Agri-Mark, repairs for the corn chopper, the baler; grain prices up. Taxes due in November and fire insurance coming up in October. The lawyer's fee for the divorce—although she'd made Pete pay for most of that; after all, he'd initiated it. Pete's ownership of half the farmland meant more negotiating, manipulating, but it was the only way she could make out until the hemp, the Christmas trees—or whatever else she'd diversify with—paid off a little. Well, she'd let him see the bills. There'd be an argument, of course, there had always been fights over money—though he'd been happy enough to let her keep the books. He was always there in the end, though, for the second-guessing.

"Hi, there," he said, coming through the door without knocking; and came on as though he'd kiss her. She instinctively swerved—she didn't need his ingratiating "gift" and the kiss landed on her ear. He was dressed to the nines, she saw: shiny brown loafers, pressed pants, and what looked like a new brown tweed jacket. His hair had receded even farther since she'd last seen him, there was more gray around the temples. "Mr. Developer," she said, and he smiled as though she'd paid him a compliment.

"As a matter of fact, we've just made a bit of a coup," he announced. "We've bought the Larocque farm next door."

"No! Lucien would never sell!" A few years ago his wife had died as the result of a break-in, and old Lucien had been carrying on alone. He'd vowed to farm till the death.

"He'll go live with his daughter. He's almost crippled now, Ruth, he had a heart attack last year, Marie says. He can't live alone."

"Oh." She put her head in her hands. She hadn't thought Lucien would give up. She'd tried to help, she'd sent Vic over, and her own hired man, but, well, she'd neglected him this past year. It was partly her fault. She hadn't even known he'd had a heart attack. She might have helped out. Damn her own busyness!

Pete was pouring himself coffee, reaching for one of her doughnuts, making himself at home as though he still lived here. "So what are you planning to do with Lucien's land? If you dare develop it, turn it into a hundred houses . . . a hundred cars that will race by and spook my cows . . ."

"Come on," he said, "you know I wouldn't do that. Six or eight houses, that's all. There's only a hundred acres left—he sold off some himself to pay taxes after Belle died. Twenty, thirty acres apiece, room for a hobby farm, a nice house, everything they're looking for."

"They?"

"City folks, wanting out of the rat race, back to the land. It happened in the sixties, seventies—but they were purists, craftspeople, content with the two-holer, the woods. Today's buyers want something more sophisticated, more urban, a place they can do their trading from—stock market, Internet, you know, without having to face the ugly hordes—the crime. Vermont's got one of the lowest crime rates in the country."

"Till you developers got in here."

He laughed, patted her hand, and she pulled it back. "Come on, Ruthie. Get with it."

She didn't want to get with it. She pushed back out of her chair. She needed distance, height, away from him. She swallowed her coffee, struggled with her thoughts, her attitude. Was she so immature that she still couldn't accept him as a friend? Or was she beginning to see Pete as he was, as an immature person himself? Charming, something of a character, others always said. But they hadn't had to live with him.

"Please, please," she said, "just stay away from Earthrowls' orchard. They're trying to recoup. Don't harass them."

"It used to be Uncle Howie's," he said thoughtfully. "I know every inch of the place. We'd visit there as kids. Uncle Howie never had all that trouble. He knew apples, he made money."

"And made all the wrong investments. Went broke. I heard about that from your mother." She took a breath. "So promise me you'll stay away from it. Leave them alone."

He stood up. He was jangling the change in his pocket; he was a little nervous, she supposed she'd made him that way. He was six-foot-one, she had to look up at him. She turned away. "I can't promise anything, Ruth. I'm in business now. There's this other woman, Mavis, in the partnership, she has her eye on that place. I'll try to hold her back."

"You'd better. You'd just better." She was close to tears now, she didn't know why. She hated herself when she got emotional, the tears would defeat her. She was glad when she heard Vic coming down the stairs. It was Saturday, he had no school.

"Hi, Dad," he said, sounding cool, like the seventh-grader he was now. He started out the door and his father pulled him back.

"Is that all you got to say, young fellow?"

Vic waited obediently. She knew he'd be glad if his father were to come back. But for now the boy had counted him out. It was Vic's defense, his shell. He wasn't going to get hurt again. The boy folded his arms. He was growing out of his pants—she'd have to find a little cash for new ones. She hated having to ask Pete—the alimony wasn't much. She saw Pete eyeing him.

"Maybe an inch?" Pete said, measuring with his hands. But Vic was still one of the shortest in his class.

"He's growing. He'll catch up," she said, and Vic looked uncomfortable in the face of this assessment.

"Mom," Vic said, "I gotta meet Garth. He's coming with his mother to help with the sheep. I said I'd help so we could go to town."

"What are you planning to do in town?" Pete asked, sitting down in a chair, tilting back, his hands clasped across his chest. Pete missed his son, she knew that. She was—almost—sorry for him.

"I did my chores. Fed the calves. Swept the barn." He appealed to his mother. She was the one he was taking orders from now.

"Have a good time," she said. "Behave yourself in town." The boy ran out with a nod at his father, and collided at the door with Emily.

"Dad," she said, and ran to give him a hug. Already Pete was pumping Emily about the Earthrowl orchard, with an occasional glance at Ruth as though he were the naughty boy and they'd both have to accept that. Now she wanted to kick him, but her foot wouldn't reach. And Emily's face was shining.

"Things are getting bad over there," she announced, "Bartholomew—he's the head Jamaican—is ill, a heart condition, Ms. Earthrowl says. And Derek—he's my favorite one—says somebody is putting obeah on Bartholomew."

Pete winked at Ruth, as though this was all foolish stuff Emily was talking about—though he obviously loved the thought of things going wrong in the orchard. All the more fuel for him and his woman developer. But there were three of them, weren't there? "Who's the third partner?" she whispered, but he just looked smug. He turned his attention back to Emily.

"What's obeah?" he asked.

"It's a kind of voodoo," Emily explained. "Derek says it's the way they put a curse on somebody they don't like for some reason. But Derek says not everybody knows how it's going to work. So you can do something to someone because only you know how it works, and when you do it to them, only you know what it is you're doing. The person you're doing it to then has to find out how it works to counteract it. It's a secret. It's never done out in the open."

Pete winked again at Ruth. "I guess I better stay away from those guys, then." He reached for another doughnut.

"But it works, Dad. My friend Adam Golding says so. He was down on the islands for a couple months. He says he knew a man who was told he was going to drown and the only way the man could keep from drowning was to cross the sea to another island and leave the curse behind. And he did, and he didn't drown."

Pete laughed aloud. "He wouldn't have drowned if he'd stayed on land."

"Yes, but his brother didn't cross the sea, and he did drown, the very next week, out fishing, when a big wind blew up."

"Bullshit," said Pete, and rocked back in his chair. "Now tell me who this Adam Golding is, who believes all this stuff."

Emily looked defensive. "A friend, that's all. A guy who picks apples with me. And I have to go back, Dad. I forgot to take my sandwich. I've made one hundred fifty dollars already, I'm putting it in the bank. I'm getting interest."

"Good girl." Pete understood banks and interest. He gave her a slap on the fanny as she whirled over to the refrigerator and took out her lunch bag. Emily didn't seem to mind. He offered her a ride over to the orchard. The place was on his schedule for the morning. He wanted to talk to the Earthrowls. The woman was all right, he said, the other developer, but she didn't quite have the finesse. It took someone who knew Vermont, who knew the land. Who knew that orchard.

"But you just said you'd back off!" Ruth cried, and Pete winked at Emily—who smiled, though she obviously didn't know what her mother was alluding to.

"Well, not exactly that. I meant we'd play it cool. Nobody's *forcing* anybody to do anything."

Ruth gasped, and he smiled.

When Ruth got up to hand Emily a couple of doughnuts for her lunch bag, Pete said good-bye and slapped *her* on the butt. "Get some sex, now, you need it," he whispered.

He was already out the door before she could kick him. And they hadn't talked about Emily's college fees.

She couldn't face the bills after that, so she poured herself a third cup of coffee, and sat there with the cup clasped in two hot shaky hands.

Thirty-one

The trees were sick, Stan could see it. The leaves were turning a deep brown, a contrast to the ripe red Winesap apples. "Seven trees, Stan," said his neighbor Don Yates, counting, looking sympathetic. Rufus stood by stony-faced; his impassivity made Stan even angrier. "What is it?" he cried. "What did this to the trees?"

"Herbicide," said Rufus, holding an apple up to his eye. "Could be paraquat. It's a defoliate, it won't kill the trees, no. Just—"

"Poison the apples," said Don.

"Well, I wouldn't advise tryin' to sell 'em." Rufus gave a sideways glance at Stan, then looked away as Stan advanced on him.

"Where'd they get it? How? We have paraquat in the storage shed, but it's locked. Or should be." Stan felt the heat rising inside his chest, crawling up his neck like a dozen maggots. He was about to explode from the heat. Rufus's voice sounded far away: He always kept the shed locked, he said, he and Stan had the only keys . . . he'd lent his to Bartholomew once or twice. He had to trust the pickers.

Stan said, "You can't trust anyone anymore. No one!" He thought of that boy who'd befriended his daughter, how nice he was to Stan and Moira when he came to dinner one time, how ingratiating, drinking his wine, and then . . .

"Put a new lock on it. Now," Stan bellowed, and Rufus just folded his arms and stared at the ground.

Don Yates said, "I'll see to it. Rufus will probably want to get a crew to pick the bad apples, destroy them, right, Rufus? If Bartholomew hadn't eaten two of them, well, we might have an epidemic on our hands. Apples going out, giving a bad name to the place. You wouldn't like that, Stan. Locals coming in soon, to pick the drops."

"Already got a bad name," said Stan, thinking of that woman developer, leaving another message, coming twice to bother Moira. He was suddenly furious at Rufus for lending out the key at all. "It's your job," he told him. "I hired you to run this orchard right. We've had trees slashed and maggots and worms and, my God, now poisoned apples, one of my men down sick, somebody coming in here at night spraying paraquat—is that a way to run an orchard?"

"Not the way I run an orchard, no," said Rufus, his voice a low hiss. "You're the boss here. You don't like the way I run it, then sell. Go back to schoolteaching."

Stan didn't like the deprecating way Rufus said "schoolteaching." Stan had heard him mouthing off about unions, when Stan himself had belonged to a union. People didn't understand about teachers, they thought they were overpaid when they had the most important job in the world: teaching the young, caring for them when their parents went off to make money.

"You get out, then. This is my orchard. You're the one to get out," Stan said, almost suffocating now, and felt Don's hand like a crate on his shoulder.

"Calm down, now," said Don, "both of you. You'll regret these words later. I'll call the police, shall I?"

They both turned on him. Stan didn't want any police called in on this. He'd had enough of police. They'd impounded his car, they were accusing him of running that woman down. He didn't need any more police.

Neither did Rufus. "Wait on the police," he said, his round face reddening. "Talk to the Jamaicans first. Other apple pickers. Someone might have seen somethin'. There's a fella in another orchard near here I can talk to. It had to be someone knows how to spray. A ground rig did this, doubt it was a plane or you'd have heard it—two nights or so ago, I figger. Takes time for paraquat to do its work." He drew in a whistly breath at the end of the unaccustomed long speech.

For once they agreed. Stan grunted; he didn't want to give Rufus the satisfaction. "We'll line the men up," he said. "After lunch. See what they know. It was someone who knew the orchard, all right. Knew where that paraquat was kept. Wanted to hurt us. Me." He felt heavy, heavy and hot, like any minute he'd have a meltdown. He couldn't deal with Rufus, was glad the man was turning away. Yet he depended on the manager. Who else could he get in the middle of the season? He felt Don's hand again on his shoulder, squeezing; at least he had an ally.

"Anything I can do," Don said, "you just call on me. I'll try to be over here more often. Since the retirement, you know, I've got time on my hands. Okay?"

"Okay," Stan said, feeling as though he was under water, like he was drowning in his own sweat. Though sometimes he just wanted to give in to it, let go. If it wasn't for Moira . . .

But when he got back to the house Moira looked as though she needed help, too. She had a visitor, introduced him as Pete Willmarth, Ruth's ex-husband. It was the last straw, Stan wasn't in the mood for small talk. He'd heard of the ex-husband who'd run out on his wife. What was he here for, anyway? The man was taller than Stan, younger, big-jawed, big-shouldered. He was trying to shake Stan's hand, and Stan put his out, limply.

"You may know that my uncle owned this orchard—Howard Willmarth? He bought it from a cousin of mine." He paused. Stan waited. What was he getting at, anyway? He could see that Moira was hesitating about offering coffee. Was this a personal visit or a business one?

"I played here as a boy," Willmarth went on. He was a good-looking fellow, Stan supposed: rather large nose—plump, one might call it. Losing his hair, though. Used Grecian formula on it, Stan recognized it. He'd tried the stuff himself, it looked phony, he let his own go gray. He let Willmarth talk on. Moira was finally bringing out coffee. Stan wasn't sure what the man was saying, his mind was centered on those trees, that poison spray, the question of who was responsible. There was the feeling of claustrophobia, as though he were in a tunnel, or one of those rooms he'd read about in Poe as a schoolboy, where the walls closed slowly in on you.

"It's hot in here," he said suddenly, a non sequitur, he knew, to Willmarth's ramblings, but he needed air. He went to a window, flung it open. Moira frowned at him. "It's chilly out," she said. "Do you really want it open?"

He did, yes. Willmarth was looking at him now, smiling a little, like he was a child. Damn the fellow anyway! "What do you want here?" Stan asked. "Why did you come?" He saw the deep flush of pink crawling up Moira's neck. Moira and her sense of hospitality . . . she'd take in the smelly tramp, Moira would, and listen to his story. She wanted everyone content. But he couldn't be content. Who could, in this situation?

"You've had a few problems," Willmarth said, and Stan drew in a breath, ready to explode. "I can understand. My farm—or was, I own a share of it now, to help Ruth out till she can get back on her feet—nearly went bankrupt at one point, you know, we nearly sold with the first herd buyout. We should have. It was Ruth wanted to keep it. Against my better judgment." He smiled at Moira, and Stan saw her face grow solemn. Of course she was on Ruth's side now, she wouldn't want to hear any bad-mouthing.

Willmarth was handing Stan a card. Stan stared at it: something about real estate, farming, developing; his vision blurred. Three Partners, it read. "We can offer a good price," the man was saying. "These are mostly old trees. You haven't planted too many young ones, I see."

"Oh yes," Moira said, "in the lower orchard, the west quad. We put in a hundred small trees just last year. They're doing beautifully." Her voice sounded belligerent. What was *her* problem? Stan thought. But he'd back her up.

"She's right," he told Willmarth. "We did. We've put all our savings into this place."

"That's why you should get out while you can," Willmarth

said, smiling, his attitude easy, relaxed. "Before you lose it all." He held up his hands, palms out. "Now, I'm not trying to rush you. Push you. I just heard about your troubles, is all. Thought you might need a helping hand. To pull you out. A hand I could have used a few years back. Mavis and I . . ."

Stan was confused. Who was Mavis? But Willmarth was going on, apologizing for something: "I'm sorry if she annoyed you. She means well, but sometimes . . . I mean, we don't want to—" He laughed, coughed, and Moira stood up.

"We don't intend to sell. Do we, Stan?"

Sell? Was that what this fellow wanted? Stan couldn't seem to think straight. He was still hot, for one thing, even with the window open; he was boiling over. That paraquat, Bartholomew sick. Those maggots. That woman he'd run over—so they claimed. He couldn't take much more. He needed air. He jumped up, pushed the window to the top, the wind rushed in, and he heard Moira gasp. He wheeled about. "Why not?" he cried. "Why not sell, Moira? You want to lose everything? We could take a year off. Then decide what . . ."

He couldn't think what. He couldn't think anything. He was on fire. He grabbed on to the back of a chair. Moira was running to him, and that fellow; he was dizzy, he couldn't walk, he let himself slump into their hands . . . onto the sofa. The room, going black . . .

Thirty-two

Moira tiptoed out of the hospital room. Already Stan was asleep, they'd given him Valium, amphetamine, a stimulant to knock down the blood pressure that was "off the charts," according to Dr. Colwell. He'd had a "small stroke," his left side was impaired, his speech affected. They'd give him physical therapy. No, he couldn't "predict" (as though Stan were a weather report) when he'd be able to come home. But they'd do everything they could. . . . And thank God she'd taken out health insurance nine months before. They'd had none at all for a time after Stan left teaching.

So much was happening, so quickly. She couldn't make sense of it. She drove home in a daze, the police still had the Blazer—what was taking them so long, anyway? Ruth had called to say they had that school board woman's body. No wonder Stan had a stroke! Although the damage had started before the move to Vermont: with Carol's death. That was the source. And she'd had to be the strong one. They couldn't both have gone under!

She drove past the Willmarth farm, impulsively turned in. She needed someone to talk to. There was something calming about Ruth, as though the woman were somehow rooted, like beets or carrots or turnips. She wanted to tell about the ex-husband's visit, how, before the collapse, Stan had said he wanted to sell. "Should I?" she asked Ruth. And repeated again all that had happened.

They were in the barn, Ruth was stroking a newborn calf. It was beautiful, all white except for a black tail and a black spot on the nose. Those eyes, like melted chocolate! Ruth had a calf coming each month now, she'd said. She couldn't cope with calves coming all at once every spring or fall—she spread them out. The mother cow, whose name was Charlotte, was a real love, Ruth said, a good mother. Charlotte lay panting on her haunches, exhausted from the ordeal of birth. The calf was rummaging about to find the teats. The two of them practically purring with happiness. Moira's eyes watered. Here was beauty in its natural animal state.

"It's your decision, of course." Ruth leaned back against a stanchion. She looked exhausted from playing midwife—though it had been a routine birth, she said. "Look, Moira, I can sympathize. I've been through these hard decisions. To sell the farm or try to run it on my own. I opted, as you know, to keep it. And that orchard of yours, it's really beautiful. In the spring, when it's in blossom, it's like . . . like—"

"Fairyland," Moira finished for her. "I could see my grandma's fairies weaving those pink and white blossoms into a shawl that would stretch for miles. It's still beautiful—most of it, except for the poisoned trees. I think I've fallen in love with apples myself. I'm learning about them, a new one every day—there are over seven thousand varieties, did you know that? Not in our orchard, of course, but Stan keeps grafting on new ones. I mean, myself, I'm learning how to graft Granny Smith onto Red Delicious . . . it's like weaving one color, one texture into the next. Stan was fascinated with the possibilities. But now . . ."

She thought about Stan, the magnitude of the stroke, and Stan not yet fifty. "They can't tell me how long before he recovers," she admitted to Ruth.

"You said it was a slight stroke, not a massive one?" The calf lost the nipple and Ruth stuck him back on it. It reminded Moira of the kittens her cat had in her closet when she was a child—

only cows were bigger—huge! Charlotte gave a grateful moo, and Moira wanted to hug her, but didn't quite dare. "You have to count the good things," Ruth went on, putting an arm around the cow. "I learned that. I've grown since Pete left. I never realized it so much until he came back and I saw what he was. Who he was. Not quite the strong, loving person I made him into in my head when we married. In many ways he's still the carefree fraternity boy he was in college. I want us to be friends for the children's sake. But it's hard. We have different values."

Would Stan's values change, too, Moira wondered, with all the mischief that was going on? Would it ever be the same for her and Stan? "There's still that woman's death hanging over Stan. I can't imagine him, for all his anger, deliberately running her down.

"Or if he did inadvertently hit her, well, it would have been an accident, her fault. She was running toward him, Stan thinks he remembers that. But he can't recall if he was in the car or if it was in front of the store when he saw her. He was a sick man, even then. I realize that now."

"The police are tending toward the accident theory, Moira. Colm says so. If anything, he has their sympathy. But they have to look at all angles, you know, all possibilities. They have to look at the possibility of, well, homicide. Because of his pushing that woman, I mean. That was what hurt his case."

"I know. Oh, God, I know."

They were silent a moment. The calf's sucking was soothing, like water running over stones. Being here in this cow barn was a kind of renewal. Moira liked the smell of hay, didn't mind the manure. It was earthy, it was real, you could name it and smell it. The orchard happenings were like so many dirty tricks, unnameable.

Moira rose from the pail she'd been seated on. She felt better already. She'd go back to the orchard, see Rufus, find out what was going on. See about Bartholomew. He was the one she was most worried about.

But she wouldn't give in. She wouldn't sell. Ruth was her role model here. "If you see your ex-husband," she told Ruth, "tell him we're not selling. We'll get to the bottom of this bad business and then we'll get on with our lives. I can do more than I've been doing. I'll go to work in the orchard. I want to! Have to."

Ruth nodded, she understood. She got up and put two sticky, smelly arms around Moira. "Now you'll have to go home and take a shower. Then you can get down to business. And I'll stand behind you. You mentioned interviewing the pickers in your last phone call. Can I come along and listen?"

"Yes, yes!" Moira hugged her back. She didn't care about the stickiness, the smell. She just wanted to burrow deep into the moment.

Thirty-three

When Ruth arrived at the orchard Sunday morning, she found the place in pandemonium. The Jamaican leader, Bartholomew, was dead. They were removing the body now. Colm, in his father's black funeral limousine, called out to her, "Cerebral thrombosis. They found him when they woke this morning. Evidently died in his sleep." The double doors clanged shut and the limousine roared off.

She found Moira inside the bunkhouse, along with the Jamaicans: grieving, upset, almost mute from the shock of their leader's death. A few offered explanations: obeah—"Dat old mistress bek home, wanting him dead"; another blamed the devil—"Here, in dis place. He take us all, you watch, mun!" Ephraim argued, "Heart, those poison apples—it was murder." And everyone quieted to listen and nod, their eyes huge and white with the thought of death, of murder.

"You're right, Ephraim," Moira said. "He was taking that heart medicine. It didn't mix with those apples, poor man. Zayon, have someone change the linen, will you? You're first in charge now." Moira's lips were set in a straight line; Ruth could see she was trying to reassure the men, to keep calm herself. "And mop up around where he was sick. They should have kept him in the hospital, they might have saved him. Oh, I don't know!" She bit her lip again, took two audible breaths, held a hand over her mouth as if she were about to break down herself; and, pushing Ruth ahead of her, hurried out, motioning Ruth to follow.

Behind them, there was a deep hush as the men tried to deal with this unexpected death.

"We'll have to bring in the police, Ruth. Stan didn't want them called, but I think we have to, don't you? With a death? He was such a lovely man, Bartholomew. He kept those men together, he had such a good spirit." She held two fists to her eyes, mopped her damp cheeks with a tissue. "We'll have to notify his family. There will be legal issues—it happened on our orchard. Stan would know, but of course he can't help much now. I know he has insurance. . . . Oh, Ruth, I feel so out of control. Upset for Bartholomew and his family, overwhelmed by what's going on here. I don't know if I can cope. . . ."

"I'll leave a message for Colm, when he gets back to the fumeral home," Ruth said, feeling awkward in the face of Moira's grief, her troubles. She put an arm around her friend, walked her back to the farmhouse. "He'll need to know the details. He'll inform Chief Fallon. I'd like to know more myself. I won't leave you alone in this, I promise! Tim's on duty, he has Joey, his foster boy. 'Take an hour,' Tim told me."

"Only an hour?" Moira said, and let Ruth draw her into the house, fix the coffee. At Ruth's request she told all again from the beginning. It would help her, Ruth thought, to talk about facts, events. "Stan was right, Ruth, it can't all be accidental. There are too many incidents now. It has to be someone who has a grudge we don't know about, or wants us out of the orchard. Or . . ." Moira ran a hand through her frazzled hair. It was beautiful hair, Ruth noticed, a warm shade of dark red. She had the freckles, of course, but Moira's weren't too noticeable—mostly on the hands and arms, a few visible on the cheeks when she looked at Ruth, indignant with the crimes she'd just described.

"Let's start with motive," said Ruth. "You mentioned a grudge. Who might it be? A worker? Your manager? Someone from the past?"

Moira was quiet a moment, considering. The coffee cup was

quivering in her hands. "That's just it. I don't know. Except for that school board woman, of course: Stan had been after her for persecuting poor Mr. Samuels. But she's gone now. And the paraquat incident came after her death. So . . ." She spread her fingers, shook her head. "I don't know. That's the worst of it. I don't know." She looked beseechingly at Ruth.

"The Messengers minister's not dead. Bertha's alive and crazy, you bet she is! Those other women, the praying ones. They're still possibilities, right? With that minister whipping them up? Telling them what to think, how to act?"

"I guess so. Yes. Though I haven't heard from that minister, well, for several days now. He could be just a kook—or he could be a serious threat. So many things happening—so fast."

"Then who would want you out of the orchard? That was your second thought. Somebody with a grudge." The coffee was good. Ruth was almost enjoying the discussion. Then felt guilty that she was complacent, at Moira's expense. Bartholomew, poor fellow, was dead. The Jamaicans were upset—and worried probably about themselves as well. Moira's husband was still in the hospital. Ruth shouldn't ask too many questions. But the woman did need help!

There was a pecking at the window, a flash of red as the bird flew off, Ruth could see it crouching on a nearby branch as though it were spying, deliberately provoking, waiting for the next opportunity to spring at the glass. Moira glanced at it fearfully, then gave a short laugh. "I could say *that* does. It's just a bird. But like a symbol of something worse, some fate that wants us out of here. Or wants in to get at us."

"Oh, Moira," said Ruth. Someone had to be practical here. Although Moira was no Bertha; she didn't believe in any devil. Moira was embarrassed at her own superstition. "I know, I know," she said. "But sometimes, at night . . . Anyway, well, there's Rufus. He's a silent, almost surly kind of fellow. Never owned his own orchard, but would like to, I think. He hasn't got the capital, that's the problem, he'd have to buy it cheap."

"Mmmm. He might think you'd sell cheap because of all the

problems here. And he could cause the problems. He surely knows all about what maggots and paraquat do to apples."

Moira sighed, gulped her coffee as though it would help clarify her thoughts. "He was a kind of legacy when we bought the orchard. There's no telling what Rufus thinks behind the mask he wears." She ran a hand through her thick hair, it fell back into her face. Her nose was shiny with perspiration. "Then there are those developers, your ex-husband. His uncle owned this orchard, he says."

"He did, yes. Though I can't quite see Pete planting maggots and poisoning apples. After all, I lived with the man for more than twenty years! For all his faults, well, he's an honest man. But I don't know about this Mavis he's partners with. And there's a third partner. A silent partner—I've got to find out who that one is. Pete's always been the cozy one, won't tell me something that's going on because 'women blab'—to quote Pete." She curled her fists into her lap, remembering. Maybe the divorce was a good thing after all. She was starting to grow, wasn't she? Like one of those wild rosebushes she'd planted behind the house that never bloomed until she cut away the rest of the taller, hardier bushes around it? And it went crazy the next spring with deep red blossoms.

"That minister," Moira said, her hands cupped tight around her coffee mug, "maybe he's your silent partner."

"We can't rule anything out," Ruth said. "I mean, even Bertha. She's Pete's sister, after all. Even though he's always put her down. Even Pete's father put her down. Maybe that's why she's so vulnerable to these kooky religions—needing someone to pay attention to her. I need to remember that myself. But blood is blood. And Bertha belongs to that sect."

"What's the man's background, anyway?" Moira asked. "Does anyone know where he came from?"

"No, but I'll try to find out. I'll put Colm Hanna on his case. The police would have access to old files. Maybe he's a wanted man—killed his old mother to get the family jewels."

Moira gave a choking laugh. Then put a hand over her mouth.

"I shouldn't be laughing. I'm still feeling swept away on a tide. I can't believe Bartholomew died! It seems like a nightmare I'll wake up from. And I can't sit here just thinking about my own problems. I'll have to contact his wife. Stan has an address somewhere. What kind of burial do you think she'd want?"

"You'll have to ship the body back to Jamaica, I'd think. Or the ashes. Do you know what religion he is?"

"I think Methodist. Yes, definitely Methodist. He got talking once about his childhood in Jamaica. His family was one of the few non-Catholic ones; his mother sent him to a school where he had to prostrate himself before the British flag. He had to memorize whole sections of Milton's *Paradise Lost*—can you believe it?"

"I can't. I could hardly get through Milton myself senior year in high school. I do recall sympathizing with Satan, though. But don't tell Bertha!" And both women smiled.

Ruth got up, took her empty cup to the kitchen. "I'd better let you get on with the arrangements. Maybe one of the other men knows Bartholomew's wife, can talk to her. Do you want me to help interrogate the men about the poisoning?"

"Would you? I'd appreciate that. And you're right, I'll ask the men for their help. They're frightened, that's another concern. We have to keep them calm, keep them assured, keep them safe!"

"You're all right? Do you want me to stay longer?"

"No, I'm okay. I was just feeling overwhelmed at the sudden death, the shock of it. But I can cope. The coffee helped. And talking to you."

Ruth nodded, got ready to leave. "I forgot to ask how Stan is."

"Stable. We'll be bringing him home in a few days, as long as he keeps up the physical therapy and lets Rufus run the orchard. I can't imagine him trying to deal with all this. I don't want to tell him about Bartholomew, not yet. Oh, that poor, dear man! I didn't know about that heart condition." She turned her face away.

"Call, will you, Moira? If I can do anything at all? I could at least question Rufus. I know him a little, the family goes back generations." Ruth thought of Emily. She'd be glad when the season was over and Emily was back in school full time. After all, her senior year—the girl needed to give time to her studies.

Outside on the porch she saw the niece, Opal. She was cradling her guitar, hugging it to her like a child, her eyes fixed on the mountains. When Ruth spoke, she didn't look up, just went on humming, tapping a foot, as though she were hearing the music in her head.

"I think your aunt could use your help here," Ruth said, but Opal didn't answer. She was strumming the guitar now, a jazzy reggae kind of beat, an ironic requiem for Bartholomew's death.

Ruth felt a surge of anger at the girl's indifference; then took a breath and climbed into the green pickup, revved it up with a "Thanks for starting, Green Baby." At least the old bucket was still going, in the face of too many deaths.

Thirty-four

In the morning a contingent of pickers, headed by Zayon, who was now Number One man, appeared at Moira's door. They were all talking at once, so rapidly in Jamaican patois she could only look from one to the other, say, "What? Please . . . speak slowly . . . I want to help you, but . . . one at a time, please . . ."

She had just had a tearful return call from Bartholomew's wife, who wanted the body sent home at once, and she had made arrangements with Hanna's Funeral Home. At least she hoped she had understood the whole message. The woman had kept shouting, "Heart, heart, I tell him to stay home, the bad heart!" Then she had burst into tears, and Moira wept with her.

Now, she understood, the men wanted two things. They wanted assurance that the police would find the source of the orchard malice—"Or we not to stay here, mum. You find him, find him, lock him up!" There was a chorus of yeas. And secondly, they wanted to have a funeral celebration that night for Bartholomew, even without his body present. "Music dat he love, good eating," Derek said, and the others loudly echoed the wish.

Of course she agreed to both. "The police are fully aware. They'll keep a watch on the orchard. There's a police car moving slowly past even now," and she pointed. "You'll be safe," she insisted, although she didn't know that, did she? She could only try to convince the others. The men didn't want to leave Vermont, she knew that. They wanted, needed the money. The money from this fall's picking was more than they would make in a whole year at home.

"And we want to give Bartholomew a proper memorial," she said—not knowing quite what to expect. "You tell me what to contribute in food. I'll take you into town this afternoon, we'll shop together."

They left then, pacified for the moment, talking excitedly among themselves, planning, she supposed, for the evening's wake. Could she call it a wake?

But she wasn't prepared for the noisy send-off they finally gave their leader. Of course, reggae was nothing if not loud, Derek explained, stomping his feet to the up-tempo beat. The police would visit at least once a month back home, he said, "count of de noise you make. You car radio be turn up loud so everybodies dat drive by know you Jamaican, not tourist."

Adam Golding, coming up to her, looking serious, filled her in further. Reggae was based on American soul music, he said, but with inverted rhythms and prominent base lines: "A lot of the performers are Rastafarians," he said, "like Zayon over there."

And there was Zayon, with his carefully cultivated dreadlocks, playing the drums. He seemed almost a part of the drum, his head nodding down into the taut skin. Adam was a musician himself, he told Moira, he was an admirer of Eric Clapton, who had adopted a form of reggae.

"You've been there?" Moira asked. "To Jamaica?"

"Couple of times," Adam said, shrugging, and began to play his guitar. Was there a slight odor about him and Zayon of cannabis? She hoped not, but there was the sensation that events were wholly beyond her control now, events that had been set in motion, that she couldn't stop—like that cardinal banging at her window.

Oh, but she was superstitious today!

Now, there was a new beat: something called ska, a Jamaican dance music, according to Ezekiel, a small, wiry man in his thirties. "De blue beat," Ezekiel said. "We dancing for ole

Bartholomew, he like dis music." And he whirled about in a stiff pair of new blue jeans, stamping his feet. Zayon battered the drums, coming in on the second and fourth beats. Derek played an imaginary horn, while Adam was caught up in the rhythm of his guitar.

And there was food—the men had spent what seemed a small fortune in the Grand Union and in the natural foods co-op. She'd given them the whole day off—in spite of Rufus's disapproval. Nothing, even death, must stop work, the latter's face had warned. They were already behind schedule and the Jamaicans were due to leave in two weeks. But she ignored him; the shopping trip took three hours. Every last bit of seasoning or exotic fruit had to be found. There was fruitcake, made in her own kitchen because the men needed two stoves going at the same time. It was a moist, dark, rich treat filled with tiny soft fruits and raisins. There were plantain tarts, bread pudding, and sweet potato pudding. There was salted codfish, pepperpot stew, and peppered shrimp—Moira couldn't eat it for the spicy seasoning. There was a drink made of soursop and lime juice, pineapple and orange—as far as she could identify. And Tia Marias, the delicious coffee liqueur she'd always had a fondness for.

The feast would go on all night, she feared, and then what would happen at eight o'clock Tuesday morning when the pickers were due at work? Rufus would be beside himself! *She* would go to bed, at least: She was learning to pick apples. Derek had given her lessons, grinning at her acrophobia up on the ladder, but patiently teaching her how to pick: how to leave the stem after picking, so that the apple would not dry out; how to take it with all the fingers and not just the fingertips, lifting the apple upward, then turning the hand slightly as you lift. She rehearsed it in her mind. How to break the stem from the fruiting spur without pulling the stem. There was so much to learn! And she was determined to keep the orchard going in Stan's absence. She'd never be able to take Bartholomew's place; like the other pickers, he was swift, easy, graceful. But she'd try. And she'd teach Opal, too, she would! The girl had to pull her weight around here. The orchard was in crisis. . . .

Opal passed by as Moira returned to the house, ready for bed without even a bath—she didn't have the energy for it. The girl had her guitar, lured, most likely, by the sound of the music in the bunkhouse. She stood in the open doorway of the bunkhouse, a little shy, perhaps, or maybe afraid to go in to a place where a death had so recently occurred. Or maybe unwilling to let go of her prejudice. Moira felt sorry for her—but it was hard to feel sorry. The girl had done everything she could to make things difficult for her aunt and uncle: deliberately leaving her bed unmade, refusing to eat the food Moira served her. . . . Opal was a fast-food, Pepsi-Cola addict—a product of the "modern world." And how depressing for the modern world!

At the path into the lower orchard Moira paused, suddenly needing to take a walk in the chill evening air; she veered into it. The orchard was lovely and quiet down here, only the thin sounds of drum and guitar drifting rhythmically through the trees. It was a cold late September night, partially lit by a crescent moon; the apples hung on the trees like dark shiny balls. If she picked one, a fairy might pop out and grant her three wishes.

What would she wish for then? She considered. Carol back and alive in their lives? No, that was impossible, she must choose her wishes carefully, practically. First of all, she wanted Stan well and hopeful—yes, that was the priority. Next, their world back in order again, the evil in the orchard banished—only Jamaicans crooning in the trees, and bins full of ripe red apples to take to the Shoreham Co-op. And the third wish? What? Well, her brother-in-law, Lindley, out of the hospital and in good health, and Opal back with her parents and Moira at her loom, weaving good and beautiful thoughts into every piece. Peace. In her home and in Ireland, where her relatives still lived in Ballyvaughan; and peace everywhere in the world. How many wishes was that? At least a dozen! Moira the daydreamer.

She continued on down the path toward the Winesap apples. She couldn't bear to think of some of them poisoned. They could still be—illegally—sold, Rolly Butterfield had told her that; the poison was inside the apples, it hardly showed in the skin. Last spring Stan had grafted Winesaps and Gravensteins onto Red

Delicious, and they took. Imagine! Three kinds on a single tree. It was like grafting a Jewish nose onto a Chinese face onto a Caucasian body. There would have to be tolerance then, none of this prejudice that Opal had evidently been reared on. Moira would try it herself next spring—grafting Granny Smith onto Rose Beauty; Roxbury Russet onto Elstar. The names themselves were lovely: Spigold, Paula Red, Newton Pippin . . .

Now where was she? She'd made several turns among the trees, she was a bit disoriented. It was black now, the moon had gone under the clouds. Was anyone about who could orient her? She stopped, listened. Heard a crunching sound. Man or fox? She'd seen a gray fox only last week, dashing across the dirt road in front of the orchard. She held her breath. The sound came closer. She leaned into a tree, waited—nervous now, wanting to sneeze, holding it. It might be . . . him. The one who'd sabotaged the orchard.

And then he came by, a dark figure—masked? She couldn't tell. His head was down, he had something in his hands. What was it? Should she scream? But then—he might turn on her. She waited until he was gone, down the path; then she followed, quietly as she could; every twig and dry leaf on the path shouted out. But the trees were silent; they gave out no secrets.

She heard footsteps crunching along from another direction. It was a smaller person this time—a woman, a girl? What was everyone doing out in this dark night? Were they leaving the funeral feast? Or were these outsiders, persons not associated at all with the orchard?

Again she hid in the branches of a tree and waited. But the smaller figure had retreated, had seen her perhaps. When she got back to the fork in the path, it was Opal standing there, gazing up into the night sky. Had it been Opal, that second figure? Maybe so. Then who was the first?

Or was this simply her imagination? Was it some sort of assignation? Someone Opal was going to see—perhaps one of the Butterfield twins?—and Moira was about to spoil it.

The music had stopped, for the time being anyway; the men were eating, drinking, celebrating Bartholomew's life—in their own way, of course. Food and music. Opal was only interested in the Jamaican music, not in the men.

"Opal," she called, and the girl gave a cry of surprise. "I didn't mean to frighten you. Have you been taking a walk? It's a grand night. Cool but fragrant."

"No," the girl said. "I just came from the bunkhouse. They've stopped playing. They make too much noise in there anyway. The place smells. That man died in there! I'm going to bed. You said I have to help pick tomorrow. I don't know how."

"We'll give you a lesson. And you'll need your rest. I'm sure they'll end the party early, though Derek tells me funerals sometimes last three days in Jamaica!" She rather liked the thought. Three days was not too long to celebrate a whole lifetime, was it?

Opal muttered something, ran on ahead, and Moira returned to the house, to her loom. The thought of a romantic tryst out there in the trees made her feel lonely. She needed to weave. She took up the shuttle. And gasped. Someone had pulled out a number of her threads, destroyed the pattern. Who in the world did this? She'd have to unravel the whole piece, begin all over again. She felt like Penelope, threading and unthreading the loom, discouraging the suitors, while she waited for her husband to come home. How alike they were, she and the ancient Greek, Penelope! Both with missing husbands. Except that Moira had no suitors, wished for none—heavens, no.

Opal was already pounding up the stairs; Moira took deep breaths to calm herself, and said nothing. The rethreading was wholly absorbing. Slowly a sense of relief stole over her. She couldn't worry about the figure in the orchard—it might have been one of the local pickers, after all. This was the night for Bartholomew, she didn't want to disturb the Jamaicans. In the morning she'd find out if someone had come to play another cruel trick on the orchard.

Red over gold, blue over mauve, warp over weft: This was her meditation, this was her way of coping. She'd finish the rethreading, and then she'd go to bed.

Thirty-five

Adam was late for their meeting in the toolshed, but it was all right; he'd been playing the guitar, he said, at Bartholomew's wake. Or she guessed it was a wake—already the body had been shipped back to Jamaica. Emily was sorry, he'd seemed a kind man, a gentle one; he didn't deserve to die. She couldn't really believe all that about obeah, she told Adam. "I mean, how can somebody back in Jamaica, some jealous wife or somebody, put a spell on him up here in a Vermont orchard?"

"Unless it was somebody right here in this orchard."

"No! I can't believe that, either. It was awful, awful of someone to spray that poison!"

"Probably he—or she—didn't know he had a weak heart," Adam said thoughtfully. "Derek ate one, too, and he's all right."

"Derek is young and healthy," she said. "It was still a cruel, irresponsible thing to do."

Adam nodded, took a long drink out of the bottle of Chablis he'd brought along. "There are a lot of poison apples in the world," he said, putting his arm around her. "But one day they'll all be turned into vinegar."

She smiled. Adam was clever with words. With music. With apple picking—he could pick almost as fast as the Jamaicans. He always looked gorgeous up there in the trees, his ponytail hanging down like a branch in blossom. She sipped her wine. It felt good, warm in the belly. It was Wilder Unsworth who'd introduced her to wine, her mother never let her touch it—her mother was so old-fashioned. But Wilder was probably making out with some female classmate this very minute. She didn't trust Wilder anymore since he'd fooled around with a city girl back in high school. But Adam: There was a certain intensity about him, a spirit of questing, as though there was something important he had to do for himself and the world. She liked that. She felt she could trust him. It might even be called . . . love. Or its beginnings.

She leaned against his shoulder; she fit right into a hollow there between the bones. The stars popped out of a traveling cloud as she watched, as if they had her and Adam in mind.

"Are we really going to the Valley Fair next weekend?" she asked, and Adam murmured, "Hmmm?" And then, "Sure. You bet." He leaned over and kissed her, on the mouth, a long loving luxurious kiss, while his hands wandered down over her breasts, down deep into her beltless jeans, into the moist V between her legs, and she felt as though any minute her groin would spill out sweet apple cider.

Thirty-six

Ruth had made an offer to help interrogate the pickers, so she felt she had to keep it—though she should be in three other places at once! There was Sharon's baby girl, down with an ear infection that filled the house with screeches; there was Vic's science fair—although it would go on through Saturday; there was a hearing in Montpelier of farmers wanting to ban the use of rBST, the synthetic hormone that would stimulate milk production in cows—unsafely, Ruth felt. It made her blood boil, in fact, to think of certain area farmers using the stuff and the FDA actually approving, in spite of health risks. And of course she should be in the barn—she couldn't leave it all up to Tim. When she announced her departure for the orchard, he'd tipped his ranch hat and said, "Well, ma'am, you gotta make up your mind. Are you a farmer or a detective?"

Startled, she'd said, "Does a woman have to be just one thing?" and he'd laughed.

"No, ma'am. But far's I can see, you're ten women all at once," and he began to tick off the jobs. She got out of there fast then, it was overwhelming to hear.

Moira had already interrogated Millie and then four of the seven remaining Jamaicans by the time she arrived, "and got nowhere. Though I'm probably asking the wrong questions,

Ruth. I'm not much good at this. I mean, I don't want them to think I'm suspicious, or accusing them of sabotaging the orchard. Lord! What's the right thing to do, anyway?"

She was glad, glad, she said, that Ruth would take over. There were still three men to question, and then Rufus and the other local pickers to talk to. She'd leave out Emily, since the girl was wholly above suspicion. Ruth laughed and said, "I'm not so sure about that! But sabotage—no. Though she might have seen something. I'll talk to her."

Ruth began with the Butterfield twins, but they had little to say. Like the three monkeys, they had seen nothing, heard nothing, said nothing. "Although," one of them said as they were leaving the barn—he stood there with his pail like a red-haired stork carrying a baby—"I did see Zayon—I'm pretty sure it was Zayon—go out late at night the time they found the maggots. He was headed down the path, I wondered what he was doing. The Jamaicans usually sleep tight. They're bushed, I mean, like us. But he went out of sight, you know?"

"What were you doing out?" Ruth asked. "Why weren't you asleep?"

And he laughed and blushed and said, "I had to go, well, relieve myself, you see, and my brother'd been on the toilet. He'd been eating too many apples, he had the runs. It was pretty bad, so I went out."

"What time was that?"

"Oh, I dunno. Late. Midnight. Adam was asleep, I think, but you can ask him. For me it was a case of too much cider, I got weak kidneys. My mother says—"

"Thanks. Thanks, then, um, Rolly. I think it's Rolly," she said. The brothers grinned at each other, obviously delighted at being able to confuse people with their twinship, and trotted off.

Zayon, though, was upset when she told him what Rolly had said. He ran a nervous hand over his dreadlocks—not through, she noticed, they were stiff as brooms, a contrast to the soft-looking pointed beard. She wondered how he slept with them. And got her answer.

"I sleep lak bear," he said. "I not to get up, I don' know what he talk bout. Once though mebbe—"

"Once?" She shifted balance on the upturned apple bin where she was seated as magistrate; a pain shot through her kidneys. She was getting these strange aches in odd places—surely not arthritis at her age? The shoulder pain, though, undoubtedly came from lifting bales of hay.

A bone spur, said Sharon, who subscribed to health newsletters from Harvard, Tufts, and the Mayo Clinic. "You'll need a shoulder replacement, Mother, if you keep doing that."

"And who else is to do it?" Ruth had asked, laughing anyway.

"Once, twice, I get Bartholomew's med'cine. He wake in de night, can't fin' it. I'm de nex' bed."

"But it wouldn't be outdoors?"

"No, missus. No, no. In de bunkhouse, dat's where. I neber go out. Neber!"

"All right, then, Zayon. Thank you. He must have seen someone else, he wasn't sure anyway. You'll be glad, won't you, to go home after harvest? You have a wife? Children?"

He chuckled. "No wife no more. Got my religion now. Got a mama. But I don't go home. Yet. Florida, dat where, for to pick de fruit. No bad ting goin' on dere. Here—not so good. Someting bad at work."

"Yes. Well, you can send in Adam Golding, then." She didn't want to hear anything about devils or obeah. Thank God she hadn't lived in the seventeenth century! All that witchcraft. Her own race was as bad as any Caribbean's. Worse!

The barn door swung open, and the niece Opal appeared—and, seeing Zayon, disappeared.

"Bad news, dat one," Zayon said, pointing a finger at the closing door. "Go ask dat one what, who."

Zayon was gone before Ruth could ask him why the girl was "bad news," but thought she might interview Opal herself.

It was a ten-minute wait before Adam appeared. By then Ruth was almost intoxicated with the smell of ripe apples—bins and bins of them, ready to take to the co-op. The cider press was in a far corner of the barn, it resembled a guillotine. "Off with your heads!" she said aloud, amused at her own analogy, and a voice said, "Ooh! got me!"

Embarrassed to be discovered talking to herself, she said, "I was just thinking that the cider press looked like a guillotine, skinning the apples, decapitating them," and Adam—for it was his voice she'd heard—laughed.

He had a nice laugh. He seemed less confident today, though, than when he was in her kitchen, waiting for Emily to come down. He'd come directly from picking; he had on the wide shoulder straps with the white bucket on his chest, and tall black boots like the ones the Jamaicans wore. Emily wouldn't wear boots: She claimed she could climb a ladder more easily in sneakers, and Ruth would agree, though she'd never picked apples. Adam's hair was half pulled out of the ponytail, but clean and shiny, unlike the Rastafarian dreadlocks that Zayon took such pride in. How *did* he wash his hair, anyway?

"Adam, you understand that no one is accusing you of anything here. I'm just helping out Ms. Earthrowl, with her husband in the hospital. . . ."

"I know that," he said quickly. "Emily's told me what you've resolved in the past. That body you all found in the horse hole. . . ." A dimple came into his right cheek, and she had to smile with him. It was rather ridiculous, the idea of a body in a horse's grave. Although at the time it had been quite sinister, too, and she'd made rather a fool of herself in some ways. . . .

"I just happened to be a neighbor. Neighbors help neighbors. It's that simple. Anyway, I need to ask you if you've seen anything, heard anything—no matter how simple, how seemingly unimportant. For instance, Rolly said he saw someone outdoors the night the maggots appeared."

"That's exactly what I've been asking myself," Adam said, seeming more relaxed now. "What have I seen that's different? Nothing that night of the maggots—though it happened a long way from the bunkhouses, didn't it? Rolly wouldn't have gone down there—I wouldn't think so, anyway. This is the third orchard I've worked in, you know, it's all pretty straightforward."

"Oh? Where else have you worked?" She was glad for an

opening into his past. Why not make this interrogation work twice? Last night Emily had come in late, beyond her curfew; the creaking boards gave her away. Then Vic got up to go to the bathroom, and there was a hotly whispered altercation. Could she ask Adam if he was the reason for the late homecoming? She decided it would be inappropriate.

He listed off two orchards: one in Branbury, one in New York State. "I like being outdoors in the fall," he said. "It's not a lot of money, but it's a challenge. To see how much I can make, how I can improve my skills. If I'm doing something, well, I want to do it all the way."

Ruth smiled at him. She approved of that. "How did you hear of this orchard?"

He thought a minute, a tongue poking into one cheek. She saw the fine blond hairs on his chin. She supposed he didn't have to shave as often as dark-haired men. Lucky. Pete used to hate shaving; he was a regular bear.

"In the local newspaper, advertising for local workers. That is, a friend of mine from the college lives in the county, he sent me a clipping. So I applied, got the job. Now, though, with all this stuff going on . . ." He looked worried, unsettled, as though someone had handed him a bruised apple and he didn't know what to do with it: eat it to be polite, or toss it away.

"But I haven't seen or heard anybody," he went on, "though I do remember last week, Tuesday or Wednesday, I think it was, hearing something down in the orchard: a kind of humming, like a tractor moving along. The geese squawking. I just happened to be awake, thinking. Planning. What I'm going to do with my life, I mean, besides . . . pick apples." He looked embarrassed, as though she must think him a ninny, a ne'er-do-well, with no serious purpose in mind. "I want to be a musician," he said. "A good one."

"Classical?"

The dimple reappeared. "Guitar. Writing music, too. The classical stuff isn't the only serious music. Though everyone seems to think so."

But they were getting off base. He'd heard a tractor, or something like it. "But it was a sprayer," she said, "a ground rig of some kind, or possibly an airplane, that did the damage."

"I think if it had been an airplane I'd have heard it. I'm a light sleeper. It could have been a ground rig, I suppose, pulled by a tractor. Sometimes the smaller rigs are pulled that way; I've seen them."

"Mmm. Have you ever done any spraying yourself?"

He hadn't. "Just apple picking, ma'am. That's my talent. I don't know anything about spraying. I mean, I've seen it done—who hasn't, if you've worked on an orchard? I suspect it's an art like any other work. You have to have all the stuff for it—mask, the right clothing. Breathe in that stuff, and, man, you're dead. Well, eventually."

"Yes, well." She got up, the questioning was over for now. What had she learned? Not much. Rolly had seen someone out late, but what did that mean? As Adam said, the trees they found maggots on were far away from the bunkhouse. She glanced at her watch—it was almost noon. She had to get home, clean the barn, the gutters. She couldn't depend on Emily these days for all the small chores. After lunch, though, she'd come back, talk to two more Jamaicans, to Rufus. Rufus was the crux, she thought, he was the orchard sprayer. He was the one who'd bought the paraquat. He knew about inchworms and apple maggots. But why would he want to sabotage this orchard, his own job? Unless to buy it—cheap. Was that what he wanted?

A schoolbus was pulling into the driveway as she left the apple barn. It was full of shouting children. Evidently this school hadn't heard about the spraying incident, or else wasn't worried—two other schools had called to cancel. Anyway, Don Yates wouldn't take them into the damaged areas. Don was running up to greet them; they were here, Moira had said, to learn about making cider. She watched as he herded pupils and their pretty young teacher into the barn. Watching them skip along, full of excitement to be out of school, to be in an apple orchard on a sunny fall day, lifted her spirits.

She stood in the barn doorway a moment, listening. "You can all make cider, did you know that?" Don told the assembled schoolchildren. "You don't have to use that big machine," and he pointed at the cider press.

There were murmurings, shouts. "Oh, come on," said one wise guy; and the teacher said, "Shush, now, I said, shush! Let the man talk."

But Don wasn't talking—not yet. Instead, he tossed an apple at each child. There was more excitement, more chatter, more shushing from the teacher. When the group was quiet, finally, Don said, "Take a bite. That's the way! Then chew. Go on, chew! Now see? You're making ci-der!"

And the children chewed, and giggled, and chattered some more. And Ruth went home, smiling.

Thirty-seven

"Geridoee, orshar, bagto Conec, Con . . ."

Moira was trying hard to understand what Stan was saying. The stroke had left him paralyzed on the left side, his speech so impaired he could only say: "Lishun tamee, shellee orshar . . ."

"Don't try to talk, sweetheart, save your energy." Moira knelt beside his wheelchair, held tight to his limp hands. The doctor had administered something called tPA; Stan would, with luck and the right therapy, recover most of his strength and speech. If, that is, he worked hard at it, did his exercises. But now he was just sitting there, propped up in the wheelchair, his head lolling forward, mumbling the same litany over and over: "Geridoee, orshar . . ." When the nurse came to announce, "Time for physical therapy, Mr. Earthrowl," he waved the woman away with a tremulous finger. "Cann, cann," he said, and shut his eyes. There was a nick in his chin where someone had shaved him and missed, a tiny drop of dried blood.

Moira was filled with a sudden panic. Was this Stan, the cheerful, industrious, good-humored man she'd married, with whom she'd had a bright, beautiful daughter? She gripped his fingers tightly, as if it would keep him from slipping away. He was deliberately, it seemed, moving away from her, spinning inward into an unknown center. His eyes were shutting, his head lolled on his chest; he was unaware she was even in the room.

She sat with him for a while, feeling light-headed; finally, at a nod from one of the nurses, tiptoed out. She needed to go back to the orchard, back to the trees where the Jamaican hands were fluttering like wild live birds. With the police patrolling the road on and off and no new crises since Bartholomew's death, the men had begun to recover their good spirits. It was true, of course, that "dead" to an American might not mean "dead" to a Jamaican—Derek had told her that. "Bartholomew keep me picking," Derek said. "He watching ever' minute. Won' lemme win at dominoes, Bartholomew still de champ."

Ah, the power of the imagination, she thought. She could easily begin to believe in something like obeah herself. Put the curse on whoever was doing this to the orchard. Her Irish granny would have done that!

Her heart quieted as she turned into the long orchard drive that culminated in apple-green trees and beyond, in deep lavender folds of mountains. Daisies and wild aster pushed up everywhere, as if unaware that it would soon be winter. Humming, she fed the mewling cat, poured a glass of cider, and drank it down; then bravely punched the button on the answering machine.

The voice came on, loud, gruff: It was a voice she hadn't heard before, muffled, as if to disguise itself. "Keep the Willmarth woman out of this. This is a warning. Keep her out of this."

But Ruth's green pickup was already there in the driveway. Moira ran outdoors, her heart hammering . . . and hesitated. Ruth was in the barn, interviewing one of the men. She didn't want to interfere, but she had to take these warnings seriously, angry though they made her. Ephraim was coming out of the barn as she entered; he acknowledged her presence with a vigorous nod of his head. He was one of the straight-faced ones, serious; he read books instead of playing dominoes or drums or flutes. He'd had a year at the University of West Indies in Kingston, but couldn't afford to go back, he was picking apples for his tuition. She touched his arm; she had to keep abreast of the moment. "I have a book for you," she said, "of Derek Walcott's poems. Would you like to borrow it?"

His face lit up. Derek Walcott was a West Indian who had come out of poverty to win the Nobel prize for literature. "Yes, ma'am, thank you, ma'am." Ephraim went into a trot and back to his picking as though the faster he moved and the more apples he picked, the sooner he would be back in his books.

Walcott, she'd read, was a black man with two white grandfathers and two black grandmothers; he called himself "a divided child"—he had compassion for both races. She thought of Stan's fight to save Aaron Samuels, and had a rush of admiration for her husband. Stan had chosen neither Judaism nor Christianity for his faith. He was a humanist, he said, that was all, that was enough.

"You look like Joan of Arc there in the sun." Ruth was coming out of the barn now, stretching her arms above her head. Moira admired the tanned, muscled look of them. "Positively saintlike," Ruth went on.

Moira said, "Oh, ridiculous. I was just thinking of Stan, that's all. I was ready to charge the enemy. The hate people. But I have something to tell you."

She repeated the warning message, and Ruth just laughed.

"But you must take it seriously! I don't want you to be involved anymore. We have to heed some of these warnings. We've already had one death."

"Two," Ruth murmured. "But that's why I want to go on. I can't stand by and let someone exploit you like this. And it's only two more interviews: Desmond and then Rufus."

"Let me question Rufus," Moira pleaded. "He won't be an easy one. He'll feel he's above all this. This is his orchard—at least he seems to think so. He takes anything Stan or I say—said—well, personally, like we're raising a vendetta against him."

"All the more reason why I should do the talking. Now go in and have lunch."

"Have you . . . ?"

"Done. Almond butter and marmalade sandwich, my favorite. Tim kicked me out of the barn again. I'm good for another hour. When I'm done with Rufus, I'll come in and we can talk."

"Okay, then, but promise after this you'll lie low. Someone, obviously, knows you've been over here, that you're doing all this questioning."

"I can't think of anyone outside this orchard who'd know. Except Pete—he called this morning and Sharon told him I was over here. And Pete might have told Bertha. And Bertha—"

"Might have told that minister. Who might have—"

"Good Lord," said Ruth, slapping the side of her head. "Reminds me of that Norman Rockwell painting—it was on the cover of the old *Saturday Evening Post?* I saw the original down in Arlington. A face with a telephone in the left-hand corner whispers the news to the next face, and so on, down through a dozen or more gossips. Each with a growing expression of horror. And obviously the news wholly distorted!"

Moira had to laugh with Ruth. She was less fearful somehow, afterward, when Ruth went back into the barn. She hummed again as she returned to the house, indulged the cat with a handful of dried food. Opal was sitting by a window with her sketchbook. Moira glanced down at the drawing, ready to compliment the girl. Maybe that was all Opal needed: someone to tell her she was worth something. Probably Annie May had never told her that. Ruth recalled going to their house and hearing the girl scolded—for this, for that.

The sketch appeared to be Adam Golding—a recognizable likeness. Opal had made him into a young god, with his hair loose about his smiling face. His chest was bare, down to his belly button, his eyes narrowed, full of passion—as though he were making love perhaps.

Aware of Moira's scrutiny, Opal shut the sketchpad with a little thump. She looked at her aunt as though Moira were an invader, an officious fool; she tucked the pad under her arm and jumped up. "You shouldn't have looked. Don't do it again. I—I have to have some privacy!"

She burst into tears and ran upstairs. Moira's impulse was to follow her—but then she heard the bedroom door slam.

The cardinal flung itself at the window, and she shook her fist. "Whatever you are," she cried, the panic heating up inside again, "go away. Leave us in peace!" She buried her face in her sweaty hands.

Thirty-eight

Ruth dismissed Desmond, thanking him—although he claimed to have seen nothing and then waited for Rufus. Ten minutes later he appeared in the doorway, a short muscular fellow with keen hazel eyes, hands like hay rakes, a sheaf of hay-colored hair cut short in the back but hanging in front almost to his dark brows. There was a slight tic in his cheek: the only indication that he might be nervous. Or perhaps it was irritation at being interviewed—especially by a woman with no authority that he could see. Except for the tic, the face was expressionless, the lantern jaw set in a stoic attitude. He would get through this, he would get back to work. Work, she was sure, was his life.

Was he married? There was no ring. Even so, Ruth said, trying to sound lighthearted, "Your wife must be worried with all this upset in the orchard?"

Rufus said, "Not married." Just the two words. And she was sorry she'd asked. His marital status had nothing to do with the orchard.

"You're the bossman here," she said. "You would have reported any unusual sounds or goings-on if you'd noticed. You're an excellent orchardist, I've heard from several sources. It was your father, I understand, who ran this orchard when my ex-husband's uncle owned it?"

Was he relaxing a little with her compliment? Did he take satisfaction from the "ex-husband" comment? Maybe. He leaned back against a tier of apple crates; his eyes glanced about the barn—habit, maybe, to see if everything was all right, in its proper place. He waited, his eyes averted.

"What do you make of all this?" she asked. "The maggots, the spraying, the felled trees. Do you have a theory?"

He crossed his arms. " 'S'no good," he said finally. "I dunno. I never seen the like of it. My dad he had no troubles when he was here. My granddad owned this orchard. Before he had to . . ." He paused, straightened up; drew in a breath, gazed up into the barn rafters.

"Had to sell?" she said. She knew he had, he'd sold it to Pete's uncle. She could sympathize, couldn't she? "Finances?"

"My grandmother got sick. It took the money he'd saved. Then she outlived him." He gave a short barking laugh at the irony of it.

"It's a beautiful orchard. Anyone would like to own it, I can see that. I drive past every spring just to look at the blossoms."

His glance was scornful. Orcharding was more than admiring apple blossoms. Although it was the blossoms, of course, that set the fruit, and then the work of the bees. But orcharding was hard work; so much depended on the whims of weather, even more than farming, maybe. Still, "I'm a farmer," she reminded him. And he nodded, he knew. He knew Pete, of course he did. But he hadn't answered her question. She repeated it. Did he have any suspicions, any theories?

He hung his head, thinking. He seemed relaxed now, he leaned back against the crates. The hair fell almost to his eyebrows. The smell of apples was making her woozy. Or maybe it was just that it was early afternoon, low blood sugar time. The door slid open and Don Yates walked in. He moved over to the far end of the barn, to the cider press.

"Nope," Rufus said. "Haven't got a clue. The Jamaicans—what would they want to destroy an orchard for? This is their bread and butter."

"Exactly," Ruth said, to encourage him. "What about the other pickers?"

Rufus shrugged. "Kids. Hardly worth the trouble to train 'em." He glanced slyly at her, Emily was her daughter. He shrugged again. "I think . . ." he said finally, "I think it's somebody got a quarrel with Stan Earthrowl, that's what I think. He's not exactly popular with certain . . . parties in town. They don't like a flatlander coming in, telling the school what to do, what not to do."

He seemed spent from the long speech, itchy now, he had to get back to work. He stood up, away from the crates, thrust his hands in his pockets; looked at his watch. It was a large man's watch with a wide leather band. She could hear his labored breathing, and then the cider press started up and killed the other sounds.

"Thank you," she said. "I hope you'll let Ms. Earthrowl know if you think of anything, if you see or hear anything amiss. That key—I forgot to ask—the sprayer must have used a key to get into the spray room."

"I'd used to keep it under a rock," he said, "in front of the shed—that was 'fore the troubles began, the maggots. Somebody must've seen me put it there, got it copied, I dunno. I've got a new lock. No one goin' to get in that shed now."

"Yes. Good. Thank you," she said again, and he was gone, head down and running, as though he'd try to kick a field goal in a football game.

Don Yates called out as she was leaving, feeling relieved to be done with the fruitless questioning—concerned in spite of herself at the "warning" message on Moira's machine. She knew Don from PTA: He had a young son from a second marriage, although Don must be all of fifty-five or more, retired from some job down on Long Island. Another flatlander, but a nice man, a good neighbor. She turned, and he came up to her, a cheerful-looking fellow with large round eyeglasses that magnified his myopic green eyes, ears that stuck out a little through the almost white hair, but were rather cute, actually.

"I hear you're interviewing the pickers," he said, smiling, putting her at her ease; he wasn't one to criticize. Not to criticize, no, but to advise. He wondered if she'd had a talk with the young woman Opal. "Hardly more than a girl, actually, but a weird kid. I mean, she's done some sneaky things around here."

"Oh? Such as?"

"Well, the goat. It was your Emily caught her cutting the rope second time around. Probably responsible for the first one getting loose, too."

"Emily told you?" Ruth was surprised. There was so much Emily wasn't telling these days. It worried Ruth, made her feel outmoded, useless—the way most mothers felt, she supposed, as their daughters grew older, grew away from them. But this knowledge didn't help the hurt of it.

"Nope, not her. I saw 'em together, Emily and Opal. Overheard. Didn't mean to, just happened to be in the area, picking up some Greenings for my wife's pies. Opal begged your daughter to keep mum. So I did, too. Probably just a prank. Still, with all this going on, I thought . . . someone should know."

"You think she might have done more than that? The maggots, perhaps? A young city girl who doesn't know anything about apple trees?" Ruth couldn't buy that. The girl had done a little mischief, maybe, but not the nasty stuff, the paraquat that indirectly killed a man. She didn't want to think that! Those deeds came from a higher intelligence, someone wanting to hurt, and hurt bad. And then there was that Wickham woman, run down. By whom? By Stan? Or someone else? Was all this somehow connected?

"Naw, she wouldn't have known where to get maggots, you're right. But she's bright—street smarts, I guess you'd call it—carries over to the country, doesn't it? Could have got into the storage shed. She follows Rufus around, the Butterfields, Adam—she's got the hots for him, you can bet. Sex rears its ugly—"

"Not always ugly," she said, thinking of Emily, angry now at Opal for interfering with Emily's boyfriend. Although she didn't want Adam for Emily anyway, did she? He was too old, too sophisticated. Maybe she should be grateful to this little city girl.

Don smiled. He and his wife were close, she knew that; they traveled in tandem, although both had their own interests. His wife was a dedicated volunteer: church, hospital, United Way. . . . Ruth felt guilty in that respect. She should volunteer more. But when was there time for a farmer? Except to help out neighbors. That was her volunteerism.

"I just meant it might not be a bad idea to talk to Opal," Don said. "She might have seen something. Found out something. Could find out something! She gets around in a sly sort of way. There's something pitiable about her, actually. Solitary little thing. Now her uncle's in the hospital. Father, too, I understand, the reason she's up here."

"I will. I'll talk to her. In time. Right now . . . I don't want to scare her."

"Sure. Just thought I'd mention it." He turned back to the cider press and she said, "How about you, Don? What are your theories—besides Opal?"

He threw up his arms. "I dunno. This is a hell of a good orchard. I like the Earthrowls. Up to now, they haven't had any trouble. Haven't offended anybody I can see. Stan, well, he got into a state over that Wickham woman, a little too. . . . too paranoid, I'd say, but what do I know? This is a pretty liberal town as towns go, they wouldn't have let some religious freak dictate what to read, what not to read. But Stan was obsessed. Something to do with that girl of his dying, I expect. You never know. I'm no psychologist."

Ruth knew about obsessions. Her sister-in-law Bertha, her husband Pete—that actress woman he'd run away with. Her own farm was something of an obsession now and she had to get back to it. The inseminator was coming for two of her cows; they'd freshen in the summer. And Zelda, her most recalcitrant cow, was due again in early spring. Last year the ornery cow had broken down two fences to expel her calf. Emily wasn't going to watch her—not with *her* new. . . . obsession. Ruth had to be there.

Moira was gone when Ruth walked by the house, so she went straight to the pickup. Amazingly, it started up on the first try. It sounded like a jet plane, though, needed a muffler. Lord. What else? Out in the road a tan car sped past, half in her lane: She honked and it veered left. She couldn't see the driver for the dust it threw up. Too bad one of those police cars wasn't in sight.

At the junction of Cider Mill and Cow Hill roads she saw a new sign; she swore it hadn't been there when she'd left that morning. SIX LOTS FOR SALE. 1/2 MILE, with a large black arrow pointing toward Lucien's farm. Old Lucien, who'd lost his wife to an assailant, had lost his farm as well. She couldn't bear it. Her vision blurred. It was Pete's sign, of course. A sign of the times. Too late now for Lucien Larocque. But it wouldn't happen to the orchard. It wouldn't happen to her farm. No, ma'am. She'd see that it wouldn't.

Thirty-nine

Ruth woke up the next morning to someone banging on her kitchen door. It was only four-thirty, she had another hour before she'd have to be up for milking; she milked later in fall and winter. She threw on a robe, stomped downstairs, hoping the intruder hadn't wakened Vic or Emily. They needed the extra hours' sleep more than she did.

It was still dark out; the night was quiet between raps on the door. Remembering the assault on the Larocques, she called out, "Who's there?" She wished more than ever she had one of those carry-around phones. She would put it on her Christmas list for the children.

"Ruth," a voice said, and it was quaveringly, poignantly familiar. "Ruth, it's Lucien Larocque—from next door. You got troubles here, Ruth. Your cows."

She unlocked the door, threw it open, drew him in. He was in his patched overalls, caring for his cows to the last, before the auction. But what was he saying about troubles, *her* cows?

"Catch your breath, now, Lucien. You should be worrying about your own cows, not mine. Lucien, I'm so sorry about your farm, that you're selling."

He waved away her concern. He was a short stocky man with gray wisps of hair crisscrossing his squarish head. His face was a patchwork of reddish lumps and scars and wrinkles. A French Canadian, he was volatile yet good-humored, he didn't see the need for fancy speech: just plain, straightforward discourse.

"My dog barked, the new one I got since they killed my old Raoul. I'd put him out half past three when I got up—you know, the old bladder, I can't sleep two hours without getting up."

She clucked in sympathy.

"He keeps barking, so I go out. I hear the cows. Hell, I don't sleep anyways since they come for me and Belle that night. Something's up, I say to myself, so I get out. The dog's on the border between your place 'n mine. I holler, 'Hey!' Somebody's there, running away. I can't keep up, these old legs of mine, you know."

He paused for breath. "I know," Ruth said, "I understand." She remembered her own dad at the end. She and her mother had had to pull him out of bed in the morning, prop him up on his feet to get him to the bathroom. "Sit down, Lucien, tell me about it." She pulled out a chair, her own legs shaky. Something was very wrong for Lucien to come at this early hour.

"I get there," Lucien said, waving away the chair, "it's your cow. Somebody slashed it. Knife's still there—he dropped it when he seen me coming. Look like a hunting knife, you know? I got it in the barn."

"My God," she said, sitting down herself. "Just the one cow?" she pleaded.

He shook his head. "I count two, tree, all down. But breathing, you know, they're not kilt. Just slashed or stabbed, one of them in the belly, you know. I come right over, I don't know what vet you want to call."

She sat there a moment, stunned. Then found her breath, her feet, her anger. She called Dr. Greiner. There was no time to see the cows first. "Yes, slashed. Stabbed. Lucien thinks three. Maybe more! You better bring an assistant. We'll meet you out by the road."

She grabbed a flashlight, followed Lucien to the pasture. It was a good quarter of a mile, the poor man couldn't walk fast; he told her to go ahead, he'd be puffing behind.

The bellowing brought her to the right place, the whole herd bawling and mewling. It was hard to tell how many were hurt; one would think all of them, from the noise. But on closer scrutiny it seemed to be just three, as Lucien had said. One, Gypsy, had been stabbed in the belly. A second, Elizabeth, was cut in the leg; she was pregnant, maybe eight months along. Had they hurt the calf? She was filled with fury. She felt like a giant bee, wanting to sting—anybody, everybody! Who would do this? she asked Lucien. Who would hurt a pregnant cow? Any cow. . . . Did they think these were cardboard beasts, like the Ben & Jerry figures? Gypsy was spooked. She would alternately lie down and then stumble up again, as though she'd attack an invisible enemy. It wasn't until Doc Greiner and his assistant arrived that the cow calmed down. The doc gave her a sedative. He said they'd get all three cows on antibiotics. Gypsy wasn't pregnant, thank God, but she wouldn't give milk for a while. None of them would. The whole herd, it seemed, was spooked. And here was Moll Flanders, pushing her big black head under Ruth's arm. Ruth let it stay.

"Who did this?" she asked Lucien again. "Who would do such a thing?"

Then she remembered the telephone threat. Was this her punishment?

When she got back, her foreman was there, ready to call in the cows for milking. His cowboy hat was cocked on the back of his head, he'd spilled hot chocolate or something on his shirt. She was so glad to see him, she gave him a hug; then told him what had happened. "What shall we do, Tim? What's the next move?"

"Milk 'em," he said. "Get 'em back in the routine. You look like you could use a cupa coffee. Then you can bring one out to me. Right? Get to work, the two of us."

"Get to work," she repeated. "Coffee. Right." And she dashed back to the house. She'd grind the beans; then she'd call Colm Hanna. The work would help. But she couldn't have someone slashing her cows.

What would they do next?

She couldn't think. Coffee first, she told herself. Then call Colm. She took them in that order.

Forty

The blue Horizon ground to a stop in front of the Willmarth farmhouse and Colm Hanna got out, feeling lame, feeling concerned that Ruth had ignored the warning and gone on to interview those pickers. "I know I'm being picky," he quipped, "but . . . "

"Yes, you are," she agreed when he carried his complaint into her barn, where she was finishing the afternoon milking. She appeared to be concentrating—as though she hadn't another worry in the world. "What do you want me to do, sit back and make popovers while my neighbor's orchard is being destroyed, tree by tree?"

"Exactly," he said, leaning against a stanchion where a huge Holstein was on the machine. It turned a chocolate eye on him and then lifted its head and bellowed in his ear; it sounded like a foghorn. Jeez, his back was bothering him. He'd helped his dad lay out a body that morning—a 325-pound body. It wasn't right. At that weight they ought to be made to cremate. "I just read in the *Free Press* about this guy out West who shot some other guy because the other guy's rabbit got loose on his property and the guy said he warned the other guy twice and still the rabbit hopped over to his land and feasted on his veggie garden."

"Good reason for a killing," she said, pulling on the cow's

teats—to loosen them up before attaching the tubes, she explained when he raised an eyebrow. Prime the pump. . . .

"Just a shooting, this time, in the leg. But there seems to be more concern here for listening to a warning. One killing already, right?"

"Yes, though in a slant sort of way. One might call it manslaughter, I suppose. If Bartholomew hadn't been taking warfarin . . ." Now she was squirting milk into her palm. "Thank God," she said, "no lumps. I mean, no mastitis. These poor cows are stressed out. Ripe for mastitis."

"It was murder, however you look at it, Ruthie," he said. "Look, woman, I want you to lie low, let this neighbor help herself. I mean, she'll want you to when she hears about that cow slashing. Jeez."

"It was Gypsy who got the worst of it. And Elizabeth—I'm worried about her calf. It's due next month."

"Elizabeth? The one who cornered me by the fence last spring? Practically sat on me when I slipped down in the mud? Maybe that slasher did you a favor."

Uh-oh, he'd said the wrong thing. She was disconnecting the tubes, they flashed steel in her hand. Was she going to attack him? Milk his brain? He stepped back. "That was Zelda, not Elizabeth," she said. "And I won't lie low, damn it, Colm. I won't play scared. I'll bring the cows in at night. I'm not letting any creeps intimidate me. I'm not!"

He knew better than to cross her when she was up in arms. "Okay, down, woman. Go ahead. When they set fire to your barn, don't come running to me."

"Ha! I won't. You can count on that. Anyhow, all the more reason why we should find out who's behind this orchard bashing." She smiled a diabolical smile. Sometimes he wondered what, who, he was involved with here. But he loved her, he loved this intractable woman. Maybe because she *was* so intractable. . . .

"Marry me," he said, flinging himself, unaccountably, absurdly, into a pile of hay, kneeing himself over to her. "Marry me, Ruthie, and we'll find those villains together. One of them might be Pete, you said he's trying to develop this neighborhood. We'll save the neighborhood, save the farms, save the orchards, save Vermont."

"There are Vermonters who are doing that," she said, "buying up land, putting it in common trust. Go join their team if you want to save Vermont. My team doesn't have any capital behind it."

"Oh yes, it does," he said, gazing up at her breasts. They were heaving under the periwinkle-blue shirt; her neck was perspiring, pink as a cow's teat. "Ruthie," he said, but she wasn't in the mood. She was herding the cows out of the milking room, motioning him to his feet.

"I have to see to Gypsy, she's over there in her stall. She's on antibiotics. They're all spooky today, even the ones who weren't stabbed. That guy used a nine-inch blade, some kind of hunting or survival knife. What kind of creep does that? Knifing a cow in its belly?"

She grabbed his arms, pulled him up. He was weak-kneed, getting flabby in *his* belly. "Colm, I want you to interview the suspects outside the orchard. That minister, that woman developer. Find out who the third partner is. I sense she—he—has something to do with these goings-on. Why else wouldn't Pete let on who that person is? He knows, oh, you can bet he knows." She paused, changed her mind. "No, I'll talk to Pete. But, Colm . . ." He was on his feet, she was grabbing his hands so tightly they were numb. "See those women. The ones who were praying. They might know something. About that minister, about the death of Cassandra Wickham."

"Oh no, not those women," he said. "Jeez."

"You can do it, Colm. I need you. Moira Earthrowl needs you. You can't imagine what she's been through, Colm. . . ."

"Well, I'll try. By the way, they've released Cassandra's body. There was nothing to indicate anything more than that she'd simply been struck by a car—judging from the height of the injury, a sport utility vehicle. Could be a Chevy Blazer, I suppose. The impact came from behind. I mean, she was hit in the back: spinal fracture, broken pelvis."

"Stan seemed to think she ran toward the road. Even the minister claimed she ran at the car—and he said she was hit from behind. There's a contradiction here. And he's the prosecution's star witness. He could be lying. Find out, will you, Colm? Maybe it wasn't Stan's car at all. Maybe it was another car, another sport utility vehicle. I mean, you see them all over the place. Colm? You'll do this for me? I'll help with Pete. But you'll have to take on that minister—what's his name? Turnbull? Sounds bovine. And, um, those women."

"Thanks," he said. "Thanks a lot." He didn't feel particularly amorous anymore. He just needed a drink of something strong. For that, he invited himself into her kitchen.

But he'd have to drink it alone, she said. Gypsy needed her, the other wounded cows. When Tim returned from town, Ruth was going back to the orchard—to leave a message for Emily. She had questions to ask her daughter, things to talk over with Moira.

The silence in her kitchen lunged at him, practically knocked him over. He'd left a bottle of Guckenheimer in her pantry, and it was gone. Who'd been drinking it in his absence—Pete? Damn the s.o.b. He settled for Otter Creek Ale, poured a tepid glassful. Head in his hands, he considered. Ruth was in love with her cows—the fact suddenly struck him. He didn't have a chance.

But he supposed he'd go on trying. He'd interview the reverend. He'd talk to those foolish women.

Forty-one

Stan wanted to go home; he tried to communicate this need to Moira, but the words wouldn't come out. All he could manage was, "Wacomho-o, Moi, geme ow-ere," and when she looked at him, quizzically, pityingly, he wanted to grab her, shake her. Why couldn't she understand? He was dying here in this place. Life was passing him by, he was a dead log, shunted to the side of the stream, thrown up on shore to rot.

She was embracing him now, talking about a woman struck in the back. His car? What woman? He couldn't think. "Cara, Cara," he said, weeping, and Moira said, "No, not Carol, Stan: Cassandra. That minister said you deliberately hit her. Ruth and I think he was lying. You didn't kill her, Stan, I know you didn't. I want you to get better now, Stan. Work on that physical therapy, come home to the orchard. We need you. I need you."

She held him in a grip that almost suffocated him. When he thought he'd never breathe another breath, she let go, turned. "Ta-me," he cried, "Moir, ta-me," but she was gone. Only the big nurse was there, the one who'd come to take him to the torture chamber. They would twist his legs, his arms, they would beat and batter him. And he couldn't complain. He couldn't talk. He was a dead log. He let himself be strapped into a chair, wheeled off. Out of control.

Forty-two

Chief Roy Fallon was sucking on a Pepsi when Colm walked in. It wasn't a diet Pepsi, either, Colm could see the flaccid belly swell even as the chief drank. "You want to lose your teeth, Roy, you want to get diabetes," he warned, "you keep on sucking up that sugar."

"I'm so far gone now," Fallon said, "what more can it do?" And he kept on guzzling. "Besides, I like the stuff. What other pleasures I got? The wife's got religion. The boy's gone to the city to be an actor. He drives a cab. What the hell?" He laughed that chuk-chuk-chuk laugh of his. Fallon was a hedonist. He'd live to be a hundred in spite of his bad habits: Pepsi-Cola, two martinis at lunch. Cigars.

"What kind of religion?" Colm asked.

The chief turned a little pink, as though Colm had hit a nerve. It was a sect. Harmless enough, he was sure, just kooky. "She's a quester, one of those. Always looking for something new, um . . . she's on the board of directors, they're bleeding her. She, um, complains. I think she's beginning to see the light."

"It wouldn't be those Messengers of Saint Dorothea, would it?"

"Jesus, yeah, yeah, you got it!" he said, loudly, as though he'd just remembered, and of course he knew. Hadn't he interrogated that minister after Cassandra Wickham's death? He was embarrassed because his wife was involved, that was all. But that, too, might be useful. "Messengers of Saint . . . Christ almighty," Fallon went on. "A friend got her into it. But just a passing phase. She's tried everything else. Catholics, Methodists, Unitarians, the synagogue couple times. Now she's a messenger of Saint Dottie. Dotty as hell." He guffawed. Chuk-chuk-chuk.

"Maybe she could help us," Colm said, and explained his mission. "I want to run a check on that minister. He seems to have a certain charisma, especially for women. I want to know what his background is, where he comes from. He could have been the one who hit that woman, you know. What does he drive for a car? What's his weak point—money? They tithe, you know, these outfits. Bertha Willmarth—that's Ruth's sister-in-law . . . was—pays out a couple grand a year. Oh yes," he said when Fallon opened his mouth, panicked. "You better keep tabs on your wife. See what she's putting in the basket each week."

Himself, Colm was nominally Catholic. He took in the late show now and then, dropped in a ten and took out a five. The church was wealthy enough, he figured. After all, it owned that Michelangelo ceiling in the Vatican, worth zillions for sure.

But Fallon didn't want his wife involved. "She's on the fence, I told you. Could go either way. Wait a while. But hell, I'll run a check on whazzisname for you."

"Ruth says his surname is Turnbull. Say, is your wife one of those praying ones? Who landed on Samuels's porch just before he shot himself? I wouldn't be surprised but what they drove him to it. Just to shut up the prayers."

"Prayers help," said Fallon stiffly. "When I had that heart attack scare, my wife was a Baptist then. She got a bunch of 'em to pray. I got out a week before the doctors thought."

Colm had heard of things like that happening. He guessed he shouldn't berate it. He might need a prayer or two himself one day. Still, one could go too far—especially when the prayers weren't wanted.

"Anyhow," Fallon said, "I want you to, um, leave her to me. We talk. She tells me stuff if I want. I'll let you, um . . ."

"Sure. But give me a ring when you find something on Turnbull, okay? I've got to talk to him. But I want to do a little homework first."

Fallon sighed, and chugalugged his Pepsi. He held up a fresh can. "You should try it, Hanna. You could use a little sweetening."

Forty-three

Moira was in love with apples, Ruth could see that. She had a large white porcelain bowl on the dining room table with six varieties of apples. "Here's one of my favorites, the Macoun," she announced. It was large and bright red. "A dessert apple, highly flavored." Already she was running into the kitchen for a paper bag. "For you, one each of six kinds," she said. "I want you to try them, tell me what you think. Of course everyone buys Red Delicious. But have you ever tried the Jonathan?"

Ruth hadn't. She accepted the apples, murmured over them. She had other things on her mind. "We had a small incident," she explained to Moira, trying to look unconcerned. "Some teenagers, we figure, vandals. Knifing three of my cows. Oh, they're all right," she said when Moira cried out. "We're keeping a close watch. Tim's over there now. I'm bringing them in at night. I only mention it because you might think—"

"It might stem from that warning?"

"Yes. But no. Teen vandals, absolutely, Lucien Larocque next door saw one running away. There's no connection. But even if there were—I mean, I want to help here. Besides, I've done all the interviewing already."

She told what she'd found out. "Nothing important, really, at least it doesn't seem so now. Rufus—well, did you know that his grandfather owned this orchard—started it, in fact? That may be something to think about."

"Yes," Moira said, biting into an apple, looking troubled, "that could be a reason for his wanting to own it back. And discourage us from owning it."

"Maybe. Maybe not. Then there's Don Yates. Seems a really nice guy. But . . ."

"But?"

"He knows the orchard. You have to suspect everyone, I guess. Awful to do that, but Don knows his way around this place. He knows apples. Though I don't see any motive for his destroying them. He did warn us about—well, Opal. Oh, I know she's Stan's niece," Ruth went on hurriedly, "but she was the one who let the goat go. Oh, you didn't know that?"

Moira sat still, a chunk of apple in her cheek. "No, I didn't know. But I can believe it. The first day she was here, she didn't want any part of the Jamaicans. I don't know where that prejudice comes from. Certainly not from her father."

Ruth shook her head. "Anyway, Don thinks I should talk to Opal. Unless you want to. . . ."

"No, no. You do it. I couldn't. She wouldn't talk to me anyway. She's a strange girl. You don't suspect her—I mean, hurting your cows?"

That stopped Ruth a minute. Could it be? Lucien hadn't actually identified the person, simply described a dark figure. That could be anyone. Lucien's eyesight was failing, he'd mentioned cataracts a while back. Looking at Moira's horrified face, she said, "I'm sure not. A woman wouldn't do that. Why would the girl have a hunting knife?"

Moira looked relieved. "Of course you're right. You said teenagers. Teenage boys can be awful. Once Carol was involved with a kid we worried about. She was a small fifteen, he was over six feet, on the wrestling team. She dropped him when she found he was bragging about his relationship with her, saying they were sleeping together when they weren't. Carol was furious! Then this other boy, Trevor Selleck, the one who killed her . . .

"No, I didn't mean to say that," Moira said when Ruth looked up sharply. "That's the word Stan uses. Trevor was twenty, he'd already graduated. He seemed nice enough, but she was still in high school. He'd been suspended once from school for using drugs—Carol said he'd been sabotaged by his friends. She was always excusing him! And then . . . it happened again—alcohol this time."

Moira was almost in a trance as she spoke, as though it were all happening for the first time. Ruth watched her carefully, waiting for an explosion but not wanting to stop her. It would be a therapy, talking it out with someone.

"They were at the high school prom, Carol was in a blue satin dress; it fit her like a glove—she had a beautiful body. Nothing like mine. . . ." Moira looked down at her own pear-shaped torso, a little extra flesh around the belly; she waved away Ruth's murmured protest. "She was so excited, he'd sent a corsage—a gardenia, it was like back in the fifties. Carol was on the prom committee. It was her idea to have a fifties ball, she was an old-fashioned kind of girl. Believed in people, their inherent goodness. He was late, but she understood. He had a job, earning money to go to college, he told her. He was an hour late, I felt sorry for Carol, all dressed up; the scent of gardenia filled the house. Then he arrived and it was like the world opened up, she was full of smiles, practically afloat. He'd rented a tux; he was a handsome fellow. Wore his hair a little too long for me, but Carol liked it. I thought I smelled more than gardenias as they left, I thought I smelled pot or alcohol on his breath, though he took care to stand away from me. Carol was so happy, so excited, I couldn't complain. What could I say: *Let me smell your breath, young man?*"

"Of course not," Ruth murmured, and sipped her coffee.

"So they left in his car. It was an old car—I've nothing against old cars, the young can't afford anything better, but it sounded like a tank, needing a muffler, perhaps. What could I do? The high school wasn't far, only a few miles. They got to the dance all right. She was made queen! We have the pictures. Here, I'll show you."

Moira pulled a framed photo from a buffet. The girl was lovely: lustrous dark hair framing a heart-shaped face, large luminous hazel eyes. Moira was right: Compassion shone from her face. What would she have made of all this mischief in the orchard?

"I still have the green gown she'd made for the ball, folded away. She never wore it! At the last minute she spilled grape juice on it, couldn't get out the stain; changed into the blue satin she'd worn the year before." She jumped up. "Look, Ruth, Emily is the same height. Do you think perhaps she'd like it? I had it dry-cleaned and the stain came out. It does no good in the drawer. We can't live in the past. Things should have a use. . . ."

Before Ruth could object, Moira was dragging out the dress, smoothing it in her hands, thrusting it at Ruth. Branbury High didn't have a ball like this, Ruth doubted Emily would ever wear it. But what could she say? She couldn't refuse it. She had a thought. "Why don't you give it to Emily yourself? I'm sure she'd be so pleased."

"I don't think I could explain. No, you give it to her. Please?" So Ruth took it. It felt fragile in her hands, as though it might disintegrate if anyone wore it.

But the story wasn't finished.

"They left the school at midnight. There were designated drivers, of course, but the boy seemed all right, according to Carol's best friend, Jen. He must have been drinking afterward because it didn't happen—the accident—until two in the morning. We were frantic by then. Stan was ready to call the police, but I realized the dance went on till one; they'd have gone to someone's house. It was such a big night! Graduation coming up and all. . . . And then, it must have been two-thirty, we heard a car, a knocking at the door. Stan went down in his nightshirt, I was at the top of the stairs. I remembered how dry my throat was, I couldn't swallow."

Moira dropped her head in her hands and Ruth said, "Don't, don't, Moira."

But Moira had to finish the story. "It was the police. There'd been an accident, the car had missed the turn onto a bridge, hit a tree, spun off down the bank, into the river. The boy got out a window. He couldn't get Carol out, he said, she was wedged in from the impact with the tree. He was crying, the police said—

but what good did that do Carol? The ambulance came. But Carol was gone. She'd . . . drowned."

Ruth thought of Vic, in that stolen car two years before—those fellows had been drinking. For a moment Carol was her loss, too. She pulled her chair closer to Moira's, put a hand on her friend's arm. Moira blew her nose, said, "I'm sorry. I didn't mean to get into all this! So self-indulgent of me. I don't know what launched me into it. . . ." She took a bite of an apple, tried to smile through its white flesh.

Ruth wanted to put an arm around her, but Moira seemed, somehow, separate, sitting there with her half-eaten Macoun apple.

It was almost a relief to see Opal coming down the stairs in jeans and T-shirt—had she been listening? Ruth stood up, called to the girl. "Have you got a minute, Opal? I'm helping out your aunt here, need *your* help. Could we talk? Out on the porch, maybe?" She still had the green ball gown in her hands; she laid it carefully on the table.

The girl glanced at the gown, pursed her lips—perhaps she would have wanted the dress for herself, although she was shorter, thinner than Emily—it would be a poor fit. "I don't know anything. Anything about anything. My father is dying, did you know that? They won't tell me, my mother won't tell me. But I know. He's dying, and I'm up here picking apples. They don't want me down there. Mama wants Daddy to herself. She doesn't care about me. Nobody cares about me!" Throwing back her head, she ran to the door and slammed it hard.

Moira looked distraught. "It's not true about the parents. Her mother calls every other night. Annie May may be a kook, but she loves her child, I'm sure of that. There's something else that's bothering Opal. I don't know what it is. I've tried to find out, but she won't talk. To me, anyhow."

"Keep trying," Ruth said, and prepared to leave. "I have to get back to my spooked cows. When Emily comes off work this afternoon, tell her to come right home. I need her." Moira's story had made her paranoid. She suddenly wanted to see Emily, touch her, warn her. About what? Men?

"The dress! You forgot the dress," Moira called out, and Ruth went back for it; then out to the pickup. She saw Opal coming out of the barn with an apple pail. She was small, but sinewy, she could have knifed those cows, couldn't she?

Ruth shook her head to dismiss the thought.

Forty-four

It was easier, Colm discovered, to interview the praying women in pairs. One woman would goad the other, sometimes to the point of wasted time, sometimes to an interesting discovery. For example, this morning, Saturday, he'd refereed a talking contest between one Evelyn Petcock and one Thelma Boggs, who had first tried to convert him to the Messengers, then, seeing it hopeless, had accused the other of being disloyal, sympathetic to Samuels.

"That Aaron Samuels," Thelma said, "is a pervert, a scourge on society."

"That's what I said, Thelma."

"Oh no, you didn't, Evelyn, you said you thought the boy seduced *him*. You said that, Evelyn."

"I did not! I said it was probably his mother's fault, the way he was brought up. And that teacher made it worse."

"Those teachers," Thelma argued, "going home at three o'clock, nothing to do till eight the next morning. And the outrageous salaries they get! Paid by us, the taxpayers. It's not right."

"And then they go and seduce young boys," said Evelyn, as if to prove her loyalty to the Messengers.

Colm, who had been a teacher for two years and worked at it day and night before he discovered it wasn't his calling, ignored the comments. "Why did you go to pray on his porch?" he'd asked Evelyn.

"Oh, we had to, didn't we?" She looked at Thelma, who was glaring into her lap, still upset by the "outrageous" salaries. "I mean, our pastor said we had to. And Cassandra, poor thing—she backed him up. Of course, they didn't always get along."

"How so?" Colm asked.

"We shouldn't talk about the dead," said Thelma, looking fiercely at Evelyn, and Evelyn said, "Well, anyway, we went. We prayed. And that very night Aaron Samuels went and shot himself." She shuddered, hugged her chest; then suddenly remembered a doctor's appointment she was late for, and the interview ended.

But Colm determined to pursue the question with the next group—a threesome this time. He did the paperwork on a house he'd just sold to a young couple from Poughkeepsie, New York, who wanted to get "back to nature," had a quick shot of Guckenheimer and cider, then drove to the home of Gertrude Bliss, where he found the three women drinking herb tea.

Gertrude's home was childproof, animalproof, and guestproof: The two upholstered chairs and sofa were covered with plastic, the shelves and fireplace mantel practically bare except for a dozen photographs, all of the same glum-looking adolescent girl. He saw no evidence of children or pets; Gertrude herself was probably in her late fifties. Something stuck to his cheek as he entered; his hand discovered a hanging fly catcher, full of dead flies. He tried to look blasé. Gertrude offered him a seat on a plastic-lined rocking chair; it made a wheezing sound as he sat. The other two women—Gertrude's sister Minerva Bliss, and Alma Herringbone—wheezed down together on the sofa and regarded him suspiciously. Of the three, only Minerva appeared to be under fifty—but barely.

Alma was the spokesperson, it seemed, and an interrogator. Before Colm could open his mouth, she was leaning forward, staring him down, hurling questions at him. Why was he here? What had they done wrong? Was he afraid of prayer? "Are you aware," she said sternly, "of the power of prayer? How many folks prayer has cured of life-threatening diseases? Terminal cancer, oh yes. My own uncle, in the hospital with prostate cancer, a tumor as big as a—a—" Her hands made swooping circles in the air.

"A pomegranate," Minerva offered, and Alma said, "Bigger. Bigger than a pomegranate. And every day we prayed, we had groups praying across the country. And he's still alive today!" she finished triumphantly.

"How long ago was that?" Colm asked, and she replied, "A year, a whole year. A whole long, long year."

Colm asked if he'd had radiation therapy, and she said, "Well, I don't know. But it wasn't what cured him. It was God. God, through us. God cured him." The other women nodded, marveled at the wonder of it.

"Was your minister a part of this prayer?" he asked, seeking a lead-in to Turnbull.

Alma looked at him as though he were a dullard. "He's our spiritual leader," she said. "What would *you* think?"

"He led you in prayer." Colm recalled the phrase from some long-ago Sunday school class.

"He did."

"Did Cassandra Wickham pray under his, um, leadership? I understand they had a falling-out."

There was a silence. He heard the women breathe. Gertrude's was a rasping, asthmatic sound, as though she might be in need of a prayer herself.

Finally Minerva said, "Cassandra was different." Alma gave a slight nod.

"She wanted to be in charge, that's what it was," Alma said.

"It wasn't that," Gertrude rasped. "It was personal. Something in their past. I heard them arguing once. They came here from the same town, you know."

"What town was that?" Colm asked. His back was itching, right in the center. He wiggled against the plastic rocker and a spoke snapped loose, stuck into his back. Gertrude glared at him.

Minerva started to answer and was shushed. "You'll have to ask him," said Alma. "We can't speak for him. But I can tell you he's a good person, a holy person, oh yes. I don't blame him for criticizing Cassandra. She had a—a sharp way about her, she could be pushy. We didn't all hold with her going after the school board like that. We believed in prayer to get our way."

"But Christ—but our minister wanted her to, he sent around petitions when she was running for the board," Minerva said, waving away a cluster fly.

"Are any of you familiar with the Earthrowl apple orchard?" he questioned. "Was there anything Cassandra might have had against it? Or your minister?"

"We prayed there, didn't we?" said Minerva, sucking on the end of a little finger. She closely examined a seeming imperfection in the petal-pink nail.

"I used to pick apples there," Alma said. "Before it sold to those new people. Now they don't let us go in and pick. They just use those black men. I haven't been there in three years."

"Except to pray," Colm said with a smile.

The women nodded. They didn't get his irony. The conversation switched to Saint Dorothea then, and he excused himself, making a wide path around the fly sticker. He didn't want to get into theology. But there was obviously something amiss between the reverend and Cassandra. He'd have to dig into that. He'd have to talk to Turnbull. First, of course, he'd have to do his homework. He'd see what Roy Fallon had dug up. He might even try the Internet, though he wasn't good at it, he kept running into dead ends, clicking on banner ads. But he'd persevere, for Ruth's sake.

Gertrude followed him to the door. "The millennium," she hissed as he groped for his coat. "It's here. It's on our doorstep. You have to keep praying."

"Why, what will happen?" he asked politely.

She gave him a pitying look. "You'll see," she said. "Oh, believe me, oh, you'll see."

Colm coughed and hurried out.

Forty-five

Emily was searching through her bureau drawers for something to wear to the Valley Fair. With schoolwork and apple picking, she had to think ahead. She wanted to think ahead. It was as though there were nothing beyond that weekend: two long magical days with Adam Golding.

The pink mohair sweater had a spot on it: a spray of milk or manure or something. Oh, that miserable barn! Well, the blue cardigan would do, and the pale pink shirt. The jeans needed washing, they smelled of barn. She fingered a brooch, a gold pin she'd found in the pasture—someone had dropped it there; she'd asked Wilder's mother, who rented out land, but it wasn't hers. Sometimes, of course, local kids walked through—her mother didn't mind, just so they didn't spook the cows. So Emily had kept it. But it was too fancy for the blue cardigan. What if they went out dancing—to a dance club? What then? Except for that green ball gown from the Earthrowls that was lovely but wholly inappropriate, she had only one dress, and it was too tight; she'd grown bustier in the past year. She yanked it off the hanger, held it up to her in front of the mirror. It wasn't even the right color! It was a pale yellow print; with her brown hair she needed something with warmth. She looked best in red. She needed a red dress: a swingy, sexy red dress that would make Adam feast his eyes on her. Where would she get the money for a dress like that? Where would she even find such a dress in Branbury, where the one store that sold women's clothing had just failed and folded? Anyway, there were no dance clubs in Branbury, Vermont.

She sank back onto the bed, the print dress crumpled in her arms. She was a small-town farm girl, she had to face it. You couldn't make a silk purse out of a sow's ear—she'd heard her mother say that over and over, speaking of her father. Her mother, so sure her father would fail down in the city, unable to keep up with that actress. But it had been over three years now and her father was still with that woman. Still in the city—well, pretty much, although he was back in Branbury for the time being, some business thing. She stretched her arms up over her head, wiggled her fingers. Her father had made it. If he could, she could. Feeling restless, she sprang up, stared fiercely at her image in the mirror. Oh God, she had a zit on the side of her nose! But she could be called pretty, and she had a decent figure: robust, but not too robust. She could do it. She could do anything she wanted. "You can, Emily," she told herself. "You can do anything you want."

"I've always told you that," said her mother, appearing suddenly, embarrassingly, in the doorway. "So what is it you want to do?"

Emily spun about, her neck flushed a deep pink. Why had she left her door open? "Nothing," she sputtered. "I was just thinking about . . . a test I have in chemistry. You know I'm not very good in chemistry. I want to pass it."

"Of course you will." Her mother sat down on the bed, looked at the crumpled print dress, the pink and blue sweaters. "Trying on your gorgeous wardrobe?"

"What gorgeous wardrobe?" Emily leaned against the bureau. "I was just thinking—I need some new clothes."

"Well, you're a working girl. Buy something with your orchard money."

"Mother, I need that just to live. To pay for books, snacks, movies. It isn't that much anyway."

"Go see your father, then. He's back at the inn. If he has money for a fancy room, he can give you money for clothes."

Emily didn't answer. Her mother didn't leave. "Mom, I have to get over to the orchard. I start picking at nine. I have to be there."

"It's only twenty of. I'll drive you. I need to ask a few questions. About the orchard. You know I'm trying to help out Moira Earthrowl. Find out what's going on."

"Mom, I don't know anything about that. I haven't seen or heard a thing. Except, well, Opal. Something I promised not to tell. But I don't think she has anything to do with the really bad stuff."

"What about Rufus, the manager? How does he strike you?" Her mother was making herself comfortable now on the bed, puffing up a pillow, sitting back against it. Frustration crawled up Emily's spine. Rufus was Rufus, that was all. She didn't have much to do with him. "He tells us where to pick, he does his job. He thinks Adam and me and the Butterfields are just kids, he resents us, maybe. Once he called Adam a 'rich city slicker'—Adam didn't like it, I could tell. Besides, Adam's not rich at all, he doesn't own anything except his beat-up Volvo."

"Rufus's grandfather used to own that orchard, did you know that? Do you think he might want it back?"

Emily didn't know. "He likes his work, that's all I can tell you. Though sometimes he acts like he owns the place."

"In what way?"

"Oh, I don't know. One time I heard him tell Rolly Butterfield to stay away from a certain tree that was still too young to pick. 'I don't want *my* tree spoiled,' Rufus said. I don't think he really meant, though, it was *his* tree. I mean, I've heard Tim call Esmeralda's calf *his* baby."

"Yes, sure. I know. So there's nothing else? No strangers who've appeared on the land? And Don Yates—why does he volunteer there, you think? Is he always friendly?"

"Yes, Mom. He's a nice man. He clowns around with the school kids—the few that have come since the spraying!" She stood up. "Now I've got to go, Mom. If I'm late, Rufus will be mad. He's taking stuff to the Shoreham Co-op today, he wants to make his quota."

She turned at the bedroom door. Her mother was still sprawled on the bed—it was unlike her to act so lazy. Emily had to smile.

"Mom, it's that minister to blame, that's what Adam and I think. He's got a thing against Mr. Earthrowl—like he thinks he's some kind of devil. Adam was telling about something that happened down in Massachusetts. In a high school it was, a satanic group that sprang up and put the fix on a kid they didn't like for some reason. They didn't kill him, they just played all kinds of mean tricks. Adam and I don't think anyone is trying to kill anybody here, it just happened poor Bartholomew ate that apple. The minister's trying to make Mr. Earthrowl realize he can't go around trying to do in the church or its members. But now that Mr. Earthrowl's had his stroke, we think the bad stuff will stop."

"What about my cows being slashed?" Her mother was sitting up now, looking angry. Emily knew that look. She tossed her jacket over her shoulder, glanced at her watch. It was ten of ten, she'd barely get to work in time.

"Mom, there's a gang of kids in town that vandalize mailboxes, things like that. It's probably them."

"My cows aren't mailboxes!" Her mother was up now, looming tall behind her, her cheeks were shiny-mad.

Emily took off then, she had to. "I'll be home at five. If I hear anything new, I'll tell you. But nothing else is going to happen. And next weekend, Mom . . ."

She could hear her mother waiting behind her. Breathing hard.

"I'm going to, um, the Valley Fair with Adam. Just for the day, of course," she said. It wasn't a lie, was it? It was Essex they'd spend the night in. She couldn't explain the whole thing now, but at least she'd give it a start. She'd tell her mother the truth, well, later on. Maybe. Her mother was such a fuddy-duddy!

"I'll drive you, we can talk about it in the pickup," her mother said, but Emily said, "No, thanks," and ran heavily down the stairs, through the kitchen, and out into the chill morning. She gasped it in. When her brother Vic came along and hollered, "I got two baby chicks just out of the eggs. Wanna come and see?" she couldn't answer. She couldn't seem to breathe.

"What in heck's the matter with you?" he said, hands on his bony hips. There were rips in both knees of his pants and his sneaker laces were untied. He seemed to think it made him look cool.

"Nothing's the matter," she gasped back. "No, everything's the matter. I don't know! Tie your dumb shoelaces. Or you'll fall on your silly face."

"Jeezum. Get a life," Vic said, and shuffled his way over toward the chicken pen. And then, when he saw the familiar red Ford Explorer cruising up the driveway, "Hey, Dad!" he cried. "I got baby chicks—I hatched 'em myself. Come'n see!"

Forty-six

Well, you might have spent more time with Vic. You never looked at his chicks," Ruth said, but Pete was obviously here on another mission. She knew what it was: It was an old tune on an old instrument. He wanted her to sell her half of the farm acreage. So he could sell the whole, develop it.

But he was determined to go through the amenities—something he'd apparently learned from Violet, or Iris, or Tulip, or whatever the woman's flowery name was.

"We talked," he said, "and I did see his chickens. He'd better keep them out of the barn, though—the inspectors don't like chickens in with the cows. Hey, these doughnuts are better than ever. I've missed them." He stuffed one in his mouth, smiled at her through sugary teeth. She caught the "them." He never missed *her*, of course. If he had, if he'd shown the slightest remorse for leaving her . . . they might be friends. She wanted them to be friends: for the children's sake, as well as her own. But it hadn't worked that way. Still, she coughed, tried to smile.

She watched him swallow two doughnuts; he mentioned the "unusually warm weather for late September," reminded her to tell Tim to put "more wood chips around those Scotch pines," and complained about the way the calf pens looked: "Need repairs, Ruth, a little paint would help. Barn needs painting, too, if we're going to sell." She sucked in her breath. He leaned his elbows on the kitchen table, bent his head forward, narrowed his pale blue eyes, and said, "You know why I'm here, Ruth. You know what I want."

"You're here about those slashed cows. It was in the paper." She didn't know why she'd brought that up, but she had a sudden concern. "Three of them, last Thursday morning. Gypsy was cut in the belly, she hasn't given a drop of milk since—the shock of it! What do you know about that, Pete? What do those developer friends of yours know about it?"

He drew back quickly, hands gripped in his lap; he was hurt. How could she suspect him or his colleagues? "Gypsy?" he said, as though he'd never known the cow, when he was present at her birth! Gypsy Rose Lee was a ridiculous name for a cow, he'd said at the time, the stripper would "turn over in her grave" to hear of it. "Yeah, I read about it. Kids. Ever hear about kids tipping over cows? That Unsworth kid, I bet, or one of them. Police better get on this one quick." He shook his head, shook the cow right out of his thoughts; if she was making an insinuation, he wasn't going to pick it up, he didn't want any arguments today.

"Ruth," he said, sounding overtaxed, weary—he'd come all this way to settle something and she was bringing up dry cows. He looked at her brightly. "All the more reason we should sell, Ruth. Bad stuff going on around here. The orchard—already one death over there. Our kids, Ruth. They don't care for farming—you have to face it. Emily'd love nothing more than to live in town, be like other kids. You got to think of the children, Ruth."

He reached idly for a doughnut; it stuck in his mouth like a round O. He was twisting her thoughts again. He was good at that: twisting things she said into what he wanted to hear, what he wanted for himself.

"Pete, if this visit is about selling the farm, I won't do it. I've told you that before. I'm not selling. You can't convince me that Emily and Vic are better off living in town than on a farm. Anyhow, Emily will be in college next year—with *your* help." She saw him grimace. "You can slash my cows, but you're not going to make me give up farming. Any more than the Earthrowls are going to give up that orchard—I wonder how much you have to do with that, too! They came up here to heal, and that's what the orchard is going to do for them. Now, this farm is *my* healing place. Since you left. So the subject is closed. Finished. Period."

She shoved back her chair, stood up, still waving her arms for truce. She stumbled backward into the refrigerator, folded her arms, and glared back at Pete. He was standing now, too, his big face a black cloud, his arms at his sides, fingers curled into loose fists.

"Then you'll have to buy me out, Ruth. You've got the house, the cows, but I own half the land. You agreed to that. My lawyer will let you know how much you owe me."

He grinned a pumpkin grin and went to the door. "Thanks for the doughnuts," he said, and let the screen door bang twice behind him.

Ruth sank into a chair, Pete's fists squeezing her heart. She knew how her cow felt, slashed in the belly. Unable to give milk. What was there left to pay for his half of the land—except blood?

Forty-seven

Stan was home: Moira didn't know whether that was a good move or not. On the one hand, he was in her care, in his own home, where she could oversee his diet, his exercise, his medications; where he could look out on the apple trees. On the other hand, because he *could* see the apples and all that needed to be done, he'd worry. Already he was sitting by the window, staring out morosely.

Suddenly he shouted, "He drob it! Budder drob a napple. All thumb, goddammee." The pickers were working close to the house: She saw Rolly Butterfield laughing with his brother, who was juggling two apples. She seemed to be the only one now who could tell the twins apart. It had something to do with attitude. Hally had the better sense of humor, was the clown. She smiled. What was a bruised apple when laughter was in the air? Laughter was what the orchard needed: Laughter was healing.

He was only joking, she told Stan. "He's back to work now. The brothers are good pickers. They've picked all over New England. You were smart to hire them."

He growled, pacified a little by the compliment. Opal tripped down the stairs at that moment and he swiveled in his wheelchair. She gave him a sweet smile. She could be nice when she chose. "I'm going out to pick apples," she announced.

Stan wasn't sure about that. "Ooh don' know 'ow," he said, shaking his head. "Shtayn' help Moir ina how."

Opal smiled her enigmatic smile and waltzed out the door. Minutes later Moira saw her running down to the tree Adam Golding was picking. Emily Willmarth was on a ladder in the tree beyond Adam's; Moira saw her look over at Opal. Then Adam glanced at Emily. Rufus came along and motioned Opal over to a young tree where she wouldn't need a ladder. He gave her a stick with a small basket on the end for hooking the apples, and gestured. The girl's body showed her irritation; she wanted to pick like the others; wanted, Moira thought, to impress Adam. But Rufus was firm. The girl was a liability, his face said, she'd do what he ordered. And finally Opal grimaced and hooked an apple into the basket.

The apple world seemed serene then. The Butterfields were raking the apples off with lightning fingers. Adam and Emily were picking, under Rufus's stern gaze, with solemn faces. Farther down in the orchard the Jamaicans were perched on their ladders like extensions of the trees. "Steal away, steal away ho-ome . . ." Moira heard them sing. Zayon came up the path with a bin of apples, bearing it lightly in his brown arms, his face glowing as though it were an offering of myrrh and incense.

Stan's head was dropping into his chest, he was napping in his chair—the medication made him drowsy, and Moira felt at peace. The police had stopped questioning Stan—for the time being, anyway; the interviewing was over, and there'd been no mischief for a few days now, not even a menacing phone call. She should be relieved. All seemed well with the apple world.

But then something thudded against the window. Stan's head jerked up. He said, "Wha? Whazit?" And Moira sighed. It was the cardinal again, his feathers blood-colored, slamming again and again at the window where Stan sat in his wheelchair. She pushed her husband away from the window, into the kitchen.

"It's all right," she soothed. "It's just that foolish bird. I'll get you some juice. We'll sit in here."

She settled back into a kitchen chair. The room was dim with the curtains pulled, and she closed her eyes, breathed in the moment's quiet.

Forty-eight

Colm had saved Bertha till last. Not because he wanted to savor the interview—no way!—but because he couldn't face the woman until the end. Jeez, it had been embarrassing back in high school: She'd send him notes, sidle up, bump her tray against his in the lunchroom. One day she'd knocked the tray right out of his hands and *he'd* had to clean it up, pay for more. What was it, he'd ask himself, looking in the lavatory mirror, that attracted her to him? He was a beanpole then, those hunger lines in the face . . . he was kind of homely, let's face it. Maybe that was it: Bertha had a hankering for homely men, the underdog—someone who might notice her. Well, he looked better now, he thought he did—Ruth said so, anyway. His face had filled out, he'd grown out the old crew cut. Not because he wanted to, but because Ruth said he was behind the times; today's men had a full crop of hair. He'd conformed—for Ruth's sake. And it only seemed to attract Bertha the more. Jeez.

Actually, he hadn't seen the woman for almost two years, since she got in trouble for trying to "save" young Vic Willmarth. She was on probation now. But the probation itself and the aftermath of that affair, according to Ruth, had increased her fear of the "devil" and the "images" she conjured up of that fictional figure. Colm didn't want to be any part of those images.

Well, he thought, here goes, and he rang the bell—ding dong—on the door of the pink-shuttered house on 9 All Saints Lane. Bertha knew he was coming; still she oozed surprise when he showed up. "Why, Co-olm Han-na, you're ear-ly!"

He checked his watch. It was true, he was early, damn it. She'd think he was eager. Was she really still holding the old torch? Just because he'd danced with her once at a freshman dance back in school? And she was a couple of grades above him then. He was pushing fifty now, a baby boomer. Well, he liked the sound of that: baby boomer, at least he was in somebody's swing of things. But half a century. Jesus.

She ushered him in: practically yanked him in, her fingers were steel. She was dressed in purple: a purple sweater that emphasized her saggy breasts, a purple plaid pleated skirt, a purple-and-pink-flowered scarf. Her piano legs were stuffed into shiny black pumps. He supposed purple pumps were hard to find.

"I know how you like your coffee," she murmured, trotting after a pitcher of cream.

"I don't take cream, Bertha. Haven't for years."

She expressed surprise. "Well, you don't have to worry. You're not the least bit fat, for heaven's sake. This is cream from a Jersey cow. Jerseys give the creamiest milk. I tell Pete he should raise Jerseys, 'stead of those old black and white Holsteins."

"Bertha, Pete doesn't raise anything anymore. Except maybe a little hell down in New York City."

"Don't you think I know that?" she protested. "But he's up here now, in town. He's back. He was staying with me until . . . his woman arrived and preferred the inn."

"You think he'll stay on up here? In Branbury?"

"Who knows?" she said coyly. "He has work up this way now."

"Oh, really?" Colm professed ignorance. "Doing what?" He watched her pour cream into his cup, gave up on that score. The coffee was weak as it was, a pale ocher color. He preferred Ruth's strong coffee—it had muscle.

"Oh yes. He develops things. Farms, you know. He bought Lucien Larocque's. About time, too. That old fool never did know how to run a farm."

Colm wasn't going to argue. He had other things to find out. "I guess I did hear something about that. He has a partner, I hear. Female. Maybe a third partner, too?"

Bertha looked coy again. She sank into a plum-colored sofa, patted the seat beside her. He took a seat across the room, stared ahead at a framed print of a woman in a red gown, bearing a tray of apples. Bertha's frizzled orangy head below on the sofa made an odd contrast. "We-ell, I can't say. There might be a third. He doesn't tell me ev-ery-thing. When we were young we were close as this," and she crossed two fingers. "But then he grew up—up and away." She lifted her arms as though she'd fly.

"It wouldn't be that minister friend of yours, Turnbull, now, would it, Bertha? I hear he has an *interest* in the Earthrowl orchard. Keeps calling up, I understand."

She missed his irony. "Oh, well, the church is his whole life, you see. He gives twenty-four hours a day to it, oh my, yes."

"He doesn't have to sleep like the rest of us?"

She giggled. "Oh, Colm, you haven't changed one bit. Of course he sleeps. You always had such a sense of hu-mor! But"—she leaned forward, the teacup wobbling in her hand—"he dreams the church then. Uh-huh, he tells us his dreams. Why, only yesterday he said he dreamed of a falcon swooping down and snatching up a robin that was doing nothing but perching prettily on a branch, and zing! in one snap of the falcon's beak the robin's neck was broken. Now, what do you think that meant?" She grinned at Colm, her head bent demurely to one side. She looked rather like a lady falcon herself. She'd love nothing more, he thought, than to snap him up in her big white dentures.

"Well," she said when he didn't answer, "the falcon is the devil and the poor innocent robin is us, Colm, you and me. If we let down our guard for one single minute, the devil will swoop down on us and carry us straight to hell. To hell, Colm! Think of it! And that devil, Michael said, is here. Right here in Branbury, Vermont. He saw it all in a vision."

"Michael?"

"Well, the reverend, of course. Who did you think I was talking about?" She giggled. "Want to know something?"

He wasn't sure. But lifted an eyebrow anyway.

"Well. Turnbull isn't his *real* name."

"No?" he said, pretending to a lack of interest, although his heart was pumping away. "What is his real name, then, Bertha?"

"Well, I shouldn't tell, really. But—can you keep a secret?"

He could, he definitely could. He smiled, nodded. "Good coffee," he said, gulping the last creamy tepid drop.

"Oh, I forgot the brownies! I made them 'specially when you said you were coming." She jumped up, sashayed into the kitchen, came back moments later with a plateful of chocolate nut brownies.

Colm did have a sweet tooth for chocolate, he had to admit. He bit into one, encountered something hard. She giggled. "Oh, a bit of walnut shell. I buy the whole walnuts, not the ones already opened. You can see better what you're getting."

She'd forgotten the question, it seemed—or was she avoiding it? He repeated it, not wanting to sound too eager, put her on the alert.

"Michael Turnbull," he said. "Nice name. But not his real one, you say?"

"Oh no. His name is"—her voice was hushed—"Chris Christ."

"Chris Christ?"

"Oh yes. That's why he changed, you see. People would think he made it up. It sounds almost . . . well, sacrilegious. But he told us. He doesn't think of himself as Christ, oh no. He's a modest man, he's only a disciple of Christ, he says—until—the real Christ returns. But we think of him as Christ. Oh yes, it's so fitting."

"He's a good man, you think, Bertha?"

Her sigh told him she did. "Better than the other one."

"Other one?"

"The minister before him. That one is still in prison."

She pursed her pink lips. She had thin lips, the artificial color went over the line of her natural lips to make them appear more generous, he supposed. Instead, she looked clownish.

"For embezzling funds in his former church," he reminded her. "You picked a good one there, Bertha."

She looked downcast. "Sometimes we're fooled. He seemed such a nice man. He did help me out."

"Sure. He helped you right into Rockbury." She was looking away, embarrassed. He couldn't help that one. Rockbury was the state mental institution. Bertha's lawyer had pleaded temporary "insanity" for her part in an illegal scheme, and the judge bought it, ordered her into psychiatric care. Obviously it hadn't helped. She was back to the devil again. He couldn't help adding, "You think this Chris Christ is more honest?"

"With a name like that!" she cried. It was the final proof, of course. How could he doubt her word?

"If you say so," he said. "Well, look, Bertha, I'm on my way. Thanks for the coffee and brownies." He stood up, the crumbs fell to the floor. He was sorry about that, she kept a pristine house. He tried to pick them up, but she protested.

"I have to vacuum anyway, Colm, don't worry about a few silly crumbs. But you're not going? I thought we'd have a nice talk. Not about this orchard business. I mean, I suppose that's why you've come, the other women told me. You've talked to them all, oh, I know you have. And we don't know anything, any-thing about what's going on in the orchard. Except . . ."

"Except?"

"That falcon," she said solemnly. "The devil. He's in that orchard, oh yes. That apple orchard! Apples, sacred to Saint Dorothea! And for good reason. He was called there. By that man. That Stanley Earthrowl."

"Come on, Bertha."

"It's true, Colm. He's sold his soul. He's in league with the devil. Look what he did to Cassandra Wickham!"

Bertha should be back in Rockbury, Colm understood that. He was sorry now he'd eaten her brownies. God knows what was in them. But he had one more question. He'd almost forgotten. "I understand Cassandra and your, um, Chris Christ—"

"Michael Turnbull, Colm, I told you, his real name's a secret. Oh, I shouldn't have told you."

"Turnbull, then. Cassandra and your Turnbull didn't always get along."

"But it was nothing, Colm. Just a little argument about church funds. It was just, I think, well, Cassandra felt she didn't have to tithe like the rest of us. I mean, she wanted him to pull her along on his purse strings. That's all. In the end she paid her share. Oh, we all saw to that. She had the money, too, she was just . . . well, there was some offspring, a daughter she had, who needed the money, she said. But she saw the light. She left it to the church like the rest of us."

"You're sure of that? She left it to the church?"

"Oh, definitely. We all did our wills together. It was last summer. Take some brownies with you, Colm!" she cried when he stood up to go. "Come to dinner next week! We'll have steak, there's a new meat market in town. Colm?"

"We'll see," he said, wondering if *he* was the meat market she had in mind. Then, as he paused by the front door, "Thanks, Bertha, thanks a lot," and this time he meant it.

She looked so pleased to hear his words that for a moment he was actually sorry for her. She handed him a pile of church pamphlets, and he took them. "I'll read them, Bertha, I promise I will."

"Oh, Colm." She twinkled.

Forty-nine

Emily and Adam were taking a walk through the orchard. It was a section Emily had never seen, she hadn't even realized the orchard extended this far. "Do they really own all this?" she asked, and he shrugged. "I guess so. I've never walked through here, either."

He took her elbow when she tripped over a small rock. There were only old trees here, raggedy, overgrown; they were probably not bearing apples anymore. At any rate, they hadn't been pruned. All at once the path came to an end and Emily gave a shout. "A cemetery!"

It was a small family cemetery, a dozen moss-covered stones poking up in seemingly haphazard fashion.

"Bone orchard," Adam said, and she said, "What?" But he was serious. "That's what my, um, sister used to call a cemetery. Bone orchard."

Emily understood the bone part, but, "Why orchard?" she asked. "Orchards bear fruit, they're living things." When she looked at him, he was staring down, his face pale as bone itself. "Maybe," she offered, "it's because they're planted in rows like the fruit trees. But these stones are in a semicircle."

"Bones can bear things," he said, his voice sounding almost macabre. "They bear lies, they bear hates."

She didn't know why he was so gloomy today. They were taking a walk, she wanted them to be happy; it was a prelude to their weekend together. She said, "But they're dead: Those things are buried, done with. You can't dig them up." She knelt down, rubbed the moss on one of the stones. "Adam. Look! It says 'Barrow.' That's Rufus's last name! This cemetery must belong to his family."

Adam looked interested; he dropped to his knees. "Yeah, you're right. I heard his grandfather started this orchard. There's no secret about that. Hally Butterfield told me."

"Ebeneezer Barrow, 1852–1893. Why, he was only forty-one years old! They died so young in those days."

"They die young these days, too," he said, and she felt he was talking about his mother. She reached over to squeeze his arm.

"Ebeneezer was such a ridiculous name," she said. "Though they probably called him Eben. I like that. Eben. Rhymes with heaven—well, almost. And look, this smaller stone: It was Eben's wife, Cassandra. She died even younger—only thirty-three. In childbirth, maybe? Anyway, they must have been Rufus's great-grandparents. You think?"

"Maybe. Let's get out of here." He was being impatient. She'd noticed that air of impatience about him. She supposed it was because he had high dreams that he hadn't yet realized. She wanted to help him realize those dreams. . . .

She bent to examine a marble stone—free of moss, it looked recent. She gave a cry. "This one says Earthrowl. Carol Earthrowl. Why, that's the daughter who died in that accident. Oh, how sad! And look, Adam! Oh, Adam, she was only my age!"

"I'll take *you*," he said. "You're alive. Let's get out of here." He pulled on her arm.

But she wasn't ready to go. She wanted to linger, think about this girl—her own age, who'd died so horribly. There was an inscription: *Carol O'Grady Earthrowl, b. April 7, 1979, died April 8, 1996*. "Why, she died the day after her birthday, Adam!" *Our beloved daughter, Carol, who loved the light.*

"And they brought her all this way," she said, "to bury her here instead of down in Connecticut where they come from. Why, do you think?"

When he didn't answer, she said, "To keep her with them, so they could visit her grave. That's why." She smeared her damp cheeks with the backs of her hands.

She turned to Adam, where he was examining an old gnarled tree; put her arms around his waist, her face into his neck. "That's why they don't want to lose this orchard—I mean, one big reason for it. They can't leave her behind! This is *their* orchard now."

"It's just as much Rufus's," he said, pulling down a scarred apple, even while she still held him. "All those other stones belong to him. *His* family."

"But he works here now. He lives a couple miles down the road. He can see them whenever he wants. And they're none of them his children. I don't think he's even married."

He turned around, handed her an apple. "Here. Try. It's a Gravenstein, an old variety. Fits this place, right? They don't grow them now in this orchard. Open your mouth. Bite."

She saw he'd already taken a bite himself. The flesh looked tender, juicy. She took a bite. It was a significant moment, she felt. They were sharing an apple, one of the most ancient of fruits. They were Adam and Eve. No, Adam and Emily. She smiled. Only this time it was Adam who ate the apple first.

She handed him the apple and suddenly he flung it away. "It had a worm in it. Near the core," he said, and made a face.

She laughed; she wouldn't let him break the mood. He was beautiful, her Adam was beautiful. She traced the curves of his face: the strong squarish chin, the rounded cheekbones, the pale pouches under his eyes—too litle sleep, the pouches said, the way it was with her, too, lately. The fantasies she'd been having! She was still a virgin—technically, anyway. Didn't she love him enough? Wilder would ask, and now she realized: No, she didn't, didn't really love him. She was saving herself for the right person, the real love. She was saving herself for Adam.

"Saturday morning," she said, "I'll bring my suitcase and hide it in the back of your car. We don't have to tell Moira Earthrowl we're going to the fair together, I'll just make an excuse about that afternoon, and Sunday. To my mom, too. I'll say I'm staying over with a friend."

He nodded, concentrated on her lips, ran his hands thrillingly down her breasts, her hips, held her tightly to him until she could feel his growing erection. "We could make love right here in the bone orchard," he said.

But the thought of Carol Earthrowl came between them; she couldn't, couldn't, not here. "Saturday," she promised, and pulled away—though she still had his hand—and started, dazed, up the path.

Fifty

Tim Junkins stood in the barn doorway, his ranch hat in two hands where it had blown off in the wind. He spoke haltingly, trying to catch his breath. It was six A.M.; he smelled of hay and cornstalks. "Got that fence fixed," he said.

"Good man." Ruth reached up to remove a reddish leaf that was caught in his hair. She was graining the cows—trying desperately, since Pete's visit, to concentrate on work. There was a great mewling and bawling, the cows wanted to be milked—needed to. She remembered what it had been like with her three children: her breasts full, oozing, demanding release. And she'd always had plenty. Maybe that was one reason women identified with cows, there was that affinity.

But Tim had more to say, his hat twirled with it. "Out with it, then," she said. "What now?" The old feeling of panic invaded her chest, although the children were safe in the house, eating breakfast, getting ready for the school bus.

"The hemp we put in?" Tim said. "It's gone, uprooted. It can't be woodchucks, coons. Not this time. I can understand the corn, it's a fair competition with the critters. But this is the work of human thieves." He blew out his breath, slapped his hat back on his head, leaned against the door, awaiting her reaction.

"Is that all?" she said, relieved.

"What? Lady, it took half a day to get those damn plants in. Now they're gone. It's a muddy mess. I wondered if . . . the police . . . got wind of it. A raid on hemp?"

She shook her head. She felt numbed. "Police would have come to me. This had to be vandals. Maybe the same ones who hurt my cows. . . . Kids."

"You really think that? Kids? Lookee here, Ruth, I work with kids. Kids are foolish, they vandalize mailboxes. Joey was in on that once. No more, though. I told him . . ."

He went on about the foster kids he worked with after hours. Tim was an optimist. Ruth knew what kids could do, the cruelties some were capable of; how they'd hurt Vic a few years back. "Marijuana," she said, "that's what they might have been after."

He allowed as to how that might be. "Hell, they won't get much outta these plants if it's pot they want. Ruth, we had five hundred plants in there, that's a lotta work, a lotta money. I thought you'd hit the roof. Here you are standin' there like I just told you a coon got in the corn."

"It's not Vic," she said. "Or Emily, or Sharon, or the grandkids. Or your Joey. We can replant hemp. It's just money."

Money: something she didn't have enough of—not if Pete went through with his plan to have her buy him out. She pulled at Cleopatra's teat and the cow mewled, as though it were something sexual, familiar, like taking a hot bath or having a rubdown with alcohol. "I'll do the milking this morning," she told Tim. "You go ahead with the corn. And the John Deere needs a new battery, it hardly starts. Can you go to town for that?"

"Sure, sure, ma'am, it's on my list anyway," he said, giving a hoot that brought Joey running. "You up for a ride to town?" he asked the boy, and Joey's eyes shone.

"Can we go to Ben and Jerry's?" the boy said. "Getta fudge sundae?"

"Maybe next time. Today we got business." Tim patted the boy's shoulder. To Ruth he said, "You're not going to replant the hemp, then?"

"Maybe in spring. When all this blows over."

"All what blows over?"

She shrugged. How could she explain it? Money, money to buy the farm back. Solve the orchard problems. Tim didn't know about that—not all of it, anyway. Like others in town, he probably knew about the spring spraying of Roundup, or the paraquat fiasco—it had been in the paper after Bartholomew's death. And she'd downplayed the cow-slashing for the reporter in the *Independent.* She didn't want the spotlight on her farm. She hadn't wanted anyone to know about the hemp. But someone did.

She thought of Bertha. Bertha's rouged face and her orangy-red permed hair came into focus in her inner eye. Bertha had come by just after they'd planted. For Bertha it was just a step to the minister's ear.

When Tim and Joey rode off on the balky John Deere, she called Colm. She'd woken him up—that was obvious from his mutterings.

"Hemp? Wha' hemp? You planting pot? Jeez, what time it, Ruth?"

"It's not pot!" she shouted. "Hemp. Wake up. You were there, for God's sake, you saw. Well, someone cut it down. I'm thinking that minister has something to do with it. I think Bertha told him, I'm afraid she saw Tim's HEMP tags. He might have slashed my cows, too. Get to him, Colm. Who is he, anyway?"

He was awake now. "Christ," he said.

"It doesn't help to swear, Colm. I asked you his real name. Is it really Turnbull?"

"That's his name. Christ. Chris Christ. Bertha told me. It's supposed to be a secret, so don't tell—not yet. Hey, you got coffee going? I'll come over."

"And help me milk," she said. "I've got six of them here in the barn, about to put on the machine. The others're outside, hollering." And they were, they didn't have to be called. Twenty-seven cows, pushing and shoving, bellowing at the top of their lungs. They seemed over their panic now, though Gypsy and Elizabeth were still off their feed.

"Ruthie," he said, "I'll swim the length of Otter Creek for you. Go over Branbury Falls in a barrel. I'll interview that Chris Christ today, yes, I will. But I won't milk. I can't milk, Ruthie, I don't know how to put those tubes on the teats, I'd crucify the beasts. They'd crucify me! Remember I tried it once? And Zelda kicked me? I can't face that amazon again."

She remembered. Zelda had got him in a corner, held him there with her big white rump. She'd got laughing till she wet her pants. She was laughing again now. So the hemp was gone. So Pete wanted her to buy him out. But the sun was riding up into the sky, it was the first of October: a gorgeous day, crisp and cool, the purple vetch and goldenrod thriving outside the barn door, chickadees and finches at the feeder, maple leaves turning red—practically as she looked.

"Okay," she said. "Come at seven. Coffee'll still be hot. We can talk about this Chris Christ. We can figure out ways to crucify him. The false Christ." She hung up, she couldn't believe it—she was laughing.

She attached the milkers and turned on the machine. The cows—Dolly, Esmeralda, Bathsheba—stood eager, obedient, grateful, their liquidy brown eyes on their feed, on her. She closed her eyes and it was Emily, Sharon, and Vic on her own breasts; the grandchildren, Robbie and Willa, drinking in life. She, giving it.

Fifty-one

Wednesday evening and Emily couldn't look another minute at the Shakespeare book. *Hamlet*: It had to be read by tomorrow, all five acts, and she was only through Act Two. She was annoyed at Hamlet, frankly, the way he frightened poor Ophelia, hurting her wrist, and then totally ignoring her, when all she was waiting for was a kind word or touch.

Emily would go after that word, that touch. Right now. Her mother wouldn't know: It was dark—dark so early these autumn days. But Emily liked that. You could do things in the dark you couldn't do in the light. She sighed, thinking of . . . things. Her mother was downstairs in the living room, working on farm accounts. She'd set up a table there, tired of doing it in the kitchen. That was convenient. If her mother said anything, Emily would say she'd gone out for a walk, she hadn't wanted to disturb her mother.

It was a clear cold night, a half moon hanging like a yellowy globe in the sky. The Globe: That was the name of Shakespeare's theater. His plays were full of love and lust—junior year, they'd read *A Midsummer Night's Dream*, she liked that. She liked the way the couples got all mixed up and then came back together in the end. She liked to think that was the way life worked: misunderstanding, and then finding out the truth, and coming together with a bang, a hug, a passionate caress. . . .

She got on her bicycle, bumped along Cow Hill Road, down Route 125, and onto Cider Mill Road to the Earthrowl orchard. The farmhouse was lit up; she saw Moira at her loom beside an uncurtained window, the cat curled up beside her. She heard the hum of harmonicas in the Jamaicans' bunkhouse as she rode past—but the lights were out, it was past nine o'clock; they'd be in bed except for the musician—Derek, probably. She rode up to Adam's bunkhouse; it was dark except for a single shimmering light that might have been a candle. Was he reading by candlelight? He'd ruin his eyes, that's what her mother always told her. She smiled. Probably the Butterfields were asleep, that's why the light was out. She wondered what it was Adam was reading. She grabbed up a handful of pebbles, tossed them at the window. Waited.

There was no response. She threw a second handful. She wanted to see Adam. Needed to. Had to! She'd come all this way. It was then she noticed the Butterfields' car was gone, where it was usually parked behind the bunkhouse—recalled they'd talked about a new movie in town. Adam was alone, then. He'd fallen asleep, maybe over his book. She laughed out loud, pushed open the bunkhouse door, surprised: Someone had hung a single strand of white blinking lights over the door. The bed was empty! Had he gone to the movies with the twins? Maybe. Oh, he'd be tired tomorrow!

She sat down on his bed. It was made up neatly, the way she would have expected. Adam was neat in everything: his clothing, his hair—her mother might complain about the ponytail, but it was usually combed, clean, tied back in a ribbon. He looked like . . . Hamlet. She pulled back the spread: The pillow bore the indentation of his head. She put her face close to it, embraced it; then pulled the cotton spread back over. The twins' bunks didn't have spreads, she noticed, only rough gray blankets; it was like Adam to have a bright blue coverlet. She pulled out the drawer in his bedside table—feeling a twinge of guilt, of course. Should she look inside? She was sure he wouldn't mind! What did they have to hide from each other? Although there was so much still she didn't know about him. She guessed you never really knew another person until you lived with him. And even then, her mother told her, you didn't really know him.

But her mother was thinking of her father and his taking off with that woman. Her mother was prejudiced against men, Emily really thought so. That was why her mother had closed the door against her father's coming back. Oh yes. She was sure things would have worked out if her mother had been more forgiving, more open-minded.

The drawer contained paper clips, tacks, tape, a pruning knife, several letters. Two were postmarked California, where his step-mother had moved after the divorce from his father. One of the letters was from the father. The name and address were on the envelope: *107 Park Drive, Waterbury, Connecticut.* The town sounded familiar. Adam lived in Massachusetts, he'd said. Well, she supposed the father had moved to Connecticut for business or something.

There was one letter that sparked her curiosity. It was on pink stationery. She pulled it carefully out of the envelope. She held it a moment, hardly breathing, then slowly unfolded it.

"Adam sweetie," it read, "have you broken your writing hand? It's been two weeks since your last letter. I'm still thinking of hitching up there to Vt but I can't get off work. I mean, I need the money for my dowry. Ha ha. Just kidding. Why get married these days? Work is lousy, why did I drop out of college? You were the one persuaded me, the role model. Drop out and we'll go round the world, you said. Well I'm waiting, baby. I'd go to the ends of the world with you. Sounds romantic, huh? But it's true. . . . Remember that night . . ."

Emily didn't want to know about that night. She stuffed the letter back in the drawer—it wrinkled in her nervous hand. She was flustered, she couldn't think. She looked back at the envelope for the address. *Waterbury, CT,* it read. He would have lived there, then.

The blood was up in her head now, her eyes were stinging. She jumped up, left the bunkhouse. Where was Adam, anyway? Of course she should have known he had girlfriends. A good-looking guy like that? She'd blocked out those thoughts. You still write to Wilder, at college, don't you, dummy? she reproached herself. Of course you do. Don't get after him now, you'll lose him. . . . Anyway, he hadn't written very often to that girl. Because of one Emily Willmarth, that was why.

She felt better now. She wouldn't say anything to Adam about that girl's letter. She didn't want him to know she'd been reading it! She really wasn't that kind of person, the kind who read other people's mail. Not usually. Hardly ever! She got back on her bicycle, started down the path toward the driveway. An ancient blue car was just turning in—it belonged to the twins, she recognized the sound of it; it needed a tune-up. "Hey," she cried, waving her arms, "hey!"

The car stopped and Hally Butterfield leaned out the driver's window. "Hi, sweet pie," he said. Hally always kidded her about Adam, he knew she was sweet on him.

"Adam in there?" she said, peering in the back window. But Adam wasn't there. Only Rolly, grinning beside his brother in the passenger seat.

"He was headed into the orchard when we left couple of hours ago," Hally said. "I thought he was seeing you."

"Ooh woo," Rolly joined in.

She felt a small stab in her chest, but she smiled. "He likes to play his guitar. Down in the trees where he won't bother anybody."

He was down at the toolshed, then, that's where he'd be. Playing his guitar. Two hours wasn't such a long time when you were doing something you loved.

The Butterfields drove on into the parking area and she sped down the path that led to the hut: past the pond—and woke up the geese. The large male ran after her, flapping his wings and squawking; finally gave up and fluttered, sputtering, back to his mate. There was a faint light in the hut; it would be Adam's flashlight perhaps, or a candle. Most of the songs he knew by heart. She heard a soft strumming, a high-pitched note. It was lovely, music in the night. She leaned her bicycle against a tree, listened a moment. Then knocked on the hut door. They hadn't planned a rendezvous, she didn't want to just walk in, although she knew he'd be glad to see her. He would, wouldn't he?

The music stopped. There was a hushed silence. But he'd think it was Rufus, or Moira, wondering what he was doing in there when he should be in bed, getting rest before the morning picking. "Adam, it's me, Emily," she said; she pushed open the door.

And shut it again quickly.

A moment later Adam came out. "Emily, wait—it's not what you think. Emily . . ."

But she was on her bike, speeding up the path. He was still calling to her. Then, more faintly, she heard Opal's voice: "Oh, come on, Adam, come on back in."

Fifty-two

Moira heard the whirring sound of a bicycle crunching up the driveway and peered out the window. It looked like a girl—Emily perhaps? A rendezvous with Adam Golding? Oh dear. And here she'd been weaving imagined scenarios with her own daughter into her loom. Nights were the worst, or the early morning hours: That's when the past came flooding back, crowding her mind with possible replays of that last night. Carol had the flu, she never went to that dance at all. Or she went, but was feverish when the dance ended. "I have to go home, take me home," she tells the boy, and the boy pleads, "Stay." But Carol is firm, she's sick, after all! And they go straight home. The beer, the wine, still uncapped in the car. And Carol, safe at home, in bed . . .

But Carol hadn't come home, and the liquor was consumed, and at two-thirty in the morning they'd had the call, the police at the door. An accident. Carol dead—drowned . . .

She must have made a noise because Stan said, "Moir? Moir, hel me outoo thi dam shair? Bringa goddam walker?"

She was glad, actually, for the interruption; she brought the walker, helped him up onto it, moved along with him, although he waved her away. He didn't want help now—that terrible pride of his. Stan's objective, as usual, was the liquor cabinet. He wasn't supposed to mix alcohol with his medicine, but she couldn't complain every minute. "I'll mix it," she said, "let me."

He gave a sly smile. He knew she'd make it weak. "No way, jush geme a glash. Icesh."

This time she mixed herself one, too. A nightcap. Then she'd go to bed, leave the door open for Opal, who'd taken to wandering the orchard at night—"to think," she told Moira, to play her guitar far down back where she wouldn't bother anyone. This was uncharacteristically thoughtful of the girl. Tonight, in fact, the girl had gone out in her nightgown, with only a thin sweater over it. Moira had insisted she put on a jacket, at least. The Jamaicans were all in bed, but there were others who might still be out at nine o'clock: the Butterfields, Adam Golding.

Well, she'd try to have a good night's rest—if Stan didn't need her in the night, that is. Get up at six with the Jamaicans. They cheered her up, those men. Nothing bad could happen while they were singing, shouting to each other in the trees. The weatherman called for mostly sun tomorrow. She lifted her chin, imagining it on her face.

And Stan called again for ice.

Fifty-three

When Emily came to pick the next afternoon after school, Moira Earthrowl stopped her. "I've a bag of apples for your mother," she called from the porch. "I'll leave them here. You be sure to take them to her. I've thrown in a couple of ripe pears, too. Did you know we have a pear tree behind the house?"

Emily knew, she'd noticed it. They were rosy ripe. In fact, she'd eaten one—and now her cheeks turned rosy, thinking of it. She tried to smile, but she was tired, she didn't feel like chatting. She hadn't slept well the night before; she'd tossed and turned all night, trying to make excuses for Adam, but finding few. She kept seeing Opal in her pink nightgown, squirming against Adam while he played. . . .

"Emily," Ms. Earthrowl said, sounding shy, "I hope you can use that green dress. I mean, it's all right to shorten it, anything you want to do with it to make it yours."

"Oh. Oh yes, thank you. It was so . . . so thoughtful of you. Thank you so much. And for letting me work here in the orchard."

Suddenly the woman grabbed Emily, embraced her; then let her go. "Well," she said, sounding like she was laughing and crying all at once, "you'd better get on with your picking. You're saving money toward college, your mom says."

"Yeah. That. And other things. You know." She waved her arms. She felt dumb, awkward. "I'll see you. I'll take those apples to Mom."

"They're Yellow Transparent, good for pies," Moira called after her.

But Emily's mother didn't have time these days for pies. She hadn't baked a pie, in fact, since Emily was ten years old. Sometimes Emily wished she had a mother who stayed home and baked pies. Emily might even bake with her. Instead of cleaning out cow dung.

She ran down to the apple barn to fetch her picking gear. Mr. Yates was there, heaving drops into the cider press. She strapped on her bucket, checked the schedule for her picking area, and ran out. The locals were to pick in the far south orchard today, not far from the cemetery. The apples in this area were Gala apples. Though Emily didn't feel very gala today. Millie Laframboise motioned her to an adjacent tree, indicated a crate she was to put the apples in. Opal was picking two trees away; she gave a sly glance at Emily, then smiled, slowly plucking off an apple. At the rate she was going, it would take her all day to pick the tree. Adam was in the tree beside her. When he saw Emily, he jumped down off the ladder. "We need to talk," he said.

"I don't think so," she said. She ascended the ladder; she'd begin at the top of the twelve-foot tree. The trees were taller in this area, older. She was aware of Adam below her.

"I can explain," he hissed up, and she saw Opal peer over at them. "Please, Emily, it's important. Emily, answer me."

"I'll give you five minutes," she said. "At quitting time. Down there by the . . . cemetery." The toolshed, she decided, was out of bounds. She never wanted to see that shed again! "Five minutes, that's all I'll have time for." She leaned into the picking, blotted Adam out of her mind—or tried to.

He was waiting at the cemetery when she arrived. They'd driven the apple crates to the barn; she'd helped the men load them onto the truck that would take them to the Shoreham Co-op, where they'd be packed. Derek had kidded her: "Gotta boyfriend, hey, girl?"

"No, Derek," she said. "No boyfriend. He's a snake, that Adam. The snake in the grass!"

But Derek kept grinning. "Adam and Eve," he said. "I learn all dat Methodis' Sunny school. You eat de apple, hey? Bad ting happen." He pretended to chew and then drop a crate. Then, seeing Rufus frown, he hefted it up into the truck, lightly, as though it were made of cardboard and not wood.

Adam was sitting on a flat headstone, gazing into the sky as though he wished he were up there and not down here, squatting on a dead person. She crossed her arms. He could have the first word.

He looked down and then up at her, as though surprised to see her, as though he hadn't known she was coming. "Hi," he said, and when she didn't answer, he said, "Okay, you saw us. It was no rendezvous, nothing planned, I'll tell you that. That girl has been after me since the day she arrived. She's a mixed-up kid. Needed someone to talk to, couldn't talk to the relatives. Had an abortion just before she came, she tell you that?"

"No," Emily said, sucking in her breath.

"It threw her, you know, the guy just split. She's lonely, feels guilty. Said her mother would kill her if she knew. I had to listen, that's all." He wrapped his arms around his knees, stared at the stone underneath, as though it would give him more words to use.

"You said it was unplanned? It sounds like you've had a lot of conversations." She heard her voice harsh; she might be coming down with a cold.

"Last night? Yeah. I just went down to play, that's all. I didn't know the Butterfields were out, they must have decided at the last minute. She came down, in that nightgown. I was about to throw her out when you arrived. That's all, Em." She heard him swallow, then cough. "And now. You can explain a few things, too." He stood up, confronted her. She took a step backward. His eyes lit into hers like lasers. She waited.

"You were in the bunkhouse. Well, okay, but you were going through my things. My mail. I don't care for that, Emily."

"I didn't read anything." She trembled with the lie.

"Oh yes, you did. That letter on the pink stationery was from an old girlfriend of mine. I could tell the way it was crumpled—you didn't even put it back in the envelope! We broke up at home. It was before I came up here, but she holds on, one more needy kid. I haven't written her in weeks, you read that!"

"Home? She was from Waterbury, Connecticut. You said you were from Massachusetts." She was on the offensive now. It was time to attack. He was the one in the wrong, not her! "Why did you fib? What was the point?"

He shrugged. "The Earthrowls are from Waterbury. I didn't want any 'Do you know the Pupplebuddies?'—that sort of thing. I never met the bloody Earthrowls down there. Never laid eyes on them! Besides, I really am from Massachusetts. I mean, more or less. I have a P.O. box in Cambridge. My dad still lives in Waterbury. I suppose you saw that letter, too."

"I didn't read it."

"My stepmother moved to California after the divorce. Dad hangs on, his business. Look, Em, I'm sorry about last night. But that girl, Opal—she's like a mosquito you swat, and she whips away, and then flies back at you."

He was standing in front of her now, arms limp at his sides, eyes downcast, like a small boy sorry he'd filched the cookies in your lunch box. She had to laugh. He laughed with her then, took her in his arms. "Valley Fair tomorrow, right? Couple of good bands playing—derelicts, but still got spunk. Lynyrd Skynyrd: They've got a triple guitar front, you'll love them, Em. Steppenwolf, too. I've got a room for us, friend of mine has a pad. He's gone, won't be back till Sunday noon."

She couldn't speak, filled with the thought of tomorrow.

"We'll be back to pick Sunday afternoon. Might not make it up to Montreal—the Volvo needs a part—I can't get it fixed till Monday." He looked into her eyes. She felt the red crawl up her neck, flood her cheeks. She still didn't know about the overnight. What *would* she tell her mother? Then she was angry at her mother for treating her like a child. When she was almost eighteen. Eighteen!

"Okay, Em? That Opal, she's a cruiser. That kind's not for me. I like open, earthy girls—like you, Em." He smiled at her, and though she knew he was loading it on her, she gave in, let him kiss her. But a moment later they heard Rufus's voice, the sound of Jamaicans, their chatter, two of them singing a high-pitched gospel tune. She caught the phrase: ". . . a balm in Gil-e-ad-d . . ." They'd be picking up the last of the crates. Adam grabbed her wrist, hard. "Okay, then, Em, okay?"

"Okay," she said, feeling giddy, and swerved about, ran crazy-legged back down the path, ducking between trees to avoid Derek and the blue-eyed Zayon, who were juggling an enormous crate between them. They smiled at her.

It was like she was running down a mountain toward a cliff: Any minute she'd leap off—and into what? She stopped running a moment, clasped a tree trunk. It was an old maple tree, not an apple. It felt solid, stable; she pressed her face into it, heard her breath come in raggedy gasps. Tomorrow . . .

Fifty-four

Turnbull—no, Chris Christ, though Colm couldn't think of him by that name, doubted even that was the real one—lived in a condominium, one of the more expensive ones in town, near the college. The place had old-fashioned-looking gas lamps along a curving drive. A marble walk lined with orange and yellow chrysanthemums led to the door of Number 3. REVEREND MICHAEL TURNBULL, an aluminum door plaque announced.

Colm knocked: a shiny brass knocker. His heart lurched a little: He didn't know why he should be nervous, but he was. He'd called ahead; the man had hesitated a long time before granting the interview. Colm had tried to sound laid-back, like it wasn't so important to speak to the guy. But Turnbull knew. "You're the one who's been talking to my women," he'd said, like he was king of the concubines—Colm had to smile, thinking of Bertha. Finally Turnbull said, "I'm a busy man, I have charities, I have prayer sessions." He had "important agenda"—as though a homicide (Cassandra) and an orchard under siege were of little import.

The man took his sweet time opening up. An eye squinted through an oblong slit in the door. When it finally opened, Colm saw a large rectangular living room furnished with black leather sofa and chairs, gold-framed biblical paintings, including one of the female with a tray of apples he'd seen in Bertha's house. Only this one was an oil, not a print. It looked expensive. Where had he gotten the money for it? Turnbull gave a fleeting smile through perfect white teeth. He was dressed in black: black gabardine pants, carefully creased; white shirt with a striped blue and black regimental tie; black jacket. Colm could see the belly where it pouched over the belted pants. He sucked in his own.

Turnbull was a little breathless, he had things to do, places to go. He kept glancing at his large black leather watch. He wore a diamond ring on his pinkie. Colm sat down in one of the black chairs—was suddenly tipped back. How to sabotage your interrogator. He thought he heard Turnbull snicker. "I'm afraid you pushed a button with your hand." The man creaked back on the leather sofa, he had the upper hand. Colm struggled with the switch, finally popped it; the chair swooshed up, almost hurling him onto the white carpet.

A white carpet, Colm thought, as though Turnbull never came in with dirt on his shoes. He thought of Ruth, stomping in from the barn in her "milking" boots; she'd make short work of this white carpet! Turnbull glanced at his watch again. "I have an appointment at ten," he said pointedly. He didn't say where, with whom. He gave an artificial smile. He was a handsome fellow—in his early fifties, maybe, hard to tell. He would charm the women, of course.

Colm was aware of his own open shirt. He'd dressed in a hurry that morning: had on kelly green cords with a royal blue shirt. His socks weren't the same length—jeez. Why was he nervous? Who was he dealing with here? His feet found the carpet, he sat sunk in the chair. "I understand Turnbull is not your real name," he said, hearing his voice coming from the root of the seat.

There was a moment of silence. He half expected the man to intone a prayer. "Where did you hear that?" said Turnbull. Or Chris Christ.

Colm shrugged. "One of your, um, parishioners. She said your real name is Chris—Christopher?—Christ. Why did you change it?"

Chris Christ (if that was the real name) looked down modestly, straightened his tie. The chin dropped into two folds. He didn't look so handsome now; he might have been any gray-haired minister with a parish. But the eyes, when they stared into Colm's, were cold; the pupils were like brown hard-shelled eggs. "I decided to take my stepfather's name," he said. And that answered that.

The rest of the questions he answered exactly, briefly, no elaboration. He had a deep, full-bodied voice, a slight accent Colm couldn't place—it wasn't New York, it didn't sound New England. His breath came in short gasps between answers. Colm could imagine him in a responsive reading: *Takes my breath away*, a parishioner would say. He was from Iowa originally, he said; came east to Bible college, heard the calling. He founded the Messengers of Saint Dorothea, "oh, four years ago now." He'd sensed a "spiritual need" here in Branbury, one the other churches couldn't fulfill. No, it wasn't affiliated with any other church, it was his own. It was a Christian church, yes, of course! He tithed, ah yes, one had to—twelve percent. Some pledged more of their income, of their own volition. The church was small but growing. Mostly women? Colm asked.

"Well, perhaps. Although we've a few men. Most men don't attend any church, do they? Too bad. They fall by the wayside, like that teacher, that Aaron Samuels. Jewish, of course, but had the synagogue if he wanted, didn't he?" When he said "synagogue," Colm thought, it sounded like "*sin*-a-gogue." As for Unitarians—well, they weren't a "church," were they?

But here was a nice lead-in to the real subject: Cassandra. Colm understood that "there was an, um, misunderstanding between Cassandra and, um, yourself."

This time he'd put Turnbull (couldn't call him Christ) off balance. A few fine drops of sweat sprang up on the man's forehead. The black wing tips did a soft shuffle on the white carpet. He almost spit out the words. "There was no *serious* misunderstanding. And I can't see where that would concern you." The eyes shot bullets at Colm.

"It does where a homicide is concerned." Colm was relaxing now, he rose up a little in his seat. If he'd had a badge, he would have flashed it—he wasn't exactly a full-time cop. But it only took a phone call to Fallon. He'd already explained that to the man when he set up the interview.

Turnbull sighed, and gave in. "It's nothing, really. Cassandra is—was—a relative, second cousin on my mother's side. She's one of the reasons I came to Branbury; she made over her barn for our church, helped bring in members. Cassandra is—was—a go-getter. She was the church treasurer, had been an accountant in her professional life. But I found the books weren't exactly . . ."

"Robbing the till?" Colm suggested. He was enjoying himself now. It was like being in a play, he supposed, like the one play he'd got dragged into acting in by Bertha back in high school: nervous as hell at the start, hands shaking; then by the third act having the time of his life. He'd actually tried out for another show, got turned down—fortunately. He had a hard time memorizing lines, to tell the truth.

"Borrowing a little. She called it that, she'd put capital into the church, improvements; she thought she was entitled to take it out. I'm sure she'd have paid it back. We had a few words, I made her understand. But then—that madman, things happening so fast, that Earthrowl, running at her . . ." He was waxing eloquent now: the melodious voice, the evangelist's quaver, gazing at the white ceiling as though a pair of angels would suddenly descend. "Ye have plowed wickedness, Earthrowl," he intoned. "Ye have reaped iniquity."

"The stories differ," Colm said. "There's no hard evidence. Nothing to indicate that Earthrowl even hit her. He thinks he bumped a curb in the Graniteworks; that would account for the adhesion in a front tire, a scratch on the bumper. There was nothing to indicate he'd struck a person—no hairs, no fibers."

The interview disintegrated then, Turnbull rising up, a meeting he couldn't miss; if he could be of more help, why, then . . . Oily, sure of himself, the white carpet with its black leather furnishings a metaphor for the man's mind. Black and white, nothing in between. Colm had picked up some church literature at Bertha's: anti-abortion, anti-gay, anti-Catholic, anti-Semitic, anti-black—skin, that is, not furniture. All neatly tied up with quotes from the Bible. He supposed it gave the outsiders a sense of belonging to a group; all the anti's made them feel positive about themselves.

On the way out he met a young postwoman, putting the mail in the porch box. When she left, after a surprised "Hello, there, Mr. Hanna," he riffled through quickly. Bills, bank statements—he appropriated one from a Boston bank—he'd steam it open, get it back in the mail—who would know? A neighbor, getting the wrong mail. There was a letter from a lawyer; he kept that, too, stuck them inside his jacket. Jeez, a lime-green jacket, he was a vision in Technicolor—Ruth would laugh. He'd steam the letters at her house. He was in the mood for a doughnut. Coffee. The good smells of her farm kitchen. Anyway, he had something else on his mind. He wanted her to go to the Valley Fair with him Saturday—after milking, of course. Take in the sights, eat some of that cotton candy. Go necking, maybe, on one of the whirly wheels. She'd scream, cling to him, and—

"Jeez," he moaned. "Oh, jeez."

Fifty-five

Emily was enthralled with the fair. She'd been summers to the local Field Days but never to the big statewide fair. There'd always been so much to do at home, in the barn, in the fields. Now, with Adam at her side, looking gorgeous with his blond hair tied back with a black grosgrain ribbon, the black STEPPENWOLF T-shirt he'd bought at a stall and slipped on over his red-tailed hawk T-shirt, the tight black jeans and Birkenstock sandals—oh, it was heaven. Simply heaven. And oh, the sounds and smells and colors! The cotton candy that was spreading now, like thick pink moss, over Adam's chin, the odor of popcorn, fried chicken, even the familiar animal dung. The neon dazzle of the rides, the voices hawking games: "Three shots for a dollar—pick out your stuffed animal!" Adam won an enormous furry Pooh bear by tossing a quarter into a plate in the center of a tent; she couldn't do it, her quarter bounced out each time. "You're the only one did it this afternoon," the vendor told Adam, and she glowed in his small triumph, was thrilled when he presented it to her with a mock bow.

She felt giddy, she felt free; chores, jobs, schoolwork dropped away with each moment of Adam's company. They watched the parade: A clown tossed a lollipop at her and she stuck it in her mouth, sucked down its cherry sweetness. They watched the horse pull: sturdy draft horses pulling flat sleighs full of concrete—two pounds of rock for each pound of horseflesh—it was like old-time farming, a man said behind her. "That's how it was clearing land two hunnert years ago, and no tractors, by God." She felt the immensity of it, the smallness of the self among all these people who were descended from Russian, Irish, Polish, Hungarian immigrants. She thought of them coming over in steerage with small hard potatoes and smelly cheeses in their flour sacks. Even a dozen people with Humane Society placards protesting the horse pull didn't lessen her joy.

Or the thought of rattlesnakes, when Adam said, "This is tame. I'm for the snake pit."

"Why not?" she said, feeling a frisson of cold in her spine. She let him pull her over to a tent that announced the West Texas Rattlesnake Show. They took adjoining seats close to the arena where a man in a white cowboy hat was stuffing a diamondback snake into a plastic tube. "Believe me, folks, they live better than I do," he bawled through the loudspeaker, and the crowd laughed. He told them that almost four hundred years ago Samuel de Champlain sent a dispatch to his native France from the Champlain Valley in Vermont, saying, "The snakes in this new world have bells on their tails." The crowd roared and clapped. And Emily felt history humming around her.

It was a scaly copper and brown snake, maybe two feet long—the snake man displayed its rattle, and Emily could hear the ratatat hiss; it sounded like a playing card stuck in a window fan. There were nine more snakes in a plastic garbage pail, waiting to be hooked up with a long-handled prong and shown to the crowd. They came from a man in rural Texas who was known as Rattlesnake Jim. He got his rattlers, the snake man said, by dragging them out from under the houses. There were as many as two or three hundred rattlers for every house! Emily gasped, while Adam laughed and wriggled out onto the edge of his seat, eyes squinting, to see the reptiles. It was as though he loved the danger of it. For a time he seemed to forget she was there.

After a while, though, she was ready to leave; the snakes were getting to her. She wished they hadn't gotten that front-row seat! "Let's go to the petting zoo," she suggested. Even now, at almost eighteen, she loved the petting zoo at Field Days. The soft snuggly bunnies, the goats with their silly pointed beards like Chinese mystery men, the peacocks unfurling green and blue tails like giant fans, the sweet baby lambs and chicks. Who could resist?

But Adam said there was no time for the petting zoo if they were to eat supper at his friend's place and get to the rock concert by eight o'clock. And didn't she want at least one ride—on that Flip'n Out?

Of course she did. Anything to get out of the snake pit and back into the good smells and sights and shouts of the fairgrounds. Back to the rides: the great slide, the Ferris wheel, the bumping cars, the roller-coaster, and oh, the Flip'n Out.

"Come on, scaredy pants, you'll love it," Adam said. "You'll be with me. I won't let you fall out." And he didn't, of course, though she thought she'd lose the hot dog she'd eaten for lunch, the cotton candy—it felt queasy in her stomach. Up and over and under in the long shiny bucket—for that's what it looked like, felt like, a bucket on the John Deere tractor, recklessly hurling itself into space. Even with Adam's arm tight around her waist she was a rocket heading for a black hole somewhere. "Adam! Make it stop! I'm getting sick!"

But Adam just laughed, held her tighter; she was on a one-way flight, the wind shrieking in her ears. . . .

Back down on the ground, she was physically sick. There was a Porta Potti nearby; she barely made it, heaved up everything, the basin was pink with throw-up. Afterward she was spent, she let an amused Adam lead her to the car; she didn't know where he was taking her, she was in his hands.

"Jesus," she heard him say, as he yanked her along. "Your mother and that guy. Get in the car!" She caught a glimpse of her mother and Colm Hanna, climbing out of his blue Horizon, along with Vic and his friend Gerry Dufours. Oh no, she thought, she'd told her mother she was spending the day and then the night with a friend. She'd told her Adam wasn't coming, after all. Now Vic was waving, hollering her name; bad luck. She pretended not to see him, ducked into the white Volvo. Adam threw her bag and the Pooh bear he'd won for her in the backseat—it was crowded with stuff, something spilled on the floor.

She tried to clean it up and he said, "My talc, I'll do it later," and she shrugged. They careened out of the grassy parking lot, onto the highway; she leaned back against the seat. It was as though she were on that Flip'n Out again: She gave up all control. When they parked on a side street minutes later, she gave him her hand, let him lead her up three flights of stairs. He had a key, he turned it in the lock and they were in a medium-sized room, its walls and windows hung with tie-dyed sheets. Adam flicked a switch and a dozen red and blue bulbs lit up. The room smelled strongly of pot, and for a quick moment Emily wished she were back on the Flip'n Out, soaring up into clean, bright space.

Adam went into the bathroom, stayed there for what seemed a long time, and when he came back, she saw he was bare-chested. "Aren't you cold?" she asked.

"With you in the room?" he teased, and she smiled.

She took the Pepsi he thrust at her—he was pouring something into it from a green bottle. She put up a hand to protest, she was still woozy from the rides; but when he looked at her, with scolding lips, she tasted the drink. It was bitter, but afterward, warm in her stomach. She felt more relaxed now, a little relaxed, anyway, in this strange one-room apartment; she sat down on the king-sized bed—there wasn't another place to sit in the room, except on the floor. Adam dropped down beside her, leaned back on a pillow, sipped his drink. His eyes looked bleary, tired, and she wondered what he'd been doing in the bathroom, if he was on something. She and her school friends didn't do drugs—maybe it was their 4-H training.

"Your eyes look old," she said. "Old and wise, like Father Time."

"Not me. I'll never be old," he said. "Trevor didn't get old. He didn't have a chance."

"Trevor? Who's Trevor?" she said. He was sounding maudlin—the alcohol seemed to do that to him, it made him maudlin. She pushed close beside him on the bed, she could feel his lungs working through the thin ribs.

"My brother," he said. "Was."

She said, "What? You never told me you had a brother."

"I couldn't. Not till now," he said. "I tried once—but it

hurt. . . . We were born the same day, November seventh. Weird." He turned his head away from her, seemed to drift into another world. He groped for an apple he'd brought, bit into it.

She propped herself up on her elbows, amazed. "You were twins? You never said!" Twins were like one person. When one fell in love, the other fell in love. When one died, the other . . . What had he said about not getting old? What was he thinking of? "What? What happened, Adam?"

He offered her the apple and she bit into it, it was warm and sweet-tasting where he'd eaten.

"Not twins," he said. "We were half-brothers. My father was in love with another woman the time I was born—she had his son. Then when my mother died, he married her—the other woman, Julie's her name—she was good to me. That's what was so weird about it, so sort of . . . predestined. She brought Trevor to the marriage, we pretty much grew up together. I didn't know we were half-brothers till I was eighteen! Then they told me. We were close right from the start. Trevor had brown hair. When I was twelve I dyed my hair brown. I wanted to *be* Trevor. Sometimes . . . I was."

"Really?" She couldn't imagine wanting to be Vic and run around chasing stars and chickens. She gave back the apple, and Adam turned it around to the place where she had eaten. He bit into it with a crunching sound.

"You can't imagine what he was like. He had smarts, more than me. Great looks—the girls went bonkers over him. He played the piano, the guitar—like the music came out of his soul. That was Trevor—all soul. We did everything together. Music, drugs, we thought alike. If he wanted to leave a party, it just took one look and we were gone. Like that." He snapped his fingers. "It was his car, the old Volvo. And then—then he fell for that girl, that Carol. . . ."

She was beginning to understand. The girl took Trevor away. Adam was hurt. Alone. It was like he was half a soul. Oh, the loneliness! She wanted to help him, to show him he wasn't alone, that he had her. She didn't want him to talk about Trevor anymore. She'd be his Trevor. She stroked his chest, traced the soft hairs down to his belly button. She felt bold now, needy, like she was swimming through wild seas. She unbuckled his belt and he let her; he lay back like a baby. She slipped her hand down into his underpants, felt the thick wiry hairs. He was still eating the apple. She touched his penis. It was like a small animal, pulsing, growing under her hand. She felt her own chest expand, her breasts taut and heavy, like a whole tree full of apples.

He dropped the apple; she heard it squash on the bare floor. "You going to wear that chastity belt?" he said, leaning over her, and she smiled, of course she wasn't. She got up and pulled off her shirt, her jeans. She felt suddenly shy, standing there in her bra and panties. But he pulled her down on top of him, he'd take care of the rest, he said, slipping on a condom. And he did.

After that it was the Flip'n Out again, she was out of control, spinning dizzily; he was inside her, they were going sideways, upside down, an upheaval of love and pain and blood—and then, as suddenly as it started, the ride stopped. There was that sensation of flipping off into an aching space, of floating in cramping sheets, sinking. . . .

The spread was damp under her buttocks, but it was all right; finally she was at peace. She tried to make herself believe it had been wonderful, beautiful, but it hadn't been—not for her. Maybe next time it would be better. Of course it would. It was nice just lying here with Adam, being part of him the way his brother had been part of him. She felt an enormous tenderness for him. He'd lost his brother. Could she fill that space? After that girl took him away? What was her name—Carol?

Carol, she thought. That was the name of the Earthrowl girl. Carol. Could it have been the same? No, too much coincidence. She'd bring it up another time, not now. Not while they were lying here together; not when she was beginning to feel so warm, so beautiful, even—she tried to think of pink and white apple blossoms. She could smell what was left of the apple, the sweetness. . . . She bent over to kiss him—and discovered he was fast asleep. Asleep . . .

Why, then, did *she*, all at once, feel so alone?

Fifty-six

I saw her, I did, getting into a Volvo," said Vic, who knew his cars, and Ruth pressed her lips together. Emily had said she'd changed her mind about going to the fair with Adam, was spending the night with her friend Hartley Flint. And Hartley had a Colt, Ruth had seen it only a month ago. Not a Volvo.

"So they borrowed someone's car," said Colm, "decided they'd go to the fair. She's not a kid anymore, Ruthie. Jeez."

"It was just that I invited her to come with us, and she said no, that fairs were boring. That's what she said, 'boring'! She didn't say that when we all went to Field Days this summer." She walked on ahead of Colm, she didn't want him making excuses for Emily.

He caught up with her, of course, with one more excuse. "With us it's boring. With one of her peers it's not. Right, Vic?"

"Right," said Vic, who admired Colm and for the moment was planning to be a policeman one day—an astronomer on the side, of course, maybe a veterinarian. These careers were more exciting to him than farming.

"Oh, I guess so," said Ruth, and waved away the worry. It was silly, of course, Emily had her own life now. It was just, well, all these things that had happened lately. And in her own life: the cows slashed, Pete's demands, the hemp torn up—although now she was convinced that Bertha and her cronies had something to do with the hemp.

Vic and his friend Gerry wanted to go to the petting zoo, so that would be the first stop. Then they'd take in the sheep shearing, her friend Carol Unsworth was taking part in it. There was the cattle tent, of course, and for Vic, the demolition derby. She'd had her choice, Colm said, between the Lynyrd Skynyrd concert and the demolition derby, and since neither was exactly a priority, she let Vic decide.

She loved the petting zoo herself: all those furry baby animals with the huge wild eyes. Vic and Gerry headed for the angora bunnies, while Colm pulled her over to the llamas. "This is what you ought to breed, Ruthie, instead of growing hemp. They're an all-purpose beast. You can milk 'em, breed 'em, ride 'em, shear 'em for wool. They make good golf caddies, too."

"I don't play golf," she said. "I don't have time."

"They're a clean animal," he went on, ignoring her indifference. "They use a communal potty pile. You can bring them indoors for parties. Vic's next birthday: a llama in the kitchen."

"No, thank you. They roll. They spit."

"Only when they're mad. You got to humor them. You'd love the milk."

"Can you sell the milk? Whoever heard of drinking llama's milk?"

"That's just it, Ruthie. You have to use your imagination. Start a trend. I'll bet it would go over big in the natural foods stores."

"And you'll help? Buy me one to start?" The price for a baby llama, she saw, was two thousand dollars. Whoa! "Fork over," she said, holding out her hand, and saw him grin, pull out his wallet, flutter a dollar bill in his fist. Colm was so impulsive, so impractical. Back in high school he'd treat ten kids to hamburgers and milkshakes, then go without lunch for three days.

Was this why she wouldn't marry him now? His impracticality? She didn't want to downright discourage him. She loved Colm, she truly did, but in a sisterly way—at least for now. After all, she'd only been divorced for a short time; divorce was like a little death, it took months, years, it seemed, to come back to life.

Besides, she liked her independence. Admit it, Ruth, she told herself, you like being in control, the one to decide what to do on a Saturday night, to decide whether you want to grow hemp or Christmas trees—or raise llamas on your dairy farm. Or make cheese . . . that might be her next diversion. Though she could never compete with Cabot Cheese. . . .

"No llamas," she told Colm. But she might give in on the angora bunny.

"I'll do extra chores," Vic pleaded. "I will, I promise. You'll see. I'll clean the stalls, I'll take care of all the calves—not just Madonna."

"Though Madonna will get special attention, I know that," she teased. They'd named the latest calf after Madonna because it sang, Emily said; it lifted up its nose and warbled, while its white head and hips waggled back and forth.

"Mom, they're only fifty dollars. I can pay half of that, I've saved up." And when she gave in: "Thanks, Mom, oh thanks!"

They had hot dogs, fried dough, and candied apples for supper, and Colm got molasses on his glasses; she had to lead him to the toilet while he spit on the lenses and rubbed them on his kelly green corduroys. He looked like a nerd, she told him, and when he asked her to marry him, she said, "How can I marry a man who can't even find his way to the potty?"

When they came back into the grounds, headed for the rides—she'd promised the boys two of their choice, and not the Whip Lash!—she saw Colm cringe under a heavy hand on his shoulder.

"Jeez," he said. "What are you doing here, Fallon? Heading for the Ferris wheel?"

It was the Branbury police chief, all right, with his wife; he chuckled his freight-train chuckle. "Treating the wife here to a night out. She loves that fried dough. Don't you, Honey?"

Honey giggled. She was a small woman with gray-blond hair scooped up in a disheveled bun; the bangs fell, poodlelike, into her eyes. She knocked the hairdo further askew with her hand and patted her plump belly. "You bet I do," she said. "It beats cooking at home. All this man wants to eat is meat and potatoes, potatoes and meat. Mention vegetables and he walks away from the table."

"Besides, we're celebrating," the chief said, and winked at Colm. "Honey's quit that Messengers group. Though it lasted longer than the last one you joined, right, Honey?"

"I was duped," Honey said. "I thought they had something. I was taken in by that lovely Saint Dorothea." She patted her chest with her pudgy fingers. "Then I discovered Reverend Turnbull wasn't Reverend Turnbull."

"S'the truth," Chief Fallon said, and nodded significantly at Colm.

But Ruth knew that. His real name was Chris Christ. Or was it? Roy Fallon was going on, "Name is Arnold Wickham, married—you won't believe it—"

"I will," said Colm, and glanced at Ruth. She'd helped him steam open a letter he'd found in the minister's mailbox that indicated a pending divorce: from one Cassandra Wickham. He'd meant to tell Fallon.

"Born in Bristol, Vermont, son of a hippie actor came up to get away from a rap down in New York City." Fallon's voice changed to a soft rasp as he went on with the story. "Arnold Wickham's wanted for bombing an abortion clinic over in Oregon. He was seen hanging around another one before a shooting in Buffalo. S'the truth. I got it from the FBI. He's out of town, but I got the word out—Vermont, New York State, you know. We'll nail the sonofabitch. He doesn't know that we know. Yet, I mean . . ."

"You'd better," Colm said. "Jeez, he could get wind of all this, take off to Afghanistan. I mean, there are things we have to resolve here in Branbury. That orchard, Roy. Turnbull, Wickham—whatever his name is—sent threats, you know. I'm wondering about that tray of apples in Saint Dorothea's hand."

"Oh, she wasn't mixed up in that," Honey assured him. "Dorothea lived way way back—in the fourth century."

"It's our anniversary," Fallon went on. "The little woman here, um, wants to ride the Whip Lash."

Honey giggled. "I've never ridden it, that's why. It's a challenge." She leaned closer to Ruth. "That's why I joined the Messengers. I'd never done it. I thought it might give me something I'm looking for."

"And what's that?" Ruth asked politely. This woman wasn't exactly Bertha, but a kook on her own account.

"The secret of youth," Honey said. "Ways to stay young. Oh, I don't mean *this* kind of young," and she patted the inflated cushion of her belly. "I mean the mind. The psyche. *Change*. We all need *change*, new ideas, to come *alive*!" She lifted her chin toward the glittering white way, the neon rides. "The Whip Lash," she said with a toothy smile. "That's what I need."

Chief Fallon smiled apologetically at Ruth. "She's nuts, but I love her," he said, and chuckled his freight-train hahahahaha.

"So you're riding the Whip Lash, too?" Colm said.

"Hell no," said Fallon. "You think I'm suicidal? I'll stand and watch, that's all." And the chuk-chuk-chuk started up again.

"By the way, Roy," Colm said as Honey trotted off, "how did your *wife* find out Turnbull's real name? I only knew from a letter I, um, happened upon—I've been meaning to give it to you. And is Wickham the real name, or one more alias?"

"Ask her sometime," Fallon said, winking, and disappeared with his Honey through the crowd.

Fifty-seven

Adam ordered pizza and they sat side by side on the bed, eating it. It was as if they were husband and wife; Emily luxuriated in the warmth of it. She could imagine spending months, years, in this room, with this gorgeous man, eating pizza. It was a tomato and cheese and pepperoni pizza, the cheese stuck in her teeth; she turned and grinned at Adam; he was slurping up long strings of cheese still attached to the crust. She kissed him and their cheeses mingled. They washed it all down, finally, with beer that Adam had found in his friend's refrigerator.

"Shouldn't we replace it?"

"Nah," he said, "Jimmy owes me. Drank me dry one time when he came down to Waterbury." He was slurring his words a little, but she was feeling woozy, too. It was all right. She'd make coffee if she could find some.

The mention of Waterbury made her think again of that dead girl, Carol Earthrowl. She said, "The Earthrowls' daughter who was killed in that accident was named Carol."

She felt him stiffen beside her. "Is that right?" But then he took another slug of beer and his body slumped back into the pillow.

"It was a boy from Waterbury who was driving the car—a Trevor, yes, Mother mentioned the name." If it was his Trevor who caused the accident, she had to know. She had to know everything about Adam—he'd been keeping too much back. Good and bad. Better or worse. "Was it your . . . ?"

He turned and looked at her. His eyes were dilated a little, blurry. Or was it her vision that was blurred? "Putting two and two together, aren't you?" he said. "You're a regular little spy."

She was hurt; she moved to the edge of the bed and he put an arm around her, yanked her back.

"Okay, it was Trevor. But he was really, really gone on that girl. I tried to talk him out of it, she wasn't worth it. Sure, she was a nice girl, but that was it. A nice girl. Not a drop of music in her bones, she wasn't even a good dancer. I saw them together. She didn't have the rhythm."

Emily winced. She wasn't such a good dancer herself. Singer, either: She always went flat on the high notes. But she loved good music, she did!

"But he still loved her?"

"Yeah, yeah, I guess you could call it that. It was the first real thing for him, he didn't have the experience. Shit! He didn't know what was good for him. He could have had it all. Women, music, a full life. And that girl took it away. His whole goddamn beautiful life."

Emily was confused. "But it was Trevor who took it from *her*."

She'd said the wrong thing. He jumped up off the bed, he was staring down at her, his eyes blazing blue-black. "She kept calling him up, you know that? She did! The parents didn't want her going out with him. He wasn't good enough, they said. 'Cause he drank a little, did a little stuff—though she didn't tell her mother that. But they found out. 'Cause he wasn't headed for some fancy degree. The princess and the swineherd, that's what they saw. But the princess was after Trevor. I'd almost opened his eyes for him, we were going to move out, head for the city—after I quit college. Then one day after school she shows up in our doorway. Ooh la la! Here she comes, long red hair, that Snow White look. Fairy-tale stuff. Wanting him to take her to the ball. He fell for it. He said he'd go. Whose fault was it he went?"

She shook her head. She didn't know. She couldn't get it straight in her mind.

"Well, think, and you'll see," he said. She tried, but could see only Carol with her long auburn hair, in that shimmery green gown—the one she never really wore. It was Emily's dress now.

He was quiet, he sat back down on the bed. He had an anguished look on his face as though he were seeing the accident—or maybe it was the half-brother's death—all over again. She wanted to know more then; she had a right, didn't she? They were lovers now, lovers—that strange, grown-up word—and she wanted to know everything. She wanted to look deep, deep into his soul.

"How did the accident happen? I mean, I know you weren't there, but what do you know about it?"

He gazed at her with those tragic eyes. They were heavy-lidded, his full lips quivered. "It was after the gig—the ball, they called it—huh, ball! I'll bet there was a little balling." The dimple flickered in his cheek. He said, "They took off for her house, that's all I know. Trevor said she had to go home right after, he fell for that stuff, she was still the princess. She'd lose her slipper at midnight, you know. Only it was two in the morning when it happened. Her fault, you can bet! Trevor would've gone along with the parents—he told me that. The way she came on to him that time she arrived at the house! You know she would've wanted it, wanted him to park someplace, make love. I suppose they did. Drank a little."

"He was on something that night?"

He looked sternly at her, the way her mother looked when Emily said she had to stay after school and couldn't help with chores. His voice was thick, like he'd swallowed maple syrup. "No. No, he wasn't. She was the princess, remember? Trevor was clean. A little bourbon, maybe. I don't know. Maybe she brought it—that Carol. I wouldn't put it past her. They were drinking some, yeah, Trevor admitted that. But mostly, well, it was icy, you know, slick roads. It was late, he was probably driving too fast. I mean, he had to get her home, didn't he? Already two hours past the curfew?" He sighed heavily, dropped his head between his knees. The ponytail was loose from their lovemaking, his hair streamed down his back. She stroked it.

"That's all I know about that night," he said. "The car skidded into a tree, they were near a bridge, it rolled down the embankment, into the river. The steering wheel got bent when they hit the tree, the girl was wedged in. Trevor got out his window, tried to get the girl out—he couldn't."

"How long . . . how long," she asked, "before he—he—"

"Long enough for the torture to knock him out. He would have been all right, I was with him. He talked and talked, you know, all that guilt stuff, couldn't get that girl out of his head. Like he was guilty! Guilty of what? I said. Laying that ice on the road?"

Adam was crying now; it was a strange, feral sound. She took his head in her hands, cradled it, stroked and stroked his hair, smoothed it with her fingernails. Crooned to him, until finally he quieted.

There was one more thing she had to know. "How did he—how did Trevor die?"

For a long minute there was no answer. Her lap was damp from his face. Finally he said, "Killed himself. I found him. I was playing music down on Pine Street. I wanted Trevor to go, he wouldn't. He'd stopped playing since the accident. That was the worst, that I was gone. He'd been drinking a lot since . . . the girl. I couldn't make him see she wasn't worth it. Well, I came back, it was three in the morning, I found him. He was . . ." He took several quick breaths, as though he were seeing the scene all over again. She waited.

"Hanging," he said in a thick voice. "He hanged himself. With the telephone cord. My God, I didn't know those cords were strong enough! Trevor was big, he was six-two, but it held him. He'd drilled a hole in the beam, it was that deliberate. I mean, he must've been thinking about doing it all night. He'd knocked the stool off, he was just . . . hanging there."

"What did you do?" she whispered.

"What could I do?" He was almost shouting; she shrank back. "Cut him down, called an ambulance. It was too late, of course.

He'd been dead a couple of hours. If I'd come home early that night . . . if I hadn't gone . . ."

"You didn't know," she soothed.

He was quiet for a long time. She heard a siren outdoors, a child calling a dog, a woman's shrill laugh.

Suddenly Adam gave a shout, jumped up. "Hey! Let's go back to the fair, kid. See Lynyrd Skynyrd." He was suddenly manic, leaped about the room, loading beer, booze, potato chips, pizza into a paper bag. She tried to follow, to act happy, but somehow she didn't have the heart, after all she'd just heard—lived through, it seemed. If the truth were told, she just wanted to go home. Home. She didn't want to spend the night in this room that seemed terribly small now, as if the walls were trying to close in on her.

But he was pulling her up. "Get dressed, girl. You want us picked up by the fuzz? I'm not exactly your innocent boy." He laughed, and she knew he *was* on something.

"Can we get some coffee?" She was sounding like a prude, like her mother, who said, "Oh no, oh those crazies, those irresponsibles," every time Emily told her about some classmate busted in school for selling marijuana or something. And yet her mother grew hemp; hemp was a close cousin, she'd heard, to pot. That is, her mother did grow hemp—past tense.

"Somebody pulled up my mother's hemp plants, did I tell you that?" she said, pulling on her underpants.

Adam looked surprised at her suddenly mentioning hemp, then said, "I think I know who did that."

"What! Who?"

"Our little friend with the guitar? Back at the orchard? Had something to do, I think, with those cows getting slashed. I saw her with a knife the morning after it happened. Looked like blood on it, too."

"No. Opal? I thought of that, actually. But she's so petite. How could she? And why? Why would she do that?"

"Jealous," he whispered, and kissed her ear; and then, "Don't worry, I'll keep an eye on her. She's harmless enough, just a little mischief maker. Of course, you never know when she's telling the truth—or a big plump lie."

"Harmless? Slashing our cows?" she cried. They were her cows, too, hers and her mother's. She was furious at the girl. If Opal were to appear in the doorway right now, there was no telling what she'd do. Grab her, yank her hair, knock her down. "Oh . . . oh!" She stood up, balling her fists. "I hate that girl!"

"Now, now," he said. "Calm down. I shouldn't have told you. Don't say anything to her. Let me take care of it. Get on your shirt like a good girl and let's go. Please? Please, now, Emily, love?"

Love. He'd never mentioned the word "love" before. She looked at him and he gazed back at her; his face was full of sadness again, and she felt she was the only one who could help him, bring him back to some kind of peace.

She threw her arms around his neck. "I love you," she said, "I do love you, Adam," and he hummed in her ear, but didn't say the words. But it was all right, she could wait.

Fifty-eight

Emily wasn't home yet and Ruth was worried. "Did she call? Did she leave a message?" she asked Sharon, who was backing out of the refrigerator, holding up homemade chocolate ice cream.

"I just had to have some, Mother. Jack's home with the kids, I can't eat it in front of them. You put sugar in this, Mom, too much. It gives the kids a high."

"I might mention that this is my freezer. Who asked you to come and eat it anyway? And I asked a question. About Emily."

"Mother, I just got here. Ten minutes ago. I'm leaving in another ten. Ice cream, Vic? Colm?" She smiled pleasantly at the two males. Or was it insinuatingly? Sharon was fond of Colm; she couldn't understand why Ruth wouldn't marry him. Of course, Vic and Colm accepted Sharon's offer without waiting for Ruth's approval. She wished Colm and Sharon would go home. She just wanted to be alone. She wanted to worry in peace.

Sharon put a bowl of ice cream in front of her and she ate it before she realized she didn't really want any.

She was in such a funk! When Sharon finally did leave and Vic trotted up to bed, she saw she hadn't checked the answering machine. Of course. There was probably a message from Emily, an explanation.

It wasn't Emily, it was Pete. "Ruth, I've seen the lawyer. I'll be more generous than he suggests. A mere hundred thousand for my share of the land. Shall we say, monthly payments, to be finalized in two years' time? That's a generous offer! But there's an alternative, Ruth. You know that, Ruth. Think of Vic, think of Emily." And the machine beeped off.

She stood there, stunned, her finger still shaking above the button. Colm was behind her, holding her around the waist. "Is it what I think it means? He wants you to buy him out? He wants a hundred grand and he might as well ask for the moon?"

She let him hold her. She needed that. "The moon," she said, "you've got it exactly. Will you go up and get me a piece of it, Colm?"

"For you, anything," he said. He led her into the living room, to the old shabby sofa, sat her down. For a moment she felt safe, secure: She was in her own farmhouse, she could hear the cows serenading the night. What was Pete planning to do if she couldn't come up with that moon? Would he foreclose? Drive her out? "What can he do, Colm?"

"Nothing," Colm said. "He won't do a goddamn thing. Not over my dead body. We'll get an appraiser, see what the farm's worth now, how much half is. How many acres—total?"

"Two hundred sixty. I rent fifty of it out for sheep."

"You could rent more, you think? Just for a time? To make the first payment? I can throw in a little. I've got some stashed away in the bank. Course, I was planning on a cruise, you and me, to celebrate our honeymoon. . . ."

"That bloody moon again."

He smiled, squeezed her shoulders. "You can get a loan."

"Huh. I'm still paying off the last loan, to build back after the barn fire. The loan before that for the forage harvester. We're dirt-poor, Colm. Who's going to loan us anything more?"

"But I'm clean. Dad and I can take out a loan. Building improvement? Dad likes farms, he likes you. He wants me married. He wants grandchildren! He'll go along."

"I smell blackmail."

"No, no, Ruth. Honest to God. No strings attached."

"Humph. Anyway, I won't let you do that. Not with your dad's business. If he goes bankrupt, who'll bury the dead? But . . . I could sell some of the cows. They'd bring in a few thousand." She sighed. "But not enough. Not enough to buy him out. He wants this farm. So he can sell it. Build houses on it. That's all he wants. To sell his own heritage! Sell his ancestors down the pike. Imagine his father, his grandfather, looking down on this. They'd walk the universe for an eternity. Isn't that what Hamlet's father's ghost did? Emily was just talking about it. Couldn't rest while his murder was unsolved? Well, this is the same thing. Another little death. Another little homicide."

"We'll find a way. We won't let him do it."

They sat there, unspeaking. Until the phone rang, and it was Emily. "Mom, I'm at Holly Brown's house. Oh, I know you know—I went to the fair with Adam. But his car broke down. And we ran into Holly, and I went home with her. Adam's staying up there till he can get his car fixed. I can't ask Holly to bring me back tonight, Mom."

"What? Holly Brown? Who's she? Where does she live?"

"Her father wants the phone now, Mom. I'll be home for chores. I'll be there by seven. I promise. I mean, I'll try. Mom, I'm fine. Night, Mom." And the phone clicked off.

There were sixteen Browns in the local phone book. Ruth couldn't call them all—not at this late hour. "She's all right. She called you, didn't she?" Colm assured her. And she had to believe him. She had to believe Emily.

Fifty-nine

Let's go to Montreal," Adam said.

"Wha?" Emily squinted at her watch. It was six in the morning, the light was just starting to filter through the thin window hangings. She sat up, caught the echo of what he'd said. "Montreal? But you said we weren't going. I told my mother I'd be home by seven. I lied to her about Holly. We're late already!"

He propped himself up on an elbow, looked hard at her, waggled his head. "You're just a kid, aren't you? Tied to Mama's apron strings. Can't think for herself." He yanked her up by the upper arms, pushed and pulled her in a crazy dance around the room.

"You're hurting me, Adam. Let me go!" Tears were welling; it was so silly, so babyish of her, but she couldn't help it.

He threw her back on the bed. He was annoyed—she'd seen that temper once or twice before. She didn't want to be thrown about. Annoyed herself, she sat up, pulled on her socks, while he leaned against the wall and watched her. "All right, then," he said. "I'll take the baby home. This time. I forgot, actually—I have some mail coming in. I need to pick up my check. But then we'll go to Montreal. You and me. Tomorrow night. No, Wednesday. Wednesday's my afternoon off. We'll go then—spend the night. You can pack a suitcase. With a lot of clothes.

Say you're coming." He stood over her, a blond giant. She was strangely afraid of him. She had a chemistry test Wednesday, but she didn't dare say so.

He dropped to his knees, embraced her thighs, buried his face in her lap. "Come with me, Em, Wednesday," he begged. "We'll have some fun, do some stuff, a little life. I need you, Em. Say you'll come with me, Emily—love. Say yes."

She put her face down into his hair. It tasted like beer and cotton candy. "Yes," she said. "Yes, I'll come."

What else could she say?

Sixty

Late Sunday afternoon after work, Emily discovered Opal down by the pond where the geese lived. The girl didn't know Emily was there; she was throwing out bread crumbs and then sketching the geese when they rushed to feed. Emily stood gazing into the pond a moment. She needed to steel herself. It was the first of two confrontations for that day: She hadn't gotten home until eleven—Adam had insisted they go out for breakfast—and then her mother had lit into her. Luckily she had called Holly Brown, and when her mother finally made contact with that family, Holly vouched for her. Emily didn't like to lie, it wasn't her nature. But it wasn't her fault, either; if she could have sat down with her mother, made her understand about Adam, she wouldn't have had to lie. But she couldn't do that; her mother was so . . . so Neanderthal.

And now there was this second confrontation. For her mother's sake, actually; her mother would thank her when she knew. It was something Emily just had to do, ever since Adam had told her about Opal. She was nervous, she stretched up on her toes, drew in long, deep breaths, then faced Opal.

Opal didn't look up, she just kept on sketching. She was dressed in black tights with a long loose shiny pink sweater. She looked glamorous, self-possessed. Emily's heart was racing.

"Opal, we need to talk," she said. "Now."

Finally Opal looked up, like it was a Jehovah's Witness at the door and she couldn't be bothered. "You don't have to shout. I have ears."

Emily got right to the point. "You hurt our cows, you came through the gate and deliberately slashed them with a knife. Oh yes, you did, don't look so innocent. Someone saw you. I have a witness."

"Who saw me?" Opal said, looking so blasé that Emily wanted to grab and shake her. And when Emily just stood there, breathing hard, not wanting to say Adam's name, Opal said, "You don't know, do you? You're making it up. Because I never slashed any stupid cows. I never set a foot on your smelly farm. I wouldn't even know how to get there. I don't know what gate you're talking about."

"It was Adam. He saw you." Emily drew three quick breaths. She told about the knife, the blood. "It was a terrible thing to do! One of the cows, Gypsy, still won't give milk. Her belly was slashed. How could you? A helpless cow!"

Opal stood up. She seemed to grow and grow; then Emily saw she was standing on a flat rock. The geese were watching with sharp yellow eyes. Opal tossed out more crumbs, then crossed her arms over her small pointy breasts. "You're lying. Adam never said that. He couldn't. Because it ne-ver hap-pened."

Emily's heart was full of fists. She almost choked on her frustration. "But he did. He did say it. Just last night. It was the truth, he swore it." She turned away, she couldn't look another minute at this stony-faced girl.

She felt steely hands on her shoulders, spinning her about. "Why would he tell you, anyway?"

Emily pulled her shoulders back, thrust up her chin. "We're . . . together now. We've started a relationship." That was all she was going to say. But she wanted Opal to know. Opal could keep her hands off.

Opal released her and sat down. Her voice was low and hard. "I know why he said that. He's trying to put the blame on me. For something he did. Oh yes, something I saw. Down in the orchard, the night before those trees got sprayed. I didn't tell on him then, but now . . . well." She ran a pink tongue over her thin lips. "Adam was coming out of the storage shed, he had a key. He's not supposed to have a key. I didn't realize it at the time, but now I know. He was after that spray. That paraquat."

Emily gasped. No one went in that storage shed except Rufus and the Earthrowls. Rufus was a tiger about that. She sank down on a crate. Someone was lying here, about something. It had to be Opal. Still, she was shaken by Opal's words. She looked down at her own hands; they looked like oblong stones in her lap.

"I don't believe you," she said. "Adam wouldn't do that."

Opal smiled her thin-lipped smile. "Then ask him. I wasn't going to tell. But I don't like what he said about me. About those cows. Because it isn't true. Why go to all that bother anyway? Why would he say that about me?" She was holding a black pen in her hand, twisting it. Her hands were trembling, she seemed on the edge of tears.

"I don't like any of it, what's going on here in this place," Opal went on. "It's voodoo. Those blacks set it on; they do voodoo down there in the Caribbean, my mother says so. They got Adam to do that spraying, oh yes. If one of them died, it's their own fault. I know. I had one for a boyfriend once. Oh, he was mixed, he was mostly white, he had a black grandmother. He was handsome. I thought I loved him." The pen dropped on the ground, but she didn't seem to notice.

Emily sat down on a stone, her hands gripping her knees. She didn't want to listen, she wanted to go home. Yet she was drawn into the story. . . .

"He got me pregnant, you know, and it was okay. I was going to keep the child, I was going to marry him. He said we would. We made plans. I told my mother."

"That was brave," Emily murmured, thinking of her own mother, whom she'd have to face again when she got home. She'd told a lie; now she'd have to make it right, or it would eat away at her. She suddenly felt like going home, taking a hot bath, getting squeaky clean.

"She helped make plans, it was going to be in the church—

she's strict Catholic, you know, so I agreed. Aureliano agreed, we got everything ready. We had a party the night before. The next day was the wedding. Then that night, after the party—Aureliano dropped the bombshell. He couldn't do it. He was already married. Oh, he hadn't seen her in two years, she lived down in Jamaica. Jamaica! But she wouldn't divorce him, her religion wouldn't let her. He wanted to tell me before that, he said, but he didn't want to upset me."

"So he waited till the day before your wedding?" Emily couldn't believe it. "How awful! So what happened?"

Opal was quiet a moment. Then she said, "What could happen? I ended it. What was the point of going on with the relationship?"

"What about the baby?" Emily whispered. "How far along were you?"

"Oh, three months. It didn't show. I went to a clinic. I had to. I couldn't tell my mother that! She'd kill me. She and my father argue about it all the time. My life is in danger, too, you know, because of what my father does."

"In danger? What *does* your father do?"

Opal didn't answer that, so Emily said, "How sad—that man lied to you, then. About being able to marry you."

"He was upset I left him, he kept calling. I thought he might get violent, follow me up here. That's why I need the knife. It's just an old kitchen knife."

"But you can't label everybody bad from Jamaica just because of Aureliano. These are good men here; they have wives and children, they work hard."

Opal frowned. Her lips were set in a straight line. She wasn't going to change her mind. Aureliano was bad. Therefore, so were all Jamaicans. Emily got up; she felt unsteady on her feet. "I'm sorry about all that, Opal. I really am. I'm sure Aureliano must have been upset, too. I mean, he wanted to marry you, right?"

"*He* said so, but I don't know. He got caught, was the way he put it, he got on a merry-go-round—his mother pushed him into that marriage. But I'm not sorry for him. Oh no, I'm not!" She picked up her sketchpad and started off. "I'm not sorry for Adam, either. He's a liar. I never slashed those cows. And he said he'd take me to the Valley Fair with him. And then he took *you*!"

She strode out, chin up, her black hair floating about her head in the wind. "Rufus will hear about this. About Adam's being in the storage shed. You'll see. Adam won't betray any more females!"

"Wait, wait, Opal!" Emily cried, running after the girl. "Don't tell Rufus. It isn't fair! What evidence do you have? So Adam was in the storage shed. He works here. It was probably something he needed. You didn't see him do anything."

"Who says I didn't?" Opal threw back over her shoulder, and ran on up the path, a slight figure who looked like she might blow away in the next breeze. The geese followed her, squawking, and Opal yelled, "Shut up. Shut up, you stupid beasts, or I'll wring your scrawny necks!"

Sixty-one

Emily stood for a long time at the fork in the path, and then took the left one to the bunkhouse. Adam was there alone, writing something in a notebook. He looked up, startled. She sat on his bed, grabbed his hand. "It's Opal," she said. "She's on her way to see Rufus. To tell him what she saw."

"What? Saw what?" He looked tense, as though something were trapped inside him, something he couldn't get out. His fingers drew circles on the notebook paper.

"You. Coming out of the storage shed. The night before the paraquat spraying. With a key, she said."

The cheek muscles relaxed. "Oh that. I was looking for a bandanna I'd left in there. I'd gone in earlier to help Rufus put away some insecticide; I was in a hurry, the bandanna got caught on a nail. I knew where he hid the key." He smiled at Emily. "She thinks I was getting the paraquat?"

Emily smiled, too. She stroked his palm. Of course that was all. She remembered now: She'd been there herself—it was two weeks ago, she thought he was meeting Opal and he wasn't, he was going after that bandanna. Why, he'd waved it at her! She squeezed his hand.

"What were you doing anyway," he asked, his eyes narrowing, "talking to Opal? I thought you two didn't get along."

"Well, I—it was those cows you said she slashed. I couldn't get it out of my head. I thought she might have pulled up the hemp, too. I wanted her to know I knew. I didn't want any more damage. My mother's running the farm alone, you know. It's not easy for her!" She heard her voice rise. Then realized she was actually defending her mother, and she said, "Oh," and then coughed.

She decided, too, at the same moment, that Opal hadn't slashed her mother's cows at all; for one thing, the girl was too petite. She had no car. She kept a knife for protection, not for slashing cows. Anyway, why would she walk all the way over to Cow Hill Road in the dark? Adam had got it all wrong.

Emily thought of Opal on the eve of her wedding and then that man saying he couldn't marry her. She couldn't imagine the humiliation, the pain of it. . . . She asked, "Why did you say she hurt our cows?"

Adam pulled his hand away, swatted a fly. "I don't know. I guess I thought maybe she did when I saw that knife. Because she let the goats go, everybody knows that. She's a mischief maker."

Emily stared at him. "Adam, you can't go around accusing people of things unless you're sure. You have to have proof."

"Don't lecture me," he said, getting up off the bed. "Opal's gone off to tell Rufus what she thinks she saw by the storage shed—without any proof, I might add, it's her word against mine—and I'm not going to be here when he comes huffing up to accuse me." He jumped up, pulled on his jacket.

She clutched his arm. "You can't hide! If you're not guilty of anything, you don't have to worry."

"I'm not hiding, damn it. I need to think, that's all. I'm going into town. I just don't want that guy bugging me. He's paranoid. He's a monomaniac. Apples, apples, apples, that's all he thinks about. How much yield? Is there a tiny bruise on that apple? Then it's only good for cider. It's your fault, Golding. You did it. You bruised that apple. He's had it in for me ever since I came here. But I stuck it out because—" He stopped, yanked at a faulty zipper.

"Because . . . what?" she said. Then, in a softer voice, standing beside him, stroking his wool sleeve: "Because of me, Adam?"

He looked at her as though surprised to see she was still there. "Partly, yes," he said.

"Only partly? What was the other part, then? Adam?" she called to him out the door, but he was already gone, waving her off, running around to the parking lot.

"Got to pick something up in town," he said. "I'll be back. I'll see you."

She followed him, still calling, wanting an answer to her question, but he was already in the white Volvo, driving noisily away.

Sixty-two

Opal waited until Adam left the bunkhouse and then she went in. She'd seen when he came back from town an hour before: He'd dropped the car keys in his pocket, tossed the jacket on the bed. When he went into the bathroom at the other end of the bunkhouse, she had her chance. She tiptoed in, snatched the keys, dashed out; crouched in the bushes, waiting, until he left with his guitar—for the toolshed, she supposed. It was so easy. He merely threw on the coat, didn't reach in the pockets, didn't need keys to go to the toolshed.

When he was out of sight, she ran to the Volvo. It was just a hunch, but she'd seen him by the post office when she went in town with Aunt Moira; he was carrying out a large box, one he stashed in the rear of his car. He'd slammed down the rear door when Moira came out of the post office, waved, and Moira waved back.

Opal wanted to know what was in that box. It could be anything: a snow parka, winter boots, books, or maybe . . . a snake. Something to turn loose in the orchard. One never knew.

But Adam had put the finger on her, and she was putting it right back. No one would ignore Opal Earthrowl. No one would get the better of her! If it was only books or boots or a snow parka in the box, it could be added to. More paraquat, maybe, or one of those other powders and sprays down in the orchard—because Opal knew where Adam kept the key he'd had made. She'd followed him back that day she saw him with the key; she'd seen him slip it under the rubber mat beneath the driver's seat. It didn't mean she was sneaky; it meant survival. You had to be cunning to survive in this world.

Quick as a weasel she unlocked the back. There was a car jack, an axe, a coil of rope. And under a gray blanket . . . the box. She slit open the outer seal with her kitchen knife. And, ahhh! saw, at once, she wouldn't have to enter the storage shed, after all. Everything Rufus would want to see was in this box. And it was—she grimaced—horrid. . . .

She taped the box shut—Opal had been prepared for any emergency; draped the blanket back over it. She shut the rear door and tossed the car keys through the open bunkhouse window, onto the floor by his bed.

As if they had simply fallen out of his pocket.

Sixty-three

Tell 'at girl t'stay outa orshard buznee," Stan told Moira where he sat at the window, and Moira said, "What?" Most of the time she was able to decipher what Stan had to say, but today she had other things on her mind. A pile of medical bills in the mail at the P.O. box, and then, at home, a police detective, waiting with a warrant to search through Stan's clothing. What had Stan been wearing the night Cassandra was killed? he wanted to know.

And why had they only come for that now? she'd asked. How could she remember after all this time what he'd been wearing? Stan wouldn't remember, either; he was on amphetamines, he was on Prozac—Dr. Colwell had put him on it to allay the depression that came with the aftermath of stroke. Finally she'd given the detective and his female colleague three pairs of pants, two shirts, an outdoor jacket, and a pair of brown loafers she thought Stan might have been wearing that night. They could analyze those for hairs or fibers or whatever.

Stan was still their prime suspect, then. It was like that British mystery series she and Stan had watched, feeling neutral at the time, above suspicion themselves. It was just a show, a TV show—that's why people watched mysteries, she supposed. They could sit, safe, in their cozy living rooms.

But this was no TV show, this was for real.

"Obul, tha nieze amine, Obul," Stan said, pointing a trembly finger, and Moira said, "Oh, dear, what's she doing now?" She went to the window, saw Opal standing behind Rufus, trying to attract his attention. But Rufus was having none of it. He was talking to three of the Jamaicans, gesticulating, waving his arms. Describing, she supposed, something they had or hadn't done. The Jamaicans just looked at him impassively. Derek had his arms folded, and Zayon and Desmond held their arms rigidly at their sides. The confrontation went on for several minutes, while Rufus lectured and pointed. Finally Opal tapped him on the shoulder and he waved her off, not looking at her.

As she wheeled about, angry as a swatted wasp, Adam Golding's white Volvo squealed to a leafy stop in the driveway. He called to Opal, and the girl came slowly over to the driver's window, stood there, a mocking smile on her face, her hands on her skinny hips. There followed what appeared to be a heated discussion. Opal stamped her foot and shook her head, her black pigtail flying about her head like a lasso. But all the while she was smiling—Moira thought of a cat, pitched into a bucket of cream. Opal started to turn away, and Adam's hand reached out and grasped her arm. For a moment they stared at one another; then the hand let Opal go and the girl laughed and spun about, and walked with dignity back to the house.

"Opal," Moira said sternly when the girl came in, "you mustn't interrupt Rufus when he's talking to the men. We're behind in the picking and Rufus takes it all personally. I suppose we're lucky he does. He's the best orchard man in Branbury, everyone says so. And we want to keep him," she said pointedly.

Stan nodded his head, frowned at his niece.

Opal waited for the speech to be over, then stomped upstairs. She had a letter to write, she said. Moira wanted to run after and shake her—the girl could be infuriating! It was Opal, she suspected, who had unraveled the scarf she was weaving for the Jamaicans—more than once she'd caught her examining the loom. She had a mind to call the girl's mother and tell her she was putting Opal on a bus. There was too much trouble in the orchard without adding more. Resolved, not wanting to ask Stan, for he was asleep now in his chair, she marched over to the phone, picked it up to call Annie May.

But the line was busy. Annie May was talking again, to a girlfriend, who knew? She banged down the phone and went to her loom. Oh no! But this time she'd made the mistake herself, she was sure: broken the pattern with the wrong color thread. Sighing, she leaned back in the chair, her hands dropped, useless, in her lap.

Sixty-four

Ruth paused on the threshold of the Branbury Inn, where her ex-husband was staying. Outside, the leaves were turning pale red and orange; it was getting on toward leaf-peeping season, he would be paying a small fortune for the room. She knew he was there, she'd seen him at the video store when she was coming out of the Grand Union; she followed in her pickup to the inn—she felt like a spy. Even so, she had to see him. She wasn't going to give in to his demands. She'd buy back her half of the farm acreage if it took her a lifetime to pay! Her renter friend Carol Unsworth had given her a small loan, enough to get her through a month's payment anyway, while she searched for other ways out. Colm would help, of course, but she wouldn't use him unless desperate. Although after three months she probably would be! Colm didn't have one hundred thousand dollars, either. She couldn't mortgage the children! She might have to sell out after all.

The receptionist rang up Pete's room; when she knocked on Number 128 the door opened, but it wasn't Pete who stood there. It was that woman, that developer, Mavis Dingman, whom she'd met at the Earthrowls'. Colm had interviewed the woman, but she was too smooth, he'd said: "Can you hold on to a handful of molasses?" She was wearing purple-flowered rayon pants with wide bottoms and a long slinky pale blue rayon top—or was it silk? Ruth wasn't up on the latest fashion. Anyway, it didn't look like business dress. Was Pete cheating on his actress friend?

"I was just on my way," she sang out when Pete introduced her. "Call me, Peter, when the lawyers settle on a closing date for Larocque's." With a knowing smile at Ruth, she flowed out.

"Animal," Ruth said to Pete. "Predator. Pouncing on an old man's farm, slicing it up into pieces like a side of beef!"

"You're exaggerating," Pete said. He was smiling, but nervous: She heard the change jiggling in his pocket, where he'd stuck a hand. "Only a few houses, I told you. It'll be an exclusive development. Ten, twenty acres apiece. Nice landscaping. You'll never see the houses for the new trees."

"And how long does it take to grow a tree? Damn you anyway."

He motioned for her to sit down, but she wouldn't. She was here on business. Anyway, there was only one small red-flowered easy chair and then the double platform bed, where Pete was settling down. She wasn't going to join him there!

"I'm here on business myself. To give you the first month's payment." She thrust a check for five thousand dollars at him. It landed on his flabby belly, and he turned it over.

He whistled. "You think you can do it, do you? Hundred thousand? In twenty-four months? Somebody give you a loan?"

"Never mind." It was none of his business how she got it.

"This could have been a check to you," he said, getting up, taking it over to the desk. "For a down payment on a town house. A flight to the Caribbean. You haven't been out of Branbury in years, have you? Not since our trip to England that time? We had a good time then, Ruth."

It was true, they had. It was ten years ago now, it was right after Pete's father died, leaving them a little money. It was like a weight had been lifted from them, the father had been part owner of the farm, was something of a martinet. He knew how the farm should be run, and Pete wasn't running it the "right" way. They'd laughed their way through the British Isles, gone to bed early nights, made love every night.

But things started to go wrong when they got back: blight on the corn, low milk prices, the herd buyouts. Then there was that film made in town, the bit part Pete had, the actress who lured him down to the city. And Pete not unwilling to go.

The old bitterness welled up in her throat again. She walked over to him where he stood by the desk, still gazing at the check as though it might disintegrate in his hands. "Before I go, Pete, there's something I have to know."

"If it's about the farm," he said, "ask Tim. He'll know. I've been out of it too long now. Got other things on my mind. This little partnership I've gotten involved in."

"That's exactly it," she said, facing him squarely, hands on her hips. She was suddenly aware that she still had on her farm boots; Pete's New York shoes smelled of polish. But never mind. "I want to know who the third partner is. Besides you and that oily woman. Why is it such a secret? I think Lucien has a right to know. So do the Earthrowls. Come on, now, tell me." She looked him directly in the eye. They'd had three children together, for God's sake! He owed her something. Some honest answers.

He turned and walked across the room, looked out the window, blew out his cheeks. She stood behind him. Finally he turned, groaned. "Okay, if you can keep it to yourself. Promise?"

She hesitated; the name might or might not be useful, one never knew. But she had to know it. She promised.

"It's Rufus Barrow. He's related to my, um, female partner. This is a small town, all these old families are mixed up together. I hate to say it, Ruthie, but I think there's a Barrow somewhere in my own past. It's not any dirty secret, damn it—that he's a partner, I mean—he just didn't want people to know. Especially the Earthrowls—and don't you go telling them! They'd just cause trouble, Rufus says. You promised, now." He gripped her arm. It hurt, and she yanked away from him.

He followed her. "Come on, Ruth, have a drink, a little sherry. You used to like sherry. Let's be friends. Talk about the kids. I—

I've missed them, Ruth. Emily, Sharon, Vic. How's Vic getting on in school now? I want to get him down to the city, show him around. Get him out of the boondocks."

But she wasn't going to let him seduce her, make her sorry for him. Pete was the enemy now. Until she completed the farm payments—if ever. Until she found out why Rufus was involved, how he was involved. Why would Rufus even want to be a partner in a development company—a fifth- or sixth-generation Vermonter, brought up on an orchard? Why would he be a party to this exploitation of the land?

But then, so was Pete a Vermonter. His father would turn over in his grave to know what his son was doing. For once she felt a certain warmth for that old curmudgeon. He'd be on her side in this battle.

"No, thank you," she said to the sherry Pete was pressing on her, and she slipped gratefully into the hall and then out into the cool leaf-bright afternoon.

She opened her mouth wide; practically drank in the fresh Vermont air.

"Hey," young Joey said when she got home: late, late for prepping the cows, "hey, Ruth, it all done. Emily got the cows all ready, Tim in there now doin' the milkin'. I'm goin' back in there t'help him, he said tell you go inside, relax. Re-lax." He grinned at her out of his sunburned face, then waved and whistled his way back into the barn. At the door he doffed his feed cap, stuck it on backward, to show how "with it" he was. Hay wisps were stuck in his hair.

She waved back. Joey was a sweetheart. He operated on five cylinders better than most people on six. How lucky she was, with Tim and Joey for helpers. How could she ever, ever consider selling the farm? And Emily: Emily doing the prepping—unasked. Although there might be a reason for that. The girl still had some explaining to do.

She found Emily in the kitchen, scrubbing the floor. She had to smile, had to remember what it was like when she went to high school. It was senior year when she and Pete stayed out till three in the morning; her mother was waiting up in the rocking chair, she'd been rocking and rocking her distress. But when Ruth tiptoed in, her mother was sound asleep. And Ruth didn't wake her, just crept on upstairs. She'd told some crazy story the next day about why she was out so late. She'd forgotten now what it was.

"Well, Em, what's this all about? You and that floor aren't usually such good pals."

"I had all this extra energy, that's all." Emily looked up contritely; stood up. She inhaled as though she were preparing to make a speech. "Look, Mom, I know I told you I wasn't going to the fair, I was staying over with Hartley Flint. And I didn't intend to go. . . ." She hesitated. "No, that's not true. Hartley couldn't come home from college this weekend, and, well, Adam Golding asked me to go with him. I didn't tell you because I didn't think you liked him. I don't know why you don't like him, except that he's older than I am. But he's a good person, he really is. And we—we had fun together—at the fair. We did some rides and we went to the snake show. Adam likes stuff like that. I mean, animals." She looked pleadingly at her mother for support.

Ruth nodded, went to the refrigerator to see what was available for supper. She hadn't thought ahead. She'd let the girl go on with her explanations, then they'd talk. Emily had to realize that she couldn't lie. True, she was older now, but communication had to be open between mother and daughter. She pulled out a pound of ground chuck, spread it on the table, began to chop onions.

"Mom, are you listening to me?"

Ruth said, "Yes, yes! You know I am. I'm waiting for you to convince me that you had to tell an untruth, knowing it would worry the hell out of me if I found out the truth!"

"I know. Mom, you were worried I stayed out overnight without telling you. You see, it was because of the concert. I thought maybe . . . you and Colm and the boys would go, too. I thought we'd all be late. I didn't realize how late it was. And then Adam's car started acting up and I . . ." She paused, and Ruth waited. "When I'm with Adam . . ." she began, and then sighed deeply and sat down beside her mother; took a second knife, and began chopping.

"I think I—I think I love Adam. I know I do. He's had such a hard life. Mom, he had a stepbrother—a half-brother—who hanged himself. He told me all about it, it was awful. I want to—to fill that hole for Adam. Mother, will you look at me? Will you talk to me? Do you hear me?"

Ruth put down the knife. The onions were getting to her anyway, she had sensitive eyes; they were watering. "I hear you, Emily. I do! I'm sorry about the stepbrother. It must have been terrible for him." She took Emily's hands. "Look, Em, I'm sure Adam is . . . a responsible person. Just promise me you won't . . . do anything rash. Without telling me, that is. So we can talk, we can listen to each other." She looked questioningly at her daughter.

"Mom, don't look so worried! I'm not getting married. I mean, there's been no talk about that. I'll finish school, I'll apply to college. Everything after that is, well . . . uncertain. But I won't do anything rash."

Ruth got up, her eyes stinging from the onions. She felt there was more that Emily wanted to tell her, but it was all right, she could wait. "I know you won't. I trust you. And thanks, Em, for helping with the cows. I'd been to see your father, I was late."

"What did he say?" Emily pounced on the turn in the conversation. She was still hoping to get her parents back together, Ruth knew that. But it was time to tell Emily about the deal she'd made. So she told her, and Emily was aghast.

"But how will you get all that money? Is it worth it? We could move into town, it's all right, I wouldn't mind. I could walk to school, I—"

"I gave him the first payment, that's all I could—can—do. We're keeping the farm, Emily. Somehow. And that's that. We're keeping it." She found herself standing with the knife in her hand. She laid it down, the onion bits splattered on the table. She took a deep, shuddering breath. Emily's hand was on her shoulder.

"I understand, Mom. I mean, I think I understand. And I'll prep the cows every day when apple season's over. I'll clean the barn."

"I know. I know. So how was Gypsy? Still skittish, I think. I'm wondering if she'll ever get back to normal."

"Adam told me . . ." Emily began—she obviously had something other than Gypsy on her mind. "Adam told me he thought Opal did it, hurt our cows. He says she has a knife, she keeps it with her. And I know why she does! I confronted her, you see. About the cows. She got pregnant by this guy. She was going to marry him, but it turned out he had a wife back in Jamaica. So she rejected him. But he's been trying to get back together. Stalking her, maybe, I don't know. So she's afraid."

"Opal? Why would she want to hurt our cows?"

"But she didn't, that's the thing. She said she didn't, and, well, I believe her, Mom."

"But why did Adam say she did?" Ruth was concerned now. "Did he see her over here? If not, it seems odd he'd say that." She didn't like it at all, the boy accusing Opal. Why would he make such an accusation? She sighed, tried to busy herself with supper. She felt Emily breathing into her neck.

"Come on, now, Mother. He was just trying to help. He was upset about the slashing, he was! He said so. Adam just saw her knife, that's all, with a little blood on it—she probably cut her finger or something. He wondered why she'd have it. You wonder about things, too, Mom, I've heard you and Colm. Suppose this, suppose that . . ."

Ruth turned, gave her daughter an oniony hug. She guessed she *had* played the supposing game. Probably that's all Adam was doing. She had to think that.

"The only thing is," Emily was saying, getting a Pepsi out of the refrigerator, "Opal wants to get back at Adam now. She saw him with a key once in the storage shed, and now she's planning on telling Rufus. To put suspicion on Adam for that spraying."

"Oh? She has no proof of anything, has she?"

"Of course not! Don't get any false ideas, now. I shouldn't have mentioned it. I mean, I was there, Mom, when Opal saw him. He was just going after a bandanna he'd left when he was in there with Rufus. Why, I saw it in his hand myself." She started up the stairs with the Pepsi. "Where's Vic?" she called down. "Isn't it time for his chores? The barn needs sweeping—you wouldn't believe the mess. It's that crazy Zelda. She knocked over the wheelbarrow when I went to grain her. I don't know why you keep that cow, Mother."

Ruth had to smile. She'd knocked over a few wheelbarrows herself lately. Her ex-husband was still trying to turn his upright. And what about Opal? Was she getting people in trouble—Adam, for example? Or was she right about Adam—that he had something to do with the poisonous spraying? She wondered. Maybe she should see Rufus *and* Adam. Before there was some kind of explosion.

Emily was in the upstairs hall, hollering down. "Don't you get any crazy ideas in your head, Mom. I know you. Don't you go suspecting Adam of anything. He's a good person, a sincere person. I love him, Mother! Don't you do anything to hurt him."

Ruth froze in front of the refrigerator. What could a mother do after an impassioned speech like that? But good God—her cows knifed, her hemp torn up, that old man dead from a poisoned apple . . . Could love excuse all that?

But now she was supposing again. What would make her think that Adam was behind the malice at the orchard, at her own farm? There was no evidence. Only a mischievous girl's report that she'd seen him in the storage shed where the paraquat was kept. Opal had let the Jamaicans' goat loose, hadn't she? And never owned up. Maybe Adam was right, and it was Opal, after all, who'd come after the cows with her survival knife. Jealous of Emily, maybe.

"Hey, I was about to call you," Colm said when she phoned him at his real estate office. He was writing up a contract for a trailer, he told her, it was a cobroke with another Realtor. "It means beans, not real cash. But what does mean something is the latest report from headquarters. Fallon got word from the FBI—some abortion clinic task force they've put together—that Turnbull and Chris Christ might be aliases for a guy connected with a rash of bombings—and shootings—of abortion providers over the past dozen years. Jeez, you wouldn't believe it. An Army of God, Lambs of Christ. Lambs with rifles?"

She shuddered at the thought: the world gone sick. "Have they picked him up yet? Whoever he really is? Is he aware they're looking for him?" She thought of Moira and Stan, any involvement the minister might have with their orchard. "I don't want him getting away!"

"They're on their way right now, couple of FBI guys. I'll keep you posted. So what's on your mind, Ruthie?"

"It's Rufus, Colm. He's the third partner. Pete told me this afternoon."

"You saw Pete?"

"I went for that purpose, damn it, Colm. No other reason. And to give him the first payment on the farm. He wasn't happy. He still hopes I'll sell. I said no way."

"Good. I'd like to have seen his face. They'll be building on Lucien's farm soon. I'm sorry, Ruth. They'll be using your road. Cow Hill Road. Not so many cows now, though."

"Mine! My cows will still be here."

"You're shouting, Ruth."

She didn't care. Her nose was running—those damned onions. She wiped it on a paper napkin. She wanted to talk to Colm about Adam, about Opal. But Emily was upstairs, she heard the girl in the bathroom, running a bath. She'd want a hot bath after working in the barn, she'd want the smell off her body. Ruth understood. She hadn't had the problem when she was a girl, hadn't been raised on a farm herself. Now she understood.

"I've something else to talk to you about," she told Colm. She listened: The water had stopped running in the bathroom. She lowered her voice. "It's about the orchard. Another thought, another possibility. Besides Rufus. Have you talked to Honey Fallon? About Cassandra and that minister? I half thought *he* might have been the third partner. I don't want the FBI running him out of state till we find out what he's involved in here. He'd been married to Cassandra, we know that. And she's related to Rufus, I think."

"What? You didn't tell me that."

"Emily's seen the family cemetery. At least there's a Cassandra buried there, and that's an unusual name. There might be some connection. With Cassandra's death, I mean, with the orchard mischief. All of them, mixed up together: Cassandra, Rufus, that alias-alias minister?"

Colm was quiet a minute. "Could be a connection. But what?" He said he'd look up Rufus's background anyway. And then, yes, he'd go see Honey Fallon. "Pump her a bit."

She smiled. "Pump her? Really? I thought you and Fallon were friends."

He snorted. "You have a dirty mind, you know that, Ruthie?" She didn't know why she'd said that. Sometimes dumb things dropped out of her mouth. But sex was on her mind more often of late. Maybe she wasn't the prude, after all, that Pete said she was.

But here was Tim coming up the back steps, that meant another problem. He had something metal in his hand, a broken part. Good Lord! His shirt was bloody. She put down the phone with a quick " 'Bye," flung open the kitchen door. "What happened?" she said, running to get a clean towel, to see where the blood was coming from.

"Brakes gone," Tim said, waving away her concern, "on the John Deere." He sank down into a chair, holding his chest. "We were going down a hill, Joey and me, Joey sitting on the fender. That hill behind the barn, you know, where we planted a new acre of balsams? I left him in the tractor, had it in gear, but angled, I thought, so it wouldn't move—while I went to check the trees, next thing I hear Joey yelling, damn thing's moving! Joey's on his way downhill. He jumps in the driver's seat, but the brakes are gone! Ruth, I'm in a sweat! Joey's hollering his head off. No brakes! I'm running after, running like hell, grab the wheel, my shirt's caught. I'm dragged along and the back tire rolls over me before it runs into a clump of bushes. Probably busted a couple ribs." He dabbed at the blood with the towel. The blood she saw was largely surface, but he was undoubtedly right about the ribs.

"We've got to get you to the hospital."

"Christ no, no hospital. No way! I'm alive, I'm okay, Ruth. But somebody did this, I bet. Somebody messed with the brakes." He swallowed the coffee she'd handed him, grinned at Joey, who was bursting through the kitchen door: excited, breathless with the tale he had to tell. "I woulda been kill without Tim, he save me, Tim!" he shouted through his whistly teeth. "Tim, you aw right, Tim?"

"What is it? Who's hurt?" Emily dashed down the steps in her blue cotton bathrobe. "Tim, what happened?" Then Vic clomped in, home from soccer practice. And Tim and Joey had to tell the tale all over again. They were laughing now, as though it were nothing: tampered brakes and a heavy tire rolling over the chest . . .

"See the marks? See, Ruth, see Emily, see Vic, where it rolled over on 'im?" Joey bawled, pointing at Tim's chest, the mauled shirt. "Lookit. Big black tire marks. An' blood!" Awed, he sat down beside his foster father, stroked his arm. Ruth would keep an eye on Tim—at least make him see a doctor, bandage those ribs.

She put an arm around Vic. It might have been Vic in that tractor, or Emily, Ruth thought. They knew how to drive it; there might not have been a Tim there to throw his body at it, stop it in time.

"Quit squeezing, Mom, you're hurting me," Vic complained, but Ruth couldn't let him go.

Sixty-five

Colm met Honey Fallon at Calvi's, the local soda fountain, established 1910. You could get a black and white soda there, or a butterscotch sundae with nuts and cherries—which was exactly what Honey did. Colm had a moment of panic that he didn't have enough cash and ordered a glass of water for himself. "It's all right," he told Honey, "I've already had my sugar fix for the day. At work, you know."

Honey said, "At work? I thought it was a funeral parlor, not an ice-cream one."

That remark set the tone for the interview. Honey was in a jolly mood, she'd just won one hundred fifty dollars from the state lottery. "A hundred fifty!" she squealed. "Now I can buy that new winter coat I've been wanting. It's seal. Roy likes me in fur, but he never puts up the money. He's getting chintzier with every new year." She giggled and dove into the sundae; her nose came up butterscotch.

"Why I'm here," Colm began, "is about Turnbull—uh, Wickham. I'm wondering exactly how you did find out. I've a couple more things I want to know about him. But first—"

"Oh, that was easy," she interrupted. "I went to see him, you see. It was before that high school thing, my niece was in that teacher's class, the poor guy who . . . you know." She made a motion as though to slit her throat, although it was a bullet that wounded Samuels, they both knew that. She popped a cherry in her pink mouth. Colm waited, while she smiled at him through cherry teeth.

"It was at Michael's house, he didn't like us coming there—we held church meetings in Cassandra's barn. I was already getting disillusioned, you know, because of the way he treated that young woman."

Colm shook his head, confused. "What young woman?"

"Oh, the one with the seizures. A pretty girl. She couldn't help it, of course, it came on her suddenly, one time, in the middle of one of our meetings. She fell down on the floor, it was frightening—for her, for us. But Gertrude was a nurse before she got religion, she knew how to deal with her, how to pull the tongue out so she wouldn't swallow it. She called the girl's mother, she came and got her. Then afterward—afterward, Christ—that's what he liked us to call him: Christ—said she couldn't come back anymore, her seizures were a curse. Imagine that. A curse! On that pretty talented girl! She wrote poems, did I tell you? Had some of 'em published. She gave me one, it was about a waterfall. She only joined like me, she was looking for something special, spiritual. Well, after that comment about the curse . . . I started wondering. And then, oh, there were other things."

"Such as?" Colm was interested, though he resolved to keep the original question in mind—what was the original question? He couldn't remember—oh yes, how she knew his real name. But he had a question out on the floor. Didn't he?

"Goodness gracious," Honey said, spooning up the sundae. A squirt of vanilla ice cream landed in Colm's water glass. "Where do I start? Well, a lot of stuff about a nursing home he was going to start up, how prayer was going to cure the old people, cure us. Stuff about picketing Planned Parenthood, all that anti-abortion thing. He handed out literature about Lambs of Christ. It was such a sweet name! I love lambs. But I discovered they were pretty nasty lambs. That's how I found out his real name. Umm,

I lo-ove butterscotch. How many calories you figure in this sundae? I'm keeping count on a chart I have at home."

Colm shrugged. "Just enjoy it. You said you found out his real name?"

She patted her bun, it was falling down, a soft gray curl swung like a pendulum in front of her nose as she spoke. "I went to his house like I told you. That woman was there, that Cassandra—oh, and I found out something else, too!"

Colm was dizzy with the sudden swerves in the dialogue; he swallowed his water, choked on it, coughed.

"That Cassandra, she was his wife! She wasn't his cousin at all like she told us. She was his wife. Well, Roy said you knew that. You steamed open a letter or something. Naughty, naughty." She shook a finger at him. "Anyway, they were arguing. It was the cleaning lady let me in. I could hear them in the kitchen. The cleaning lady didn't even announce me—well, it wasn't her job, I guess, she wasn't a butler or something." Honey giggled. "There was a pile of mail on the front table. Something from Lambs of Christ."

She leaned across the table, peered into Colm's face. Her eyes were a deep hazel, he could see the powder on her nose that was slightly sweating with what she had to tell. "It was addressed to one Arnold Wickham, at that same address. It had been slit opened, that's how I knew it was him. He wasn't Turnbull or Chris Christ at all, but Arnold Wickham! Not that I knew who in hell—pardon my French—Arnold Wickham was, it was just that now he had three names, and that was two too many for me. But that argument was going on, and being a policeman's wife, well . . ."

She licked her spoon, slurped up the last of the butterscotch. "You wouldn't be a good boy and get me a drink of water, would you?"

Damn, he thought, just when she was getting to the meaty stuff. But he got up obediently, waited while the kid gave change to an adolescent boy, then took the water back to Honey. She was practically gasping. "Mmm," she said, and swallowed it down as if she'd been walking through a desert. She blew her nose into a tissue. "Where was I?"

"The argument. Between, um, Wickham—and Cassandra, who's not his cousin but his wife. Or was."

"Was, yes, now I remember. She had a daughter by a husband before Wickham. And he wanted Cassandra's money for himself, not for the daughter." She looked triumphant at the realization. Her voice was thick with butterscotch. "The vacuum was grinding away in another part of the house. They thought the cleaning lady couldn't hear. They didn't know I was there!" She marveled at her exploit.

"Money? For what purpose?"

"For development! For Cassandra's cousin. And Cassandra's cousin was—guess who?"

Colm waited.

"Rufus Barrow, that orchard man." She leaned across the table as though Colm were hard of hearing. "She wanted her money—*her* money, mind you—not just for the daughter, but to invest in houses on the orchard. Because Rufus was into a development firm now, she said. But our dear minister wanted the orchard left alone; he wanted the money to go into his causes. Lambs of Christ, that Creator's Rights party site on the Internet—you know that one? I had Roy look it up. Why, they've got our own Senator Leahy on their hit list!"

"But she wouldn't give in."

"Nope. She would not. Uhn-uh. Not only that, but it turns out she controlled the money. He'd married her for her money—she was yelling that at him now. He wasn't getting a penny of it for himself, she said, for she had other causes, too. She belonged to some White Citizens' Council—'keep Vermont pure' is their motto. Oh, it ain't maple syrup she was talking about, or milk." Honey winked at Colm. "Hate groups. No blacks, no gypsies, no gays, no Jews. Roy looked that up, too: They want to homogenize Vermont—can you believe it? Turn us into skim milk! Well, that's when I got out. Out of the house, out of the church. I didn't want to be on that hit list. I've got Jewish friends, I mean! For that matter, I've got pro-life friends, too, when I was in the

Catholic church—but they don't want violence, either. Well, Colm"—her voice was a low hiss—"I didn't want to be in the house if one of those two offed the other, 'cause they were getting to that point. What would I do with a dead body on my hands? It's bad enough being married to a policeman!"

She was finally quiet, drank her water, struggled up; she had a hair appointment, she said. "My hair is falling out, handfuls, every time I comb it! My hairdresser has some special shampoo supposed to keep it stuck to the scalp." She grinned. "I'm already late."

He thanked her, watched her scurry out; she reminded him of a rabbit the way her rear end wiggled. He liked her, though, she had sense. She got out of that church—if one could call it a church. He was suddenly hungry, decided he'd have a sundae after all. A chocolate fudge sundae. "With nuts, with whipped cream," he told the kid behind the counter.

Then discovered he'd forgotten to bring his wallet.

But it was all right, the owner said, and had the sundae brought over by the kid. He knew Colm; Colm had sold his daughter a couple of acres. Colm could bring in the money later.

"And another glass of water," Colm told the kid. Now, though, he was sorry he'd ordered the sundae. He wanted to call Ruth, tell her about the interview. Was there a phone in here? The sundae would have to wait. . . .

Sixty-six

But why would Turnbull—whatever his alias was—bother the Earthrowls?" Ruth asked over the phone; she was confused. "I mean, if he didn't want Cassandra's money going to the developers?" She was in the barn, tending to a brand-new bull calf. Poor thing, he'd have to be sold. But Oprah thought he was beautiful, she was licking him down, her moist brown eyes focused on the spindly, sweaty fellow. Oprah was her newest cow, named after the TV queen. She'd named the cow that partly because the name Oprah reminded her of Opera, and this cow sang. She was humming even now, in a mezzo-soprano mewl. It was a duet with Madonna, in the next calf stall. "Can you hear her, Colm?" She held out the receiver.

He wasn't interested in the bovine duet. "Jeez, I don't know," he said. "There must be a reason. There must be a link between him and the Earthrowls. Are they Jewish? Gypsies? Not gay, I don't think."

"Well, Moira's Catholic. I don't know Stan's background. The name sounds Anglo-Saxon—Beowulf comes to mind. I could ask, I suppose." The bull calf wasn't sucking, she saw, she'd have to get him started. "Can I call you back, Colm? I've got a newborn here. It needs a helping hand."

"Look, see what you can find out, okay? About the connection with Earthrowl? A visit to Moira? This afternoon, maybe? The FBI guys are lying in wait for Wickham—he seems to be out of town. I told Roy he shouldn't wait, the son of a gun! When—if—they hook him, we'll have some tough questions to ask."

"Colm, don't rush me. My work comes first. My cows. Then I'll go. Come on, baby, catch hold." With her free hand she pushed the calf toward the nipple.

"Catch hold of what? Wickham? We're trying, we truly are. Call me, then, Ruthie, when you know something. My sundae is melting."

"Your what?" she said. But the line had clicked off.

Finally the calf caught hold, sucked. Oprah was a good mother, she had plenty of milk. She nursed and licked, licked and nursed, bellowing all the while. Ruth gazed at the pair for a few more minutes. This was the reward of farming, this mother and calf—even if it was a bull calf and had to go. But she had to be practical, she'd get a good price for the calf, put it toward the fortune she owed Pete. She could sell a few more cows, too, she supposed. And part of the land. She could do without so many acres, couldn't she? She could sell them to a government trust. Some farmers she knew in Shoreham had. Then no one would put houses there; it would keep Vermont green.

She washed up and then drove the pickup over to the Earthrowls'. She'd intended to go over anyway, she was worried about that last incident, the tractor brakes. Brakes that might have been tampered with. It wasn't Moira she'd tell, but the girl, Opal, although she couldn't imagine that petite girl doing it. But the girl might know who did, or have a suspicion. Opal seemed a complicated girl: mixed up in the head, selfish—though Emily seemed a little sorry for her because of some love affair. Emily was sorry for the boy, too—Adam Golding. Ruth wasn't sure of him, either, her instincts churning away inside her.

It was hard to imagine anything wrong with this orchard, though, or its workers. There was something fresh and earthy about the smell of it. Most of the apples were picked now; the

Jamaicans, she understood, would be going home after the weekend, after their harvest ritual, and the orchard would be open to the public for drops—if anyone dared come, after the bad publicity. A few trees were still heavy with red apples, the green leaves dazzling with late sun, daisies and goldenrod growing at their roots. It was autumn's last gasp before it chilled down into winter, its leaves falling and dying. It was autumn when Pete had left with that actress. She'd thought she would die herself then. But here she was, still alive.

She found the girl on the porch, wrapped up in a blanket—it was nippy, only fifty-five degrees out. "Aunt Moira's gone to town. She should be back, though," Opal said. "Uncle Stan's in there. You want to see him?"

"I'll wait for Moira." She was glad for an excuse to talk with Opal; she planted herself in an Adirondack chair. "No, don't go," she said when the girl got up. Opal looked wary then, zipped her lips together, sat down on the edge of the porch rocker.

"Are you enjoying it here?" Ruth asked, then winced at the cloudy glance. "Of course, it's not Texas—is that where you're from? I believe your aunt mentioned . . ."

"Mentioned what?" the girl demanded. "What did she say?"

Ruth was stammering now. She couldn't think what Moira had said, if anything. Then she remembered—something, anyway. "Only that your father is ill. I'm sorry. Is he any better?"

Opal sank back into the rocker, it creaked with her weight. She sighed; she would milk out all the drama she could. "I don't know. He had heart surgery, but it might not help that much. And he's a doctor, too! But . . ." Her voice petered out.

"I didn't know he was a doctor. Does he specialize?"

Opal shrugged. "Yeah, I guess. Women. He's a gynecologist. Can't help his own daughter, though, when she needs him. My mother wants him to quit what he does. I think Mama's glad he's sick. So he will quit. Mama wants to move to California, he can practice there, she says. I want to stay in Texas. I have friends there. One of them has a ranch. When Mama sends the money, I'm going back."

"A ranch? Horses? Cows?"

"Sure, all those things. I ride, you know. I've been around cows." She glanced slyly at Ruth. "Not *your* cows," she said. "I know what Emily told you. That's why you're here, isn't it? You think I did all that stuff to your cows? That's what Adam told your daughter, right? And you believe him." Her voice was rising. "Oh sure, I know what you're thinking!"

She stopped. Ruth was up out of her chair, hands on her hips, confronting the girl.

"You're sorry for yourself, aren't you, Opal? Making excuses because you're out of school and still living with your parents—oh yes, Moira did tell me that. Your father's ill and you have to live in this backwoods state on this miserable orchard. An orchard most people would kill to own . . ." She stopped, aware of what she'd said. But she plowed on. "And now you've been accused of damaging my cows and you assume I believe that and I understand you're accusing others in your turn. . . ." She was out of breath. The girl's arms were hugging her chest, shutting Ruth out. Ruth sat back down.

"Adam, you mean," said Opal, unruffled by Ruth's tirade. "And I've already told Rufus. He's too busy to talk to me, so I left him a letter. And a certain key. You see, I found out some things. Adam's the one did that spraying, oh yes. I told Adam I knew and he just laughed at me. I hate people laughing at me! He says I don't have any proof. But I do, you see, I do have proof. Something terrible that Adam's going to do to the orchard. Maybe even tonight . . . But Rufus will stop it. When he reads my letter."

"What proof, what?" Ruth cried. "Tell me!" But the girl's eyes were half shut; she was rocking away in the wooden rocker, smiling.

The front door opened and Stan Earthrowl stood shakily in the doorway; he was wearing a plaid wool robe over blue pajamas, and brown leather slippers. "Wazzall the yelling?" he said. "Obul, wazzit?"

"I need money, Uncle Stan," she said, leaping up, sending the rocking chair spinning. "I want to go home. If you don't give it to me, I'll hitch a ride. I want to see my daddy. I want to see my friends. I don't have any friends here. Everyone hates me." She glared at Ruth and brushed by her uncle, nearly knocking him down.

Ruth steadied him. "I was coming to see Moira, Stan. Somehow we got into this brouhaha, Opal and I. She'll calm down."

Stan's face had a lopsided smile. "Neber calm dow," he said, and let her turn him around. He was walking better, though, she noticed, without the walker: a fairly straight line toward the refrigerator. When she tried to help him, he waved her off. He was freshly shaved, Moira would have seen to that. Or maybe he did it himself. She hoped so. She couldn't imagine being dependent on another person for one's basic needs: food, elimination, dressing.

She heard a truck then, coming from the road, glanced out the front window. It stopped by the apple barn; two Jamaicans jumped out the rear, Rufus out the front. He was heading for the barn. Was that where Opal had left the letter? What proof did the girl think she had?

"Tell Moira I'll call her tonight after milking," she told Stan, who'd grabbed a hunk of cheddar cheese, was trying to slice an apple on the cutting board. She hesitated. Should she help? But now he'd done it, hadn't cut himself; was heading to his chair with a plate.

"I teller," he said, and leaned into his snack, a forlorn figure in pajamas on a late afternoon when others were cleaning up from a day's hard work.

But just when she'd almost reached the door, he stumbled on the edge of a rug. The plate flew out of his hand; it cracked on the floor, the knife flying. "Shi, shi, shi!" He'd cut his finger. She ran to the bathroom for a Band-Aid, found one. "You're fine, you're alive," she said, sticking it on him. "I've done that a hundred times."

But it didn't help. He'd made the mess, he was furious with himself. When she'd finished, swept up the pieces, placed a new plate of cheese on his lap, he wouldn't look at her. "I'll wait," she said, "till Moira comes."

It was the wrong thing to say. "No, no! I okay, dammit. Go!" He waved her off.

At the door of the pickup she hesitated, thought of that letter to Rufus; wheeled about, strode over to the barn. What *had* Opal said in that note? She didn't want Rufus running after Adam; after all, the girl could be lying. Opal had worked on a ranch, she could have been the one to slash the cows. Adam may have been right after all. Emily loved the boy; Ruth had to support her daughter, didn't she?

"Rufus?" she called. She'd catch him before he read the letter, warn him. "Rufus?"

"Not here. In a heat about something." It was Don Yates, cleaning out the cider press.

"It wouldn't be a letter he'd read—does he have a message box here or something?"

Don indicated a scarred desk in a far corner. "Yeah, he was reading something. Seemed awful excited about it." He shrugged. "Your guess is as good as mine. Hey," he called after her, "try some cider? Freshly brewed!" He was holding out a paper cup.

But she couldn't speak, her heart was beating in her throat. She ran out, knocking over a bag of apples. And collided with her daughter.

"Mother! I've been looking everywhere for you. I called and Mr. Earthrowl answered the phone. But I couldn't understand a word he said." It was the new bull calf, she said breathlessly, it was sick or dying, she didn't know which. She'd called Dr. Greiner, but he couldn't come right then, he was in East Branbury, treating a calf with the scours. "You have to come right now, Mom. Sharon's holding the fort. And she's got to get home to the baby, the sitter has to leave. What were you doing in the apple barn, anyway?"

"Came to see Rufus," Ruth managed to say, but Emily was hurrying her back to the pickup. She'd have to go. She needed that bull calf, needed the money it would bring in. Whatever Opal had said in the note—well, they'd have to work it out, Rufus and Adam, she couldn't be held responsible for the world's ills.

"Aren't you coming?" she asked the girl, but Emily shook her head. "I did my chores. Tim's coming to do the milking. I'll be home in an hour to help with supper."

Which meant, Ruth thought, she was going to see Adam. Something welled up in her throat. "Don't—" she started to say, but then realized she was talking to the air, Emily was already on her way.

Maybe it was just as well. Emily's presence would soften Rufus, postpone any false accusations. If indeed that's where Rufus had gone. And if Adam was even there!

Sixty-seven

Emily was smiling as she walked down the path to the bunkhouse. It was late afternoon, cool but sunny: She loosened her bandanna. She was content: She'd made amends with her mother, she was convinced it was Opal who was the liar. She didn't believe for a minute that Adam would do anything so cruel as to poison apples, tamper with tractor brakes. She waved at Derek as she passed by the Jamaicans' bunkhouse. He was sitting on the steps, talking to the goat. Soon, though, there wouldn't be a goat. The harvest supper was in five days; the goat would be curried stew.

"How can you do that to this poor goat?" she said. "Make a beef stew instead, Derek." Then, thinking of her mother's sick bull calf, she said, "No, chicken stew." Chickens were dumb. Vic's chickens ran in silly squawky circles. "Please, Derek, chicken stew?"

But Derek only laughed, his gold earring glittering in the sun. "Trad-i-tion," he said. "Jamaica trad-i-tion. No harvest widout curry goat. You like it, you see, missy." And he tossed an apple core at her. She ducked, smiling. She heard the other men chattering inside the bunkhouse, preparing supper. As she moved on, Derek called to her.

"Where you go? See dat boy? Adam? Better wait. Rufus on his

way dere, I seen him, awful mad 'bout someting. You wait. Let dem argue it out."

She stood still a moment. Something balled up in her chest: fear. Opal, she thought, doing her dirty work, telling lies. Angering Rufus, turning him against Adam. She could hear them already, inside her head: Rufus accusing, Adam defending himself. She pushed on, but her feet were slower than her mind. Afraid of what she'd hear? Oh, the power of rumors, suspicion. She shook her head free of them. But the voices held on. Her feet plodded along, up the path to the bunkhouse, where a half-open window let out quarreling voices. The voices were real, not just in her head. It seemed they might shatter the glass.

"It was you, you," Rufus was shouting. "Webworms. Fall webworms! Enough to destroy half this orchard! She found them in your car."

"No—no—unless she planted them there!"

"Where'd a girl like that get webworms? Know what they were? Let's go out now. Let's take a look at 'em. Huh? Don't tell me you know nuthin'. You had a key made. For what? T'get into the storage shed? To steal that paraquat? By Jesus, I do the sprayin' around here. Not you. This is my orchard. My granddad's orchard. Everything done right, by God. I want things done right. Then you come with the Roundup—"

"No, no!" Adam was yelling.

But Rufus shouted over his voice. "My apples! My Jamaicans! It was you killed my man Bartholomew. I want the proof now. Unlock that car, damn it, I'm callin' the police. You're a murderer, a murderer!"

Emily pushed through the door. She had to see Rufus. She had to make him see that, no, Adam wasn't a murderer. That whatever it was had been planted by Opal, couldn't he see that? "Rufus," she cried, clutching his elbow as he sprang at Adam. "That's not true!"

A hand thrust her aside. She saw a pruning knife: It gleamed in the glare of sun. "No, Adam, no!" she screamed. But Rufus was down, something gone wrong with his head, his blood pooling on the rough wooden floor, leaking into the cracks. She opened her mouth once more to scream, but nothing came out. She dropped to her knees beside Rufus. "Adam, get help!" But Adam was grabbing her, yanking her out of the bunkhouse, over to his Volvo; she had blood on her shoes. A thornbush caught her; she crashed through it.

"Where, where . . . ?" she mouthed, but he shoved her in, slammed the door; the engine shrieked to life. They careened down a grassy back road. Geese squawked. Apple trees flew by on both sides.

"Montreal," he said. "You got your suitcase?"

"You know I don't!" she cried. "You can't just leave Rufus. Go back, Adam! Why did you do that? Why, Adam?" She was speaking of Rufus, but he was talking about something else as he drove: fast, so fast she found herself clinging to the door handle. She couldn't look at the speedometer. Mechanically, she reached for a seatbelt, but couldn't find it. They raced past the sharp bend where West Street cut in, the old cemetery on the right where her dad's parents were buried; on up to Addison 4-Corners, careening on three wheels, so it seemed, around the curve and out toward the lake, past farms and orchards and falling-down barns.

"Earthrowl," he was saying, "he's the one killed my brother. He's the real murderer. Hounding, hounding Trevor months, years after the accident, letters, phone calls, lawsuit—you wouldn't believe the harassment—long after they moved up here. Till Trevor—he couldn't take it, he—"

Adam coughed, and coughed; mechanically she rubbed his back. The trees were racing past the window, the world was a greenish blue blur, she could only look at Adam, there was blood on the steering wheel. Blood on the bunkhouse floor where Rufus was lying . . . "Adam, go back, we have to go back."

But Adam was talking again, entreating her, trying to make her understand something. "I had to show him, he couldn't do that to Trevor. He had to be punished. It was killing me that he got away with it. Finally I saw how. Saw in the paper about someone spraying Roundup—a friend sent it on, said it might've been an accident. I knew then—knew I'd finish the job. I knew how to pick apples. I had a different last name, he never caught on why I was here. . . ."

She sat frozen to her seat, her hand numb on the door handle. The late sun was in her eyes, the clouds shone like the bright headlights of cars, she was dazed with it. Rufus was right, she thought, and Opal, too: It was Adam all the time.

"All those bad things, Adam: the paraquat, the maggots, those disgusting worms . . . the Roundup spraying last spring?"

"Someone else did the Roundup, I said. Are you listening to me?"

"The paraquat, though. Poisoning the apples. And Bartholomew died, Adam, he died because of what you did. Adam, how could you?"

But Adam was there behind the wheel, nodding, nodding, not smiling, not looking triumphant or anything, just nodding, like it was out of his hands, like he was the instrument of some outer force he had no control over.

"Not the cows, though, Adam, not my mother's cows . . . Say you didn't do that!" But he was humped over the wheel, like he was glued to it, his foot solidly down on the accelerator.

"Adam, stop, stop the car, Adam! I want to get out. I want us to go back. Turn back, Adam, turn back." A sign flashed by: Route 125, they were still on it, it was twisting and turning toward Lake Champlain. The Crown Point Bridge loomed up suddenly through the trees, its steel girders glazed with sun. The lake was a blue blade, knifing northward. "Adam, stop," she screamed. "Let me out!" But he was racing toward the bridge.

Sixty-eight

The barn phone rang and Sharon ran back to pick it up, leaving Ruth with the sick bull calf and her grandson Robbie asking, "Why it won't get up, Nana?" The calf was having convulsions. Doc Greiner was finally on his way. "It's all right, it'll be all right," Ruth told Oprah, knowing it might not be, Oprah would lose the calf no matter what. She imagined her own son destined for slaughter—she shuddered. But it happened in wars, didn't it? What a mad world.

Sharon was standing over her, repeating her name. "Mother! Mother, you'd better talk to Moira. She's sounding hysterical. Something bad . . ."

Things exploded in her head then, everyone wanting her, needing her: Moira's panic on the phone—something about Rufus, an ambulance. Doc Greiner arriving and Oprah butting him, the vet giving a yell, an oath. "She won't let me near the calf. Get her away, Ruth!" Sharon shouting at the toddler to move: "Robbie, out of the barn, you hear me? Mom, my sitter has to leave. The baby—"

To Moira: "I'll be over in a minute, soon as I can." To Sharon, who was pushing the boy out the barn door: "Help me with Oprah. She doesn't want to move. Let's get her in the stanchion. So Doc Greiner . . ."

The doctor, a graying, robust man, overworked but cheerful, his shirt daubed with excrement from the convulsing calf, was poking a needle into the animal's flesh. "It doesn't look good," he said, "not good, but we'll give it the best try."

"I have to get the sitter," Sharon shouted, "then I'll come back. Vic's home," she added, squinting out the door. "Tell him to clean up this mess, put down more hay. That calf has wrecked the place."

Ruth was torn, between calf and orchard. Then realized: Rufus. It was Rufus who was hurt. What had Moira said? Bleeding! She recalled that word now. Rufus, on his way to accuse Adam of something. Of poisoning those apples? And where was Adam? Had he done something to Rufus?

"Doc," she said, "can you hold the fort? I'll get Tim, he'll be in to milk in a couple minutes anyway. Vic's here to help. Sharon'll be back. Maybe Emily." Emily? Where was Emily? What had she seen? Good God. Ruth remembered. Emily was on her way to the bunkhouse. "Get Tim, tell him to get to the barn, on the double," she screamed at Vic, who was running up the steps into the house, schoolbooks banging on his back.

"Mom, I have to pee."

"Get Tim, I said, he's in the east pasture, and pee on the way."

"Jezum." The boy veered off in the direction of the east pasture, unzipping as he ran.

The ambulance was shrieking off as Ruth arrived; she wondered if Colm was in it, on call. But the doors were shut tight, she could see only the shapes of two medics, leaning over what must be Rufus. Was he hurt bad? Was he alive? So many questions . . .

Then Moira was on her, shouting in her ear. "Knifed, unconscious. I don't know the medic, it wasn't your Colm Hanna." Moira looked like a madwoman, her hair wild in the wind, she was hissing out the words. "I haven't said anything to Stan, I don't want him to know. Not yet."

"Who did it? Who hurt Rufus?"

"We don't know who, but it was in the bunkhouse where Adam Golding lives. The twins found Rufus. Adam's gone. What other conclusion can I come to?" She stroked back a mass of snarled hair; there was blood on her hands. She held them out, looked at them blankly, as if they were a stranger's gloves she'd pulled on by mistake. "The police are in the bunkhouse now. They seemed upset we'd moved him, but my God, we had to get help!"

"Emily," Ruth said. "Have you seen Emily?"

And Moira looked at her blankly.

Sixty-nine

Colm was at the mortuary, trying to get through to Ruth, to tell her they had Wickham, alias Turnbull, alias Chris Christ; he was pleased with the litany of names he recited in his head. They'd caught up with Wickham in Malone, New York, at a Burger King—a nurse from the Planned Parenthood clinic had spotted him, phoned the police. He was wanted in that town, too, for disrupting the flow of traffic into a clinic, knocking down a male nurse, giving him a concussion. They were investigating other complaints: a clinic in Birmingham, Alabama, another in Buffalo, a wounded doctor in Canada—the list was long. At Colm's request they'd impounded the man's Blazer—they found it at the local Chevrolet dealer's with a busted alternator; Wickham had taken off in a blue Beetle with Vermont plates. They'd brought him back to Branbury.

First the line was busy, then Vic answered. "We've got a sick calf here, I'm helping the vet."

"But where's your mother? I have some news she'll want to hear. . . . Vic, you still there?"

"Yeah, the vet needs me, I gotta help hold the calf down."

"Your mother, Vic! She's not there?"

"She's gone to the orchard." And the phone went dead.

Immediately it rang again. It was Bertha. "Colm, he took my

car. My little blue Beetle! He said he'd be back, but that was last night, Colm! He won't answer his phone. I have a grange meeting tonight. Can you take me?"

"Sorry, Bertha, I've got an appointment. I mean, right now. Can you ask one of your friends?"

"But I thought you could pick me up after. I'm done by eight-thirty. We could go have a coffee somewhere. I could tell you things about him, Colm. Things you might want to know."

Colm considered. "I'll pick you up, then, Bertha. After. I can't before. You can take a taxi."

"All right, then, Colm." She sounded triumphant. She had the trump card—or was it blackmail? "Nine o'clock, at the grange hall. I'll be waiting, Colm."

"Sure, Bertha." He hung up. It had better be good. He didn't want to hear about the time Wickham-alias-alias had stepped on her feelings.

He pulled on his coat and the phone rang again. This time it was Roy Fallon. He was talking about a Rufus. Colm did a double-take, yanked back his shoulders. "What was the name again, Roy?"

"Rufus. Rufus Barrow, that orchard manager. Thought you'd want to know. He got hurt. They got him in intensive care."

Those high ladders they climbed on to pick the apples . . . Colm could never be a picker, he was scared of heights. Jeez.

Fallon said, "A knife wound, a jagged pruning knife, in the throat. We have it now, we're checking fingerprints. An impulse stabbing, I'd say—in the bunkhouse—or the guy wouldn't have left it behind like that. That is, I assume it was a guy."

"Jesus Maria." Colm felt his legs go numb, the receiver stuck to his ear. That's why Ruth was there. What about Emily? The place would be in pandemonium. "Thanks, Roy. I'm on my way."

Seventy

Emily wasn't in the apple barn. She wasn't by the pond, she didn't answer to Ruth's shouts. Derek had seen her, he said, spoken to her "just . . . short time ago. Bad ting, bad ting going on here," he kept repeating.

"Then what, Derek? Where did she go?" Ruth demanded, out of breath from running, out of voice, feeling her skin on fire; and he pointed down the path that led to the second bunkhouse. Her breath quit, she heard herself gasping. Moira grabbed her elbow, to steady her. "It doesn't mean—not necessarily that—"

But Ruth was already past the crime scene tape, forcing her way into the bunkhouse, struggling with the detective who was holding her back. "Lady, lady, you can't go in there."

Ruth couldn't speak, couldn't explain; it was Moira who had to do the talking. "Her daughter was with that boy, that Adam, the one who we think might—might have . . . attacked Rufus. We don't know why."

"Oh, we do, we do know why." Ruth had found her breath. "It was because—because of something Opal told him, or wrote him, accusing Adam of doing all—all that's been going on. . . ." She swept her arms wide to encompass the orchard.

"No! Opal?" said Moira. "I felt when she first arrived she

meant trouble. It's what that bird was trying to tell us. But we didn't listen. . . ."

"Bird?" said the officer, raising an eyebrow. He stood firm, a solid wall. The women couldn't go in. Not until the men inside had every print, every fiber, every possible clue to what had happened. He was trying to be patient, he had a daughter himself, he understood. "Please," he said, the final rejection.

Ruth gave a shout. She saw something caught in a bush at the far corner of the bunkhouse. Something bright green with red stripes, unmistakable. It was Emily's bandanna, the one she wore for picking. It had been a present from Wilder Unsworth, her high school boyfriend. She treasured it, even though they weren't seeing each other very often. She snatched it up, waved it at the officer's face. "It's my daughter's, it's Emily's. She was pulled this way, toward his car. She would have picked it up if she'd had time, she's a careful person."

"He kept his car here," Moira said. "Adam and the Butterfields. But . . ."

The parking space was empty. "He's got her," Ruth cried, "he's got her in his car—against her will, oh, I know it, she'd never leave that bandanna behind."

Colm was suddenly beside her, running ahead, shouting back, "He peeled off, all right, you can see the tire marks in the grass. They went out that way." He pointed to a grassy road.

"It's a tractor road," Moira explained. "It winds through the orchard and exits on Route 125."

"Why haven't you gone after him?" Ruth accused the officer. "After his Volvo? This all happened—how long ago—a half hour, at least? Longer? They could be in New York State by now, over the bridge, headed toward Montreal, Albany, California—I don't know! He knifed a man, he could do it again. To save his hide."

Ruth was out of control now, she knew it, the blood was boiling in her head, her knees, her toes. This was her daughter, Emily, he'd taken. She wanted to grab the officer, stamp out his confounded patience.

Colm patted her arm. "All right, all right, Ruthie."

But the officer was motioning her down, the way you'd tell a dog to lie down, stop barking. "Ma'am, the call's out, Vermont and New York. They know about the Volvo. One of the young men told us. They'll find him. Calm down, now."

"I can't just stand here, I can't just wait," Ruth told Colm, and, against his protests, ran back toward her pickup. A policeman swore softly as she rammed past; her boots squashed a fallen apple. She glanced at the farmhouse as she ran and saw Opal's white face pressed against the window. Was the girl satisfied now with her mischief? She picked up an apple, threw it at the image. It missed and hit the porch rocker.

Now it was Colm who was in the way, he was pushing her toward the passenger seat. "I'll drive," he said, "I don't want you running me into the lake."

"The lake," she hollered. "We'll follow 125, head for the lake. For the bridge. He might've killed a man, he knew it, he'll be half crazed, want to get out of the state. I feel that way myself. He'll be driving fast. Too fast."

"Get in," Colm ordered, holding open the dented door. She obeyed, and they were off, heading past the bunkhouse again, past the angry geese, their wings wide and flapping, down the rutted tractor road toward Route 125. A flock of starlings flew up in the air like black leaves. Already it was dusk. An apple bounced off the top of the car; its juice splattered on the windshield. She stared ahead mutely, while the apple world spun by.

Seventy-one

"Where are we going?" Emily shouted above the noise of her heart, the engine, the wind that was shrieking through the crack in her window.

He didn't answer, and she cried again, "Adam, where are you taking us? Not Montreal, Adam. Not to Montreal . . ."

The wind howled; the Volvo sounded like it would split in two if they went any faster. The speedometer was climbing past eighty. "Adam, stop, I want to get out. Adam, stop the car!"

But he was talking again. "It was murder," he cried, his voice high and scratchy with his anguish. "Earthrowl never quit. Letters in the papers, calls every day—he hounded the police. He hounded Trevor. He filled him with guilt, he wanted him in jail. He wanted him dead, that's what he wanted. And . . . and . . ." His voice cracked horribly. "He got what he wanted."

"But now, Adam, where are we going now?"

"To the ends of the earth," he yelled. "The very ends. And then we'll stop."

Emily hung on, her hand frozen to the handle.

The road turned sharply to the right, following the curve of lake; a lumber truck loomed up in their lane. Emily screamed, and Adam swerved, veered off right into a grove of bushes. The car crashed crazily among them and slowed.

"Turn back, back," Emily shouted.

Adam yelled, "Get out, then, goddamn it, get out. This is your chance," and his right arm pushed her toward the door. It sprung open. "Get," he yelled. "Get out, leave me alone." The car was still moving, through the scrub, out toward the road again. She tumbled out, fell, banging an elbow, twisting an ankle, stunned. "Adam, sto-op . . ." But he was back in the road, picking up speed, throwing dust in her face. The dust glittered with sun, it clogged her eyes and nose. She couldn't get up, her leg kept collapsing. She dragged herself over to a stump, hoisted herself up on it, held on to a branch, then hobbled out toward the lakefront. She could see the bridge, now and then the Volvo as it raced in and out of the leafy curves. Somewhere a siren shrilled. And another . . .

"Ad-am," she shrieked after him, knowing he couldn't hear her, but screaming anyway. "Ad-am, come ba-ack!"

Then, just before he reached the bridge, just before the Chimney Point site, in a boat launching area that dipped off to the lake, he veered left. For a moment the Volvo was out of sight; then it reappeared and plunged into the blue void. She screamed again and someone came running toward her. "Help you, miss?"

"Help him!" she shouted, pointing at the car. The man followed her eyes, her shaking finger. "Jes-us and Mary," he said. He crossed himself as they watched the Volvo drift out into the lake, float there a moment like a giant white buoy, and then slowly, slowly sink, until the surface was a mass of bubbles, like the slow descent of a white whale.

She dragged herself forward. She could hardly see the lake for her blurry eyes. When her vision cleared, she'd see Adam, she was sure of it, he would have got out! He was a good swimmer, wasn't he? But the man was at her back again.

"Too late," the man said. "She's gone, that white car. The driver in it. What in hell anybody want to do that for?"

She couldn't tell him. She only knew it was his brother's car, he'd told her that. The one the Earthrowl girl had drowned in. Now there were two drownings. She sank down on her knees, and the world reeled.

Seventy-two

Ruth swooped down on the battered-looking girl they found squatting on the ground by the lakefront, her back against a rock. A man in striped overalls stood nearby, with a thin angular woman. "She been like that a good thirty minutes," the man said, looking anxious. "Me and the missus tried to get her into the house, she won't come. She just stares out at the lake like that white car would come up again, drive away over the bridge."

"In the lake?" Colm asked. "A white car?"

Ruth didn't hear what the man said because she was kneeling down by Emily, wringing her hands, hugging her. "Thank God you're safe," she murmured. "Thank God." Behind her she heard the men talking, she caught the words "drove her right in . . . floating . . . sinking . . . a young man, she said."

Ruth caught the drift. "Oh, Emily, oh, Em, love," she said. "I'm sorry, I'm so sorry. But he caused a man's death—maybe two men."

Emily broke down then; whether it was for Rufus or for Adam, Ruth didn't know. She just kept hugging Emily while Colm knelt down beside her; she could feel his hand on her right shoulder, stroking.

"But he let me out of the car," Emily said finally, her first words. "He made me get out. I thought he was going over the bridge, into New York. I thought he'd go to Montreal. But he swerved off, down to that boat landing. He kept . . . going. . . ." She sobbed into her mother's shoulder. Ruth rocked and rocked her. She could hear the lake lapping, the gulls crying as they wheeled overhead. The sun was almost down behind the Adirondacks; the sky was a brilliant pink.

"I'll check in with the others. They'll want to drag the lake, pull up that car," Colm said, and his hand released her shoulder. She nodded. Of course they'd want to do that. Someone would want a body to bury. The boy had a father, a stepmother, Emily had said.

"Don't hate him," Emily pleaded, her face dampening her mother's shirt. "He had reasons for what he did to the orchard. It was wrong, I know, but he had reasons."

Ruth supposed he did. She'd hear about them later. Every killer had his reasons, she supposed, his motives: jealousy, envy, an abusive childhood. But so did other people, ordinary people, who wouldn't go about poisoning apples—just because they wanted to avenge a wrong.

"But he let you go, he let you out of the car," Ruth said, "and I'll thank him for that. With all my heart." It was her turn now to weep into Emily's tangled hair.

They sat together, not speaking, for a long time, and then, when Colm came back, waving off a police car, they helped Emily up and into the green pickup, where Ruth sat in the back with Emily, and Colm drove, carefully around the curves, as though he had a basket of freshly picked apples in the backseat.

Seventy-three

Bertha. Colm had almost forgotten in the madness of the day. He was to pick her up at nine at the grange hall. She was going to tell all. Or tell something, he didn't know what. He could think of a dozen places he'd rather be—most particularly at the Willmarth farm. But Ruth had Emily to comfort. He wasn't going to intrude on mother and daughter. The girl was back home after a brief visit to Dr. Colwell, who'd found bruises and scratches, a sprained ankle, but nothing broken. "It's the head and heart that will need watching for a time," the doctor had told Ruth, looking hard at her. Colwell was a wise old fellow, Colm thought.

Colm himself would like to be part of that head and heart watch, but the time wasn't ripe yet. At least Ruth didn't think so. Well, he'd waited a quarter of a century; he could keep waiting.

Bertha was there on the steps. She was dressed in orange: orange hat, orange coat, orange stockings. If it rained, he warned her, they'd be squeezing her for the juice.

"That's not funny, Colm," she said. "Besides, the color is tangerine. Not orange. Cassandra and I each bought an outfit. She was wearing hers the night she was killed, poor thing."

He made a mental note of that fact, ushered her into his car. He'd take her home, stop in for ten minutes, whatever it took to squeeze (he grimaced at the word) a little more information out of her.

"I thought we might have a drink," she said, "talk a little."

"You're drinking now, Bertha? Didn't I hear that you and your prayer ladies were picketing a liquor store? The night of the, um, accident?"

She leaned close to him, he could smell the perfume, it was nauseating. "I've changed, Colm. I've left those Messengers. I mean, it was such a lovely idea: Saint Dorothea and the apples and all."

"I never quite understood why Turnbull—or whatever—chose that name Messengers of Saint Dorothea. Who was she anyway?" They were almost at Bertha's house. The perfume was getting to him. At least he could sit across from her in the living room.

"Well, you see, they were going to execute her, Colm. She was a Christian—back in the, um, third, fourth century. This pagan Theoph—Theo—well, something like that, was going to cut off her head! Can you imagine how awful? And he asked her to send him back some fruit from the Paradise she believed in—you know, Heaven? There is a Heaven, Colm, there is!" She put a hand on his arm, he almost drove up on a curb. "You must believe it, Colm."

"Finish the story, please, Bertha."

"Yes, well, suddenly a boy appeared—no one had ever seen him before! And he carried a basket with three red apples—apples so beautiful they looked like rubies. 'Give these to Theo—to that man,' Dorothea said, 'and tell him there are more in Paradise where I hope to meet him.' "

"Uh-huh." They were at her house now. But she wasn't getting out yet, she wanted to finish the story.

"Well, Colm, they did it. They lopped her head right off. Unh!" She drew a finger across her neck, her head jerked forward. For a minute he thought she'd had a heart attack. Her head swung back up. "And you know what, Colm?"

"What?"

"He turned Christian, that Theo man. He realized that life on earth was only a prelude to eternal life in Paradise. And that Paradise would be reached through the doorway of death." She grinned at him triumphantly. "That's what Christ told us, Colm. That's what we were counting on, that Paradise he was going to lead us to." She put a hand on his sleeve. "Oh, Colm, what happened? He seemed so sincere. We all believed in him. We prayed with him, we did all those protests with him. And then he . . . he took my car! He disappeared without a word! Someone said he'd killed a man. I'm so disillusioned. Profoundly, Colm, profoundly."

"Why did you pray at the Earthrowls' orchard? What did that have to do with this Saint Dorothea? Was it the apples?" He sat back in the seat. He'd have all this out now, not go into her house after all. She might lock him in or something, he didn't want to chance it.

"I think it was that particular orchard," she said, "because of Cassandra. Oh, that godless man, that Earthrowl—running down Cassandra! Cassandra, in her lovely tangerine coat."

"You were praying in that orchard before she was killed."

"Oh, we were? The sequence of events escapes me, Colm. It's been so traumatic, everything. And someone stabbing Rufus. Oh, I heard about that, they were all talking about it at grange. Rufus was one of us, Colm, did you know that?"

He didn't. "He came to your meetings? Your, um, prayer sessions?"

"Oh no, he just belonged, that's all. He was Cassandra's relative, you know—some kind of relationship. She got him to join. You see, she and Rufus planned to turn that orchard into a Paradise on earth, the two of them. Cassandra told me that."

"They wouldn't sell the apples, pick them? They'd just let them hang on the trees?"

"Oh no, silly." She punched him on the arm and he cringed. "They'd still sell them and all, but not the way they do now. They wouldn't have those men there, picking, those Jamaicans. Oh, Rufus liked them all right, they were good pickers, he said. But still, he'd prefer *American* pickers, the way his granddaddy ran it. And then have it partly a pick-your-own. Like you and me, Colm, and other Vermonters. It would be a kind of church, an outdoor cathedral. An earthly path to the true Paradise."

She sighed heavily, as though a black cloud were coming over her mind. "But then Cassandra decided she didn't want the whole orchard for apples. That's where she and Rufus and Christ all disagreed. She wanted half of it to turn it into houses like the other farms they'd buy up. She needed the money for other things."

"The daughter?"

"Yes, that daughter of hers, for one. Oh, we were all so upset when Cassandra tried to take away part of our Paradise. Even Rufus was! He'd become Pete's partner so he'd be sure nothing happened to that orchard. Oh, he loves that orchard. And that's why we were all so upset when Ruth started to interfere. It's really awful, Colm, the way she does that. Interferes with other people's lives."

Colm cleared his throat, looked at her. The pot calling the kettle black? She smirked, plowed on. "Well, what business did Ruth have anyway, poking around in that orchard, asking questions? Rufus didn't like it. Christ didn't like it. So he . . ." She hesitated, coughed.

"So he what, Bertha? He didn't like it, so he went over and slashed her cows, is that it?"

"Oh no, no—I mean, I don't know that. He asked me to . . . well, I'd told him about Ruth's planting that hemp. I mean, I saw the tags. Hemp is marajuana, Colm. It's illegal! Christ said why didn't I go and pull it up, God would want me to."

"So you did. You pulled up all that hemp she painstakingly planted. Took a whole day out of her life to put in the ground and help make ends meet for the farm."

"I did, Colm." She hesitated, gave a delicate cough. "Wouldn't you?"

"No, Bertha. I wouldn't. I definitely would not. And you're not planning to do anything with that hemp? Show it around a little?"

"Oh no. Would I want to hurt my own sister-in-law?"

Colm could say something, but he held back. "You're sure it wasn't, um, your minister who slashed Ruth's cows, tampered with the tractor? She might have been killed, you know. One of the children. Vic?"

Bertha gasped, pulled out a hankie, noisily blew her nose. "Oh no, I didn't know about any tractor. I didn't, Colm! I didn't have anything to do with that! I couldn't imagine our Christ doing such a thing. He loves children. Why do you think he's so against killing babies? I only pulled up the hemp, that's all I did. I promise, Colm, that's all." She was sniveling now. The perfume was making him sick. He ran around and opened her door; he had to get her out of the car.

"You're coming in," she said, climbing out, planting a shiny pump firmly on the grass. "I was counting on it, I have wine, Colm. I've changed, I told you. I'm going back to my old church. They drink wine there for communion. I have apple wine, Colm. I bought it, 'specially." She giggled. "For you, Colm."

He sighed. "Another time. I have to go now, Bertha. It's been a very, very long day. A lot of things have happened. Things you don't even know about."

"What? What things, Colm? Have they found out who hurt Rufus? He was one of us, Colm. We need to know." She pulled at his arm.

"Listen to the late news," he said, and ushered her up the walk to her door. Back at the car, he left the windows wide open. He didn't want to smell of perfume when he got back to the mortuary. Perfume didn't mix with formaldehyde.

Seventy-four

Moira carried Opal's suitcase over to the bus, where the driver swung it down into the bottom. "You're sure you don't want to stay for the harvest supper? Your last chance," she murmured, knowing the girl was set on going home. Opal had hardly said a word to anyone since Adam's drowning.

They had pulled up the white Volvo—the only living things inside were a thousand hairy webworms, crawling about in a sealed container. Adam's body was swollen and blue, his hands still clutching the wheel as though he would drive through the water into some other world—to find his brother, perhaps, for Emily had told her mother the whole story now, and Ruth told Moira. "Because you have to know," Ruth had said. "Whatever you want to tell Stan about the brother's suicide or not is up to you."

She didn't say it accusingly, as if it were Stan's fault that this terrible sequence of deaths had followed his own harassment—a harassment that Moira, wrapped in her own grief, had been largely unaware of. But the deaths had begun with Adam's brother, Trevor, hadn't they, driving too fast, drinking, killing her child? What would a jury, a psychologist, say about cause? It was as though Adam, by drowning, had atoned for Carol's death—the final irony. How strange life was.

Stan would know about Rufus and Adam. But Adam's reasons for damaging the orchard? She'd have to think about that. She had time. The harvest supper was tomorrow night. Then she'd decide.

Opal stood behind her, her hair frizzing about her face, her red sweater pulled tight over her breasts, the Guatemalan bag thrown over a shoulder. Should she hug the girl? After all, Opal was a niece. She was such a confused girl! Yet without her mischief they might never have known the cause. Opal had been a catalyst, one of the Fate sisters. Although the girl didn't look at it quite that way, she supposed.

"Got your ticket?" Moira asked. She'd bought the girl's ticket with her own money; she hadn't wanted to ask Annie May. Her sister-in-law had been in a tizzy anyway, when Moira called to say they were shipping Opal back. "Lindley needs the rest. Opal won't give it him. She's always after him about what he does."

About being a doctor? Moira had wondered. But what was wrong with that?

The girl just nodded, and sniffled a little. She stood there a moment and Moira put out a hand, squeezed her arm. "I'm glad to hear your dad's better. You can go back to a normal life now."

"Normal?" the girl said. "With my father going back to doing abortions? Oh yes, Mama told me. Already he's talking about going back. I hate it that he's doing that! I've lost friends over it. I've lost a boyfriend. Papa's on a list. He'll get us all killed. Maybe even you, you're his sister-in-law," she said meaningfully.

Moira was stunned. She hadn't known that, about the abortions. Did Stan know? Probably. It was one of those things he wouldn't want to talk about. Annie May was Catholic. Of course there would be dissension in the family. Annie would be worried sick.

"He's a brave man, your father," she told Opal. "He's doing what he thinks is right." She realized she still had her hand on the girl's arm, and Opal hadn't brushed it off. "You take care, now. You come again."

"Up here?" Opal said. "Never. I never want to set foot in that orchard again. Never. Never!" She wrenched away from Moira's arm and swung her red-stockinged legs up onto the bus. When it pulled away out into Route 7, Opal's face was set resolutely forward. For a mad moment, with her red sweater and red bow on the back of her hair, Opal resembled the cardinal that had tormented them for so long. Moira half expected the girl to turn and hurl her thin body at the window.

Back home, Moira found Stan on his feet, painfully facing a detective. He wouldn't be caught sitting down, in spite of his condition. She wanted to run and hug him, tell him she was his partner, she was on his side no matter what they said he'd done, no matter what he *had* done. When she put out a hand to steady him, though, he shook his head. He wanted to face this alone.

For a time she didn't understand what the officer was saying. Something about the Blazer, about fibers. Tangerine fibers, the color of the coat Cassandra was wearing, a match for it. They were found on the front bumper of the Blazer. Their Blazer, the one Stan was driving the night the woman was killed? What other Blazer could he be talking about? She stood closer to Stan, she could feel his body trembling beside hers. But he stood there resolutely. And on his own. He wasn't touching the walker.

"Sit down, sit," the detective said. His name was "Bump, Orrin Bump, ma'am. I'm sorry it's taken so long. But we have that man in custody. We have his Blazer."

What Blazer was he talking about, for heaven's sake? She didn't understand. Out of politeness, she offered a cup of coffee. Coffee before handcuffs. She shivered. He wouldn't do that, would he? Take a sick man into custody? Stan was sitting down now—after, that is, the detective was seated. Independent to the last.

"No coffee, ma'am, for me. I'm on my way in five minutes. It was Chief Fallon sent me to tell you the good news. One of those apples, though, I might take that. The wife's always after me about eating fruit. You know. That food pyramid or something?" He smiled at the absurdity of a food pyramid.

Good news, he'd said? What good news? She passed him the fruit bowl. "These are Red Russets, that's what they're picking now. This is the last day of picking. The Jamaicans go home Saturday. Tomorrow night's the harvest supper. Next week your wife can come and pick drops, though."

She was talking too much. The officer was smiling. Why was he smiling? Stan's mouth was hanging open, as if it were a moment of discovery. "Is tha' tha' min-ster's Blazah?" Stan said. "His Blazah ran over tha' woma?"

"Yes, sir," Detective Bump said. He turned to Moira. "As I was explaining to your husband before you came in, it was a Blazer, like yours, only black, a year older. Same brand of tires. But belonged to that minister, the one with the aliases, Arnold Wickham his real name. We've got him in custody, but not for long. He's wanted in five states. The only thing here is, well, we can't prove if he was the one driving. He says not. Says he let some of his church members drive—now and then, you know. So . . ." He bit into the apple, murmured his pleasure through appled teeth.

It was finally coming together. Moira took a bite of the Russet she'd been squeezing in her hand. The flesh was firm and sweet, it gave her succor. "You mean," she said, choosing, chewing, her words—she had to be sure everything was clear—"that it wasn't Stan's vehicle at all that hit that woman—it was that minister's? And the fibers you found that matched the coat that woman was wearing were on the minister's front bumper? Which means that Stan"—she glanced at her husband; was he frowning, after all this good news?—"is cleared?"

"Yeth, ma'am," the detective said through his apple. He was standing now, offering to shake Stan's hand. But Stan's hands were clutching the walker, his legs failing him. "Gotto proo it," he was arguing, "proo is tha man, tha minster dri-ing. Oh course he dri-ing!"

Bump looked at Moira for interpretation.

"Stan says of course it would have been the minister driving. It was his car. It was full of women. Haven't you asked them?"

He had, he said. "Every female member. Actually there were two men among the members, but we don't have the names. The women say they don't remember who was driving. They say he'd let others drive the car to pick up signs, that sort of thing." He paused, swallowed the mouthful of apple. "But ma'am, sir, we've got him on ten other counts. He'll be punished, you can be sure of that. He's up for murder on one of the counts, if we can prove he shot that doctor down in Birmingham. We know he wounded a Canadian doctor. He goes on trial there next month. He'll get his comeuppance."

"Goto proo it," Stan insisted. "Proo he wa dri-ing!"

Detective Bump blew out his cheeks, waggled his head. He'd brought good news and now they wanted more. More than he could give. "We'll keep trying, you can be sure, sir. We'll try to determine who was driving. That's the best we can do."

At the door he looked to Moira for help. "We've questioned every active member," he said. "No one will talk. I don't know what more we can do. At the least he was an accessory to the fact." He had the apple core in his hand; she wondered if he wanted to go home and plant it. "We can't even call it homicide, you know, ma'am, it could have been an accident. She could have run out, sudden-like, into the road and the driver didn't see."

"But she was struck from behind—the autopsy determined that. And the car wouldn't be going too fast in that parking lot—it could have stopped for a woman passing. It had to be deliberate. Well, keep trying," she said, and held out her hand for the apple core. He smiled, and put it in his pocket. He didn't want to trouble her.

"Thank you anyway," she said, "for coming to tell us," and he took her outstretched hand.

When he left, her palm was full of apple seeds. She took it for a good omen.

Seventy-five

It was time, Moira decided, to talk to Stan. He'd had good news, he might as well hear the bad. "Sit down, Stan," she said. "I want to tell you about Adam Golding. About why he did this to us. Not that what he did excused anything, oh, not at all!"

"The poin'," he said, "get to the poin'."

So she would—she did, and quickly. "He hanged himself," she told Stan. "That boy, Trevor, hanged himself. Adam told Emily Willmarth that. Trevor was his half-brother, you see. I never knew that, did you? That Trevor hanged himself?" Stan's shocked face told her that he didn't. "He was young, Stan, and full of remorse, hurt, guilt—oh, I'm sure of that! He loved Carol, that's what Adam told Emily. He loved our Carol. We have to . . ." She stopped. She was going to say, *We have to forgive, not persecute*, but Stan knew that. Deep in his heart, he knew it. He was thinking about it now, she could see from his tortured face, what he'd done: the harassment, the lawsuit. Keeping the boy away from the funeral, she remembered that, too. Stan had made a phone call. . . .

"I'll get us both a cup of hot chocolate," she said. "It's chilly out there today!" She wouldn't say any more unless Stan brought it up. But he shook his head at the mention of chocolate; turned away, head hanging. He needed to be alone, she knew that. He needed to think. He had all the pain he could handle for now. His orchard damaged, the stroke, his head man in intensive care, and the shock of hearing about the suicides, his role in them . . .

She watched him shuffle off toward his window seat. He dropped heavily into it, put his head in his hands. She sipped her hot chocolate. He sat with his thoughts for a long, long time. She scrubbed the kitchen floor, ran the dishes through the dishwasher. Finally the house was quiet, the cardinal was outside with his lady cardinal at the feeder. The Butterfield twins passed by the window with a large crate of apples. The crate tipped and an apple fell out. "Hey!" Stan stood up with a shout.

"Wano ge dress," he told Moira, "go out ina orshar. Haf to, wi Rufa gone . . ."

"Then go. Go, they need you," she said.

It was the last day of picking. The boss should be in charge. Both bosses, she decided, and she stuck a feed cap on her disheveled hair, pulled the visor tightly down on her forehead. She'd be ready when Stan was.

Seventy-six

After school on Friday Emily got off the school bus at Seymour Street, near her sister's apartment. Tonight was the harvest supper, she had to make a salad to share with the others. But first she had to see Sharon. She had to talk to her, try to straighten out things in her head, come to terms with them. But, as usual, Sharon was racing about the place, boiling applesauce for the baby girl, changing the toddler's diaper. "He has no interest whatsoever in the potty," she complained. She held up a soiled diaper. "The portable potty," she described the diaper. "For boys on the go."

"Sharon," said Emily, easing into a chair with her bandaged ankle. "I need to talk."

"Stinky, stinky," Sharon told Robbie, and the boy grinned and ran away, bare-bottomed. Sharon chased him with a clean diaper.

"I need to talk. Please, Sharon. I need your help."

"Just a min," Sharon said. "I want to hear, I really do, we're in a bit of a mess at the moment."

Sharon changed the diaper and the child sprang away, ran to the TV, and turned it on and off, on and off. Sharon shrugged. "I give up. Let him break the damn thing." She put her hands on Emily's shoulders. "Look, Emily, I know it's hard for you. I know you had feelings for that guy. I saw you together one time downtown, first at Amigo's, and then going into the Alibi. You didn't know I was there. What'd you use, a fake ID? That wasn't Pepsi-Cola you were drinking."

"Sharon, I'm not here to listen to a lecture. I need to know why he did it, why he drove into the lake like that."

"He was scared, that's all. Scared shitless. He couldn't face the bars—I mean the steel ones. A life in prison. Maybe he couldn't face his family. Have you met them?"

"No. His father came to Vermont after they dredged up the car, took Adam's body back to Connecticut. He didn't want to talk to us."

"Of course not. Terrible, what his son did. And then driving into the lake like that. My God! Maybe Adam had a death wish. It happens. It was lousy, that's all, for all of you." Sharon pulled the child away from the TV. "Enough, Robbie. Here, play with your telephone." Upstairs the baby girl was waking from her nap, screaming for "Mama, Mama."

Emily clomped upstairs behind her sister. "But he had me, Sharon. He loved me, he told me so. The night we—we were together."

Sharon wheeled about on the stairs. "You slept with him? I thought Wilder was your man. My God, Emily, you hardly knew Adam!"

"Don't get all moral on me, Sharon, I was in love with him. I don't sleep around. Wilder and me, we never once—I mean, not all the way. But Adam was different. I loved him, Sharon."

At the landing Sharon took her sister's hands. "I didn't know that, Em. Hey, I didn't know it was that far gone. Oh, sweetie . . . But you don't love him now, do you? I mean, we've got a heavy issue here. Em, you have to let it go."

The baby's cries increased in volume and Sharon released her sister. "Come tonight, okay? Around nine o'clock? When the kids are in bed, we can talk. Okay, Em?"

"Okay."

Emily left Sharon's place with the question burning in her chest. Did she love Adam now? Could you love someone who'd caused a man's death? Stabbed another man and then drove away? What if they hadn't crashed into the bushes, slowing the car so she could get out? Would he have driven her with him, into that cold lake?

What was it like, she wondered, to drown . . . ?

Out in the street a boy roared past on a motorcycle, his red hair bushed out under the black helmet.

"Oh, Adam," she whispered. "Why did you do it?" Bartholomew's kind, wrinkly face flashed into her mind's eye; then Rufus, lying bleeding on the bunkhouse floor; then Moira Earthrowl, struggling to survive a daughter's death, an orchard's ruin—the white apple flesh bruised and brown from worms and maggots.

And suddenly she felt betrayed—as though a handsome prince had opened his arms to her, but once she was inside his embrace, he'd turned into a raging, avenging beast.

The motorcycle disappeared around a bend, but long afterward, while she stood there on the sidewalk, she could hear the earsplitting grind of its engine in her head.

Seventy-seven

Colm was getting nowhere in his interview with Wickham. The man was full of false pieties. He was actually proud of what he'd done: stalking a Canadian doctor, shooting him in the leg; "saving" (as he termed it) women heading into Planned Parenthood clinics. "I wouldn't so much as offer a handkerchief," he declared, blinking those hard-boiled eyes, "to a wounded provider."

He sat there like a wounded martyr himself, a crucified Wickham. Outside the town jail, where they were holding him before giving him up to authorities in Alabama, five women, true to the end—Bertha among them, the hypocrite!—were praying. Wickham had God on his side: His squared shoulders, the upthrust chin, all declared his righteousness. Right and wrong, absolute and unchanging. Only one shiny black wing tip, fidgeting on the hardwood floor, cast doubt on his probity.

Colm wanted to walk out right then, leave the fellow to the FBI, but he hadn't asked a key question: about the Earthrowl orchard, the April spraying. Adam's father had told police his son was home at that time, not in Vermont at all. Who could have done it, then? Not Rufus, he was sure, who wanted the orchard pristine for his heavenly apples! Colm asked the question. He got an answer half expected, but nevertheless stunning.

"It was simply a matter of substituting the Roundup for the

usual fungicide," Wickham said. "Cassandra did that. She knew the orchard, she and Rufus Barrow had the same grandfather. It was my idea, of course." He smiled his pearly white smile.

"It was for the greater good," he proclaimed. "You might not understand. And you know, don't you, that Earthrowl's brother is a murderer?" When Colm made a sound, he held up a hand. "An abortionist, yes. You didn't know that?" He looked pityingly at Colm in his kelly green corduroys and scuffed boots. "Those of us destined for Paradise will do all in our power toward that glorious end."

"It doesn't matter that people's livelihoods are destroyed in the process, their lives?" Colm thought of Aaron Samuels—out of the coma, yes, but his profession lost, his good health gone.

"Lives? But that wasn't my church. When we saw that other forces were at work—"

"By 'other forces,' you mean another man? Adam Golding: felling trees, spraying more poison, spreading maggots? He worked right into your hands, did he? Did your dirty work for you?"

"God's work, yes. God works in mysterious ways, He—"

"Right," Colm said; he'd go to mass Sunday; he didn't need a sermon today. He had one more question. "Who was driving your Blazer? The night Cassandra was killed?"

Wickham shook his head, he was smooth as black ice. "Cassandra and I had stayed behind to pick up the signs and crosses. There wasn't room in the Blazer—too many church members. We arranged to go back to the church in her car. I wasn't looking to see who was driving mine." He spread his hands to show how magnanimous he was, how trusting.

"You must have seen Cassandra struck, then, if you were standing there; you must have seen the Blazer drive away. Which one of your, um, members would have done that? Would have hit a human being and then driven away like she was some small animal in the road?" Colm was angry now, angry at the man's lack of concern, his cool in the face of tragedy.

"I told the police what I saw," Wickham maintained. He sounded almost bored. "I had gone back into the store to leave pamphlets. When I came out . . . I found Cassandra." He paused, made a steeple out of his hands. "The Lord giveth and the Lord taketh away."

The black wing tip was tapping out a beat now. Colm checked his watch, switched off the tape. He'd had enough of Wickham. The man was sick. Colm was glad he'd be taken away.

Wickham called to him as he started out. "You can lock me up, but you won't stop me," he warned. "There's another soldier ready to take my place. Another soldier of God. We're at war, you see. A war against Satan. A war against sinners like you."

Outside, Colm took in gulps of fresh air.

He smiled to see Honey Fallon swinging along up the walk. She was wearing a pink pantsuit; her hair was in the usual upheaval. "Hi, there," she said. "I sure enjoyed that butterscotch sundae. It stayed with me all day. Look!" She pointed to a stain on her blouse that she'd washed "in vain," she said.

"Honey," Colm asked, "were you in that church Blazer the night Cassandra was killed?"

"Why, sure, I was. You mean before or after she got it?"

"Both. I just saw Wickham, your sainted minister. He claimed he didn't know who was driving."

"Why, honey," said Honey, "it was Rufus, that's who was driving. It was Cassandra called him, made him quit work at five-thirty."

"Whoa. Why didn't you tell me that before? Or tell your husband?"

"But you never asked! Either of you. Anyway, I didn't see anything—except Rufus when he got in the driver's seat. I was in the back—there were eight of us crammed in there, some of us on thin cushions. If someone hit us from the rear—curtains!" She drew an imaginary veil across her face.

"But Rufus didn't stop. No one saw her running out in front of the car?"

"Wee-ell, I heard someone up front holler, felt a bump. Rufus said he'd hit the curb. It was getting dark by then, you know. Then the minister started hollering, claimed Stan Earthrowl had hit her and run. But later Roy said she was hit in the back. That was weird, wasn't it? I suppose she was headed for her car. Well, it's all over now." Honey stifled a yawn. "Golly gee, I was up half the night—Roy snoring? I bought him one of those anti-snore gizmos, he won't wear it, says it pinches his nose. Well, nice to see you, Colm. Glad you guys pinched that devil. Still . . ." She hesitated. "He sure was good-looking. I mean, he could be on TV."

"Oh, he will be. He will be on TV," Colm assured her, and headed toward his car.

"Keep praying, ladies," he told the group of kneeling women as he passed by. "He's going to need your prayers."

"Colm, it's not what you think," Bertha said, getting up with a groan, stumbling after him. "We were praying for Rufus, and then someone drove us here. . . ."

But Colm waved her away.

Seventy-eight

Ruth was fixing a large leafy salad with onion rings and red pepper and ripe red tomatoes out of her own garden for the harvest supper. Emily had promised to do the salad, but the girl had come home from school and gone directly to bed. She wasn't feeling well, she said, her ankle hurt. Ruth sensed it was more mental than physical: the shock of the stabbing, the abduction, the Volvo sinking into the lake. Of course, Emily hadn't gotten completely over that boy. Even killings and suicides couldn't change feelings that quickly. When it was over, this harvest supper, she'd sit down with Emily: They'd have a long talk, mother and daughter.

The phone rang. Things always interfering: with thoughts, with resolves. If she wasn't careful, the time for Emily would slip away. And self-healing could leave scars.

"I'm coming over, Ruthie," Colm said, "just wanted to warn you. I've been invited to the harvest supper. But afterward, I want some time. With you, alone. We need to talk, Ruthie. It's hell living alone, don't you think so? No, don't answer. I won't ask now. I'll be over in ten minutes. Oh, and Ruth? I found out something. It was Rufus driving that Blazer. Yup! It was Honey told me. It was just before she defected. Honey was sitting in the rear, felt a bump, couldn't see what, who it was."

"Oh," Ruth said. "No accident, you think? From what you told me."

"My thought exactly. Great minds? Rufus didn't want his orchard turned into houses. This was his chance. Make it look like an accident."

"Will it stand up in court?"

"We'll have to see, won't we? When he gets out of the hospital. He's gaining, I understand. . . . But those women—some of them must have seen her killed. The ones in the front. Why, you could arrest the whole bunch for collusion, accessories before the fact! They all wanted the orchard for a path to Paradise, right? Hmm. I wonder exactly where Bertha was sitting in that Blazer. Don't make me go back there and ask. Please, Ruthie?"

She laughed. "Okay, relax."

"Oh, and Ruth, they found a small arsenal in Wickham's attic. Guns, knives, explosives. It could have been him slashed your cows. Jeez, I knew there was something else I didn't ask him. But he was responsible for the Roundup spraying last April, Golding took over after that. So Ruthie . . ." His voice got softer. "We can talk afterward? After the harvest supper? About you know what?" He waited; she could hear him breathing. She sighed. "I know, Ruthie. You've got Emily there. See you in ten minutes."

Ruth held the phone, buzzing, in her hand. Everyone wanted time with her, wanted a bite out of her. Who was she, Mother Earth?

"Mom," said Vic, crashing through the kitchen door, "that bull calf is gone! I hoped we could keep him, just this one—I mean, for a little longer. Why'd you get the vet and everything and get him all fixed up if you were going to sell him right off?" He looked at her through huge indignant eyes.

"You say that every time, Vic. You know as well as I, sweetheart, why we had to. We can't have a bull running around here, humping cows. Look, I need celery for this salad. Get it out of the fridge for me, please?"

There was a certain satisfaction in the thought of celery. It was green and crisp and clean, with that leafy ruffle at the end. She cut into a stalk, heard it squeak. When she looked up again, Vic was gone, she heard the TV squalling out in the living room. It drowned out the celery. It softened the memory of the bull calf.

Seventy-nine

Emily needed an ending, and it wasn't the harvest supper. She had to know something. She had to know who slashed her mother's cows, who tampered with the tractor—if it was Adam. If so, it would have been a final violation—of her heart. Adam had said he was sorry about Bartholomew, maybe even Rufus, though he *hadn't* said. It was just the way Rufus had barreled in, accusing him like that. . . . And Adam did have a temper, she'd seen that for herself. But the cows, the tractor brakes, she couldn't imagine him doing that. It would have been like striking . . . her. He wasn't *all* beast, was he? She'd been struggling with her thoughts since his death.

She sat on the porch step. Crimson maple leaves swirled about her head in the soft October wind. Colm Hanna was in the kitchen with her mother, he was helping her pack up a salad, they were on their way to the Earthrowls'. She could hear them talking through the screen door. They were talking about that minister. About Aunt Bertha, who'd pulled up the hemp. Could it have been Aunt Bertha, then, who slashed the cows? Fooled with the tractor? After all, she'd been brought up on this very farm!

She almost smiled. It was muddy in the pasture, the tractor was greasy. Aunt Bertha wouldn't want to soil her shiny pumps. It had to be a man, Colm was saying, her mother agreeing. Maybe

Rufus, her mother said—he'd wanted the orchard for himself, didn't want any interference. And he'd run down that woman, Cassandra, his own relative, her mother said.

"If it was Rufus," she heard Colm say, "how're we going to prove it? Oh, and Fallon says Wickham had an alibi for the night the cows were knifed: He was in Plattsburgh, picketing a health clinic. Most likely it was—"

The step creaked when Emily shifted position, and Colm's voice stopped. She imagined her mother giving him a signal: *Emily's out there. Don't let her hear. Poor Emily.*

She knew what they thought. They thought it was Adam who had slashed the cows, damaged the tractor. He had that knife, she'd heard Colm Hanna say. But he wouldn't hurt the farm where Emily lived, he wouldn't! Still, she had to know.

She hobbled back into the kitchen on her bandaged ankle. The doctor had given her crutches, but she could move faster without them. Her mother and Colm Hanna were talking about her father and his girlfriend now, Colm loved to hear about that relationship; he wanted to marry her mother. Emily had some reservations about that.

"I never remember her name, anyway, Colm, you know that. It's some kind of flower. I don't suppose she used that name when she was in the circus. Wrap up these carrots and celery in a baggie, would you? I want them kept fresh. The Jamaicans are fussy about what they eat."

"Circus? No kidding?" Colm Hanna said.

"Sure, she rode elephants, Pete says. It was one leap from there onto the stage. But she never was big time. I mean, the only role she had was that small part in the film they made here in town. Hi, Em, you coming with us?"

"Yeah, but not this minute." Emily was on her way upstairs. She had just thought of something—something she'd found in the pasture a week ago, something she'd put away in her top drawer.

"Mom, can I take the pickup?" she called down. "You can ride with Colm, can't you? I need to go downtown. I need to see somebody about homework."

"Now? Friday night? With that bad ankle?" Her mother sounded skeptical.

"Please, Mom," she said, coming down. "It's my left ankle, not the right. And I'm a careful driver. Why'd I get my license anyway if I can't drive the pickup? I learned on that old junk, Mother!"

Colm laughed, and her mother made a face. "You're talking about the vehicle I love," she quipped. But she fished in her pocket, handed over the keys. "The supper's at six. Moira will need your help."

"I'll be there, Mom, I said." She went to hug her mother, stopped short. She couldn't seem to hug anybody lately. It was like she was out in the lake in a small boat, cut adrift, without oars. She shut the door quickly before her mother could change her mind.

She drove to Branbury Inn. Her father was there, with that woman. They were drinking wine, watching TV. "Dad, I need to talk to you. Alone."

"Sit down and have a glass of wine with us," her father said in a jolly voice. She knew that voice so well. It would override her mother's when he wanted the floor, when he wanted his way. She used to love the sound of that voice. . . .

"No, thank you," she said to the wine. "I have to go to a party."

"Ooh, what fu-nn," said the woman, looking glamorous, looking phony in black tights and long silky caftan—something oriental. It was really too delicate for her large frame. She wasn't fat, Emily noted, just big. Maybe six feet tall, almost her father's height. Emily hadn't known till tonight that she'd been in the circus. Why hadn't they told her things like that? But elephants! You needed muscles for that.

"A new boyfriend?" the woman asked.

Even her father squelched that one. "Violet," he warned; he knew about Adam. He got up, put an arm around his daughter. "It was a tough thing," he said. "Tough thing," he repeated, not having the words to describe what she hoped he felt. He looked at the woman for support. Her father always shied away from feelings, from psychological thoughts.

"Oh yes, sweetie, I'm so sorry. But it was all for the best, wasn't it? In the long run?" The woman stood up. In her black satin heels she was taller than Emily's father.

"All for the best," her father echoed, and took another sip of wine. But she knew he was concerned. There was something about the way he frowned, his pale blue eyes searching hers. He was worried about her, but he didn't know how to express it. She was sorry for that.

But she needed to talk to him, alone. "Would you mind?" she told the woman. She couldn't bring herself to say *Violet*.

"Okay," the woman said brightly. "Dads and daughters have to talk. I understand. I'll go back in the lobby bar, have a drink there. Give you fifteen minutes, all right, Emily, dear?" Her smile glittered. Emily nodded. That was all the time she had anyway. Moira Earthrowl needed her help.

The woman left. Her father looked hard at Emily. "Em, we have to talk about this. Violet and I, well, we plan to be married. She'll be your stepmother. You have to get over this . . . this . . ." He couldn't think of the right word, but she knew what he meant.

She was worried now, she had to make her father aware. At first when she'd found the brooch she wasn't sure, she thought it belonged to Opal. But Opal hadn't recognized it when she wore it one day in front of her, and now she was certain it wasn't Opal who came through the fence that night. But the woman. She could have done it. She'd want Emily's mother to sell. She'd want houses all over their land that would bring in money. She'd want money, period, and all the luxury it would bring. Trips to Paris. To London. To the circus?

Of course, they could have been together that night, her father and the woman. She didn't want to think her dad had been there, but she'd never have thought of Adam hurting anyone, either. . . .

"I found this, Dad," she said, pulling the brooch out of her pocket. It was a gold brooch, with an elephant overlaid in ivory.

Her father appeared to recognize it. Her heart lurched. "Hey," he said, "Violet was looking all over for this. It was me gave it to her. Where in hell'd you find it?"

She took a breath. Then looked her father in his watery blue eyes. "By the fence, Dad. In the pasture where the cows were the night they were slashed. Does she have a survival knife, Dad?"

He didn't answer. His ruddy face paled; there was a slight ticking in his cheek. She knew the answer.

"She just keeps it for defense," he murmured. "I mean, she lives in New York City. She wouldn't use it to . . . my God, I can't imagine she would . . ."

"Well, try to imagine, then, Dad. Imagine her coming a second time, and fooling around with the John Deere. Does she know anything about tractors? You don't, Mom knows that. Our tractors and cars were always breaking down and she had to take them in town to be fixed. Till we got Tim. Your girlfriend ever take a course in mechanics? Some women do. Mom always means to, she hasn't found time."

She was taking a chance; she felt nervous and bold at the same time. She despised this woman. She didn't want her for a stepmother. For that matter, she didn't know that she wanted her father back, either. That is, with her mother. At least Colm Hanna's voice didn't override her mother's. He wouldn't make her sell her farm. Pay a hundred thousand dollars for the land.

"I'll talk to her," her father said. "I'll find out. I can't imagine . . ."

"Okay, Dad. Dad, I need to go. I just wanted to know if she did it, that's all. Just to be sure she doesn't do anything like that again. It's not fair to Mom. Vic drives that John Deere sometimes. He's not supposed to, but he does."

Her father seemed bewildered, then angry. He got up and phoned the bar. He told the bartender to send Violet back to the room. Emily didn't want to be there when she got back. " 'Bye Dad," she said, and put a hand on his arm. He was her father, after all; he'd had a setback, a disillusionment. Emily could understand that.

She limped out to the pickup, feeling strangely exhilarated. The tears were wetting her cheeks. It wasn't Adam. It wasn't Adam! a voice shouted inside. He wouldn't have hurt her animals. They could have had something together, it just hadn't been the right time, that's all. He had too many other things on his mind, heavy things that weighed down on his very soul. He was sick—she realized that now.

She went straight to the orchard. Her mother and Colm were already there. Ruth cried out in surprise when Emily flung her arms around her. Emily hadn't meant to do that, she just did it, that's all. Moira and the twins were coming out the farmhouse door, carrying trays of food: salads, corn on the cob, cheeses, fruit. Emily relieved Moira of a casserole of apple pan dowdy; it looked delicious. Even before she and the twins arrived at the bunkhouse she breathed in the fragrance of curry, garlic, spices she couldn't recognize but that smelled heavenly. Heavenly, she thought, remembering the story Colm told her mother about why the church wanted the orchard.

Derek was out on the grass, grinning, stirring an enormous pot of goat stew. He was wearing a red and purple hand-woven scarf around his neck. "Tek it, eet it, girl, dee-lee-cious!" he told Emily. Don Yates and the other men were crowding about the pot, smiling and chattering. Desmond, in a pink and yellow scarf, was playing a harmonica, Zayon was setting up the drums. Derek held out a bowl of curried stew. She shook her head.

"Come on, Em, we have to try it. You eat beef, don't you?" her mother said. "The old law of hospitality?"

"Break goat together," Colm Hanna said, and Ruth said, "Honestly, Colm." He had his arm around her mother's waist, but Emily didn't mind.

She accepted the bowl Derek was holding out. It was more a soup than a stew, but it was warm, it smelled savory. "Ole goat he sacrifice for us," Zayon said, whispering in her ear, and she nodded, tipped up the bowl, and she drank.